POSSUM BOY

BATTLES THE MULEFOOT MENACE

SWIFTY SLOWPOKER

ISBN: 979-8-88640-373-2 (sc)
ISBN: 979-8-88640-374-9 (hc)
ISBN: 979-8-88640-375-6 (e)

THE EWINGS PUBLISHING

One Galleria Blvd., Suite 1900, Metairie, LA 70001
1-888-421-2397

Local Coon Hunters Spot "Possum Boy"

By Murphy Kearns

Two local raccoon hunters swear they encountered the so-called "Possum Boy" last Thursday night. The "Possum Boy" creature has been sighted a number of times throughout the Upper Cumberland region in the last few months.

Spurgeon Baker, 43, and Buford Richardson, 45, both of the Defeated Creek community, say they were raccoon hunting on the Hugh Maggart farm in Elmwood when they were confronted by the " Possum Boy."

"We were sitting around the campfire, listening to the dogs," said Baker, "When my dog, Ticker, starting baying like he had treed a coon."

"Actually, I believe my dog, Speck, got the scent first," added Richardson.

"So we went running up to where they was at," continued Baker. "We were expecting to see just a regular coon, like always. But when we shined the flashlight up into the tree, we saw this ... critter, about the size of a two-year-old baby, hanging from a limb by his tail. It didn't have any hair on its body except some spiky white hair on the top of its head. It was definitely a male."

"It all happened so fast, it's kind of hard to give a really close description," said Richardson. "But I would guess it was about two and a half feet tall and its tail was at least as long as its body. It didn't have on any clothes and it was a cool night."

"The dogs was going crazy, trying to climb the tree," said Baker. "Then the creature hissed at us and swung off through the trees using its tail, like a monkey. But this wasn't no monkey."

Both hunters say they were too shaken to take a shot at the creature.

"I just stood there with my .22 dangling in my hand," said Baker.

Smith County Sherriff Sidney Harper and Game Warden Bob Ford of the Tennessee Game & Fish Commission investigated the scene where the hunters say the incident occurred. "We were unable to find anything out of the ordinary," said Ford. "We did find a few scuffed places on some tree limbs, but any number of things could have caused that."

Still, Ford does not completely discount the hunters' story. "There have been sightings of the 'Possum Boy' creature in Cumberland, Putnam, and Jackson counties. These people are seeing something."

Sheriff Harper remains unconvinced. "We found a pile of empty beer cans at Baker and Richardson's campsite," Harper said. "These boys just had a little too much to drink and got spooked out here in the dark."

"LOCAL COON HUNTERS SPOT 'POSSUM BOY'"
THE CARTHAGE COURIER,
SEPTEMBER 28, 1966 Carthage, Tennessee
By Murphy Kearns

Two local raccoon hunters swear they encountered the so-called "Possum Boy" last Thursday night. The "Possum Boy" creature has been sighted a number of times throughout the Upper Cumberland region in the last few months.

Spurgeon Baker, 43, and Buford Richardson, 45, both of the Defeated Creek community, say they were raccoon hunting on the Hugh Maggart farm in Elmwood when they were confronted by the "Possum Boy."

"We were sitting around the campfire, listening to the dogs," said Baker, "When my dog, Ticker, starting baying like he had treed a coon."

"Actually, I believe my dog, Speck, got the scent first," added Richardson.

"So we went running up to where they was at," continued Baker. "We were expecting to see just a regular coon, like always. But when we shined the flashlight up into the tree, we saw this ... critter, about the size of a two-year-old baby, hanging from a limb by his tail. It didn't have any hair on its body except some spiky white hair on the top of its head. It was definitely a male."

"It all happened so fast, it's kind of hard to give a really close description," said Richardson. "But I would guess it was about two and a half feet tall and its tail was at least as long as its body. It didn't have on any clothes and it was a cool night."

"The dogs was going crazy, trying to climb the tree," said Baker. "Then the creature hissed at us and swung off through the trees using its tail, like a monkey. But this wasn't no monkey."

Both hunters say they were too shaken to take a shot at the creature.

"I just stood there with my .22 dangling in my hand," said Baker.

Smith County Sherriff Sidney Harper and Game Warden Bob Ford of the Tennessee Game & Fish Commission investigated the scene where the hunters say the incident occurred. "We were unable to find anything out of the ordinary," said Ford. "We did find a few scuffed places on some tree limbs, but any number of things could have caused that."

Still, Ford does not completely discount the hunters' story. "There have been sightings of the 'Possum Boy' creature in Cumberland, Putnam, and Jackson counties. These people are seeing something."

Sheriff Harper remains unconvinced. "We found a pile of empty beer cans at Baker and Richardson's campsite," Harper said. "These boys just had a little too much to drink and got spooked out here in the dark."

CHAPTER ONE

Who He Is and How He Came to Be!

If you ever read a local newspaper in East Tennessee, you've probably heard of me. I'm "Possum Boy!" But nobody wants to believe me because I am eleven years old and also because I'm a resident at Clover Bottom Hospital and School. That's a State school for slow learners, but I'm not a slow learner. I read the *World Book Encyclopedia* from *Volume A* to *Volume WXYZ*. They captured me and cut my tail off! And I can prove it.

PROOF NUMBER ONE: My name. My name is Delphus V. White. Now usually, when a newborn baby is dropped off at a hospital or an orphanage, they type *Baby John Doe* on the birth certificate. Or if it's a girl, they type *Baby Jane Doe.* Then on the line for the momma's and daddy's name, they type in *Jane Doe* and *John Doe.*

So when that baby gets adopted, they print up a new birth certificate for him, one that's got his new name on it and that's also got his new momma's and daddy's name on it, too.

But I never did get adopted. Possums ain't cuddly.

So I've got a Welfare check for as long as I can remember. Actually, Clover Bottom Hospital and School gets it. But you can't fill out a Welfare application with the name *Baby John Doe* on it. There'd be too many of 'em! So they have to give you a real name.

On a birth certificate for an abandoned baby, in order to explain why the baby's momma and daddy's names are listed as *Jane Doe* and *John Doe*, they type the letters *D.I.* before your name. That stands for *Deserted Infant.* So the actual name that is typed on my birth certificate is *D.I. Delphus V. White.*

Didelphis is the Latin genus name for the American Opossum. Look it up! I promise I'm telling the truth!

Plus, the word *opossum* is a Powhatan Indian word that means "white dog" or "white beast." So that is how they come up my last name, White.

Now the "official" story is that I got my first name from the sheriff's deputy who captured me and brought me into Clover Bottom Hospital. He must of been pretty dang smart to catch me alive 'cause I ain't got no bullet holes in me. Later on, I heard that deputy became the first colored sheriff that there ever was in the State of Tennessee.[1]

PROOF NUMBER TWO: Right above my heinie, I've got a big white scar where they cut my tail off.[2] I can show you right now! It is about as-big-around as my right arm and it looks like a frowny face. Maybe you believe I should thank them for making me "normal." But how would you like it if somebody cut your nose off? And what can you do with a nose, really? I used to could swing from tree limb-to-tree limb with my tail! I can still remember swinging through the trees with my little possum brothers and sisters, naked as a jaybird.[3]

PROOF NUMBER THREE: I have special Possum Powers. I am invulnerable to rattlesnake bites, just like a possum. I ain't actually tested that one out yet, but I'm pretty sure it works. Also, when I get into a dangerous situation, I drop into what I call my *Possum Mode.* When I am in *Possum Mode*, I lose consciousness and my muscles go all stiff

---

1 No county in Tennessee has ever elected an African-American sheriff.

2 White's medical records indicate that upon his arrival at Clover Bottom Hospital and School, he was diagnosed with spina bifida occulta, a congenital defect of the vertebral column, and underwent surgical correction for this.

3 Although opossums use their prehensile tails to assist in climbing, the muscles of the tail are not strong enough to support the weight of an adult opossum. However, young opossums have been observed hanging by their tails for brief periods.

and hard.[4] You can kick me or poke me and I don't feel a thing! I'm invulnerable to pain, just like Superman. It's just like when a possum is "playing possum." But I can't make myself go into *Possum Mode*, it just has to come on by itself.

One time in an experiment, I got my pal Sammy Blount to smack me in the forehead with a piece of pine two-by-four. Sammy didn't want to do it at first, but I talked him into it, in the Interest of Science. I was gonna try to force myself to go into *Possum Mode* before the two-by-four made contact with my forehead, but it didn't work.

On the second try, Sammy knocked me clean unconscious with that two-by-four, but I still couldn't make myself go into *Possum Mode.*

ADDITIONAL PROOF: I have snow-white hair on my head just like a possum. How many eleven-year-old kids have you ever seen with white hair - not blond – white? Plus, I have six more teeth than most folks do. You can see 'em right here under my gums. Finally, I ain't even gonna tell you what they did to my ding-a-ling! But, I will tell you that I can still pee in two streams at one time if I squeeze it just right.[5]

Now, you're probably wondering what my Secret Origin is? To tell you the truth, I ain't for sure. But I have two competing theories:

The first one is just plain old hillbilly inbreeding. It can do funny things. There's a kid in here named Perry Lee who's got two thumbs on his right hand. It has a little fingernail on it and everything! It's kinda gross. Plus, I did come from East Tennessee.

But the second theory seems a lot more likely to me. You ever head of the Oak Ridge National Laboratory? It is a laboratory in a Tennessee town called Oak Ridge, about thirty miles west of Knoxville. They made part of the Atomic Bomb there.[6]

---

4 White's medical records indicate he was diagnosed with epilepsy: atypical type with tonic seizures.

5 White appears to be referring to the fact that the male opossum has a bifurcated (forked) penis. However, the male opossum does not pass urine through its penis. White's medical records make no reference to anything other than a conventional circumcision.

6 The plutonium used in the Manhattan Project was extracted from enriched uranium at the Oak Ridge National Laboratory.

Well, I read about this study where the Oak Ridge National Laboratory gave these people some milk to drink that had gamma-irradiated stuff in it. And you know what gamma rays caused? That's right -The Incredible Hulk! They didn't even tell them people what was in the milk!

So, I bet my momma was one of them people that they gave that gamma-radiated stuff to, and it mutated her genes. I reckon I'm a mutant like one of the X-Men. And then I run away because I was a little baby and didn't know what I was doing. I figure The Government knows this and that's why they're keeping me here. So they can keep an eye on me. Sometimes I wonder if my momma is out there looking for me right now. Sometimes I just wonder if she is still alive.

CHAPTER TWO

From his Hidden Lair, he keeps a constant vigil

Remember how I said I lived at Clover Bottom Hospital and School? Well, the Stones River forms a big "S" before it joins the Cumberland River, just east of Nashville. The bottom loop of that "S" surrounds about a thousand acres that people call "Clover Bottom."

John Donelson, one of the founders of Fort Nashborough, which went on to became Nashville, led about two hundred settlers on flatboats down the Cumberland River in 1780.[7] After Donelson dropped them people off at Fort Nashborough, he poled his flatboat back up the Cumberland River, and then took a hard right at the Stones River. Donelson figured that he needed to plant hisself a whole lotta corn to feed them folks he had just deposited off at Fort Nashborough.

Donelson didn't have the time to cut down a bunch of trees or to clear the land. What he needed was a big, flat space with no trees. On the west bank of the Stones River, he run up on a huge, flat river bottom that was covered with white clover. Now white clover ain't really white, it's green just like a regular St. Patrick's Day clover. But here and there,

---

[7] Colonel John Donelson (1725 – 1785) was a member of the Virginia House of Burgesses before moving to Tennessee. His voyage, from Fort Patrick Henry, down the Cumberland River to Fort Nashborough, covered more than one thousand miles.

it's got little white blossoms that look like popcorns. Anyway, John Donelson named that place "Clover Bottom" and he planted a big, huge corn crop on it.

The Indians[8] who actually owned that land sure did appreciate this White stranger planting all that nice corn on their land for them.

They was really disappointed when that White man came back about six months later with a big boat, a dozen men, and the sole intention of stealing their sweet corn![9] So the Indians waited until all the corn was loaded up onto the boat and then they slaughtered every last one of them White men. Only a couple of guys managed to escape. The flatboat drifted down the Stones River, winding back up at Fort Nashborough, The starving settlers buried the dead men onboard, washed the blood off the corn, and ate it.

John Donelson decided to relocate to Kentucky until things cooled down a little bit.

After the Revolutionary War, Clover Bottom got parceled out to three guys as payment for them fighting in the War. One of them fellows was named Hoggatt and he bought out the other two guys.

By the time of the Civil War, Clover Bottom Plantation was over 1,500 acres. The Hoggatt family owned more than a hundred slaves and raised corn, wheat, cows, and hogs.

Dr. John Hoggatt was a bony man who roamed around his plantation smoking his pipe like he was in a dream. Although he was a medical doctor, he didn't do much doctoring except every now and then on his family. He lived in a big fancy house that his slaves called the "White House" with his two nieces and his second wife, Mrs. Mary Ann Saunders Hoggatt. Mrs. Hoggatt was the granddaughter of John Donelson.

Mrs. Hoggatt was a short, beefy woman who stomped around the plantation in a long black dress. She always carried a three-foot rawhide whip with her. It had a tiny leather band that circled her plump wrist.

---

8 The Chickamauga Cherokee

9 It was actually Captain John Donelson III (1755–1830), the son of Colonel John Donelson, Sr. (1725–1785), who led the party to harvest the corn.

If you looked at Mrs. Hoggatt crossways, she would wallop you with that rawhide whip. That is, if you was a slave. I don't reckon she ever whipped any white people.

One of the slaves that the Hoggatts owned was a little boy named Johnny McCline. Johnny lived with his Grandma Hanna and his three brothers in a two-story frame house. Another family lived upstairs. Johnny's momma had died when he was two years old and his daddy had been sold to another plantation several miles away. Johnny got to see his daddy every now and then. His daddy would always bring him a little something, like a pocket knife, or a whistle, or maybe some candy.

Even though Johnny was just ten years old, he had to work like a full-grown man. He was a "cow-boy." He had to get up early in the morning and ride a black mule named "Nell" to round up about forty cows that had to be milked. Then, after they was milked, he had to drive them cows three or four miles back out to the pasture so they could graze. While they was grazing, Johnny had to hitch Nell up to a cart and haul fresh water from the spring to fill up a big metal tank by the kitchen door.

When he got through with that, Johnny had to carry the workmen's dinner out to them in the fields. Then at four o'clock, he had to round the cows back up to be milked again. One time, a cow wandered off and Johnny couldn't find her. Phillips, the evil overseer, whipped Johnny's bare back with a rawhide strap.

Then the Civil War broke out. One time, General Nathan Bedford Forrest and 3,000 of his cavalry troops camped out at Clover Bottom. Mrs. Hoggatt threw them a big barbeque supper.

One December morning, Johnny was setting up on Nell at the fence, watching a regiment of Union troops march up Lebanon Pike into Nashville. Some of the Yankees called out to him, "Hello, buddy!" and "Hey, little chap!" And then one of them Yankee soldiers hollered out, "Come on up North with us, Johnny! We'll set you free!"

At first, Johnny wondered how that soldier knew his name! He didn't know that Yankee soldiers called all Southerners "Johnny" or "Johnny Reb."

And right then and there, setting up on top of Nell's back, Johnny decided he had had enough of Mrs. Hoggatt's rawhide whip, enough of Clover Bottom Plantation, and enough of Slavery in general. So he slid down off of Nell's back, hopped over the fence, and fell in line with them Yankee soldiers.

Just think about that! He was eleven years old, the same age as me. He gave up the only life he had ever known for the dream of something better. Even with my special Possum Powers, I don't know if I would have been that brave.

Johnny went on to see some famous Civil War battles. He mostly took care of the mules and horses. During the war, one of his army buddies taught him his ABC's and some reading and writing. After the war, Johnny moved to Michigan, where his captain was from, but he came back to Nashville to go to school. Johnny went on to become a schoolteacher and taught school for a little while. Johnny travelled everywhere! He lived in Chicago, Colorado, and New Mexico. Eventually, he managed the governor's mansion for the Governor of New Mexico.[10]

Maybe you are wondering how I know so much about Johnny McCline and everything he did. None of this stuff is in *The World Book Encyclopedia.*

One night, I was out on my nightly patrol. Possums are nocturnal. I was looking for a solid wooden box to hold my comic book collection. Although the staff locks the doors to the dormitories, there ain't no fences around Clover Bottom School. So I was exploring around the house that Johnny called the White House. Today it's called Clover Bottom Mansion.

Clover Bottom Mansion is not white. Maybe it used to be. It's a big three-story house which is a regular red-brick color. It has fancy windows and doors that are round-shaped at the top. The Mansion does have white porches and balconies, but the paint is cracked and chipping

---

[10] Herbert J. Hagerman (1871 – 1935) was the 17th Governor of the New Mexico Territory from 1906 to 1907.

off pretty bad. The porch has fancy wood curlicue decorations on it.[11] It kind of looked like Herman Munster's[12] house. Setting just behind the Mansion was three or four small white buildings. They was too close to the Mansion to have been slave quarters, so I am not sure what they was used for. I think one of them may have been a smokehouse. The second building had a rusted tin roof and the wind had blowed back the corner on a sheet of tin, exposing the gray wooden shingles underneath. I quietly eased inside the building and immediately spotted a dingy chest o' drawers. In the top drawer was a cedar box that would be perfect to store my comic book collection! Inside the cedar box was a big stack of papers tied up in a dirty white string. The top sheet read:

HALLECK, KETRON & BILLINGS
LAWYERS
213 East Palace Avenue
Santa Fe, New Mexico

August 22, 1938

The Hoggatt Family
Clover Bottom Farm
Donelson, Tennessee

To The Hoggatt Family:

This office represents the Rydal Press book publishers of Santa Fe, New Mexico. Our client is considering

[11] Clover Bottom Mansion was built in 1852 in the Greek Revival style. After a fire in 1859, the Mansion was rebuilt in the Italianate style. By 1975, it had fallen into a state of serious disrepair.

[12] Herman Munster was a character featured in the television program, *The Munsters*, which was broadcast on the CBS television network from September 1964 to May 1966, and afterwards in syndication. The program depicted the life of a benign family of monsters who lived in a haunted Gothic-style mansion. The program featured Fred Gwynne as Herman, Al Lewis as Grandpa, and Carolyn Jones as Morticia.

a manuscript for publication submitted by Herbert J. Hagerman, former Governor of Territorial New Mexico.[13]

The manuscript, "Slavery in the Clover Bottoms," recounts the memoirs of John H. McCline, a former bondman in your family's service.

McCline's narrative offers a less-than-flattering depiction of his tenure of service to your family, particularly in his interactions with Mrs. Mary Ann Saunders Hoggatt. A copy of the manuscript is enclosed for your perusal.

Our client hopes to forestall any unnecessary litigation should it proceed with the publication of "Slavery in the Clover Bottoms."[14] This office would be eager to discuss this matter with your legal advisors to explore what accords may be reached.

Please have your legal counselors contact us at their earliest convenience.

Very truly yours,

Harrison B. Ketron, Esq.

---

[13] The Rydal Press had previously published Herbert J, Harriman's *Letters of a Young Diplomat,* Herbert J. Hagerman, Rydal Press, Santa Fe, 1937

[14] Before the 1965 case, *Gruschus v. Curtis Publishing Co.*, 342 F.2d 775 (10th Cir. 1965), New Mexico law was unclear whether the right to sue for defamation survived the death of the party who was defamed, i.e. whether the survivors of a defamed person could bring a lawsuit after his death. Had the Hoggatts filed a defamation lawsuit in federal court, the case would likely have been decided under New Mexico law.

So Johnny wrote his autobiography. It is one of my favorite things to read. I read it over and over! I don't know if it ever got published, I ain't never run across it.[15]

I read a lot of books and magazines. The library in Progress House, the dormitory where I live, don't have a lot of books. It has an old set of *The World Book Encyclopedia,* which I have read from *Volume A* to *Volume WXYZ*, like I told you, but it does have not much else.

But I have a Secret Weapon! The Tennessee School for the Blind is just down the road from Clover Bottom Hospital and School. The Blind School gets all kinda books. They take them books and turn them into Braille books for the blind kids, and then they just throw 'em away. Behind the Blind School is a big Dempster-Dumpster,[16] which is a big square garbage can that you dump regular garbage cans into. Then a special truck with mechanical arms comes along and dumps all the garbage into the back of the truck. So about once a week, usually on Saturday nights, I climb into the Dempster-Dumpster and pick out all the books and magazines I like. I like science books, fiction, and history. My favorite is history, I read a lot of history.

That's how I know, for example, that the Hoggatts sold Clover Bottom Plantation to a congressman from Louisiana. When the congressman died in 1919, his wife sold the property to the Stanford Brothers, A.F and Robert Donnell.

The Stanford Brothers had gone out west and made their fortune in the furniture building business. Since Lebanon Road split Clover Bottom Farm right down the middle, Robert Donnell took the property on the west side of Lebanon Road, and A.F. took the property on the

[15] McCline, John, 1852-1948 and Jan. Furman. 1998. *Slavery in the Clover Bottoms: John McCline's Narrative of His Life During Slavery and the Civil War.* Knoxville: University of Tennessee Press.

[16] The Dempster-Dumpster system of waste handling was developed by the Dempster Brothers, Inc. of Knoxville, Tennessee. Introduced in the 1950's, the Dempster Dumpmaster was the first commercially successful, front-loading garbage truck in the United States. In 1975, dumpsters were not as ubiquitous as they are today and many Tennesseans continued to use the trademark name, rather than the generic term *dumpster.*

east side. A.F.'s side of the property had the Mansion and all the barns and buildings. Together they started a big dairy farm, raising Jersey and Guernsey cattle.

In 1921, A.F. sold about three-hundred-and-fifty acres of the southeastern corner of his property to the State of Tennessee. Two years later, the State opened up the Tennessee Home and Training School for Feeble-Minded Persons. I reckon A.F. wasn't too worried about the "feeble-minded" living so close to him.

Robert Donnell built hisself a fine brick house on his side of the property and then started subdividing the rest. He got into the real estate business.

A.F. Stanford died in 1939 and his second wife kept on running the dairy farm until 1947. In 1949, she sold the property to a mortgage company and then they turned around and sold it to the State of Tennessee. So, now the State of Tennessee owned all of A.F.'s half of Clover Bottom Plantation. The State opened up the Tennessee School for the Blind in 1952.

The Tennessee Home and Training School for Feeble-Minded Persons was built according to what they called the "Cottage Plan." Instead of one big hospital building, they built a bunch of little buildings called cottages.

By the time they got around to building Progress House, which is where I live, the fashion had gone back to big institutional buildings. Built downhill from the original campus, Progress House is a huge one-story brick building shaped like a "T," with three different wings. A-Wing is where all the grown-up men live. The B-Wing has all the girls. And C-Wing has all the young guys like me.

So up on top of the hill is a bunch of little red rectangle buildings, and at the center is the Steam Plant. The Steam Plant generates the heat for all our buildings. A huge black smokestack rises up out of the top of the Steam Plant. Just a little further up the hill is a tall white water tower. The whole view kinda reminds me of Isengard. Did you ever read *The Lord of the Rings*? Isengard is the place where they cut down all them trees and made the Tree People mad. Clover Bottom kinda reminds me of that. A huge black Tower, surrounded by a bunch of short, squat buildings and then a gleaming White Tower stands off in the distance. But maybe I'm making it sound too scary, Clover Bottom ain't scary.

Sometimes, in the winter, when they have the Steam Plant really cranked up, it makes a white cloud overhead as far as the eye can see. It looks like the roof of the sky has dropped down about two or three thousand feet and it makes the world feel really small.

CHAPTER THREE

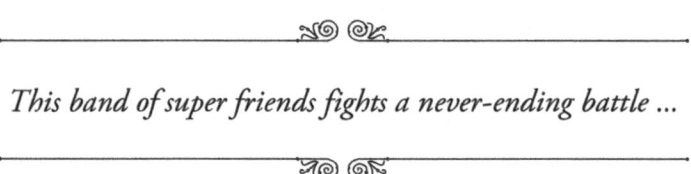

This band of super friends fights a never-ending battle ...

"DC Comics is just better than Marvel," I told Ferlin. "That's all there is to it."

"Nossir!" Ferlin said. "Marvel characters is a hundred times better than DC!"

Me and Ferlin Blount was setting on our beds across from each other. For years, I had been trying to make him listen to reason.

"Whenever the police show up, Spider-Man always runs away. What kinda hero does that?"

"Yessir, I think that in the real world, if the police rolled up on a crime scene and saw a man in red long johns, they would chase him. Yessir, the first thing they would do is try to pull his mask off."

"Plus, Spider-Man's creepy looking," I said. "He's all knees and elbows and when he takes off his mask, he has a widow's peak in his hair. And you know who else has a widow's peak? Dracula!"

"Nossir! Spidey don't look like that no more!"

"The Incredible Hulk looks like Frankenstein," I said. "His skin's green and he's got that big bulge on his forehead. All of Marvel's characters look like monsters. The Thing looks like a big pile of orange rocks."

"Yessir! My favorite part is when The Thing yells, 'It's Clobberin' Time!' Yessir! You just know there's fixing to be some action."

"That don't seem kind of silly to you?"

Ferlin craned his head back and peered at me from the space beneath the rims of his coke-bottle eyeglasses. "Yessir, I'll tell you what's silly. Superman once destroyed an entire solar system by sneezing too hard!"[17]

"I never read that one."

"Yessir, Mr. Mxyzptlk gave him some magic sneezing powder." Then, as if to emphasize his point, Ferlin lifted his right cheek off the bed and pooted. "Scobey," he said.

That was a game we played. If I had said, "Three Jacks!" before he said "Scobey," then I would have got to hit him on the arm. It all started when our Developmental Technician, Mr. Anderson, which is kind of like our schoolteacher, started making us say, "Excuse me" after we pooted. "Excuse me" turned into "'Scuse me" and then somehow evolved into "Scobey." So, if you pooted you had to say, "Scobey." If you belched, you had to say, "Otis!" If you didn't say it, someone could call "Three Jacks!" on you and punch you on the arm. The rules permitted you to say "Otis" at the same time you was belching. Almost everybody who lived on the C-Wing of Progress House played the game. The only one who didn't play the game was Frank Blount, Ferlin's brother. Frank didn't like to be touched.

"Yessir, do you reckon Superman's farts could destroy an entire solar system?" Ferlin said.

"I think yours could," I told him. "Man! What did you eat?"

Ignoring my question, Ferlin continued, "Yessir, Marvel's characters are regular fellers, just like me. They have real problems. DC heroes are basically gods."

"Batman's just a regular guy."

"Yessir, but I have three words for you: *Holy Guacamole, Batman!*"

"Now, you know good and well that Robin moved off to Hudson University in 1969. Batman works alone now!" I said, fumbling through the stack of comics beside me on my bed. I held up *Batman #227* to show him. "Look at this cover! That right there is a work of art! Batman is overlooking that spooky castle, looking all scary and mean! Marvel's artwork can't touch that!"

---

17 Action Comics No. 273, February 1961

"How's it hanging, boys?"

I felt my *Possum Mode* coming up on me. It was Billy "Earz" Grissom. He didn't live in Progress House, but Progress House was the only dormitory where they had a rec room with a pool table, so people was allowed to hang around there.

I lived in absolute mortal fear of Earz. He was only fifteen, but he already needed to shave every day. Ferlin was bigger than Earz, but Earz was a whole lot meaner.

Nobody knew for sure how Earz got his nickname, but I think I know how. One time, I was hiding in the bushes watching Earz beat up a kid. Earz stopped to smoke a cigarette before going back to punching him. He had worked up a sweat and he pushed his hair back behind his ears. Earz had a cauliflower on the top of each ear. Do you know what a cauliflower ear is? Boxers get them. When a boxer get punched on the ear, it can make a blood clot in the cartilage. When it heals, it looks like a cauliflower, all shriveled and lumpy. The tops of both of Earz' ears had cauliflowers, but his hair usually covered them up.

I never even dreamed of revealing his secret.

Earz sauntered through the door and slapped a one-arm headlock on me, not a tight one, but I could feel the *Possum Mode* coming on hard.

"Whatcha doing', Delly?" he said, letting me go. "Looking at your little funny books?"

"Uh-huh," I squeaked out.

He snatched *Batman #227* from my hand and he wasn't careful with it at all. He immediately bent the spine.

"Yeah," he said. "You reckon if I wore my drawers on the outside of my fucking clothes, they'd make a book about me?"

"I dunno," I murmured.

"They could call it 'The Skidmark!'" he said, cackling and tossing *Batman #227* back down on my bed. "You boys are funny," he said. "See you around." And then he swaggered off towards the rec room. I heard him yell, "Hey, you fuckin' retard! Gimme that goddamn pool cue!"

"Whew," I said. *Possum Mode* aborted.

Before we could even catch our breath, Frank Blount, Ferlin's middle brother, stomped in and plonked hisself down beside Ferlin.

Ferlin Blount, Frank Blount, and their little brother Sammy, looked like identical triplets born several years apart. Ferlin was fifteen, Frank was thirteen and Sammy was ten. The Blount Brothers was descended from one of the guys who signed the United States Constitution. One of their great-great-grandmothers was a Cherokee princess. The Blount Brothers all had thick black hair which they had cut in bangs straight across their forehead. They thought it made them look like Mr. Spock, but once it grew out even a little bit, I thought it made them look like Moe on The Three Stooges. All the Blount Brothers had horrible eyesight and got their glasses from the State Dispensary, so their eyeglasses was all exactly alike. That made them look even more identical. They had Clark Kent glasses with lenses so thick, I don't know how they saw through them. In fact, all three of them had a habit of craning their head back and peering out beneath the little space underneath their frames. They would make kind of a beaver face when they did that. It was kinda funny. Except when Frank did it. When Frank did it, it meant you needed to find something to hide under.

"Frank, what's the matter?" Ferlin asked his younger brother.

Frank shook his head vigorously. Frank was not a big talker.

"Frank, did somebody hurt your feelings?" Ferlin asked.

Frank just shook his head.

"Frank, you ain't gonna make a 'Number Two' in someone's locker, are you?" Frank did that sometimes. I yelled at him one time and he ruined a good pair of tenni'shoes.

Frank shook his head.

For a minute, I wondered if "Earz" Grissom might have said something to Frank that upset him. But if Earz had said much, Frank would have just straight-up attacked him. Frank could be a bit high-strung at times.

But before we got to the bottom of it, Sammy Blount came bounding into the room. He struck a kung fu stance and announced, "The spirit of the crane resides within the stillness!" Sammy never missed an episode of "Kung Fu."

"Say what?" I said.

"We require weightlessness to rise above our crises."

"What in the world are you talking about?"

Still in his stance, Sammy replied, "Ladybird is farrowing."

Ladybird was one of the hogs we took care of. Clover Bottom was a working farm. We raised pigs, dairy cows, corn, beans, and all the vegetables. Each dormitory, or cottage, took care of a certain thing. The C-Wing of Progress House took care of the hogs.

"How can you tell she's farrowing?" I asked Sammy.

Sammy dropped out of his crane stance and said, "She's making herself a nest and she's leaking out of her you-know-what."

"Yessir, we should call Mr. Anderson," Ferlin said.

"It's Mr. Anderson's thirtieth wedding anniversary tonight," I said. "He was taking Miss Zelda to the Golden Corral. He wouldn't be home even if we did try to call him."

"We could go get Mr. Birdwell," suggested Sammy.

"Mr. Birdwell don't know nothing about hogs," I said. Mr. Birdwell was our nighttime Development Tech and he didn't do much work around the hogs. "We can do this our ownselves. Ladybird has had two or three litters before, so she knows what to do. We just have to be there to help her and take care of the babies."

So me and the Blount Brothers rushed off to the hog barn. There were a dozen other boys in C-Wing that helped take care of the hogs, but they wouldn't be much use with this kind of work. They were the little boys and mostly just shoveled manure. They had difficulty "staying on task."

When we got to the barn, Ladybird was already laying down on her side. We had put her in the special farrowing stall two days ago, but we didn't think she would be having her babies just yet. The stall was about four-feet wide and ten-feet long and had two-by-fours nailed edge-down along each side to help keep Ladybird from accidentally laying down and squshing one of her piglets.

"Okay," I said. "We need plenty of rags, the big and little side cutters, the iodine, the soap, and buckets of warm water."

"Yessir, all the stuff is locked up in the storeroom," said Ferlin.

"When has a lock ever stopped Frank Blount?" I replied.

One paper clip and a few minutes later, we had our little production line set up. Once the piglets started coming, they would come about 15 to 20 minutes apart. Ferlin was in the stall with Ladybird and would hand them out to us. If a piglet had to be pulled out, I could hop in there to help him. My hands and arms was smaller than his, but I wasn't sure I would be strong enough to pull one out. But we both washed our hands real good, clipped our fingernails short and had the slippery stuff handy in case we had to pull out a piglet.

"Yessir!" said Ferlin. "And here's the first one! Nossir! He's not breathing!"

"Okay, wipe his nose and mouth out real good," I said, handing him a clean rag.

After he did that, I yelled, "Now, swing him, Ferlin!"

Standing with his feet wide apart, Ferlin swung the little piglet, head down, between his legs. That would get the water out of him.

"Yessir, there he goes! Yessir! He's breathing now!" Ferlin said, grinning from ear-to- ear, and wiping the piglet's nose and mouth again. "Nossir, you didn't like that at all, did you, little feller?" he said to the piglet. Then he handed the pig to Sammy.

Sammy bathed the piglet in warm soapy water and then put the iodine solution on his belly button. The belly button is one of the first places that infection can get into a baby pig. After he dried him off, Sammy told the piglet, "Cleanliness is a Pillar of Enlightenment," almost like he was saying a little prayer over it. Then he gave him to me.

My job was to clip the "wolf teeth." Baby pigs have eight little teeth called "wolf teeth" or "needle teeth" that are sharp as little razors. There are four on the top jaw and four on the bottom jaw. I had to take the small pair of side cutter pliers and clip them down to the jaw line. I reckoned the Blount Brothers didn't have good enough vision to do this. If I didn't clip these "wolf teeth" down, then it would hurt Ladybird when the piglet tried to nurse. And then she would not let him nurse and he would starve. So clip, clip, clip, clip and I handed him to Frank Blount.

Frank Blount's job was to clip the piglet's tail with the large pair of side cutter pliers. You had to cut off a half to two-thirds of the tail. Since I had had my own tail cut off, I was a bit squeamish about this procedure. At this age, a pig's tail is just soft gristle. There's hardly any blood, if any. But Mr. Anderson says if you don't clip the tail, other piglets will chew on it and it will get infected and make him sick. Still, every time Frank squeezed down on them pliers, I felt a sting in the scar on my back.

We went through this process eight more times and I am here to tell you that we did not lose a single pig! Ferlin didn't have to swing any more piglets, the rest of them came out breathing. Sammy told each one of them that "Cleanliness was a Pillar of Enlightenment," I clipped all of their teeth and flinched every time Frank cut their tails off.

We had to let Ladybird pass her afterbirth and get back on her feet before we could let the piglets nurse. If she didn't get back on her feet, she would get constipated, then she would stop eating, and die.

We had to wait a long time for her to pass the afterbirth. It was purpley and gross. "Yessir, we got to get her up now," said Ferlin.

We coaxed and we pleaded, "Get up, Ladybird." I tried to bribe her with an apple. Exhausted, we sat down in a circle wondering what to do next. Without a word, Frank stood up and walked to the storeroom. He came back with a four-foot wooden stake with a sharpened point. He walked over to Ladybird and poked her with it. Not hard, but it got her attention. He did it again and she squealed and jumped up. Boy, was she mad!

Sammy jumped up and struck a kung fu pose. "Hard like steel and soft like a rope of silk," he said.

Finally, Ladybird pooped. I have never been so glad to see a hog poop in all my life. She would be getting special feed to help her while she was nursing. We cleaned out her stall and put down some fresh straw. Finally, after she had laid back down, we placed each of the little piglets down to a teat. Each one started sucking as soon as he hit the ground.

"Yessir, we better get washed up and go to bed," said Ferlin. "It'll be daylight here 'fore too long."

CHAPTER FOUR

You can't fight injustice on an empty stomach, chum ...

After sleeping a couple of hours, I got up to check on Ladybird and her litter. Momma and babies were fine. I hiked over to the cafeteria to eat my breakfast. It would be a couple of hours before we had to go feed and water all the other hogs. It took me a while to get set down. I had to help a guy in a wheelchair get to his table. All we have around here are hospital clunker wheelchairs and they are pretty hard to drive balancing a tray in your lap.

We have those square kind of plates that with those little dividers that separate each kind of food. I don't mind my food touching, but I only want them to touch on my terms, when I say so. I opened up my red-and-white carton of milk and started cutting my biscuit in half. I was going to eat me some biscuits and gravy.

"Well, look, it's little Delly," said Earz Grissom as he crashed down across the table from me. I could feel my heart pounding in my ears. I did not want to go into *Possum Mode* right here in the cafeteria. "You work with them fucking hogs, don't you, Delly?" he asked.

"Uh, yeah."

"Well, you're a lucky little cocksucker then," he said. "I have to take care of them goddamn cows, and I have to get up at three o'clock in the fucking morning to milk those fuckers."

"Oh."

"And you would think that if I have to get up at three o'clock in the goddamn morning," he continued, "I could get a cup of fucking coffee." He yelled that last part extra loud, looking around the cafeteria, like somebody might hear him and rush a cup of coffee over to him. No one did.

"Coffee makes me jumpy," I said.

"Yeah, this whole goddamn place makes me jumpy," he said. "Anybody ever bother you?" Without waiting for my answer, he went on, "Because, if one of these booger-eatin' motherfuckers ever lays a finger on me, I'll stick a fucking shiv in his ear!" He lunged at me across the table with a fork in his hand! He swung his arm around like he was going to stick it in my ear. But he stopped short.

It all happened so fast, I didn't have time to flinch or even go into *Possum Mode.*

Settling back in his chair, he looked around the room and howled with laughter.

"I mean, you burn down one goddamn church and they stick you in a place where you can't even get a cup of fucking coffee."

"You burned down a church?"

"Yeah."

"Why would you burn down a church?"

"I like to look at the colors."

"You know, if you like to look at different colors, Mrs. Batson has a real good painting class on Thursdays."

Earz exploded into laughter. "Fucking painting," he said, shaking his head. "Hey, you're not eating them goddamn eggs," he said, sliding his tray over next to mine and raking my scrambled eggs onto his tray. "And you ain't touched them grits either," he said, raking the grits over onto his tray too. I wouldn't really miss the grits, but I love scrambled eggs.

We sat in silence for a while as Earz stuffed my scrambled eggs into his mouth. He hunched over his breakfast, with his arm in front of his plate, like somebody was going to try to steal it away from him. My heart started to slow down, but I think I had peed a little. I took a bite out of my biscuit, but I had kind of lost my appetite.

I saw Mr. Anderson come in through the cafeteria doors and get in the serving line. My stomach stopped churning. *Possum Mode* averted! Me and Mr. Anderson usually had our breakfast together every morning.

"Good morning, men," Mr. Anderson said, setting his tray on the table and sitting down. "How are we doing this fine morning?"

"Anderson," Earz said.

"Great!" I said.

Mr. Anderson bowed his head for a quick little prayer. He did that.

"Well, I gotta take my morning dump," Earz said, standing up and wiping his mouth on his sleeve. "Hey, Anderson, you got a cigarette you can spare?"

"Nah, I gave them up," Mr. Anderson said, grinning. "They were ruining my good looks."

Earz nodded his head, picked up his tray and headed out.

If Santa Claus shaved his beard, he would look pretty much like Mr. Anderson. I don't really believe in Santa Claus, but you get what I mean. Mr. Anderson was bald on top and had a horseshoe of snow white hair around the back of his head. But above his glasses, he had jet black eyebrows. I used to suspect that he dyed his eyebrows. But then I noticed he also had these luxuriant tufts of hair growing out of his ears and nose. And they were jet black too! Why would anyone dye their eyebrows, nose and ear hair, but then not bother to dye the hair on their head?

I reckon I thought about hair dye a lot because my own hair is so white, like a possum's. I ain't never dyed it though.

"You got a haircut," I said.

"I sure did," said Mr. Anderson, taking a bite out of his biscuit.

I couldn't see his little ear tufts, so I stuck my finger in his ear to see if he had just maybe stuffed them down into his earholes or something.

"Quit that, Delphus," he said, shooing me away with his hand.

"Your ear tufts are gone," I told him.

"Yes, I know," he said. "The barber took care of them for me."

"Will they grow back?"

"I'm sure they will."

"Good," I said. "'Cause I don't like things to change."

"I know that about you."

"Don't Miss Zelda miss your ear tufts?"

"You know, Delphus, we haven't really discussed it."

"I thought they kind of made you look like a bear."

"A what?"

"A grizzly bear. Or like a were-grizzly bear. Which is like a werewolf, only a bear. 'Even a man who is pure at heart and says his prayers by night, may become a Bear when the salmon run, and the moon is full and bright.'"

"Calm down, Delphus," he said, taking another bite. "I'm not a werewolf."

"A were-bear."

"I'm not one of those either."

"Did you hear about Ladybird?"

"I sure did," he said. "I stopped by to check on her and the little 'uns before I came here. You men did an amazing job."

"We didn't lose a one."

"I know."

"Ferlin had to swing one that wasn't breathing."

"Sounds like y'all had a big night! I checked on the Blount Brothers and they were still sawing logs."

"We didn't want to call you because it was your wedding anniversary."

"It would have been okay if you had called. We got home by eight-thirty. You probably should have called."

"Did Miss Zelda have a good time?"

"She said she did."

"Did they have candles?"

"What?"

"At the restaurant, did they have candles?"

"No, it was the Golden Corral. They don't have candles."

"You should have taken her to a place that had candles. Women like candles."

"When did you become such an expert on women all of a sudden?"

"I saw it on TV. Women like candles on the table. And they like it when a man comes to your table and plays you a song on the violin."

"My three grown sons, my daughters-in-law and my granddaughter were there."

"That don't sound very romantic."

"We been married thirty years, Delphus," he said, looking at me grinning. "It's a different kind of romantic."

CHAPTER FIVE

The eerie music . . .
causes odd accidents to happen ahead of him.

On the third Thursday of every month we had music class. I enjoy music class because I have an excellent voice, if I do say so myself. We have it in one of the classrooms in Roberts Hall. It looks like any other classroom, I reckon. At least like all the ones I've ever seen on TV: a blackboard with a border across the top showing the ABC's, and a bulletin board with construction paper people.

I designed that particular bulletin board myself. I am a pretty good drawer. Boy, I sure do sound stuck-up, don't I, bragging on myself so much? Mr. Anderson says you shouldn't brag on yourself. This bulletin board's theme was the Wizard of Oz, which I chose because this room is not used very much. If you go with Santa Claus or the Easter Bunny, then the bulletin board is out of date in a month or two. I had some help on this one, a little kid named Chester. He pasted the Cowardly Lion's mane on wrong. The Cowardly Lion looks like he's wearing a brown football helmet. By the time I realized what Chester had done, the paste was already dried. I couldn't fix it because there wasn't no more brown construction paper and also because Chester had eaten the rest of the paste. So there's the Cowardly Lion with a football helmet on.

Our desks were the desk-and-chair-all-in-one-piece kind. People had carved and drawed a lot of stuff here on the top. I don't know how they carved that stuff, they don't let us carry knives in here. Maybe they used to. There was a heart with "C.A.M" inside it. One carving said, "If I had a home in Hell and a farm in Memphis, I'd sell the farm and go home!" Another person had etched, "Denise is a Hore," and finally, one person had scratched out, "I love Bloomer Pudding!"

I wondered where all them people was now.

The Penguin pranced into the room lugging his big record player. It folded up and had a handle like a suitcase. Two boys followed him, each carrying a cardboard box. The boxes held the hardbacked songbooks that we would sing out of. It was kind of a big deal to get to carry the boxes. I don't why. You also got to pass out the books at the beginning of class.

The Penguin went from school to school in Davison County teaching Music Appreciation classes. He only came to Clover Bottom one day a month. He would set his record player on the big wooden desk up front and play songs from all over the world. And we would sing along with the songs. The words and the music was in the songbooks but we couldn't read the music, just the words. Before he played each song, he would tell us a little story about it, like if it was a "shanty," which is a kind of pirate song they would sing while they was pulling on their ropes.

The Penguin's real name was Jerry D. Popper. But there was this book we'd all read called *Mr. Popper's Penguins,*[18] and everybody always asked him where his penguins was. That really seemed to upset him, so we did it even more. Finally, we just started calling *him* The Penguin, but not to his face.

The Penguin did not look anything like the villain on the *Batman* TV show. He was tall and boney and wore wireframe glasses. He was losing his hair, but a stubborn little island of hair right at the top of his forehead refused to let go. So he made like a little bridge of hair from the island to the back of his head.

---

18 Atwater, Richard, Florence. Atwater and Robert Lawson, *Mr. Popper's Penguins.* Boston: Little, Brown and Co., 1938.

The Penguin was the most nervous-looking man I ever saw in my whole entire life. He looked like he needed to use the bathroom really, really bad all the time. He always seemed to be twitching and straining to hold it in. I always thought that if one of us pushed just the right button, he would pee and poop hisself right there in front of us. I wondered if he was that nervous around all kids, or if it was just us, because we was "different." But, I didn't mess with The Penguin, because I liked music class, like I said.

"Three Jacks!" I choked out, as a rancid fart cut through the smell of chalk dust. I turned around to Sammy Blount, who was sitting in the desk behind me. "Three Jacks!" I said again. "Did you do that?"

"It is written, 'He who smelt it, dealt it,'" said Sammy. "It wasn't me."

I saw Frank sitting in the desk behind his brother, slyly grinning with pride. Frank did not play the Scobey/Otis/Three Jacks game. If you hit Frank on the arm, he would probably head-butt you. Or take a Number 2 in your locker. It was best not to touch Frank at all, if you could help it.

"Good afternoon, boys and girls," said The Penguin, "Let's begin our enchanted excursion around the globe through the magic of traditional folk music. Now, if you'll all turn to page 24 of your songbooks, we'll begin our expedition right here at home, in the Old West with 'Git Along, Little Dogies.'"

"Git Along, Little Dogies" was a good song, I could really get down on the "Whoopie Ti Yi Yo!" part. But that was not the song I was hankering for. I wanted "Señor Don Gato!"

While we was singing "Git Along, Little Dogies," I thought I would go ahead and try to take control of The Penguin's mind and make him play "Señor Don Gato." I did not have mind-control powers, as far as I knew, but you never knew when them latent psychic powers might manifest themselves.

"Señor Don Gato, Señor Don Gato, Señor Don Gato," I telegraphed to The Penguin.

As the song ended, I held my breath, waiting to see if it worked.

"That was lovely, boys and girls," said The Penguin. "Now if you'll turn to page eight, we'll travel across the ocean to the emerald isle of

Ireland for the traditional song of the 'Rattlin' Bog.' This is a 'cumulative song' like 'The Twelve Days of Christmas,' where each verse get longer as the song progresses."

Again, this was a good song. It got faster and faster as it went along. By the end of the song, most of us were just singing "Blah, blah, blah, blah," because we couldn't keep up. But it wasn't "Señor Don Gato," and I wanted "Señor Don Gato." Since mind control wasn't working on The Penguin, I decided to quietly whisper "Señor Don Gato" over and over again and see if The Penguin would pick up on it subliminally.

"'*Señor Don Gato, Señor Don Gato, Señor Don Gato.*'"

"Very good, boys and girls," said The Penguin as we finished. "Now, if you'll turn to page 54 in your books, we'll venture to the exotic land of Czechoslovakia for the beautiful song, 'Waters, Ripple and Flow.' There are many different translations of this song, but this version is about a person yearning for freedom."

This song was nice, but it made me sad. I had tried mind control and subliminal suggestions. What else could I do? I was about to pop a gasket. If we didn't sing "Señor Don Gato" today, it was gonna be a month before I could hear it.

As the song ended, The Penguin said, "Lovely, boys and girls. Now if you'll turn to page 174, we'll travel to Old Meh-he-co,[19] for the tale of 'Señor Don Gato.'"

AT LAST! FINALLY! I love this song, as you can tell. It goes like this:

Oh, Señor Don Gato was a cat
On a high red roof Don Gato sat
He went there to read a letter
(Meow! Meow! Meow!)
Where the reading light was better
(Meow! Meow! Meow!)
T'was a love note for Don Gato.

[19] Although of Spanish and Sephardic origins, "Señor Don Gato" is identified as a traditional Mexican folksong in *Making Music Your Own*, Volume 4. Beatrice Lundeck, Elizabeth Crook, Harold C. Youngberg, Otto Luening. *Making Music Your Own,* Volume 4, New York, Silver Burdett Co., 1968.

"I adore you," wrote the lady cat
Who was fluffy, white, and nice and fat
There was not a sweeter kitty
(Meow! Meow! Meow!)
In the country or the city
(Meow! Meow! Meow!)
And she said she'd wed Don Gato.

Oh, Don Gato jumped so happily
He fell off the roof and broke his knee
Broke his ribs and all his whiskers
(Meow! Meow! Meow!)
And his little solar plexus
(Meow! Meow! Meow!)
"¡Ay, caramba!" cried Don Gato.

Well, the doctors all came on the run
Just to see if something could be done
And they held a consultation
(Meow! Meow! Meow!)
About how to save their patient
(Meow! Meow! Meow!)
How to save Señor Don Gato.

But in spite of everything they tried
Poor Señor Don Gato up and died!
Oh it wasn't very merry
(Meow! Meow! Meow!)
Going to the cemetery
(Meow! Meow! Meow!)
For the ending of Don Gato.

As the funeral passed the market square
Such a smell of fish was in the air
Though his burial was slated

(Meow! Meow! Meow!)
He became re-animated
(Meow! Meow! Meow!)
He came back to life, Don Gato!
(For he had nine lives, Don Gato!)

Ain't that song awesome? It's got everything! I half-yelled, "Play it again!" and somebody behind me yelled "Yeah!" but The Penguin ignored us and went on to the next song. The rest of the songs were forgettable, but I did my best to enjoy them.

At the end of the class, The Penguin said, "Now, I need two strong boys to collect the books and carry them out to my car for me." He looked down the class roll and called out, "Delphus White!"

Hey, I was having a good day!

Then The Penguin called out, "Earz Grissom?"

Uh-oh.

As Earz stood up, The Penguin smiled nervously and asked, "Why do they call you 'Earz?'"

Earz looked at him like he was an idiot and said, "You know, them things that stick out of the side of your head ...?" and started picking up the songbooks.

After we had all the books collected and stacked inside the cardboard boxes, we headed down the hall to The Penguin's car. My box was kinda heavy. As we walked, I thought maybe a little small talk would ease the tension and I might get away without Earz doing me any bodily harm. I noticed a red pocket-sized Gideon Bible[20] in Earz' shirt pocket. The Gideons' headquarters was just down the street and there was a ton of Gideon Bibles lying around everywhere at Clover Bottom.

"Hey, Earz," I said. "I see that Gideon Bible in your shirt pocket. I didn't know you was a Bible-reading man."

---

[20] Gideons International is an evangelical Christian organization that distributes copies of the Bible free of charge. Since 1908 the Gideons have distributed more than 1.8 billion Bibles and New Testaments to hospitals, schools, colleges, hotels, motels, and prisons.

"You fucking with me, Delly?"

"Uh, No."

"You really don't know what that shit's for?"

"No."

"Well, I'll have to show you," he said, as we used our backs to push open the glass doors. "You see, the dumb shits that work around here, they don't bother to smoke their butts all the way down to the filter. Or, I dunno, maybe they just get interrupted.

"See? There's one right there," Earz continued, setting his box of books down and picking up a half-smoked cigarette butt off the ground. "That ought to be enough. Set them books down and come on over here," he said, leading me behind some hedges in front of the building.

Earz squatted down and carefully tore a page out of the small Gideon Bible. I think he was already down to the Book of Luke. Holding the Bible page in his left hand, he carefully rolled it into a half-tube. Taking three or four cigarette butts out of his pants pocket with his right hand, he ripped them open and poured the tobacco into the tube. Then he expertly rolled the Bible page into a little cigarette.

"See?" Earz said, "It's the perfect size." He pulled a lighter out of his pocket and lit it up. He inhaled deeply. "Here," he said. "Take a drag."

"Uh, I don't really smoke," I said. I was pretty sure Earz was going to bust Hell wide open for what he had just done.

"Take a drag!" he said again, looking at me menacingly.

So I did. I didn't inhale a whole lot, but I sure did cough. And then I coughed some more.

Earz laughed. "I knew you was gonna do that," he said, looking around, making sure nobody was watching. After he finished his cigarette, he flicked away the still-burning butt, and said, "Well, let's put them fucking books away."

The Penguin drove a brown Dodge Colt four-door sedan. It was spit-shined. He left the trunk lid down, but it was unlocked, so we wouldn't have to get inside his car to unlock it. Earz lifted up the trunk lid with one hand and I carefully placed my box of books inside. Earz pitched his box of books inside and it slid the carpet around.

"Fuck me, Delly, is that a goddamn box of Trojans there in the back?"

"A box of what?" I said.

"There, way in the back."

"I don't see anything," I said, leaning inside the trunk to see what he was talking about.

Earz grabbed me by the seat of my britches, shouted "Whoa, Nellie!" and hauled me into the trunk of the car! Then he slammed down the lid before I could get out! I could hear him cackling like a crazy person as he ran away.

"Okay," I said to myself, "This ain't so bad. This trunk is big. There's plenty of air in here. I just need to …"

Possum Mode in 3, 2, 1 …

CHAPTER SIX

Tell me, O muse, of that ingenious
hero who travelled far and wide ...

When I come out of *Possum Mode*, I was still laying inside The Penguin's trunk. I could tell we was driving down the road at a pretty good clip. I had plenty of room to move around, so I was comfortable enough, but I could barely see. I found that "Trojans" box that Earz was talking about. It was full of them individual packets of moist towelettes like they give you when you eat barbeque ribs at a restaurant. Mr. Anderson took us to eat ribs a time or two. I reckoned The Penguin liked to bring his own moist towelettes when he ate ribs.

Then I had a crazy thought. What was it that Earz had said when he hauled me into the trunk: "Whoa, Nellie!"? Why did he say that? Bozo The Clown used to say that in the cartoons. But Nellie is just a longer version of Nell. And Nell was the name of the mule that Johnny McCline used to ride when he was a slave at Clover Bottom Plantation. As a matter of fact, Johnny was sitting on top of Nell's back when he decided to escape from Clover Bottom and join the Yankee army. I was eleven years old, the same age as Johnny when he run away. Maybe this was a sign, kinda like an omen. Maybe this was my "Moment of Destiny!"

Maybe The Penguin and his wife needed a kid. Maybe one time they tried to adopt a kid, but State adoptions take forever. So they just gave up. Maybe The Penguin would take me home and I'd meet his wife. She would be a plump woman, who could cook good fried chicken. Maybe we'd have supper, play some *Parcheesi,* and listen to some records. Who knows what could happen?

So I decided to let The Penguin know I was inside his trunk. I pounded my fist on the inside of the trunk lid. Not too hard though, I didn't wanna dent it. If I dented his trunk lid, that would sure get us off on the wrong foot.

The Penguin didn't hear me at first, so I banged the lid a little harder. Finally, I could tell he was slowing down and pulling over. He stopped the car and I heard the car door open. I pounded the lid a couple of more times just to reassure him. Well, here goes nothing...

When he opened the trunk, I said, "Howdy, Mr. Popper, I'm Delphus V. White!" flashing him as big a smile as I could muster.

"Ahhhh," he gasped, stepping back. After he caught his breath, he said, "Yes. Yes. You're the little boy who sings so ... loud and clear." The Penguin forced a smile onto his face. "Stay, uh ... Stay right there. I'll find a...a phone. Yes, I'll find a phone and I'll call the school. Stay right there. Well, of course, you can get out of the trunk. But stay right there. You remember that I...I didn't put you in the trunk, right? You do remember that, right ... son?"

"Sure," I said. This was not quite the reception I was hoping for. I could see we had pulled off into the parking lot of a shopping center.

"Stay right there," he said again. Now he was talking extra loud and slow. "You understand, right? ... Delphus?" he said, nodding his head. "I'll be right back."

I flipped him a thumbs-up sign and said, "Take your time."

As The Penguin went running off toward one of the shops in search of a telephone, I clambered out of the Colt's trunk and thought for a minute. Finally, I decided I wasn't ready to give up on my "Moment of Destiny!" just yet. Although it was a little cloudy, it seemed like a nice day for a walk, so I headed out walking. After a while, I decided to run so I could put a little more distance between me and The Penguin.

A street sign said I was on Old Hickory Boulevard. That could mean anything. "Old Hickory" was the nickname for President Andrew

Jackson, who they said was "as tough as old hickory." I reckon whenever the City of Nashville builds a new road and they can't think of what to name it, they just call it "Old Hickory Boulevard." In some places, Old Hickory Boulevard runs east-and-west, other places it runs north-and-south. Old Hickory Boulevard will stop on one street and then pick back up several miles away.[21]

I finally passed an old muffler shop that I recognized. I was in Lakewood, a community in Donelson, just ten miles east of Clover Bottom. I had not been in *Possum Mode* as long as I thought. Mr. Anderson said Lakewood was a notorious speed trap. Reckon what he was doing?

As I slowed my pace, I came up on a liquor store. Its glass windows was all covered up with posters advertising Thunderbird, something called Wild Irish Rose, Canadian Mist, and of course, Jack Daniels. Steel metal grates protected the glass windows and rusty brown gates rode in metal tracks on each side of the door. The metal gates was rolled back now. A sign posted on the side wall said, "No consumption of alcohol on the premises." Underneath that, someone had written in magic-marker, "That includes the parking lot."

Right next to the liquor store sat a dingy green building surrounded by stacks and stacks of car tires. Above the door, someone had spray-painted, "Loutie's Used Tire."

Scooted up right up next to the very edge of the liquor store parking lot, like they was trying to make some kinda point, sat a cracked concrete picnic table. About a half-a-dozen bums and hippies was congregated around it. All of them bums and hippies had bottles stuffed into brown paper sacks setting in front of them. They was all smoking cigarettes and it didn't smell like no kinda tobacco I ever smelt. A gray cloud of smoke floated above their heads.

"Hey, little dude," one of them with a bushy red beard hollered out to me, "You wanna hit?" They all laughed at this.

"Shut up, man!" said one hippie without a shirt, "He's a narc!"

[21] Originally Old Hickory Boulevard formed an unbroken loop around the city of Nashville. By the 1970's, it was so interrupted by lakes and rerouted sections that many Nashvillians believed that there were many roads in Nashville with this name.

"No, man, look at that hair! That little dude parties!" All the other bums laughed.

"No, man," said the one without a shirt, as he staggered to his feet. His hair hung down below his shoulders and he was wearing a ladies' necklace. "They're recruiting them younger and younger these days. It's like the Hitler Youth, man. I say he's a narc. What about it, little dude, you a narc?"

Now, I didn't know what a "narc" was, but I knew how to deal with trash like this. "Your momma didn't think I was a narc last night," I yelled at him. The rest of the bums exploded with laughter. There was a good twenty feet between us, so if he made a move toward me, I had a good head start. I was pretty sure I could outrun that drunken bastard.

"Yeah, well,... You just watch yourself, you little narc!" he said, sinking back onto the concrete bench.

I flipped him a bird and said, "Up yours, hippie!" Then I decided to hotfoot it out of there. After a while, I got a stitch in my side, so I went back to regular walking. None of them bums was behind me.

Then the bottom dropped out of the sky! It came a flood! The raindrops hit me so hard, they was like beestings on my skin. My clothes got soaked through-and-through in less than a minute. My jeans felt so heavy, I thought they was going to fall down around my ankles. So I hitched them up to make sure that didn't happen. I finally came up on a long row of buildings that had a covered sidewalk, so I ran up under there to get out of the rain. I strolled down the sidewalk looking in the windows of a junk store, a pawn shop, a little doll store. When I got to the end of the awning, I paused for a minute to decide what to do next.

Then I heard a deep "Wooof!" behind me. I turned around and there was a massive Basset Hound winking at me through the shop window. "Wooof!" he repeated.

"Goddammit, Rooster, get down off that window!" yelled a man from inside the shop. "You'll break through it, you fat bastard! It'll cut you in half like a guillotine." A man appeared at the door and he looked kinda surprised. "Well, hello, young man!" he said to me. "What are you doing out here?"

"Just watching the cars go by. I wasn't hurting nothing."

"Well, of course, you weren't." he said. "It's a free country, isn't it?"

"I reckon."

"Why don't you come on in here for a minute and get dried off?" he said. "You're as wet as water."

I stepped inside the store and there was every kind of vacuum cleaner that you could imagine stacked on metal shelves from the floor to the ceiling. A wooden roll-top desk sat sideways against the back wall.

"I'm Ray Olis," he said and he reached out his hand for me to shake. But I just stood there and looked at it for a second. I don't have much occasion to shake hands at Clover Bottom. Finally, I snapped out of it and shook his hand.

"Howdy! My name is Delphus V. White," I said.

"Pleased to meet you, Delphus," he said. "This is my shop, Aerus Vacuum Cleaner Sales and Service." Ray Olis looked like he was in his fifties and he needed a shave. Although his arms and legs was skinny, his fat belly stretched out the front of his white T-shirt. Pointing to the Basset Hound, he said, "That fat monster's Rooster. Say hello, Rooster!"

Rooster jumped up, putting his paws on my chest, and knocked me right down on the tile floor. Then he straddled me and starting licking my face as I laid there. It was fun!

"Get off, Rooster! You're gonna smother that boy," he said, helping me to my feet. "You're soaked" he said, looking around the shop. "Well, I'm clean out of shop towels. Here, stand right here."

Mr. Olis plugged the cord of a giant, blue vacuum cleaner into a hook light overhead. He turned the power on and aimed the hose at me. A gust of warm wind blanketed me. It was like sticking your head out of a car window on a summer day. In just a few minutes, I was completely dry.

"Now, how was that?" Mr. Olis asked.

"That was great!

"You look good as new, except your hair. Here's a comb."

"No, sir, my hair always looks this way," I said.

"Well, take a comb anyway. It's a promotional item. See? It's got my company name and phone number right here on the side. A traveling comb salesman caught me here at the shop one day and I was bored. I got boxes of these damn things."

Rooster bumped my hand for me to pet him so I did. "Rooster ain't got but one eye," I said.

"Yeah, he got glaucoma when he was a younger man. Bassets are especially prone to getting glaucoma. Nothing they can do but take the eyeball out."

"Why did you name him Rooster?"

"He is named for Marshal Rooster Cogburn in *True Grit*. John Wayne. Did you see that one?"

"Yes, sir, that's my favorite John Wayne movie."

"Mine too. When we first got Rooster, he was still wearing his eyepatch. So we started calling him 'Rooster Cogburn.' Then we just shortened it to 'Rooster.'"

"Have a seat," Mr. Olis said, pointing to a chair. Rooster came over, plopped down on top of my feet, and leaned against my legs.

"You know, you oughta feel honored! Rooster doesn't like most people, especially kids. I have a houseful of kids and they make him a nervous wreck. That's the reason he's here with me today at the shop, to give him a little break."

"I reckon I smell different from most people."

"I hadn't noticed that."

"Dogs can smell about a million times better than people."

"That's what they say."

"I'm part possum."

"Is that right?" Mr. Olis smiled.

"Yessir, I had a tail but they cut it off. I can show you," I said, getting up out of my chair. Rooster grumbled when I moved.

"No, no, no," said Mr. Olis. "You don't have to show me. I'll take your word for it."

I sat back down and Rooster got hisself situated back on my feet again.

"Now, I've read about people born with tails, in India or somewhere," Mr. Olis said. "In India if you're born with a tail, they consider you a holy man."

"I ain't too holy." I said.

"Yeah, well, none of us are as holy as we oughta be, are we?" Mr. Olis said. "Hey, Delphus, are you hungry?" he said as he examined a brown paper sack on his desk that was tied up with sparkly silver twine. The twine looked like tinsel from a Christmas tree. Removing the silvery twine and opening the bag, he said, "Let's see what the Missus fixed for lunch. Hmmm. Egg salad! Fart sandwiches!" he said, winking at me. "Here you go." He tossed me a sandwich neatly wrapped up in wax paper.

"Thank you very much."

"So, Delphus," Mr. Olis said, after taking a bite out of his sandwich, "You got a momma or daddy out there looking for you right now? They're probably worried about you."

"No, sir. I don't have a momma or daddy."

"I'm sorry. That must be tough," he said. "Well, where do you live then?"

"I live at the Clover Bottom Hospital and School," I said, taking a bite out of my sandwich. It was pretty dang good.

"Ohhh, I see. Do they treat you okay there? 'Cause, you know, I've heard rumors."

"No, they treat me real good. Me and my Developmental Technician, Mr. Anderson, are pals."

"How come you decided to run away then?"

"A mean kid stuffed me into a car trunk. I thought it might be my 'Moment of Destiny!'"

"You want me to give you a ride back? Clover Bottom is not far from here."

"I don't think I'm ready to go back just yet."

"I bet your buddy, Mr. Anderson, is probably out there looking for you right now."

"They're supposed to let the police do that."

"Well, I still bet he's worried about you."

"Probably." I took another bite of the sandwich.

"Hey, watch this!" Mr. Olis said. "Catch, Rooster!" he called, as he pitched a bite of his sandwich toward us. Rooster watched it drop on the floor right in front of him. Then, he slowly leaned over and licked it up.

"I reckon it's hard for him to catch things with just one eye," I said.

"Nah," Mr. Olis said. "He's just lazy." He finished his sandwich and said, "Okay, Delphus, what are your plans then?"

"I was thinking about joining the Army."

"The Army?"

"Yeah, my hero, Johnny McCline, joined the Army when he was eleven years old."

"I've never heard of him."

"He was a slave boy at Clover Bottom Plantation during the Civil War, but he got tired of being a slave. So he run away and joined the Yankee Army."

"At eleven years old?"

"Yeah."

"Wow. I can't believe I haven't read about him."

"Ain't that something?"

"Well, nowadays, I think they have age requirements for the Army," Mr. Olis said.

"I was thinking maybe I could be a mascot, like Bucky in *Captain America*."

"I'm sure you'd make a good one, but I don't think they actually do that anymore."

"I was also thinking about going to East Tennessee and seeing if I could find my kinfolks."

"White is not that common a last name," Mr. Olis said. "You might have some luck with that."

"White's not really my last name. I don't know what my real last name is."

"Well, that's going to make it tough."

"Yeah, I know."

"Listen, Delphus," Mr. Olis said, "I gotta let somebody know you're here so they can stop worrying about you."

"I know."

"Do you know the telephone number out there at Clover Bottom?"

"No," I lied. I did know some of the dormitory numbers, but I didn't know the Main Administration number by heart. So maybe technically, that wasn't a lie.

"I'm gonna go get the phone book," Mr. Olis said, standing up, "It's back in the back room." He stepped out to a room in the back.

I still wasn't ready to give up on my "Moment of Destiny!" Rooster groaned a little when I got up. He had drifted off to sleep. "Bye-bye, Rooster," I whispered to him, and then I was out the door and back out into the rain.

The rain had slacked off a little bit, but it was still coming down good and steady. In just a few minutes, my clothes was sopping wet again. After walking a while, I came to a huge gold-colored laundromat building. On each side of the glass doors sat two kiddie rides that were exactly alike. You know the kind I mean? Where you put a kid in the seat, drop in a quarter, and it rocks back-and-forth. These were these shiny yellow cartoon dogs with a friendly grin on their face. They was perched on polished metal pedestals and they looked like they was guarding the entrance. Why would you want two just exactly alike?

At any rate, I figured I could go in there, get out of the rain and warm up a minute. Goosebumps was starting to come up on my arms. I opened the doors and stepped in. I didn't want to track water all over the laundromat floor and there was a thick welcome mat right inside the door. It read, "Welcome to Fashion Laundromat!" I decided I was just gonna wait by the door until I stopped dripping water so much.

I stood at the door and watched cars go by. Now, you might think that would be boring, but at Clover Bottom, the only kinda cars I get to see is trucks and plain white State cars. It's interesting to see all the different kinds of cars there are, with various colors and shapes. You can see them on TV, but it's not the same. Although it was nice and warm inside the laundromat, a chill shook through me. I folded my arms across my chest so I could rub some warmth into my arms.

My britches immediately dropped down to my ankles and took my drawers with them! I yanked 'em back up as fast as I could and looked around to see if anybody had seen me. A woman and a little girl was behind me, standing at a table folding clothes and giggling as hard as they could. The woman said something to the little girl and the little girl picked up a towel and started walking over towards me. Oh, sweet mercy!

Before the little girl could say anything, I said, "I'm sorry, ma'am, I didn't mean to moon y'all. It was a complete accident." *Why in the world did I call her "ma'am,"? She looked like she was about my age.*

"I know," she said, smiling. "It looks like your jeans might be a little too big for you."

She was the most beautiful girl I had ever seen in my whole entire life, including on TV. She had long blond hair, almost as light as mine, under a blue baseball cap. She had on shorts and knee socks, and a white baseball jersey with "Wildcats" embroidered in blue. Her white uniform contrasted with her dark suntan. She had a little patch of freckles across her nose and cheeks. But her eyes was what really caught you off-guard. They were huge and the lightest blue you ever saw. She seemed to have a glow that radiated off her. She was a little bit taller than me, so I tried to stand up as straight and tall as I could.

"Yeah, well, uh, ma'am," I stammered. "I still didn't mean to do it." *I said ma'am again!*

"It's okay," she said, smiling. "I have five older brothers," she whispered, "And I have seen boy's underwear and *everything*." I tried to smile, but I wasn't sure my mouth was working right. "Do you need a towel?" she said, holding one out in front of me.

"Well, I wouldn't want to put you out."

"Don't be silly. Here!"

I took the towel from her and it wasn't nothing like the towels we have at Clover Bottom. It was white and fluffy and about two-inches thick. It had just come out of the dryer and was still warm. I dried myself off and felt a hundred percent better. I handed it back to her, but she said, "Why don't you hang on to it for a little while?" draping it around my shoulders.

"You want to sit down?" she said. "You look bushed."

We walked over to some of those hard plastic chairs that look like they belong on *The Jetsons*.[22] Bronze-colored clothes dryers lined the walls of the laundromat with bronze-colored washing machines in the center. There wasn't a scratch or dent on any one of them.

As we sat down, the girl said, "I'm Bernie."

"That's an interesting name," I said. *Mr. Anderson says you can't never go wrong complimenting a woman on her name.*

"It's short for Bernadette. What's yours?"

"My name is Delphus."

"Now, *that's* an interesting name."

"Well, it's kind of a long story. I'm part possum."

"Ha! I think my brother Hal is part gorilla."

"That's funny," I said.

"I was supposed to play softball this afternoon, but then it blew up this terrible thunderstorm," Bernie said. "So I had to help my mom do the laundry. Our washing machine is broken and my Dad owns this place."

"I like doing laundry. I like the smell. One time, my buddy, Sammy Blount, climbed into a dryer and he rode around inside it while it was running. He got into a lotta trouble, but he said it was worth it."

"I think about doing that every time I come to a laundromat."

"Yeah, me too."

"I go to Donelson Christian Academy," Bernie said. "Where do you go to school?"

"Clover Bottom Hospital and School."

"I don't believe we play y'all in softball," she said. "That's a special school, isn't it?"

"Yeah, but I'm not a slow learner."

"I know that, silly," she said and she smiled that smile again and I melted inside. "You have to stay overnight there, don't you?"

"Yeah."

---

22 The Eames Molded Plastic Armchair is a polyester and fiberglass chair designed by Charles and Ray Eames. Introduced in 1950, the chairs have become a mainstay in schools, airports, restaurants, and laundromats.

"Don't you miss your family?"

"I don't have any family that I know of."

"Oh, that's terrible," she said and patted me on the arm. "Did you run away from Clover Bottom?"

"Kind of," I said. I decided that sharing the story of Earz Grissom manhandling me would not make a good impression on her.

"Where on earth will you go?"

"I was thinking about joining the Army," I said, "But I hear they have age restrictions. I may just travel around and have adventures."

"But how will you eat?"

"I don't eat too much."

"Maybe you should stay at Clover Bottom until you get a little older."

"I dunno," I said. "I feel like there's this ... Destiny waiting for me out there, something I'm supposed to do."

"You're just what eleven, twelve?"

"Eleven-and-a-half."

"You have your whole life ahead of you," Bernie said. "Your destiny will be there waiting for you, when you're ready."

"I reckon," I said.

"Won't you miss all your friends at your school?"

"Yeah, I'd miss my Developmental Technician, Mr. Anderson, and my pals, the Blount Brothers. They make me laugh."

"Let's go talk to my mom and dad," Bernie said, "I'm sure they'll be glad to help you get back home."

We walked over to the table where her momma was folding a purple sweater. Bernie's momma was a tall, thin woman whose hair looked like a blond Dairy Dip ice cream cone. She had on a humongous diamond ring. I don't usually pay attention to stuff like that, but you couldn't help but notice this one.

"Mom, this is Delphus," Bernie said.

"Nice to meet you, ma'am," I said. "I'm sorry about what happened earlier, I failed to adjust my accoutrements." I got that line from Daffy

Duck,[23] but I wasn't trying to be funny, I was trying to sound smart for Bernie's momma. It never hurts to impress the momma.

"Don't worry, honey," Bernie's momma said, smiling. "That happens to all of us from time to time. I'm Rita Sinnott. Did you get dried off?"

"Yes, ma'am. It's nice and warm in here," I said. "Thank you for the use of the towel. It's a nice one." I handed her back the towel.

"Mom," Bernie said, "Delphus would like to ask you favor."

"What's that, darling?" Bernie's momma said.

"Well, ma'am, if it's not too much trouble," I said, "I would appreciate it if you could give me a ride home. I think I've been away from my friends for too long."

"Well, sure, honey," Bernie's momma said. Then she called over to a man reading a newspaper, sitting in a row of *Jetson* chairs against the wall. "Al, honey," she said, "This little boy needs a ride home."

The man got up, folded his newspaper, tucked it under his arm and walked over to us.

"Hello, sir," I said, extending my hand for him to shake. "I'm Delphus V. White." I had decided I liked shaking hands.

He leaned down so we was eye-level and shook my hand. "Hello, Delphus V. White," he said, "I'm Al Sinnott. Pleased to meet you." Mr. Sinnott smiled a big smile and stood up. Putting one arm around Bernie's mom, he held the other arm out wide and said, "Welcome to Fashion Laundromat! Mrs. Sinnott and I are the owners! And Delphus, this is just the beginning! We have a new laundromat opening up in Madison in three months! And after that, who knows how many?"

I looked over at Bernie and she just rolled her eyes.

Mr. Sinnott had kind of a pointy nose and a big fluffy beard. On top of his head was a bright orange bucket hat, like fishermen wear. His khaki jacket and pants made him look like he wearing some kinda uniform. He leaned back down and, "So, where do you need a ride to, son?"

"Clover Bottom Hospital and School."

"Oh, you go to Clover Bottom?" Mr. Sinnott said. "Are they treating you okay there?"

---

23 *Drip-Along Daffy*, Dir. Charles M. Jones, Warner Bros., 1951. Film.

"Yes, sir, they treat me fine."

"Well then, Clover Bottom is right on our way," he said. "We'll have you back there in no time. I think Mother's about finished with the laundry, aren't you, dear?"

"I will be if y'all would help me," Mrs. Sinnott said.

So we all pitched in to finish folding the laundry. It was fun. Mr. Sinnott watched me folding a t-shirt and said, "That's some mighty fancy folding there, Delphus."

"My Developmental Technician, Mr. Anderson, showed me how to do it this way," I said. "It's how he learned to do it in the Service."

"I thought I recognized it," he said, smiling.

We finished up and loaded the laundry in the Sinnotts' car. They had a Ford Country Squire station wagon, with fake wood panels. Mr. Anderson says that back when they used real wood panels, you would constantly have to go around and re-tighten all the bolts and screws because the wood would expand in the summer and then contract in the winter. Bernie and me sat in the back seat, but there was a laundry basket between us.

As we were driving down the road, Mr. Sinnott called over his shoulder, "Hey, Delphus, look at this." I was sitting behind him and leaned over the front seat to watch. "I push this button right here ... and the car drives all by itself. See? My feet aren't even touching the pedals." He lifted his feet up to show me they wasn't on the pedals. "It's called cruise control.[24] Have you ever seen anything like that? By the time you're ready to start driving, cars probably won't even have steering wheels."

"Yes, sir," I said, "That sure is something!"

"Honey," said Mrs. Sinnott, softy placing her hand on Mr. Sinnott's shoulder, "Why don't you play with your gadget when it stops raining? The rain is still really coming down."

She was right. And it had gotten dark as we drove along. I settled back into my seat and looked over at Bernie. She was smiling. "You have a great family," I whispered.

---

[24] Cruise control became a popular option for production vehicles after the 1973 Oil Crisis.

"Yes, I do," she whispered back, "Thank you."

The ride to Clover Bottom was way too short. We got there in no time. I directed Mr. Sinnott to Johnson House, the administration building, at the entrance of the campus. It was covered in red brick and had four big white columns on the porch.

"Well, I guess it's time to face the music," I said, under my breath.

"Delphus, would you like me to come inside with you? Could make thing go a little more smoothly," Mr. Sinnott said.

"Oh, no, sir!" I said. "I'll be fine."

"Wait a minute," said Mr. Sinnott. He turned in his seat and handed me a card. "This is my business card. It's got our home telephone number written on the back of it. You do have access to a telephone, don't you?"

"Yes, sir."

"Well, if you need anything, anything at all, you just give us a call. Okay?"

"I sure will. Thank you." I shook hands with Mr. Sinnott and he turned back around.

I looked over at Bernie and she was not smiling. She looked sad. "You better not forget me," she said, "Because I saved your butt." Then she smiled.

"I know," I said. "You're my guardian angel!" Then she reached over and squeezed my hand, which was resting on top of the laundry basket. It was as good as a kiss.

"We'll wait to make sure you get inside," Mr. Sinnott said.

"Good-bye, hon," said Mrs. Sinnott, "You take care of yourself."

I got out of the Wagon and tromped over to the porch. The rain was still coming down by the bucketfuls. I opened the door and held my breath. Thank heavens! Mr. Farley, the night watchman, was not at his desk. He liked to take little naps during his shift. I waited until I heard the Sinnotts' car drive away and then I went back outside the door. Progress House, my home, was just two buildings away. I ran through the rain and made it to the door. And it was locked. What time was it? I pounded on the doors but nobody answered. I went around to the windows and couldn't wake up the Blount Brothers. I had to find a phone. If I could wake somebody up in Progress House, they would let me in.

I checked the doors on every cottage on our street: Harpeth, Stones, Cumberland, Caney Fork, and Clinch. I couldn't find a single one unlocked. And the rain just kept pouring down. I ran back up Progress Street. Rosewood Building - locked. I tried the door on the Magnolia Building. Bingo! It opened. I quietly eased into the entryway and there it was, right there on the wall, a pale yellow telephone. As I tiptoed over to the phone, I heard someone say, "Who's there?"

I turned around to see a woman in deep blue nightgown rolling toward me in a wheelchair. Her dark hair stood out in every direction. She suddenly rolled to a stop. "Oh, it's you," she said and her eyes welled up with tears.

"Just borrowing your phone," I said. I had never seen this woman before in my life.

"I knew you'd find me," she said, the tears now streaming down her face. "I knew you'd come back to me."

"I live just down the street," I said.

"Don't you remember me?" she said, rolling herself closer. "Don't you remember your Mum, Little Tater?"

"My name is Delphus," I whispered.

"They told me you had died," she said. She was crying so hard now that I was having trouble understanding her words. "But I knew you didn't die." She grabbed me and hugged me close to her, so tight I couldn't get away. She kissed me on top of my head and her breath smelled like garlic. Her armpits stunk. It's a weird feeling getting that much love and affection from a complete stranger. But it's not altogether terrible.

"Zoey, who is that?" squawked a woman from a side room.

"It's my boy, Tater," the old woman answered. "He's come back to me!"

Could this be my real momma? Living just a block away from me all these years? "Are you sure I'm your son?" I asked her. "Do you remember me being born with a tail?"

"A tail? You mean like a puppy dog?"

"Yes, ma'am," I said.

She guffawed and all her teeth was capped in gold. "No, Tater, you wasn't born with no puppy dog tail."

"Then I don't think I'm your kid, lady."

"Oh, don't talk that way, Tater," she said, loosening her bear hug on me. "Of course, you are a lot paler than I remember. 'Cause when you were born, you were brown as a little tater. Because your daddy was ... She took a deep breath, and whispered real low, "Mr. Maxwell." She let me go and stared down into her lap. "They took him away. He's been gone a long time now."

"I just need to use the phone," I said, "And I'll be out of your way."

She grabbed me by the hand, but then she let me go so she could push her wheelchair. "Let me show you to the girls."

I followed her. I reckon I felt sorry for her. Inside the room she said, "This is Florry. Florry, this is my boy, Tater." Florry was a humongous blonde woman sprawled on the couch. A sty had almost closed her left eye.

"That ain't no baby," Florry said. "That's a little old man. That's my Grandpa Whalen! Oh mercy!" she said starting to rock back and forth on the couch. "The dead are rising from the grave! It's the end of the world!"

Another lady in a wheelchair rolled in from the hall. She was pale and bony and had that orangey-pink color hair that older woman have. She was in a navy nightgown and had a little white sailor's hat on her head.

"Kitty," said the lady who thought she was my momma, "This is my baby, Tater! He's come back to me!"

The pink-haired lady with the sailor hat rolled her wheelchair beside the lady who thought she was my momma. She gently put her hand on her arm and said, "Zoey, honey, this can't be your Tater. That was a long, long time ago. Tater would be a grown man by now. Tater didn't make it, honey. Remember, we put some nice flowers on his grave back then?"

The lady named Zoey buried her face in her hands, hunched over in her wheelchair, and wailed!

The fat lady named Florry rocked back and forth on the couch, crying, "This is the end of the world! The end of the world is coming!"

I squatted down by Zoey and said, "Maybe I could come see you sometime. I live just down the street."

She didn't reply.

"I don't believe that would be a good idea," said the pink-haired lady.

I stood up and looked at her and said, "I'm sorry. I didn't mean to cause all this trouble. I just wanted to borrow your telephone."

I walked back out to the entryway and picked up the phone. Then I heard a door open down at the end of the hall. I peeped around the corner. Earz Grissom came swaggering down the hall, zipping up his britches. I slammed down the phone and ran out of there as fast as I could.

I hid in the bushes at the corner of the building. It had stopped raining.

I walked down to the hog barn. Ladybird was lying in her stall, with her little piglets. The pen next to her was clean and filled with fresh straw, so I just went in and laid down. As tired as I was, I couldn't go to sleep. I thought about everything that had happened to me today and all the people I met. I realized why there wasn't no fences around Clover Bottom Hospital and School. Out in the real world, there ain't no place for us to go.

Questions for Class Discussion

1. *Was Delphus locked inside a "Trojan Horse?" Why or why not?*

2. *Was Delphus captured by a one-eyed monster?*

3. *Did Ray Olis share a "bag of wind" with Delphus? Why or why not?*

4. *Have you read another story that included Zoe Higgins, Kitty, and Florry?*

CHAPTER SEVEN

The jagged flint edge sawed at the crimsoned breast, and thin bony fingers, ghastly dyed, tore out the still twitching heart. "The portents are dire!" exclaimed the priest wildly ... "Here from the pulsing heart of a captive Roman, I read – Defeat for the Sons of the Heather!"

"Well, it looks like we got us a new pig," said Mr. Anderson.

"Good morning, Mr. Anderson," I said looking up from the straw.

"You get locked out of Progress House last night?"

"I couldn't wake up Ferlin."

"He is a sound sleeper," said Mr. Anderson. "You better get on up out of there before somebody comes along and tries to make a barbeque sandwich out of you."

I got up and brushed the straw off my clothes and Mr. Anderson dusted off my back. "Okay, let's go get us some breakfast," he said. After we had walked a while, he said, "So, you decide to take a little trip yesterday?"

"Not exactly."

"So, what happened?"

"I went into *Possum Mode*." That was not exactly a lie, I did go into Possum Mode after Earz hauled me into The Penguin's trunk. If I snitched on Earz Grissom, he would kill me. Literally kill me.

Graveyard dead. I was more scared of him than any punishment that Clover Bottom could hand out.

"So, are you telling me you had one of your spells, fell into the trunk, and then somehow closed the lid down on top of yourself?"

"I don't know."

"'Lying lips are an abomination to the LORD,' Delphus."

"What's his position on snitching?"

"Don't you blaspheme around me, son."

I cogitated for a minute and said, "Doesn't Proverbs 17 say, 'Whoever would foster love covers an offense, but whoever repeats the matter separates close friends?'"

Mr. Anderson laughed a belly laugh. "I guess you got me there, you little stinker!" he said, messing up my hair. "So that's all you're gonna tell?"

"All I can tell," I said. "Do they know in Johnson House that I'm back?"

"Yeah, I found you in that pen a little while ago and I went over and talked to them."

"You didn't wake me up."

"Nah, I thought I'd let you sleep a little longer. You looked pretty comfortable and I figured you had had a big day."

"Thanks."

"You've lost your rec room privileges for a month."

"Okay." *I didn't use the rec room much anyway.*

"You had us worried there for a while," Mr. Anderson said. "They said The Penguin, uh, Mr. Popper, was about to have a conniption fit when he called yesterday afternoon. He finally came back here and me and him drove all over Lakewood trying to find you."

"Did you get a speeding ticket?"

"That place ain't nothing but a speed trap," Mr. Anderson said. "That Popper is a good fella, though. I never had really talked to him much before. He was a Marine, he played in the Marine Corps Band."

"He don't look like a Marine."

"Folks can surprise you, Delphus."

We reached the cafeteria and there wasn't many people in line yet because it was so early. I asked Mrs. Crawford, the breakfast lady, for extra scrambled eggs. After we sat down at the table, Mr. Anderson said a short blessing and we started eating.

"Did you work with Spanky on his trick last night?" I asked. Spanky was Mr. Anderson's English Bulldog and Mr. Anderson was teaching him how to go the refrigerator and fetch him a coke-cola.

"No, I tied a rag onto the refrigerator door handle and Spanky has mastered opening the refrigerator door with it. But after he gets the door open, he just stands there and stares at all the food inside."

"He probably likes all the smells."

"Spanky never takes anything out. He just looks at all the little Tupperware containers in there."

"What does Miss Zelda think about Spanky being able to open the refrigerator door?"

"She doesn't think it's as funny as I do."

"I can see that."

"Spanky still hasn't learned what a Coca-Cola is, though. I got those Cokes in a can because I figured they would be easier for him to carry in his mouth."

"I think a bottle might hurt his teeth."

"Yeah," said Mr. Anderson said. "That's what I figured."

"Why didn't you work on the trick?"

"Because I didn't get home 'til late."

"What were you doing?"

"I was out looking for your goofy behind."

"Did Miss Zelda get mad because you was late?"

"No, she understands when I have to work late."

"She's a good wife."

"She sure is," he said. "I hit the jackpot on that deal."

"I met a beautiful girl yesterday, Mr. Anderson. Her name was Bernie, which is short for Bernadette."

"Did you get her phone number?"

"Her daddy gave me their phone number."

"Well, don't you go running off to visit this Bernie," he said smiling. Then he changed his tone. "Seriously, Delphus, you can't run off like that again. I almost had a heart attack. I'm not a young man."

"I won't run off again," I said. "I didn't mean to this time."

"Did anybody hurt you?" Mr. Anderson asked. "'Cause, you know, we can take care of things like that?"

"No, everything's fine," I said. "I don't think I'll be calling Bernie though. We're just from two different worlds. But I can still think about her from time-to-time."

"No more running off?"

"I promise."

"Who would help me take care of the hogs if you left?" he asked.

"The Blount Brothers."

"And who would keep the Blount Brothers out of mischief?"

"You."

"Speaking of the Blount Brothers, here they are!" Mr. Anderson said, as they joined us at the table.

"Yessir!" said Ferlin Blount. "It sure is a fine morning."

"'Each morning we are born again,'" said Sammy Blount. "'What we do today is what matters most.'"

Frank Blount stuffed a biscuit into his mouth.

"Good morning, men," said Mr. Anderson. "I hope y'all are ready to castrate some pigs this morning."

We all groaned.

"Do we have to do that, Mr. Anderson?" I asked. "Ladybird's little pigs seem so happy."

"You know we have to," he said. "If we don't, their hormones will taint their meat. They'll get the 'boar taint' and the meat won't be fitten to eat. Plus, we gotta do it by the signs, so there will be a minimum of pain."

"Yessir," said Ferlin. "I have heard farmers talk about planting and harvesting 'by the signs,' but I ain't sure I know exactly what that means."

"Well, my daddy and granddaddy always planted and castrated by the signs," Mr. Anderson said. "The old-time folks always swore by it. It really is scientific and a *Farmer's Almanac* could explain it to you better than I could, but I'll try. What is a man mostly made up of?"

"Spirit!" I said.

"Chi!" said Sammy.

"Yessir! Muscle and blood!" said Ferlin.

"Water," said Mr. Anderson. "A man's body is made up of about three-quarters water."

"Yessir," said Ferlin, nodding his head. "I think I heard that somewhere before."

"And we know that the gravity of the moon has an effect on all the water on the Earth," continued Mr. Anderson, holding up a biscuit like a small imaginary moon above the table. "We know this because the moon's gravity makes the oceans' tides go in and out each day.

"But the moon's gravity pulls on all the water in your body just like it pulls on the oceans," continued Mr. Anderson. "And it pulls just the same on the water in a cow's body, or in a pig's body. And what is blood mostly made out of?"

"Yessir! Water," said Ferlin.

"That's right!" said Mr. Anderson. "And the pull of the moon's gravity is strongest when the moon is full. I used to go out with a little girl who was an Emergency Room nurse and she said that people always bled more and it was harder to get them to stop bleeding when it was a full moon."

"That could explain why werewolves come out when there's a full moon," I said.

Mr. Anderson ignored me.

"Now, depending on where the moon is in the heavens," Mr. Anderson continued, "The pull of the moon is stronger in a particular part of your body. For example, when the moon is in the Taurus part of the heavens, the moon is pulling harder on your neck, so your neck is more sensitive. When the moon is in the Virgo section of the heavens, the moon's pull is stronger on your belly, so your belly is more sensitive."

"Yessir! When does the moon pull on your privates?" asked Ferlin, in all seriousness.

"That's Scorpio!" said Mr. Anderson. "And that's exactly the time you would *not* want to castrate pigs. It would hurt them more and there would be a good chance that they'd get an infection."

"How do you remember all this, Mr. Anderson?" I asked.

"I was reading *The Farmer's Almanac* last night before I went to bed," he said. "I knew the right time was coming up, but I wasn't sure exactly when it was. It almost slipped past me."

"So the best time is ..."

"Today. When the moon is waning, that is, getting smaller, and it's pulling hardest on the legs, or in Aquarius."

"I don't know, Mr. Anderson," I said, "This all sounds kinda ... magical."

"Well, I do know that the Good Book says, 'And God said, Let there be lights in the firmament of the heaven to divide the day from the night; *and let them be for signs, and for seasons,...*'

"And then you read that in conjunction with Ecclesiastes," Mr. Anderson continued, "'To everything there is a *season, a time for every purpose under heaven*: ...'"

"Okay."

"So I figure this is just the Good Lord's way of letting us know when the time is right," said Mr. Anderson. "Plus, my daddy and granddaddy swore by this stuff. Now, let's go castrate some pigs!"

We emptied our trays and hiked down to the hog lot, which was about 200 yards away. The hog lot was not a part of the original Clover Bottom Plantation, they built it just for the School. I reckon they built it so far away from the campus because they was worried about the smell. The smell ain't really that bad because we kept the lots pretty clean. We had about an acre fenced off for pasture. Four metal hog feeders sat out in the middle of the pasture. They looked like shiny outer space probes that had crashed down out of the sky.

The hog barn was a long, low wooden building with a tin roof. We wanted to paint the outside walls red, but we never could get together enough red paint. So the walls was just a faded gray wood color. At the back of the barn was a big silver galvanized silo where we stored the hog feed. Inside the barn we had six different pens, one for each of our

Ladies: Ladybird, Mamie, Bessie, and Jackie O, which included space for their litters. Plus, we had two extra pens for when anybody got sick. The farrowing shed, which is where they had their babies, was built onto the outside of the barn.

We didn't have a boar. When it was time for one of the Ladies to get "in a family way," we would take her to visit a boar at Rudy's Farm,[25] a gigantic hog operation not far from Clover Bottom. Rudy's Farm donated their boar services to Clover Bottom. We loved to go with the Ladies on their trips to Rudy's Farm, because the farm had a petting zoo. They had buffalo, llamas, and a bear. The llamas was the only ones you could actually pet. One time, a llama named Peaches spit in Frank Blount's face. We had to hold Frank back until he got calmed down. Frank wanted to strangle Peaches.

Our Ladies are Chester White hogs, which are the best kind there is. They are known for being good mothers. They are colored white and have drooping ears. You can tell what breed a hog is by what color he is and what kind of ears he has. For example, a Yorkshire hog is also white, but he has erect ears. A Duroc hog is red and has small drooping ears. A Berkshire hog is mostly black, with some white points, and he has erect ears. So you can see what I mean.

When we got to the barn, Mr. Anderson said, "Ferlin, go get us a bale of hay out of the barn. Frank, get that metal bucket that is hanging on the peg in the barn. Delphus, get the antiseptic spray out my office. And Sammy, would you get the knife out of my truck? It's in a paper sack sitting on the seat." We always used the disposable kind of castration knives. That way, it was a new blade each time and it would be good and clean and sharp.

When everybody got back with the stuff they was supposed to get, Mr. Anderson got the knife out of its plastic packaging. It was shiny

---

[25] Rudy's Farm was a family-owned sausage company established by Daniel Rudy in 1881. At its height, the farm covered twelve-hundred acres. By 1962, the company was producing hundreds of thousands of pounds of sausage each year. In 1976, the company was purchased by Kahn's, which later became a subsidiary of the Sara Lee Corporation. In 1990, the Rudy Sausage Company plant was moved to Newbern, Tennessee.

and kinda curved. He said, "Okay, men, we'll do this like we always do it. Watch closely, y'all might be doing this on your own someday. The other boys probably aren't ready to be seeing this just yet." He was right. Castrating pigs gave me nightmares whenever we did it.

"Ferlin, you get on the right side of the bale. Frank, you get on the left. You can each hold a leg and keep the pig from squirming around. I'll cut 'em and then, Delphus, you spray 'em with the antiseptic spray. Sammy, you can bring the pigs back and forth from the pen one at a time." It didn't really take two people to hold down a two-week-old pig, but Mr. Anderson wanted us to learn how to do it. I reckon he thought we was all gonna grow up to be pig farmers.

When Sammy brought up the first pig, Mr. Anderson picked him up and laid him on his back on the hay bale. "Okay, men," he said, "Ferlin, you get that leg. Frank, get the other one." The pig squealed a little bit in protest and Frank gently patted him on his little chest with his free hand. The pig quieted down. Mr. Anderson narrated what he was doing because the Blount Brothers couldn't see too good. "Okay, you find the nut with your thumb and forefinger, you raise up on it just a little bit, then you take the knife and make a tiny, little cut on his sack, and then pop! The nut will pop right out of the sack. Then you pull up on the nut just a little ways and cut this connector cord. And it'll just reel back in. Now, some people say just rip that nut out. But you don't want to do that. It can give the little pig a hernia, and you don't want that." He tossed the nut into the bucket. "Now, we're gonna do the other side," he said. "Pinch the nut up, slit the sack - tiny cut, and cut the cord. Okay, spray him, Delphus." I jumped in and sprayed his sack with the antiseptic spray. The pig started squalling again. The antiseptic spray was very cold. Frank and Ferlin let the pig go and he went running after Sammy back to his brothers and sisters. "Now, you want to try to make the cuts low down on his sack to allow for drainage." Mr. Anderson said, pitching the other nut into the bucket.

We castrated four more pigs. It was always seemed funny to me that the pigs squealed the most when I sprayed them with the antiseptic. One time, I cut my arm and Mr. Anderson sprayed some of the antiseptic spray on my cut. It didn't burn. It was just cold. Maybe it was because of my special Possum Powers? Who knows?

Sammy came walking out of the barn, holding the last pig in his arms like a baby. "This little man decided that he wanted to sleep late today," Sammy said.

"Is he injured?" Mr. Anderson asked. "Can he walk okay?"

"Oh, he can run like the wind," Sammy said. "I almost couldn't catch him."

I inspected the little pig wrapped in Sammy's arms and said, "Congratulations, Sammy. He looks just like you!"

"Yessir!" Ferlin said, "Sammy Jr."

"Sammy Davis Jr." said Mr. Anderson, laughing. We wasn't really supposed to name the little pigs, because that made it harder when they grew up and had to go to the processer, but Mr. Anderson was the one who said it. "Well, come here, Sammy Davis Jr.," Mr. Anderson said. "Let's get you cut."

After Sammy Davis Jr. was cut and I sprayed him with the antiseptic, Frank set him down on the ground. I swear that little pig gave Sammy Blount the meanest look you ever saw and then went running back to his little brothers. Mr. Anderson tossed the last nut into the metal bucket. Blood stained his hands, but not as much as you might think.

"Great job, men," Mr. Anderson said. "I know we're all glad to have that over with. Y'all did real good work!" He stooped over to pick up the bucket of little nuts. "What in the world...?" he said, looking down into the bucket.

"What is it, Mr. Anderson?" I said.

"Oh, I just thought I saw something black down there in the bottom of this bucket," he said. "I thought maybe one of the little nuts had busted open somehow. I don't see it now, though. I guess it was just rust on the bottom of the bucket. Hmmmm."

We cleaned up our worksite, which didn't take long. Then we went about our daily chores of feeding and watering all the hogs. "I'm going to go get the other boys," said Mr. Anderson, "Before they get into shenanigans."

But before Mr. Anderson could leave, a gleaming white truck towing a long white stock trailer pulled into the driveway towards the hog barn. Both the truck and trailer looked like they had just rolled off the showroom floor. The truck started backing the stock trailer up to the loading chute at the rear of the barn, where we loaded and unloaded hogs. I could see a single black mass crouched deep in the shadows of the trailer. When the driver had lined the trailer up even with the loading chute, he killed the truck's ignition and got out. The passenger stayed inside.

"Morning, fellas," said Mr. Anderson. "What's going on?"

"Delivery for you, sir," said the Driver, studiously avoiding a huge black puddle of pig poop. He didn't look like any kind of stock truck driver I had ever seen before. His bleached uniform was starched stiff and there wasn't a speck of dirt on him.

"I'm Ed Anderson. I run the hog operation," said Mr. Anderson, extending his hand for the Driver to shake. The other man didn't shake it. Ignoring the snub, Mr. Anderson smiled and said, "There must be some kind of mistake. I didn't order any kind of stock. I place all our feed and stock orders."

"No mistake, sir," the Driver said. "The superintendent of the school has already signed for the delivery." He held out a clipboard with some papers on it for Mr. Anderson to look at.

"I can see that's a boar on that trailer and I'm sure it ain't no Chester White. We don't need a boar here and we dang sure don't need a boar that ain't a Chester White!" Mr. Anderson was starting to get a little angry now and I ain't never seen Mr. Anderson get angry before. "There's no immunization record here!" said Mr. Anderson, pounding his finger on the clipboard. "I don't know where that boar came from. I don't know what kind of diseases he might be carrying."

"If you have a problem with the delivery, sir, I suggest you take it up with your superintendent," the Driver said.

"You bet I will," Mr. Anderson said. "I run this hog operation! You do not unload that boar 'til I get back!" Then he shot us a look to make sure we understood. Mr. Anderson practically ran to his truck and scattered gravel as he sped off for the Johnson House Administration building.

So we were all just standing there looking at each other. To break the silence, Sammy Blount sauntered over toward the Driver's direction and said, "Sure is a glorious morning, ain't it?"

The Driver ignored Sammy. He just stood there leaning against his truck with his arms folded across his chest.

"I hear that Cedar Grove Hog Farm is real nice," Sammy said. "I hear they have their own processing plant right there on the farm! Is that where you boys are from?"

"Beat it, Retard."

Sammy took a few steps back like he had been kicked. Ferlin and Frank came running up behind Sammy. If you fight one Blount Brother, you gotta fight 'em all! In unison, the Brothers craned their heads back slowly and surveyed the truck driver beneath the rims of their spectacles.

But Sammy turned and calmly placed a hand on Frank's chest. "'Not engaging in ignorance is wisdom,'" he whispered.

Sammy paced two steps forward and then one step to his left. Then, he struck a Kung Fu Tiger Stance. Holding the pose for a millisecond, Sammy exploded into a single fluid spin! His left foot hammered down into the huge puddle of pig poop!

The puddle exploded! The pig poop went sailing through the air, describing a perfect arc! Pig poop rained down all over the Truck Driver's starched clothes and his stupid white truck. Me and the Blount Brothers ran into the barn to hide, laughing so hard we almost couldn't stand up.

"Come back here, you little bastard!" screamed the Truck Driver. He was soaked in pig poop from head-to-toe!

We hid in the barn until Mr. Anderson got back. But if the Truck Driver had come looking for us, he could have found us pretty easy, we was giggling so hard.

"Amazing shot, Sammy!" I whispered across the barn.

"'The greatest victory is that which requires no battle,'" he whispered back.

We heard Mr. Anderson's truck come barreling back down the drive and we eased out of our hiding places. His truck tires scattered gravel everywhere as he slammed to a stop. Stomping into the barn, we could see Mr. Anderson's face was blood red. "Ferlin," he said, "Open that gate to the back pen."

"Yessir," said Ferlin, as he rushed to the gate. The gates on each of the pens would swing open wide enough to completely block the hallway which ran between the pens. The gates had a hook on them that would let you hitch the gate to the pen directly across from it. That way, you could just herd the Ladies and their little pigs into whichever pen you wanted. Ferlin hitched the gate open, blocking the hallway, and stood outside the gate.

Mr. Anderson went back outside to talk to the Truck Driver. We peeped through the door at the top of the loading chute.

"What happened to you?" said Mr. Anderson.

"You should keep those little bastards in a cage!" screamed the Truck Driver.

"Watch your language, son," Mr. Anderson said. "This is a school. We've got youngsters here."

"Yes, sir," he mumbled.

"Open up the gate," Mr. Anderson said. "Let him out."

The Passenger got out of the cab of the truck carrying an electric cattle prod. "You won't need that, son." said Mr. Anderson. They opened the trailer's gate, but the boar just sat there. Mr. Anderson came back inside the barn and got a wooden plank. Returning to the trailer, he slid the plank through the bars. Mr. Anderson nudged the boar on the butt. The boar snapped at the plank and bit a chunk out of it. Mr. Anderson smacked his butt a little harder with the plank. The boar snarled, but he rose up and headed slowly towards the loading chute. Mr. Anderson continued to prod him along with the plank.

The loading chute was an eight-foot ramp that ran from the level of the stock trailer gate down to the barn floor. The chute was made of thick seasoned wood and was about thirty-inches wide. It had wooden partitions on each side. It was designed to be narrow enough that a hog couldn't decide to turn back around and go back the way he came.

The wooden chute creaked and popped with the massive weight of the huge boar. We heard the boar's angry huffing and puffing as he stomped down the chute. His gargantuan black shoulders popped the partition's wooden boards out of their nail holes.

As soon as the boar reached the bottom of the ramp, he charged at Ferlin, standing outside the gate. The boar moved quick, in spite of his enormous bulk. Although the bars got dented, the strong aluminum gate held fast. The boar looked unfazed and he just stood there, glaring at Ferlin.

The delivery men got back in their poop-speckled truck and drove away without saying a word.

"Just stay right there, Ferlin," Mr. Anderson hollered. "I'll be inside in just a second," as he closed the door of the loading chute.

Sammy and Frank and me slipped out from our hiding places in the adjacent pen.

It was the most enormous boar I had ever seen in my life. He made all other boars look like piglets, and Rudy's Farms had some huge boars. The muscles of his hips and shoulders stood out beneath his black skin.

When Mr. Anderson got back inside the barn, he said, "I bet that boar'll weigh six hundred and fifty pounds. Jet black. Ain't a white hair on 'im."

The boar's eyes gleamed with an evil fiery glow. "He's got vampire eyes," I said.

"Well, now that you say that, his eyes do have kind of a reddish cast, don't they?" said Mr. Anderson. "Never seen that before."

"Look at his feet, Mr. Anderson!" said Sammy.

We all looked down at the boar's hooves, which had partially sank into the soft dirt floor. Instead of having a cloven hoof split into two toes, like all pigs have, this boar had a solid hoof like a horse!

"He's mulefooted!" said Mr. Anderson. "See that? He's got a solid hoof like a mule. I've seen pictures of Mulefoot hogs, but I've never actually seen one up close. There's a breed of hog called Mulefoot, but that can't be what he is. His ears are all wrong. Mulefoots are supposed to have medium-sized, floppy ears or ears that are pricked forward."

"Yessir," said Ferlin. "Them ears are definitely erect."

"They're so pointy, they look like devil horns," I said.

"Yessir, look at that scar running down his side," Ferlin said. A blazing red scar ran from the boar's shoulder down his right side, and stopped right before it got to his hip. "Reckon what did that?"

"Considering his disposition," said Mr. Anderson, "Probably another boar."

"He don't smell like no other hog I ever smelt," Sammy said.

"He smells like that disinfectant they use to mop the floors with when somebody pukes."

"Yep," said Sammy. "That's it!"

The Mulefooted boar and Frank was engaged in a staring contest. They were at a draw.

"Yessir, Mr. Anderson," said Ferlin. "I was thinking maybe me and the fellers need us a hog-butchering class."

"No can do, " said Mr. Anderson. "Orders from headquarters. But I think I got it figured out now. Mulefoots, real Mulefoots, are an endangered species.[26] I figure somebody's planning on waiting until Mulefoots go almost extinct, and they're gonna charge somebody else a whole lot of money to use him as a stud boar."

"But, like you said," said Sammy, "He ain't a real purebred Mulefoot."

"I doubt the person who bought him knew that," said Mr. Anderson. "And I 'spect they got a bargain price for him."

"The superintendent?" I asked.

"Naw, I think he's just doing a favor for somebody," said Mr. Anderson. "More importantly, the school is getting a hefty donation for keeping him around."

"So we're keeping him?" Sammy asked.

"It looks like we got us a new pig."

---

[26] The Mulefoot pig is the rarest of American swine breeds and was all but extinct by the 1970's. Only one purebred herd continued to exist on a farm owned by R.M. Holiday of Louisiana, Missouri. In 1976, the breed registry closed and all pedigrees and registration information were lost.

CHAPTER EIGHT

Can the Archfiend be rehabilitated?

We ended up calling the Mulefoot boar "The Mulefoot," because nobody could think of a better name. Sammy campaigned for "Bodhidharma,"[27] but none of us could say it. Plus, I don't believe Mr. Anderson liked that name very much. The Mulefoot was a pain in the neck to deal with and made a whole lot of extra work for us. We couldn't let him be around the other pigs. All the other pigs had to be gathered up into their pens before we let The Mulefoot go out to the pasture. Mr. Anderson wouldn't let nobody but Ferlin help him move The Mulefoot. The rest of us had to stay behind the fence.

Mr. Anderson made about a dozen "hurdles" or "handling panels," which are four-by-four sheets of thick plywood with a small oval hole cut out at the top to make a handle. Him and Ferlin never went inside the pen with The Mulefoot unless they was carrying a hurdle. They always kept a hurdle between themselves and The Mulefoot whenever they was moving him around.

[27] Bodhidharma was a Buddhist monk who lived during 6th century CE. He is traditionally credited with the establishment of Zen Buddhism in China. According to Chinese legend, he also began the physical training of the Shaolin monks which led to the creation of Shaolin Kung Fu. In traditional Buddhist art, Bodhidharma is usually depicted as a wild-eyed barbarian with a bushy black beard.

Instead of penning everybody up every time we had to move him, Mr. Anderson finally decided that we should just fence off a separate pasture for The Mulefoot. Mr. Anderson tied a string to a wooden stake and we pulled the string tight so the fence would be straight. Then he measured out every sixteen feet and drove wooden stakes where the fence posts would go. Since me and the Blount Brothers wasn't very good with the post-hole diggers, he got one of the older residents to help him dig the fence post holes.

Mr. Catfish lived in the A-Wing of Progress House and was in his thirties. He always wore a baseball cap pulled down too tight on his head. It made his ears stick out funny. Mr. Catfish always walked in kind of a squat with his feet wide apart.

Me and Sammy Blount had finished watering the pigs and we thought we would go see if we could help them with digging the holes.

When we walked up, Mr. Catfish reached into his shirt pocket and held out a pack of Juicy-Fruit chewing gum. "You fellers nant sum gumm?" he said. Mr. Catfish didn't talk real plain and it was hard to understand him sometimes.

"Don't mind if I do," I said. "Thank you, Mr. Catfish."

"Thank you, Mr. Catfish," said Sammy.

"Hey, Mr. Annerson!" Mr. Catfish hollered to Mr. Anderson, who was digging a hole down from him. "How long you been nigging on nhat hole?"

"Oh, I don't know," said Mr. Anderson. "About ten or fifteen minutes, I guess."

"Now, if a nan-anna-half can nig a hole-anna-half in an hour-anna-half, how long does it nake one nan to nig one hole?"

"Okay, lemme see if I got this, 'If a man-and-a-half can dig a hole-and-a-half in an hour-and-a-half, how long does it take one man to dig one hole?'" Mr. Anderson repeated. "I don't know. An hour?"

"Nope."

"I don't know then. How long?"

"You can't nig halfa-hole!" Mr. Catfish said, his face breaking into his broken grin.

Them two cut up like that all day. Me and Sammy wasn't much help. While he was digging, Mr. Catfish started singing a song that went:

"I'm nout in the pasture
An' I'm nigging a hole!
I'm beating Mr. Annerson
'Cause he is so ol'!"

(Mr. Anderson just laughed at that part)

"I'm nigging a hole!
An' look what I foun'!
Nere's a pirate treasure
Right nunder the groun'

"I'm nigging a hole
All the way down nu China!
See if nem Chinese women
Have a sideways va-

"Whoa! Whoa! Whoa!" said Mr. Anderson. "That song sure is something else, Catfish. He ought to be on the Grand Ole Opry, oughten he, boys?"

"You bet!" we agreed. "How do you come up with them songs right on the spot like that, Mr. Catfish?" I asked.

"Ney just come nu me," he said, shrugging his shoulders, a bit embarrassed by all the praise.

"Do another one!" Sammy yelled and we all agreed.

He stopped digging for this number and started bobbing his head up and down to get the beat. He sang, "Nell, I got a gal inna county jail, nakes her living ny shaking her tail..."

"Whoa, Catfish!" said Mr. Anderson. "I'm not sure the boys here are quite old enough for a song like that. Maybe you oughta' sing something a little more traditional."

So Mr. Catfish sang "On Top of Old Smokey" and it was nice, but I really wanted to hear about that gal who made her living by shaking her tail.

Before too long, they was finished with the digging and needed to put concrete in the holes to set the fence posts. Me and Sammy drug the hosepipes over to help mix the concrete. I tried to make a Batman head out of the leftover concrete, but it was too thick. Sammy made a little pile of dog poop. It looked real except the color wasn't right. They let the posts sit in the concrete overnight and me and Sammy took the concrete dog poop back to Progress House. Our plan was to paint it brown if we could scare up some paint.

The next day, Mr. Anderson and Mr. Catfish put up the fence. Mr. Anderson had found some used hog panels for sale. Hog panels are sixteen-foot wire metal mesh panels that you attach to fence posts and they make a fence. They had the fence up in just a couple of hours.

The next day, we built The Mulefoot a hog house. It was seven-feet by eight-feet and we made it out of white oak. Plywood can get wet and slippery for a pig to walk on, plus treated wood can irritate their skin. It even had an insulated roof because if you don't insulate the roof, condensation will build up inside and drip down on him. When it got real cold, we would still have to put The Mulefoot in the big barn, but he could stay in his own pasture most of the time.

The Mulefoot's hog house stood in the shade of a humongous bodock tree.[28] The gnarled old tree looked like it was made up of four or five smaller trees that got squashed together at the bottom. Ashy-brown bark covered its trunk. There wasn't no limbs directly above the house, so we didn't have to worry about hedge apples dropping down on the roof.

Mr. Anderson put a shiny metal hog feeder over right next to the fence. That way, you could pour The Mulefoot's feed into the feeder

[28] *Maclura pomifera*, commonly known as the Osage orange, hedge apple, bois d'arc, or bodock, is a deciduous tree, ranging up to 50 feet in height. The tree is notable for its sharp thorns and its inedible bright yellow-green fruit. The fruit is variously referred to as hedge apples, horse apples, or monkey-balls.

without having to get inside the pen with him. Mr. Anderson set The Mulefoot's galvanized water trough at the corner of the barn so it would be in the shade most of the day and stay cool. Moreover, it would let me and Sammy run a hosepipe through the side of the barn and just water him that way.

So we rounded up Mamie, Bessie, Ladybird and Jackie O and all their little ones and got them inside their pens. Then Ferlin and Mr. Anderson herded The Mulefoot to his new pasture. The Mulefoot immediately went over to the old bodock tree and started rubbing his sides up against the tree's scaly bark like he was trying to knock it over.

"Yessir! He sure looks like he's happy," said Ferlin.

"Well," said Mr. Anderson, "As happy as *he* ever gets."

Everything seemed to be going fine. Everybody stayed on their side of the fence and the little ones was gaining weight every day. Then I thought I would try something. I stole two carrots out of the vegetable garden and washed them off real good. Then I went over to The Mulefoot's pasture. He was laying down under his bodock tree. Standing at the fence, I hollered out to him, "Hey, Mulefoot, come here, I got something for you!"

The Mulefoot jumped up and came charging toward the fence like he was mad that I had disturbed his rest. He was snorting like he was going to eat me up. Each step he took jarred the ground! As he got closer, he saw the fence and pulled up short. I don't think The Mulefoot's vision was all that good. I never had been this close to him before and didn't really realize just how massive he actually was. When he raised his head, I had to look up at him.

"Look what I have for you," I said, sticking one of the carrots through the fence. He wanted the whole carrot but I wasn't about to let him have the whole thing all at once. Our tug-of-war broke the carrot and The Mulefoot only got the end. After he chomped up that bite, he rammed his face up against the fence and snarled like he was demanding more.

"Well, if you're gonna get ugly," I told him, "You ain't gonna get any more."

After a bit, The Mulefoot calmed down and just stood there glaring at me with his evil vampire eyes. I pushed the carrot through the fence and let him have another bite.

"You wasn't born mean, was you, boy?" He just stood there watching me, chomping on his carrot. "It was them men with the electric cattle prods, wasn't it? Ain't no telling what they did to you. They made you like this, didn't they?" By now, he had orange foam oozing out both side of his mouth. I offered him the second carrot. This time he seems content just to take a bite out of it, but he still eyed me warily. "Ain't nobody here at Clover Bottom gonna hurt you," I told him. "If you're a good boy and you behave yourself, I'll bring you a treat every week." I thought about reaching through the fence to try and pet him on the snout, but I decided against it. If he tried to bite my hand off, I couldn't jerk it back through the fence fast enough.

"See how that works?" I said. "You're a good boy, you get a reward." I gave him the last bite of carrot. Then I held up both hands to show him there was no more carrots. "Okay, that's all there is," I said.

With a mighty Harrumph! he sprayed carrot-colored slobber all over me. Then he wheeled around and stomped back to his tree.

The next morning, me and Mr. Anderson was having breakfast in the cafeteria.

"Did you and Spanky work on y'all's trick last night?" I asked. "Where he gets you a coke-cola out of the refrigerator?"

"Nah, Miss Zelda exercised her veto power on that last night," Mr. Anderson said glumly.

"What happened?"

"Well, Miss Zelda was cooking a pork tenderloin for supper last night. It's kind of expensive, but it's one of her favorite things. She ties up the tenderloin with a piece of white string so that it looks like a big wienie. Then she mixes up a special sauce and lets the tenderloin marinate in a Tupperware container in the refrigerator overnight.

"So last night, Spanky decided to practice the trick unsupervised. Spanky had the best of intentions. I honestly believe he was planning on getting me a coke because I was in the den watching the news.

"Spanky used the dishrag on the door handle to open the refrigerator door. But before he could get that coke out of there, Spanky was overcome by temptation. That pork tenderloin just smelled too good to him. He pulled it off the top shelf and that Tupperware container popped open as soon as it hit the floor. I will say, in Spanky's defense, that Tupperware lid had gotten warped in the dishwasher.

"Spanky scooped up that tenderloin in his jaws and carried it into the den, where I was. I wasn't paying no attention to him, because I was watching TV. Spanky sat right there in the corner of the den and ate that pork tenderloin, string and all."

I laughed.

"Yeah, it's funny now," he said, "But it sure wasn't funny last night. Miss Zelda hardly ever loses her temper, but when she does, Katie bar the door! She was mad at Spanky for stealing the pork tenderloin, she was mad at me for just sitting there and letting him eat it, and she was mad at me for teaching him how to open the refrigerator door in the first place."

"If you had got the pork tenderloin back away from Spanky, would you have wanted to eat it?"

"I brought up that point," Mr. Anderson said, "But it was like throwing gasoline on a fire. Sometimes in a marriage, Delphus, it's just best to keep quiet."

"So what finally happened?"

"I had a baloney sandwich for supper last night."

"Ugh!"

"I'm lucky I got anything."

"Are you still in the doghouse?"

"Well, I did get a good-bye kiss this morning, but I'm still in the hole. I need to do something to make it up to her."

"Like what?"

"I don't know. Take her out to dinner or something."

"Marriage sounds hard."

"It *was* last night," he said, laughing and shaking his head. Then his face changed and he said, "Uh oh."

Sammy Blount stumbled into the cafeteria. He was crying so hard he couldn't stand up straight. Sammy hardly ever, ever cried. Mr. Anderson scooted his chair around and put a hand on Sammy's shoulder. He said, "What's the matter, son?"

"He ripped him to shreds," cried Sammy. Tears were running out from behind his glasses and snot was pouring out his nose. Mr. Anderson give him a napkin to blow his nose. "He didn't even bother to eat him, he just killed him for fun."

"Who?" asked Mr. Anderson.

"Sammy Davis Jr."

"Who killed him?" asked Mr. Anderson.

"That monster, The Mulefoot."

"Okay, Sammy, why don't you go back to Progress House and lay down for a little while? Take the day off. Delphus, you go back with him. I'll take care of things down at the barn."

I walked back to Progress House with Sammy. As we walked, I don't know why, but I reached up and put an arm around his shoulder.

"I was teaching him tricks, Delphus," Sammy said.

"We're not supposed to do that," I said.

"I know, but he used to follow me around like a little dog. I always wanted a dog."

"Yeah, me too. What kind of tricks could he do?"

"He could sit and play dead," said Sammy. "I was teaching him this one where I would pretend to shoot him with my finger, like a gun, and then he would fall over like he was hit by the bullet and play dead."

"That's a pretty cool trick."

"We hadn't perfected it yet," said Sammy "Sammy Davis Jr. was smarter than most pigs."

"I'm sorry he got killed that way."

"'He who loves fifty people has fifty woes.'" Sammy Blount said.

When we got back to Progress House, Sammy laid down on his bed. He didn't seem to want to talk no more. So I headed down to the barn. I run into Ferlin and Frank Blount along the way.

"Yessir, we just heard about Sammy Davis Jr." said Ferlin. "How's our brother doing?"

"He's okay. He's laying down and resting right now."

"Yessir, we're gonna go up there and see if we can do anything for him."

"Y'all are good brothers," I said.

When I reached the barn, Mr. Anderson had picked up all the pieces of Sammy Davis Jr. and put them in a plastic bag. He was inside The Mulefoot's pasture washing away all the blood with a hosepipe. Just within arm's reach, he had a pig hurdle leaned up against the fence. He had leaned pig hurdles up all around The Mulefoot's fence so there'd always be one handy.

"The Mulefoot got ahold of him through the gate," said Mr. Anderson, pointing. "Pulled Sammy Davis Jr. through the gate and tore him apart like a ragdoll. Didn't bother to eat any of him. Just did it for sport, I reckon."

"We should get a big stick and beat him," I said.

"He's just a dumb animal," said Mr. Anderson. "He wouldn't even know what it was for."

"It'd make me feel better."

"Beating a dumb animal to make yourself feel better. That ain't very Christian, is it?"

"I ain't feeling very Christian right now."

"Well, that's when you have to work the hardest at it, I reckon," said Mr. Anderson.

I looked over at The Mulefoot, lounging beneath his bodock shade tree. I swear that monster was smiling.

Later on, I asked Sammy Blount if he wanted to have a little funeral for Sammy Davis Jr.

"'The world is afflicted by death and decay. But the wise man does not grieve, having realized the nature of the world,'" was all he said.

Ferlin and Frank Blount buried Sammy Davis Jr. quietly behind the barn.

CHAPTER NINE

Disaster is averted ... or is it?

Sometimes, I think our tragedy could of been avoided if I just hadn't read that article in the *Reader's Digest.* Other times, though, I reckon that Doom was always there, hiding behind a tree, waiting to pounce.

I found that old *Reader's Digest* in the Dempster-Dumpster behind the Blind School. It had an article about water conservation.[29] It said we was gonna run out of clean water to drink if we didn't start conserving. I got pretty excited about that. You see, me and Sammy's main job was to keep the hogs' water troughs filled up with water. But when we was filling up The Mulefoot's trough, we wasn't allowed to get inside his fence. So we had to snake a hosepipe between the boards of the barn wall to fill it up. It was a lot of trouble. We couldn't never tell when the trough was getting full and we run it over just about every time. We wasted a lot of water. Then I had a brilliant idea. The Mulefoot's water trough sat at the corner of the barn roof. If the barn roof had a gutter that emptied out over The Mulefoot's water trough, then every time it rained, it would fill up his trough. But then it occurred to me that we didn't need no store-bought gutter. We could just bend up the edges of the tin sheets on the barn's roof to form a little gutter. And as long as we

---

[29] Likely James Nathan Miller, "Battle Tactics for Conservationists." *Readers' Digest* 98 (January 1971): 175-180

turned up the edges at the back of the roof a little higher than the edges at the front, then the water would drain right down into The Mulefoot's trough. And me and Sammy wouldn't have to water him so much.

I shared my plan with Sammy Blount.

"That's a great idea," said Sammy, "But I'm dunno if Mr. Anderson will go for it."

"Yeah, I know," I said. "I was planning on doing it without telling Mr. Anderson. It would be a surprise! Mr. Anderson don't have time to do it his ownself. On the other hand, we ain't allowed to climb on the barn roof. What do you think?"

"In the words of the Master," Sammy said, 'One must obey the principles without being bound by them.'" Then he struck a Kung Fu Tricky Leg Stance.

"Yeah, I really think Mr. Anderson will like it when he sees it."

So we headed to the hog barn to start our project. As we walked along, I smelled something foul.

"Three Jacks! You farted!" I yelled and punched Sammy on the arm.

"Yeah, Scobey!" he said, laughing. "My brakes slipped." Then he stopped in his tracks, struck a Kung Fu Dragon Stance, and another fart exploded loudly. "Scobey!" he yelled, before I could call "Three Jacks!" on him.

All the tools that had to stay nice and clean were locked up in Mr. Anderson's office at the front of the barn. But the regular tools, like to work on fences, was hanging on a pegboard on the wall above the workbench. Frank Blount kept the tools on the pegboard organized and, boy, was Frank good at organizing! We needed a pair of pliers to bend the tin sheets on the roof.

"Hey, look up there," I said, pointing to a pair of pliers up at the top of the pegboard. These pliers had four-inch arms that stuck out on each side of the nose. It looked like a hammerhead shark. "Them pliers would be perfect."

"That's called a 'hand seamer,'" said Sammy Blount.

"Well, smell you, Rosebud!"

"What?" Sammy said. "You're not the only one who knows things."

Neither of us was tall enough to reach the hand seamer, so we used the wooden stool to reach it. After we got it down, I glided it through the air toward Sammy, opening and closing the wide jaws. "Watch out, Sammy," I said, "The hammerhead shark is coming to bite you."

Sammy casually struck a Kung Fu Spreading Pillars Stance.

"Kung Fu don't work on sharks," I said.

"Yeah, but it's perfect for a nincompoop with a pair of pliers."

"It's a hand seamer."

"You didn't know that until I told you, smarty-pants."

"You know, I think it's a good omen for our project that we found this hand seamer," I said, abandoning my shark offensive. "We'll have that roof done in no time."

We walked around to the back of the barn and I climbed up on the outside of the loading chute. Scaling up the wall, I said to Sammy, "You know, back when I still had my tail, I had excellent balance. I could swing from tree limb to tree limb. Now my balance is only average."

"Then maybe I should climb up there," said Sammy. "I have excellent balance."

"That's okay." I said. "The pitch of the roof is not steep at all." The hog barn didn't have a loft and the roof's pitch was almost flat.

"Then I'll stay down here and catch you if you fall," Sammy said.

"You couldn't do that. I weigh more than you do."

"Sure I could, if I was braced for it."

"Okay, I'll warn you if I'm fixing to fall."

I set to work with that hand seamer and it didn't take no time at all. The edges of the tin roof bent up easily. Before long, I had a perfect little two-inch gutter running down the length of the roof. Sammy and I talked as I worked.

"Bruce Lee's not dead," Sammy said. "The Chinese Triad Gangs tried to poison him because he was challenging them. So he went ahead and faked his own death to protect his family. Now, he's fighting the Triad Gangs undercover. He's got a secret island headquarters in the South China Sea. Once he finishes them off, he's gonna go back to making movies."

"What about Count Dante?"[30] I said. "It says in the comic books he's 'The Deadliest Man Alive.'"

"Count Dante is a joke," Sammy said. "He's just says that because he knows Bruce Lee can't challenge him without revealing to the world that he's still alive. Bruce Lee has to remain in hiding to protect his family."

"You bought Count Dante's book."

"Yeah, it did have some useful stuff in it," Sammy admitted. "And I did master the 'Dim-Mak,' the Touch of Death. At least, I'm pretty sure I mastered it. It's kinda hard to practice something like that."

"Yeah, you wanna be careful with something like that."

We finally got to the part of the roof that overlooked The Mulefoot's pen.

"Well, we're up to The Mulefoot's fence and I can't cross it," Sammy said. "So you can't fall now."

"There's only about ten feet left to the corner," I said. "We're almost done. Look at The Mulefoot over there under his shade tree. He ain't even paying attention to us."

A minute or two later, I was right over The Mulefoot's water trough. All I had left to do was to shape a little water spout that so the water would pour right down into his trough. I leaned back to catch my breath and put my hand down on the tin roof. Something stuck me! A rusty nail had worked its way up out of the sheet of tin and was sticking up about a quarter of an inch. I wasn't bleeding or anything but it did kind of hurt. I tried to tap it back down with the side of the hand seamer. The nail did not want to go back down into the wood. So I decided I'd just pull it out. I put the jaws of the seamer under the head of the nail and pulled. It was not coming out. It did not even move. But I thought I'd give it one last try. I gave it one more good pull and the nail head broke off! Suddenly, I realized I was leaning way too far over the edge of the roof. I was going to fall.

---

30 Count Raphael Dante (born John Timothy Keehan, Chicago, Illinois, 1939-1975) was a controversial martial arts instructor. He gained notoriety in popular culture for his mail order advertisements in comic books. For $4.98 one could purchase his instructional booklet *World's Deadliest Fighting Secrets* and receive a free Black Dragon Fighting Society membership card.

Time froze.

I am falling. My feet are above my head. I believe I can somersault and land on my feet. My body is rolling over and over in the air. Fire explodes in my right leg and it feels like my ankle has shattered into a million pieces. A dull gong clangs in my ears! My ankle has hit the water trough. I land on the ground on my shoulder blades, and the impact has knocked the wind out of me! I cannot breathe!

I hear Sammy screaming for Mr. Anderson. Now I roll over onto my side and The Mulefoot comes into my view. The sound of my ankle striking the water trough has outraged him! The Mulefoot is charging towards me! The blows of his hoofbeats striking the ground resound in my chest! White slobber streams from his jowls!

I am getting to my feet but it is hard because my ankle hurts so much. The Mulefoot is getting closer to me. I am trying to make it to the fence. I realize I am not going to be able to climb the fence because of my shattered ankle. The Mulefoot is closing in on me!

I spy a plywood hog hurdle leaning against a fence post. I scramble toward the hurdle and swing it over me. The Mulefoot is almost upon me! I try to curl my body up as small as I can and cower behind the hog hurdle. The Mulefoot slams into the plywood! He is pounding it! The plywood is splintering!

I go into Possum Mode.

When I came out of *Possum Mode*, I was in my bed at Progress House. I still had on my clothes but my shoes was off and my right pants leg was rolled up. My ankle had a plastic bag of ice on it. The Blount Brothers was sitting on the edge of the bed.

"You look like you been eat up by a wolf and pooped over the edge of a cliff," said Sammy Blount.

"I kinda feel that way too," I said.

"Nossir, your ankle's not broke," said Ferlin. "Mr. Birdwell took a look at it and he said it wasn't broke."

"Mr. Birdwell is a poot head."

"Yessir, he was a medic in the Army," said Ferlin. "He looked at your ankle and wiggled your foot around and said your ankle wasn't broke."

Frank Blount poked the bag of ice on my ankle with his finger. The ice shifted around inside the bag.

"You missed the big show," said Sammy.

"What happened?"

"Yessir, Mr. Anderson and me was changing the spark plugs on the truck when, all of a sudden, we heard Sammy screaming blue murder. We walked around the edge of the trees and we could see The Mulefoot had you pinned behind that hog hurdle. Yessir! He was going to town on that hurdle like he was gonna smash it to bits."

"I jumped up on the fence and was yelling at him," said Sammy, "I was trying to distract him away from you."

"Yessir, Mr. Anderson took off running," continued Ferlin. "I wouldn't a thought a man his age and his size could move that fast. I was trying to run along beside of him, but I couldn't keep up. And, Delphus, when Mr. Anderson came up to the fence, he placed one hand on top of a fence post and jumped! And he cleared that fence in a single bound. Yessir!"

"Is Mr. Anderson alright?" I asked.

"Oh, yeah, he's fine," said Sammy, "But here comes the good part. Tell him, Ferlin!"

"Yessir! Once he cleared the fence, Mr. Anderson scooped up a pig hurdle that was leaning up against the fence. He held that hurdle out in front of him, like he was Captain America holding up his shield. Yessir, he's still running ninety-miles-an-hour! Then he slams right into the side of The Mulefoot. Yessir! You ain't seen nothing 'til you've seen a 240-pound man hit a 600-pound hog at full bore. Mr. Anderson's shield broke right in half and it made a sound like a clap of thunder! The impact knocked The Mulefoot over on his side! Yessir! And for a second or two, The Mulefoot just laid there on the ground stunned. And then he roared he was so mad! But while The Mulefoot was laying there, Mr. Anderson grabbed you up from behind the hurdle and tossed you over the fence. Then, as The Mulefoot was scrambling to get back to his feet, Mr. Anderson was climbing back over the fence hisself. But, before he got all the way over, The Mulefoot bit a plug out of Mr.

Anderson's leg. Yessir, got him right here," Ferlin said, clapping a hand on his calf muscle.

"Is Mr. Anderson gonna be okay?" I asked.

"Sure," said Sammy. "Mr. Birdwell thought he might need some stiches and he definitely needed a tetanus shot. There was a lot of blood, but Mr. Anderson said it didn't hurt that bad."

"Yessir, at first, Mr. Anderson wasn't gonna go to the doctor at all," said Ferlin, "But Mr. Birdwell talked him into it. Mr. Anderson couldn't remember the last time he had had a tetanus shot. So he went."

"Was he mad at me for being on the roof?" I asked.

"Nossir, I think he was more mad at the superintendent for letting The Mulefoot stay here in the first place."

Frank poked my ice bag again. It hadn't melted much.

"I don't know," I said. "I got a bad feeling."

"'Everything in the past died yesterday,'" said Sammy. "'Everything in the future is born today.'"

CHAPTER TEN

An essential part of this complete breakfast ...

The next morning, my ankle was still pretty sore. But I was able to hobble up to the cafeteria. I got a load of scrambled eggs, a biscuit, and two sausage patties. Ordinarily, I don't eat a lot of sausage, but today I was going to have my revenge on all hog-kind. One of them tried to eat me yesterday, so I figured I was gonna eat one of them today. Then we would be Even-Steven. Don't get me wrong, I wasn't mad at Ladybird, Bessie, Mamie, Jackie O, or any of the little ones. I was only mad at that monster The Mulefoot. And I hated his guts!

Mr. Anderson set his food tray down on the table across from me, sat hisself down, and said, "Good morning, Delphus." He looked terrible.

"You look like a man between pukes, Mr. Anderson. You shouldn't have come into work today."

"Well, you ain't no Cary Grant, yourself," he said, laughing. He bowed his head as he gave a little silent prayer of thanks for the meal. I went ahead and bowed my head too, out of respect. It seemed like he prayed a little longer than usual.

When he got done, I asked him, "So, how are you feeling today?"

"Oh, I'm feeling fine! I hope you are!"

That is exactly what he always said when he didn't want to tell you how he was really feeling.

"Heard you went to the doctor yesterday," I said. "What all did they do?"

"They gave me a tetanus shot and sewed up my leg. I got twenty stitches, and then they drew a bunch of blood."

"Can I see your stitches?"

"Maybe later. People here are trying to eat. We don't want anybody losing their breakfast."

"Did it hurt?"

"Not too bad, but I'm afraid I won't be able to wear short britches anytime soon."

"That was a pretty brave thing you did, fighting a monster hog. Ferlin said you looked just like Captain America."

"I don't know who that is," Mr. Anderson said. "Is that someone in your comic books?"

"Oh, yeah! He has a big red, white and blue shield and he fights people with it." I sang, "'When Captain America throws his mighty shield, all of those who chose to oppose his shield must yield!'"

"I didn't throw the hurdle at The Mulefoot."

"I know," I said. "You charged at him, holding the hurdle in front of you. Captain America does that too sometimes."

"You do know comic books aren't real, don't you?"

"I know, but they do have real things in them sometimes, like the science parts."

"I'll have to take your word on that."

"Earz" Grissom walked by our table. He extended his index finger like the barrel of a gun and shot me with it. Earz had that scary grin on his face. I had been trying to stay out of Earz' way since he stuffed me in the Penguin's trunk. By now, he had to know that I hadn't snitched him out.

"Thank you for saving me from The Mulefoot," I said. "I reckon I should have said that first thing."

"Don't mention it," Mr. Anderson said. "That's the most important part of my job here, keeping you boys safe. That, and maybe teach you a little something."

"You're not mad at me?"

"You're a kid, Delphus," he said. "Kids do silly, childish things. It would be like being mad at a pig for squealing. That's just what they do. It's in their nature."

"I'm glad you're not mad at me."

"But," he said, wagging a finger at me, "You broke the rules, climbing up on the barn roof. You know what happens when you break the rules?"

"You get punished."

"That's right," he said. "I imagine you'll lose your rec room privileges for another month."

"Okay." I tried to not look too happy. I never used the rec room.

"Before you get too cocky," he continued, "You ought to know if you get into trouble again, Johnson Hall will probably want me to take your comic books away from you."

"But that's my own personal property, Mr. Anderson," I said. "I bought them with my own money."

"Don't backtalk me, Delphus," Mr. Anderson said very calmly.

"Yes, sir. I didn't mean to."

"But we're not gonna have to worry about that, are we?" he said, smiling. "'Cause you're not going to get into trouble again, are you?"

"No, sir."

"You're going to obey the rules, aren't you?"

"Yes, sir!"

"Good man! I'm glad we got that settled," he said. "What were you doing up on that roof anyway? Playing Superman or something?"

I told him about my water-reclamation plan.

"Well, that is a good idea, but you should have come to me with it first."

"I know, but you was busy," I said. "And I wanted it to be a surprise."

"It was a surprise alright."

"Are we going to be able to get rid of The Mulefoot now?"

"I doubt it," he said. "I'm going to talk to the superintendent about it, but somebody is paying a whole lot of money for The Mulefoot to stay here. The superintendent is not gonna want to let go of that money.

And the school does need it. I'll probably talk to him about it tomorrow. To tell you the truth, I don't really feel up to a big fight today."

"You shouldn't have come into work today."

After breakfast, we went to feed and water the hogs. I wasn't much use with my sore ankle. Sammy had to do most of the hard work, hauling the hosepipes around. I stayed away from The Mulefoot. I had a lot to say to him, about him being a bully and that I wasn't scared of him. But I figured I would keep my distance. I guess I was feeling like Mr. Anderson was: I wasn't up for a big fight today either.

When we finished with the hogs, we took to raking the leaves on the campus lawn. It was the fall of the year and crispy golden maple leaves was everywhere. Only a few stubborn leaves was still clinging on the branches. Raking was something even the slower boys could do. In no time at all, we had a leaf pile that was as high as my head. While we was taking a break, Ferlin picked up one of the little boys named Cordell and pitched him right into the middle of that leaf pile. Cordell giggled and wallered around in the pile of leaves, burying hisself deeper and deeper. Pretty soon everybody was taking turns, getting a running start and diving on top of the leaf pile. Sammy Blount got a running start, jumped high into the air, did a kung fu "Naughty Monkey Kicks Tree" move and landed in the leaf pile. That show-off!

I didn't feel like jumping in the leaf pile. Have you ever got up in the middle of the night to make a Number Two, but you didn't turn on the lights to keep from waking somebody up? So, with the lights turned off, you don't realize that somebody left the commode seat up? You know that feeling you get when you go to sit down and then you realize, "Uh-oh, I'm going down too far," but before you actually hit the water? That was the feeling that I had. I was just waiting for my heinie to crash into the water.

CHAPTER ELEVEN

This little piggy went to market,...

Mamie's litter had to go to the processor today. They was about six months old and had gotten up to about 240 pounds. We always bred the girls in the same order they was First Ladies: Bess Truman, Mamie Eisenhower, Jackie (O) Kennedy, then Ladybird Johnson. We all hated sending a litter off to be processed. Even amongst ourselves, we didn't talk about what we was really doing. The pigs, I reckon they was too big to be called "pigs" anymore, they was "hogs" now. The hogs would be driven in a truck to a meat processing plant north of town, shot in the head, cut up into pieces, ground up, and stuffed into cloth tubes. Other parts would be wrapped up in thick brown paper and frozen hard as a brick. The processor gave us a deal on the processing costs 'cause it was for the School and they could write it off on their taxes as a charitable donation. At least we didn't have to handle the hog parts when they got delivered back to Clover Bottom. The cafeteria workers did that.

It was a cool morning and I had on my wool C.P.O. jacket.[31] It was itchy and smelt like pig poop. But it was good and warm.

A pale snot-yellow stock truck backed up to the loading chute at the back of the barn. Its sides was covered in pig poop and the rear axle squeaked so loud that it made your ears hurt. The Driver climbed down

[31] A casual woolen jacket based on the design of a Navy Chief Petty Officer's jacket

from the cab and he was the skinniest man I ever seen. He had on a pair of greasy coveralls unzipped to his waist. Under that, he had on a dingy t-shirt. He didn't have a hair on his head and his cheeks was so sunken in, his face looked like a skull.

"Name's Azra," he said in a low raspy voice to Mr. Anderson. "You got some hogs for me?"

"Good to meetcha, Azra," said Mr. Anderson, shaking his hand. "I'm Ed Anderson. Yeah, I got twelve hogs heading to the Joelton Locker."

"We can sign the paperwork after we get the hogs loaded," The Driver said.

"Well, let's get on 'er, then," said Mr. Anderson as he hurried back around to the front of the barn.

I stood right there, staring at The Driver, which I know was rude, and I shouldn't of done it, but I wasn't thinking.

"You don't wanna be eyeballin' me for too long, boy," said The Driver, almost whispering.

Hearing that, I scurried back to the front of the barn. As soon as I caught up to Mr. Anderson, I noticed his britches was all bunched up around his back belt loop. I hooked a finger around that belt loop and swooshed his britches from side-to-side. "You're getting skinny, Mr. Anderson!" I said.

"Quit that, Delphus," he said, waving his hand behind him. Then he said, "Oh? Yeah? Thanks."

Earlier that morning, we had herded each litter of pigs, Bessie's, Jackie O's, Ladybird's, and Mamie's, into their individual pastures.

"Sammy, open up that back stall gate toward the ramp of the loading chute," said Mr. Anderson. "Then take some of them rubber tie-down straps and tie up the gate up real good."

Sammy Blount did as Mr. Anderson instructed. The back gate came up exactly to the ramp for the loading chute. Whoever had designed that hog barn sure had been smart about planning things out. It made a perfect funnel right up to the ramp of the loading chute.

"Okay, Delphus, open up the gate," Mr. Anderson said, and I opened up the gate to Mamie and her litter's pasture.

Mr. Anderson and Ferlin and Frank Blount all had pig hurdles in their hands and they started slowly herding Mamie's litter toward the barn. I distracted Mamie with an apple I had in my pocket. After the litter was out of the pasture, I closed the gate back up with just me and Mamie inside it.

The Mulefoot stood watching all this from his side of the fence. I walked over to face him. "I wish they was taking you to be processed, you monster," I told him. "I would eat every bit of you, boar taint and all! I would eat your ears, your eyes, and *even your wanger.* And then I would laugh and laugh and laugh because you'd be gone and I would still be here and the world would be a safer place."

Mulefoot just made a Harummph! noise, walked back to his bodock tree and laid down. I gave Mamie another apple and then joined everybody else in the barn.

When I got there, Mr. Anderson was gently nudging the first hog up the ramp of the loading chute. Frank Blount was midways outside the chute, gently patting the hogs on the bottom, encouraging them to hurry on up the chute. Soon all the hogs was loaded onto the stock truck. Ferlin walked up the chute and quietly fastened the truck's trailer gate. Mr. Anderson practically run back out to the stock truck to sign the paperwork. Mr. Anderson never got in a hurry about anything. We all chased after him. The Driver was leaning up against his truck picking his teeth with a gigantic hunting knife.

"Well, we got 'em loaded," said Mr. Anderson.

The Driver opened the truck's door and reached inside. A shiny metal pick-axe hung in the gun rack in the back window, and for a second, I thought The Driver was reaching for that. But instead, he just pulled out a clipboard with some papers on it.

"Just sign here, and here," said The Driver.

Mr. Anderson signed the papers and handed the clipboard back to The Driver. He ripped out the yellow page and handed it back to Mr. Anderson.

"Good to meet you, Azra," Mr. Anderson said, extending his hand.

The Driver shook Mr. Anderson's hand and said, "Be seeing you soon." Then he grinned. His teeth was nasty.

As the snot-yellow truck drove away with Mamie's litter, that rear axle shrieked out a shrill two-note song.

Mr. Anderson wheeled around and hotfooted it back to the front of the barn. We all stared at each other. Mr. Anderson never rushed anywhere, so we hurried after him. By the time we caught up to Mr. Anderson, he was in his office, chugging down a bottle of Pepto-Bismol. Sweat poured off his forehead.

"You feeling bad, Mr. Anderson?" I asked.

"Oh, I've just got a little tummy ache," he said. "Listen, I've got to leave early today. I've got an appointment I have to go to. Ferlin, you're gonna be in charge."

"Yessir," said Ferlin, nodding his head.

"What kind of appointment?" asked Sammy, peering out beneath the rims of his eyeglasses.

"None of your beeswax," said Mr. Anderson, laughing and drilling his index finger into Sammy's belly. Sammy giggled. Then Mr. Anderson seemed to consider for a minute and said, "I've got another doctor's appointment. They want to run some more tests."

"Are you sick, Mr. Anderson?" I asked.

"Oh, heavens, no!" he said. "Doctors just like to run a lot of tests and then they send the bill to your insurance company. That's how they make money."

"Yessir," said Ferlin. "Is Miss Zelda gonna go with you?"

"No," said Mr. Anderson. "They're just drawing some more blood. No big deal! There was some funny results on my blood tests when I got my leg sewed up. They just want to make sure everything's okay. It's no big deal."

"You didn't mention any of this at breakfast," I said, pointing a finger at him.

"Because I didn't want y'all to worry," he said. "It's no big deal."

"Do you want one of us to go with you?" said Sammy. "Ferlin could drive you, in case you get sick."

"Then my life *would* be in jeopardy," laughed Mr. Anderson and he slapped Ferlin on the back, to make sure Ferlin knew he was joking. Ferlin could see well enough to drive the truck around on the Clover

Bottom campus, but he had had a few fender-benders. On the highway, Ferlin would be lethal.

"Yessir," laughed Ferlin, wagging his head.

"Now, y'all go on about your regular day and everything will be fine," said Mr. Anderson. "I've got to go. I don't want to be late for my appointment."

I grilled Mr. Anderson about his doctor's appointment the next day at breakfast.

"How did your doctor's appointment go yesterday?" I asked.

"It went fine," Mr. Anderson said, sipping his milk. "They just drew some blood."

"Do you like your doctor?"

"He's fine."

"What are they looking for in your blood?"

"I don't know," Mr. Anderson said. "I don't want to talk about it."

"When do you have to go back?"

"I don't want to talk about it."

"Are they gonna call you on the telephone with the results?"

"I don't want to talk about it."

"Did you tell Miss Zelda about your appointment?"

"I don't want to talk about it."

"So, basically, you don't want to talk about it?"

"That's right," Mr. Anderson said.

I thought for a minute. This was going to be harder than I thought. "Mr. Anderson, I can see some white hairs in your ear tufts," I said. "That can't be good."

Mr. Anderson had laid out the newspaper next to his food tray and was pretending to ignore me. Without taking his eyes off the paper, he said, "I'm an old man, Delphus, I'm supposed to have white hair."

"Your ear tufts have been jet black as long as I've known you."

"I'm getting older every day, Delphus."

"Your eyes look kind of yellowy, Mr. Anderson."

"That's just the tint on my glasses, Delphus."

"You know, that's one of the symptoms of a werewolf," I said. "Do you reckon you might be turning into a werewolf?"

"Yes, I'm turning into a werewolf," he said, "And I eat little boys who bother me when I'm trying to read the paper."

"Werewolves only come out at night," I said, "And you're at home during the night."

"I'll make a special trip."

"I think you might wreck if you tried to drive your truck while you was a werewolf," I said. "And the hospital would call us on the telephone and say, 'What's wrong with this werewolf? Is he sick?' and we would have to answer, 'We don't know! He never tells us anything!'"

"I'm not sick," Mr. Anderson said. "Stop worrying. You worry too much, Delphus."

"I'm not worrying. I'm just ... contemplating."

"Contemplating?"

"I like to plan ahead."

"Did you read 'Charlie Brown' this morning?" he asked, trying to change the subject.

"I did," I said. "Charlie Brown is never going to get to kick that football, is he?"

"I don't think so."

"You haven't touched your breakfast, Mr. Anderson."

"I'm not very hungry. I guess my eyes were bigger than my stomach."

"That would be very scary looking."

"It's just an expression."

I kept on him like that for the rest of the week. Mr. Anderson would not tell me anything. He wouldn't even tell me his doctor's name. I think he was afraid I would call his doctor. He was right about that.

Then, that next Monday, Mr. Anderson did not come into work.

CHAPTER TWELVE

The Batman topples into the uncaring waters ...

We had a few cold nights, so they fired up the Steam Plant. I paused for a minute on my way to the cafeteria and watched the smokestack spew up the thick black smoke. The smoke blotted out the sky over Clover Bottom Hospital and School.

I got me some scrambled eggs and milk. I was peppering my eggs when Mr. Anderson came up to the table. I practically shouted, "Where were you yesterday?"

"Good morning to you too, Delphus," Mr. Anderson said. He set his food tray down, sat down, and said his prayers.

"You didn't even call!"

"I called the office at Johnson House and told them I wouldn't be coming in."

"But you didn't call us," I said. "You didn't call me. I sat here in the cafeteria for forty-five minutes waiting for you, Mr. Anderson."

"I'm sorry, Delphus," he said. "You're right, I should have called you. I've had a lot of things on my mind lately, not sure which way to go. But I had a long talk with Miss Zelda last night and we prayed about it, and I've decided I'm not doing you boys any favors by keeping you in the dark." He let out a long sigh. "So, what would you like to know?"

"Where were you yesterday?"

"I had to go to the hospital. I had to have a procedure done called a 'liver biopsy.'"

"What did they do?"

"I had to put on a hospital gown and they made a little incision right up here on my belly." He pointed to the spot. "Then, they stuck a needle in the incision and took a little sample of my liver."

"Did they put you to sleep?"

"No, they just numbed the spot where they made the incision."

"Did it hurt?"

"A little bit, not too bad."

"Were you scared?"

"Nah, Miss Zelda was there to hold my hand." He grinned.

"What was they looking for in your liver?"

Mr. Anderson let out another long sigh and said, "Well, my liver's not working right and they're trying to figure out what's wrong with it."

"So, what do they think's wrong with it?"

"Well, that's why they did the biopsy, to try and figure that out."

"When they find out what it is, can they fix it?"

"I hope so," he said smiling. "But it's in The Lord's hands now. We'll have to let him handle it. But whatever happens, you and all the other boys are gonna be safe and everything's gonna be alright. So there's no need for you to worry."

The next week was just a blur. The days was long, and each day seemed like the day before. They all ran together.

On Monday, Mr. Anderson was late again for breakfast. I was already done, and the Blount Brothers has showed up and finished their breakfast by the time he got there.

"Good morning, men," Mr. Anderson said. He did not get a food tray. "Y'all finished with your breakfast?"

"Yessir," said Ferlin Blount. "You missed some good biscuits here, Mr. Anderson."

"Well, I'm watching my girlish figure," he said, patting his belly. Mr. Anderson had lost a lot of weight, but I don't know if anybody else had noticed. Still, we all laughed at his joke. "Why don't we head on down to the barn then?" he said. "I wanna talk to you men before we get started with our day."

As we hiked down to the hog barn, the sky was black with all the smoke from the Steam Plant. It looked like a tornado was gonna blow up just any minute! When we got to the barn, we gathered in the little storeroom that served as Mr. Anderson's office. He slumped forward in his wooden chair behind the desk and we all leaned up against the shelves along the walls.

"Well, men, y'all know I been feeling poorly," began Mr. Anderson, "And I had that biopsy last week. My doctor called me last Friday with the report on that and I'm afraid he give me some bad news. I got liver cancer." He fished a piece of paper out of his shirt pocket and read, "*Hepato-cellular carcinoma*, they call it and it don't look too good. They figure I got about six months."

"What about surgery or a transplant?" I asked.

"Well, they said it was too widespread for surgery and they don't really do liver transplants," Mr. Anderson said.

"Can't they use radiation sometimes for cancer?" said Sammy Blount.

"Yeah, sometimes, and I might try some of that," said Mr. Anderson, "And it might give me a little more time."

I could feel my heart pounding in my chest and I felt my *Possum Mode* coming up on me, so I collapsed into a chair.

"Now, you boys know I think the world of y'all and I want to keep working here as long as I can ..." Mr. Anderson continued, but I didn't hear him. All I could think about was Mr. Anderson dying, and why couldn't it of been me instead? Nobody would miss me, but everybody would miss Mr. Anderson.

I heard Mr. Anderson say, "Why don't we pray for just a minute? *Our Heavenly Father, thank you for today and for all the days we have together. Please give us the strength to bear the burdens we have ahead of us. Please give us the wisdom and understanding to see the plan that you have for each of us. And give us the courage to follow that plan. In Jesus' name we pray, Amen.*"

Everybody said *Amen,* even me. But I don't think God was there. I reckon Mr. Anderson was just talking to hisself.

My *Possum Mode* had passed. I suppose Mr. Anderson's prayer had calmed me down.

"Now, let's get to work, men!" said Mr. Anderson, with a big smile on his face.

We all shuffled out of the Mr. Anderson's office like dead robots. Sammy Blount and me went through our chores, dragging the hosepipes to the water troughs without saying a word. The Mulefoot stood in his pasture watching me. I wheeled toward him and said, "Why couldn't it be you? You're an evil monster! Mr. Anderson is good. It's not fair that good people have to die and a monster like you gets to keep on living. It's ain't fair!" My face was cold and I could feel hot tears rolling down my cheeks. The Mulefoot smiled his evil smile. I know y'all don't think a hog can smile, but I swear he did. Then he turned and slowly walked back to his bodock tree. He sauntered like he thought he was a lion or a king or something. I wiped my face on my sleeve. My C.P.O. coat stunk. This whole place smelled like pig shit!

I didn't want the Blount Brothers to see that I was crying so I rushed back to Progress House. As I hurried along, I heard a familiar voice behind me. "Hey, Delly, how you doin', motherfucker?" It was "Earz" Grissom!

"Leave me alone!" I cried, without even turning around. I started running as fast as I could. After a while, I glanced over my shoulder and "Earz" hadn't even bothered to chase me. I don't know why I run. I wouldn't of cared if "Earz" had beat me to death standing right there.

I didn't stop running until I got back to Progress House. Inside, I dropped down on my bed without even taking my shitty boots off. I pulled my pillow over my head and I cried like a big baby.

That next Sunday, I went to Church, which I never do. We got a little white chapel here on the Clover Bottom campus, but I don't go much. The preacher, Brother Donnelly, talks down to us. Maybe with a congregation of slow learners, he has to do that. But these things are more important and a whole lot more complicated than he likes to make out.

I went to Church with the intent of begging God to heal Mr. Anderson. If anybody ever deserved a miracle, it was him. Mr. Anderson was the best man I ever knew and he worked hard to follow *all* of God's rules.

"Farther Along" played on the piano and everybody sang along:

Farther along, we'll know all about it
Farther along, we'll understand why
Cheer up, my brother, live in the sunshine!
We'll understand it, all by and by

I looked around the church, studying all the different kinds of people setting in the pews. Some of them was ancient and some was just kids. Many of them was in wheelchairs or on walkers. But they all seemed happy! Or at the very least, content. Some of them was so content, they had already dozed off. Whatever it was that they felt, I wished I could feel that too! If there was a pill I could swallow, or a book I could read, that would make me feel like them people, I would do it in a second. I had read The Bible several times and I had a right smart of it committed to memory, but it just didn't do the trick.

I started to pray to God to give Mr. Anderson a miracle. And then I thought, Shit! God is the one who give Mr. Anderson cancer in the first damn place. That is, if God even exists. And even if God does exist, he don't strike me as the kind of fella who would change his mind once he's got it made up.

So I didn't pray to God and I marched right out of that Church in the middle of "Amazing Grace."

CHAPTER THIRTEEN

What treasures ...
or horrors lie inside the emerald green box?

The next Saturday night, the Blount Brothers was all asleep, so I decided to go out on patrol. After I got locked out of Progress House that time, Frank Blount made me a key to the Progress House door. It's a just little metal cut-off spoon handle with some grooves cut into it. Not only will it open the Progress House door, it will also open up every door on every building on Clover Bottom campus. At least, it has opened up every door I have tried it on so far.

On Saturday nights, I go to the Blind School. The Blind School is a little less than a mile away from Progress House and it takes me about ten minutes to walk there. The Blind School has a seven-foot-tall metal fence around it. I know where there's two or three places where you can just slide right under the fence.

I was going to the Dempster-Dumpster to see what books the Blind School had throwed away that week. Like I told you, they take regular books, turn 'em into Braille books for the blind students, and then they just throw 'em away. Perfectly good books! I had my book bag with me. I had made me a book bag out of an old long-sleeved shirt. I tied the sleeves together to make a strap to go over my shoulder and then I sewed the bottom shirttails together. You feed the books down through the neck hole. At first, I just glued the shirttails together, but the books kept breaking through the glue, so I had to sew the shirttails together. Mr. Anderson showed me how to sew one time. I reckon everything that I know that's worth knowing, I learned it from Mr. Anderson.

That's all I can think about anymore, that Mr. Anderson is gonna die. It just don't seem real. Like it's all a dream, and one day I'll wake up and everything will be alright. But I don't never wake up. Whenever I try to picture how it's gonna be, it's always bad. I'm gonna have to start eating breakfast all by myself.

I could feel the tears rolling down my cheeks as I walked along in the darkness. I used to never cry, but now it's all I do. I try not to do it in front of the Blount Brothers. I don't want them to think I'm a cry-baby. I wiped my eyes on the sleeve of my coat.

I reached the place in the fence where I could crawl under. I slid under with no problem. A glowing security light lit up the empty parking lot and the Dempster-Dumpster was setting right in the corner. It was a green eight-foot cube with a sliding metal window. I scrambled over to the Dempster-Dumpster and quietly slid back the window cover. Pulling myself up to the window, I somersaulted headfirst inside it. Didn't make a sound. They didn't throw food or anything stinky into this Dempster-Dumpster, so I didn't have to worry about getting anything grody on me. It didn't even smell bad in there. And the security light was at the perfect angle to shine in right through the window.

And now to the books! I used to take every book and magazine I could find back with me to Progress House. But I started running out of room. I snuck some of them into the bookcase in the rec room at Progress House. But nowadays, I have to be more selective and just take back the books that look interesting.

There was a big black hardcover one with *The Boy's King Arthur*[32] printed in gold. It had some really cool painted pictures in it. I put it in my book bag.

I saw one about talking rabbits that sounded like it was for little kids, so I didn't get it. There was a ton of geography books in there.

---

32 Malory, Thomas, Sir, 15th cent, Sidney Lanier and N. C. Wyeth, *The Boy's King Arthur: Sir Thomas Malory's History of King Arthur and His Knights of the Round Table.* New York: C. Scribner's sons, 1922.

Why would a blind kid need a book on maps? Can they make Braille maps? I hate geography so I didn't take any of them.

I picked up a paperback that looked like it was a copycat of James Bond. The cover read, "*On Hazardous Duty*,"[33] The thriller that introduces America's most ingenious spy – playboy PETER WARD... An electrifying new espionage novel by a former C.I.A. agent." It looked dumb, so I tossed it back on the pile.

There was an orange hardcover one with black lettering that said *King Conan*.[34] He's in comic books. I hadn't read any of them, but you know it's got to be good if they make comic books about it. I jammed that one in my bag real quick. I saw *The Wind in The Willows*,[35] but I already had a copy.

And then I spotted one that might really be something! It was a dark blue hardcover and in gold lettering it said *The Merck Manual, Eleventh Edition*.[36] It was a medical book that had all kinds of information about every kind of disease you could ever think of. Maybe I could find something in there that could help Mr. Anderson! And then he could keep on living and I could be a hero. I hurriedly stuffed it down into my bag.

I somersaulted back out the window and rolled across the pavement a few times. Even without my tail, I can still be pretty nimble when I have to. I slid under the fence and hotfooted it back to Progress House.

Everyone was still asleep on our wing when I got back. I changed into my P.J.'s like a flash. I was chomping at the bit to get at that medical book. There had to be something in there that would help Mr. Anderson. I got my flashlight and pulled the covers over my head so I wouldn't wake Ferlin up.

Propping the flashlight between my neck and shoulder, I dived into the book. *The Merck Manual* was split up into chapters for each

---

33 St. John, David. *On Hazardous Duty*. New York: Signet Books, 1965.

34 Howard, Robert E., *King Conan*. New York: Gnome Press, 1953.

35 Grahame, Kenneth, 1859-1932, *The Wind in the Willows*. New York: Scribner's, 1954.

36 Merck Sharp & Dohme, Charles E. Lyght, Editor, *The Merck Manual of Diagnosis and Treatment*, 11th ed. Rahway, NJ. Merck Sharp & Dohme Research Laboratories, Division of Merck & Co., Inc., 1966.

part of the body: blood, heart, bones, and like that. "Liver and Biliary" (whatever that is) was in Chapter 13. There was only one page on liver cancer (or "neoplasms"). Out of 1,850 pages of that whole book, there was only one page on liver cancer. It said cancers starting in the liver are relatively rare and "In about 1/2 of reported cases they are associated with cirrhosis." I knew what "cirrhosis" was. That is what people get when they drink too much booze. They talk about it on TV. Mr. Anderson never drunk booze. Mr. Anderson is a deacon at the Methodist Church and one time, somebody said they oughta start using real wine instead of grape juice when they had Communion. Mr. Anderson voted against using real wine. He thought God would be okay with them just using grape juice. He did not want to drink real wine because it had alcohol in it.

The Merck Manual had more terrible news. It said, "Radiotherapy to the liver is of no value" and "In a few instances, successful surgical removal of the tumor has been achieved." But Mr. Anderson had already said that his doctor told him that his cancer was too spread out for him to have surgery.

Finally, there was one sentence I wasn't exactly sure about. *The Merck Manual* said, "Treatment is palliative." Just three words. I didn't know what *palliative* meant. I turned off and flashlight, climbed out of bed and tiptoed into the rec room where I had stashed a humongous *Merriam-Webster's Dictionary* in the bookcase. I dragged the dictionary off the shelf and set it down on the floor, careful not to make any noise. Clicking my flashlight back on, I crouched down over it.

"Palliative," the dictionary said, "*adj.* 1. serving to palliate... See palliate." So I found *palliate,* which was the word right above it. The definition read, "palliate *v.t.* 1. to relieve or lessen without curing; mitigate; alleviate..."

So there was no cure for Mr. Anderson.

I sat there for a few minutes looking at the illustration for *Palladian window*. It reminded me of the windows on the old Clover Bottom Mansion, but they wasn't exactly the same. I slid the dictionary back on the shelf, shut off my flashlight and went back to bed. I didn't reckon that tomorrow was gonna be any better.

CHAPTER FOURTEEN

"Heroes and villains, their identities concealed by colorful masks, mix and mingle around the canapés..."

"I have a great idea about who we can be for the Halloween party," I told Sammy Blount. We was playing in a mud puddle. A truck's tire treads had mashed a perfect castle wall design into the edge of the puddle. We had made little ships out of leaves and were in the process of bombing them with gravel. "I can go as Batman and you can go as Robin."

"I ain't wearing short pants," said Sammy, "For it is written, 'Buddhas do not practice nonsense.'" Then he splashed the puddle with a big rock.

"You'd make a good Robin."

"Also, it's too cold for short pants," he said. "I have a better idea. You could be The Green Hornet and I could be Kato, as portrayed by the immortal Bruce Lee."

"Bruce Lee played Kato?" I asked, tossing a gravel at a leaf ship and missing completely.

"On *The Green Hornet* television show," Sammy said."

"Yeah, now I remember them," I said. "They were on *Batman* one time. They got turned into a giant postage stamp."

Sammy picked up a rock as big as my head and dumped it into the deep end of the mud puddle. "Typhoon!" he yelled.

"I don't think I wanna be The Green Hornet," I said.

"Well, I don't wanna be Robin."

"You'd make a good Robin."

"Holy Hard-of-Hearing, Delphus! I don't wanna be Robin!"

"We could go as Batman and Kato," I said. "It could be part of a sidekick-exchange program."

"You really want to spend the whole night explaining that?" Sammy asked, as we headed back up the hill toward Progress House.

"I reckon not."

"Scobey!" he said. It must have been a silent-but-violent, 'cause I hadn't heard a thing.

"It'll sure be good to see Mr. Anderson," I said. "He ain't been to work in almost two weeks."

"You reckon he'll come to the party?" said Sammy.

"I hope so. He always brings Miss Zelda. They dress up like cowboys."

After we walked a while, Sammy said, "Delphus, I'm still not going as Robin."

But I still went as Batman. I found a brown paper grocery sack that fit my head perfectly. I cut out some eyeholes and a place for my mouth. After I glued on the ears, I sprayed the whole thing down with a can of blue spray paint I found in the barn. I found a blue towel to make a cape with.

Sammy Blount ended up going as Bruce Lee. He wore a tight yellow sweat suit with black electrical tape running down the outsides of his sleeves and legs.

Frank Blount was a ghost. At first, he just cut eyeholes in a sheet, but then he realized he needed a mouth hole if he was gonna eat anything at the party. Frank was not all that big on Halloween.

Ferlin Blount found two cork bottle stoppers, covered them with tin foil, glued them to his neck, and went as Frankenstein. He slicked his hair back and painted a big red scar on his forehead for where they put his brain in. He also stuffed a pillow under his shirt to make it look like he had big muscles.

It was already dark when we headed over to Roberts Hall, where they was having the Halloween party. Luckily, the weather wasn't too cool, so we didn't have to wear coats and ruin the whole effect of our costumes. We was taking along the little boys who shared our wing of Progress House: the twins, Ernest and Bernest, Corpy, Floyd, Cordell, and Skippy Dean.

Ferlin Blount was in charge of watching the little boys and herded them along. He had also helped them with their costumes, which is why he didn't have as much time to spend on his own. Ernest and Bernest were baseball players. Corpy was a car, he had two headlights on his chest. Floyd wore overalls and went as a farmer. Cordell was either Peter Pan or Robin Hood. And I ain't got no idea what Skippy Dean was supposed to be.

With Mr. Anderson gone so much, more and more responsibility had been heaped onto Ferlin. He was practically running the hog operation. Remember, Ferlin was only fifteen years old. I imagine all that responsibility was weighing heavy on Ferlin's shoulders, but he didn't let on.

Roberts Hall was just next door so we didn't have too far to walk.

"Yessir!" said Ferlin. "You little fellers make a straight line so I can keep sight of you. Nossir! I don't want to lose none of y'all in the dark."

"Hey, there's Nellybelle," said Sammy, pointing at Mr. Anderson's green-and-white truck in the parking lot. "Mr. Anderson got to come." Mr. Anderson had named his Ford F-100 truck "Nellybelle" after Roy Rogers'[37] jeep.

The staff had really decorated the auditorium in Roberts Hall up nice. A life-sized scarecrow with a real pumpkin head stood just inside the door. A couple of hay bales sat at his feet and a big sign read, "Happy Halloween!" The lights was dimmed real low and orange and black crepe paper streamers hung all around the walls. A bedsheet ghost on a wooden frame stood guard in each corner of the auditorium. More hay bales sat around the edge of the walls and the sweet smell of straw filled

---

37 Roy Rogers (born Leonard Franklin Slye; November 5, 1911 – July 4, 1999) was an American singer and cowboy actor who was one of the most popular Western stars of his era. Known as the "King of the Cowboys," he appeared in more than 100 feature films and six seasons of *The Roy Rogers Show* television program.

the air. A Halloween record played in the background, you know, that kind that has the wind howling, and cats shrieking, and chains rattling loud. Later on, they would start up the music and play "Monster Mash" about a million times.

All the tables had black tablecloths and a lighted jack-o-lantern in the center of the table. And, sure enough, sitting at the closest table was Mr. Anderson. Like every other Halloween before, he was dressed up as a cowboy. Which meant that he put on a beat-up cowboy hat and dressed like he always did. Miss Zelda was standing behind Mr. Anderson's chair. She had on a pink cowboy hat and a blue-jean skirt that came down to her boots. Miss Zelda had white hair and big blue eyes. She was a beautiful lady and so she didn't really wear a lot of makeup.

The little boys made a break for the refreshment table and Ferlin chased after them. The rest of us hurried over to Mr. Anderson's table and I shook his hand. "Greetings,... Citizen," I said. "I'm glad you were able to make it to tonight's ... festivities."

"Well, hello, Batman," Mr. Anderson said, "It's good to be here. You better watch out, I think I saw The Penguin around here someplace."

"I shall remain ... vigilant," I said.

"Well, Kung Fu," said Mr. Anderson, leaning forward in his chair to pat Sammy Blount on the arm, "You ain't gonna karate-chop one of these tables in half, are you?"

"Not unless someone starts trouble," said Sammy, grinning.

"Is that Frank back there?" asked Mr. Anderson. "Son, I wouldn't of known you. I think you've grown a foot taller since I saw you last."

Frank Blount stuck his hand out from under his sheet and shot Mr. Anderson with his index finger, crooking his thumb.

"It really is good to see you, Mr. Anderson," I said. "You look great." Which was a big fat lie. Mr. Anderson looked terrible and his shirt hung off his shoulders. Then putting my Batman voice back on, I said, "Who is this alluring ... creature ... standing behind you?"

"Oh, that's just some young girl I hired to drive me around." Miss Zelda's hand was resting on Mr. Anderson's shoulder and he reached up and patted it.

"Howdy, Delphus," Miss Zelda said like a real cowgirl. "You sure look smart in your Batman outfit."

"Thank you, ma'am," I said. "When are you going to get rid of this old man and find somebody younger, like me?" Now, I know that, with Mr. Anderson being sick, maybe this wasn't the best time to tell that joke, but it's what I've always said to Miss Zelda whenever I saw her, and tonight I was going to pretend like everything was alright.

"Well," she said, pretending to think it over, "I've finally got him house-trained, so I probably better keep him around a little while longer."

We all laughed at that.

"Little Sammy!" said Miss Zelda, kneeling down, "Come here and see me!" Sammy was Miss Zelda's favorite and she petted on him. He was tiny little feller with humongous spectacles when the Blount Brothers first came to Clover Bottom. Miss Zelda was asking Sammy all about his costume and how he made it.

"So, how you been feeling?" I asked Mr. Anderson.

"Not too bad, not too bad," Mr. Anderson said. "My skin itches a lot. Don't know what that's all about. The doctor give me some cream for it and I just coat myself down with the stuff."

"Maybe you need one of Spanky's flea collars."

Mr. Anderson laughed. "I might have to give that a try."

"You need anything from the refreshment table? Some punch or something?" I asked.

"No, I'm good right now, Delphus. Thank you," he said. "I may get a little something after while."

"Yessir! There he is!" said Ferlin Blount, pumping Mr. Anderson's hand. Ferlin had helped the little boys with their plates and had gotten them set down at a table. Mr. Birdwell was watching over the boys now.

"Ferlin, son, are you staying out of trouble?"

"Yessir!" said Ferlin. "It sure is good to see you, Mr. Anderson."

"It's good to see you, Ferlin," said Mr. Anderson. "And first things first, I owe you an apology. With Miss Zelda driving me around all over the place, I've learned something about myself. Don't nobody's driving suit me but my own! So I'm sorry for all those times I criticized your driving. I reckon I'm just a bad passenger."

I never heard Mr. Anderson be harsh with Ferlin about his driving. He just kidded him about it sometimes. And Ferlin did run the truck into a lot of stuff because his eyesight was so bad.

"Nossir," said Ferlin. "No apology necessary."

"Well, I just wanted to clear the air."

"Yessir! I hate to bother you with this, but I thought I'd go ahead and get it out of the way" said Ferlin, reaching into his jacket for some papers, "I need to get your signature on some feed bills."

"Pull yourself up a chair and let's take a look at 'em," said Mr. Anderson.

Ferlin set down at the table and spread out the papers.

"Well, if you boys are going to talk business," I said, "I'm gonna go get me a bite to eat."

As I walked away, I heard Mr. Anderson telling Ferlin, "Now, you see, you don't have to worry about these 'cause we're on a quarterly billing cycle..."

Sammy and Frank Blount was standing over by the punchbowl so I headed over there and got me a cup of punch.

Looking over the crowd, I said, "Not much talent here tonight."

"No siree-bob," said Sammy Blount. "Although Miss Lakeisha sure looks nice in her Catwoman outfit."

"Yeah," I said, "But she's waaay too old for us."

"She would be out of your league even if y'all was born on the same day," Sammy said.

Putting on my Batman voice, I said, "A somber,... but astute, observation, ... old chum." I took a sip of punch. "This punch tastes funny," I said to Sammy. "It tastes like it has Ripple[38] in it." I had never even tasted alcohol and didn't even know what "Ripple" was. It was just something I had heard on TV.

---

[38] Ripple was an inexpensive fortified wine produced by E & J Gallo Winery from 1960 to 1984. Due to its low price, it earned a reputation as a beverage for alcoholics and the indigent.

Sammy set his cup of punch down on the table. "'I undertake the training rule to abstain from fermented drink that causes heedlessness,'" he said.

Frank Blount dipped his finger into Sammy's cup and then stuck it into his mouth hole.

"Enjoyin' the punch, boys?" Earz Grissom said as he rolled out from under the refreshment table. "I put a special ingredient in it." He laughed like a maniac. "Drink up, boys! Drink up!"

I figured his "special ingredient" could mean one of two things: 1) Earz had gotten ahold of a bottle of booze and poured it into the punchbowl, or 2) he had peed in it. I quietly set my cup back down on the table.

Now let me just stop right here and tell you about Earz' costume. Earz was standing there buck naked except for a pair of white jockey shorts and a pair of white tenni'shoes. But, he had another pair of jockey shorts pulled over his head to form a mask. His maniac eyes gleamed out through the leg-holes. He looked kinda like a masked wrestler on Saturday TV. And right between his eyeholes was a huge splotch of what I hope-to-Heaven was brown shoe polish.

"What do you think, Delly?" Earz said, standing with his fists on his hips. "I'm The Skidmark!" Laughing insanely, he dragged his finger through the brown stain between his eyeholes and tried to wipe it on me. I quickly sidestepped out of his reach. Thankfully, Earz decided not to chase me. Instead, he reached under the refreshment table and brought out a roll of white toilet paper. "Watch this!" he said. Then he yelled, "Shazam!" and hauled off and slung that roll of toilet paper as hard as he could, but he kept ahold of the end, so that the roll trailed a long white banner clear across the auditorium.

"You there! You there!" cried Commissioner Jordan, as he rushed over toward us. He was the Commissioner of the Department of Mental Health, which is in charge of Clover Bottom. Commissioner Jordan was a real Medical Doctor and his costume was his white lab coat over a regular business suit.

"Oh shit! Five-O![39] Gotta book!" said Earz, as he scrambled back under the refreshment table and disappeared into the darkness.

"Who was that?" said Commissioner Jordan, out of breath as he reached us.

"The fiend identified himself ... only ... as The Skidmark," I said in my best Batman voice.

"He was wearing a mask," Sammy added.

"His true identity remains ... a mystery," I said.

"I hope you boys didn't have anything to do with these shenanigans, Delphus," Commissioner Jordan said. He crossed his arms and stared down at us sternly.

Before we could answer, a bloodcurdling scream rang out from the front of the auditorium. Suddenly, all the lights came on, the music stopped, and everyone crowded toward the front entrance to see what was the matter. As me and Sammy pushed to the front of the crowd, I saw Mrs. Clarice, one of the teacher's aides, dressed like a woman from the Holy Land. She was frantically pointing at the scarecrow that had greeted us at the entrance.

"Somebody done put a manhood on that scarecrow!" Mrs. Clarice cried. Mrs. Clarice was very active in her church and her costume was her choir robe with a blue shawl over it. "Oh, Lordy, in front of all these children ..." she added.

I worked my way around to the side to get a better view. Sure enough, somebody had unzipped the fly on the scarecrow's overalls and stuck a big orange gourd in there. The "handle" part of the gourd stuck out of the zipper, took a slight bend toward the floor, and then the tip eagerly pointed straight up towards the ceiling. It looked like the scarecrow had a massive orange wanger.

Commissioner Jordan, was trying to console Miss Clarice and calm her down. But he hadn't removed the offending gourd. I don't think he wanted to touch it.

---

[39] The term *Five-O* refers to the police, a police officer, or in this context, any figure of authority. From the police drama television series, *Hawaii Five-O*, which was broadcast from 1968 to 1980.

"I saw who put it there," said Nellene Wilkerson, a notorious tattletale. She was perched on a bale of hay near the door and was dressed like Little Bo Peep. Nellene lived on the B-Wing of Progress House, where the girls and women lived. She was around my age and, there for a while, she was sweet on me. But Sammy had seen her eat a booger one time, and so I wasn't interested. Nellene was pretty odd and didn't talk much, but she could remember every single day of her life since she was a little-bitty kid. And she could remember every single detail about every single day.[40] Her memory was a pretty amazing thing and everybody at Clover Bottom knew about it.

Commissioner Jordan stepped over to Nellene, leaned forward, and peered into Nellene's eyes. She stared down at the floor, she did not like to look into people's eyes. "Nellene," Commissioner Jordan said, "Did you see who put the gourd on the scarecrow?"

"Uh-huh."

"Who was it?" Commissioner Jordan asked. "What did he look like?"

"He had a sheet over him," Nellene said. "Like he was a ghost."

The crowd parted like the Red Sea as everyone turned to look at Frank Blount. He was the only person in the auditorium dressed like a ghost.

Commissioner Jordan marched over to Frank like he was going to grab him by the arm. I couldn't let him do that! I knew that if Commissioner Jordan laid a hand on Frank, Frank would tear into him like a bushel of bobcats! And then they would move Frank into the Spruce Building, where they kept the bad boys, and we'd never see Frank again! Out of the corner of my eye, I could see Ferlin and Sammy Blount moving toward where Frank stood and Mr. Anderson had eased up out of his chair and was headed that way too.

"Hold on! Hold on! Hold on!" I cried, reaching my arm out toward Commissioner Jordan, who thankfully stopped in his tracks. "Perhaps...

---

40 The condition described here appears to be hyperthymesia, also known as Highly Superior Autobiographical Memory (HSAM). First identified in 2006, hyperthymesia is a condition wherein an individual can recall the vast majority of personal experiences and events in his or her life in meticulous detail.

we ought to get the *full* description...of the culprit!" I said, and looked around, searching the eyes of the crowd, hoping they would agree with me.

Turning to Nellene, I whispered to her, "Nellene, it's me, Delphus."

"I know that, you silly goose."

"Did you see any more... of this ghost person?" I asked out loud, "Like his shoes, ... perhaps?"

"I sure did."

"And what...did his shoes look like?"

Nellene closed her eyes for a few seconds. "They were white tennis shoes, with a little red circle right here on the back of the heel," she said loudly, hiking up her foot and tracing a small circle on the back of her patent leather shoe.

"That's it! That's it! You see?" I said to the crowd, and to Commissioner Jordan in particular. "Everybody knows...how good Nellene's memory... is. And she's describing *white* Red Ball Jets[41] tenni'shoes." And then I walked over to where Frank Blount was standing stock-still. I caught Frank's eye through his eyeholes so he wouldn't clobber me. "And everyone knows...that Frank Blount only wears...*black* Converse Chuck Taylor All-Stars," I said, lifting up the bottom of Frank's sheet so that everybody could see his black tenni'shoes. Frank had six pair, all black, and he kept them all looking like they was straight out of the box. It was the only thing Frank ever spent his money on.

"The culprit's shoes weren't like these, were they, Nellene?" I called over to her.

"Oh, no," Nellene said, "They were white and much dirtier."

Then, doing my best Batman imitation, I said, "This,... Commissioner... Jordan...is what I postulate...happened!" I swirled back around quickly, hoping it would make my cape billow out. Pointing to the entrance, I said, "The evil perpetrator came in through the front door...disguised under a common bedsheet! He placed the contemptible

[41] Red Ball Jets was a brand of canvas-and-rubber athletic shoe produced by the Mishawaka Rubber & Woolen Mfg. Co. under the trademark name Ball Band from 1951 to 1971. They were characterized by a red circle or "ball" on the back of the heel.

vegetable onto the unsuspecting scarecrow...making certain that he was observed ... by at...least...one...witness! Luckily for young Frank Blount here, that witness was one Miss...Bo...Peep!" I glanced over at Nellene. She was glowing from all this attention. Acting out the movements of the perpetrator, who I knew had to be Earz Grissom, I paced toward the crowd. "Having completed his devilish scheme, the scoundrel need only remove his sheet in the darkness and mingle among the partygoers!"

A few people clapped. But then I got an idea. It was just a hunch, but I was on a roll. "But where to hide the incriminating bedsheet?" Pointing toward the back of the room, I said, "There is a ghost figure in each corner of the auditorium. The villain could easily drape his own bedsheet over the top of the existing sheet ... and no...one...would...be... the...wiser!"

Everyone turned to the back of the room and Mr. Birdwell hustled over toward the ghost in the back left corner. He ripped the sheet off the ghost and, whaddayaknow? There was another sheet underneath! Mr. Birdwell jerked the second sheet off revealing the figure's wooden framework. Lifting a bedsheet in each hand, Mr. Birdwell, "There are two sheets!"

Everyone cheered and clapped their hands!

I had always figured that this gourd business was the work of Earz Grissom. It had his name written all over it. What I reckon happened was this: Earz came in dressed as The Skidmark, but hidden under a sheet. After he put the gourd on the scarecrow, he ditched the sheet by hanging it over one of the ghosts. But when Earz lobbed that roll of toilet paper across the auditorium, he got Commissioner Jordan on his scent. He had to disappear and couldn't come back to collect his sheet. In the darkness, he went out the side fire-exit door and had to streak[42] home to his cottage.

People in the crowd were starting to mill around, heading toward the refreshments, and moving back to their tables. Commissioner

[42] Streaking (the act of running naked through a public place as a prank or dare) was a popular American fad in the mid 1970's, particularly at college campuses.

Jordan came over to me and said, "So, 'Mr. Batman,' who did it? Who put the gourd on the scarecrow? Are they still here?"

"I surmise it was the archfiend...known as The Skidmark, whom you observed earlier," I said. "And I fear he has made good... his escape." I didn't dare snitch out Earz Grissom. He would cut my throat while I was sleeping.

"And you don't know who this 'Skidmark' is?" he asked.

"Alas! I...do...not!"

Commissioner Jordan nodded his head, and then turned and announced to the crowd, "Okay, everybody! The *Batman* show's over! Let's dim these lights, put on some music, and get back to having a good time!" He looked at me over his shoulder and said, "I'm going to go check out the refreshment table."

"Try the punch!" I called after him.

CHAPTER FIFTEEN

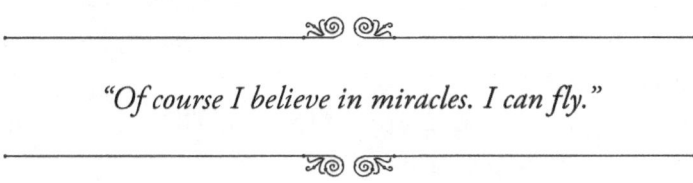

"Of course I believe in miracles. I can fly."

So I was sitting alone having my breakfast in the main dining hall. I was peppering my scrambled eggs, when I hear this voice say, "You like a little scrambled eggs with your pepper, don't you?"

It was Alvin Elliott, a kid I had seen around the dining hall, but didn't really know. Alvin was about my age and he had this humongous forehead. He was losing his hair and I imagine he was gonna be looking like Lex Luthor by the time he hit sixteen. Everybody at Clover Bottom knew about Alvin because he had an imaginary dog.

I shook the last few grains out of the pepper shaker and said, "Yeah, I like a lotta pepper."

"You mind if I sit down?"

"No," I said. "Make yourself at home."

He put his food tray down on the table and said kinda under his breath, "Fermac, sit." Then he sat down in Mr. Anderson's usual seat and said, "I'm Alvin Elliott."

"Yeah, I know," I said, "I'm Delphus V. White." I reached across the table to shake his hand. Alvin didn't understand at first, but then he shook my hand.

"I live in Cumberland Cottage," Alvin said. "What cottage do you live in?

"I'm in Progress House."

"I hear you all have a big color television in Progress House."

"It's not gigantic or anything, but bigger than regular-size, I guess. It's in the rec room," I said. "Anybody can come watch it, anytime they want."

"I may have to come check that out," said Alvin.

"There's always plenty of folks there watching it."

We set silent there for a minute as we stuffed our breakfast into our mouths. "Where do they have you working?" I asked, after swallowing a mouthful of eggs.

"I work in the garden, mostly." Alvin said. "I can't do a lot of hard work like some of the bigger boys."

"I work with the pigs," I said. "It's fun sometimes, but the smell gets on you and you can't never wash it off, no matter how hard you scrub."

"I can't smell you right now," said Alvin.

"You can't?"

"No, but I can't smell anything," he said, grinning. "I fell down in the bathtub and busted my noggin. I was unconscious for about a week and when I woke up, I couldn't smell anything."

"Not even a poot?"

"Nope, not a poot, or a hamburger, or a candy bar or ... even a biscuit," he said, glancing down at his tray, which had two biscuits on it.

"Whew! That's tough," I said.

"Oh, it's not so bad, I guess," Alvin said. "Because I got Fermac out of the deal."

"Fermac's your ... uh, dog?"

"Yep, he goes everywhere with me," said Alvin. "He protects me."

"Is he here right now?"

"Yeah, he's sitting right here under the table."

I looked under the table and didn't see nothing but our feet and legs, but I thought I'd humor this crazy kid. "Hey, Fermac!" I said underneath the table. Then sitting back up, I said to Alvin, "Yeah, that's a great-looking dog!"

"Don't be a jerk, Delphus," Alvin said, "I know nobody can see Fermac but me."

"Yeah, you're right. I'm sorry," I said. "I couldn't see him. I dunno. I was just trying to be nice."

"Well, don't," he said. "I know everybody thinks I'm crazy." He looked down at his tray and then I noticed he slowly broke off part of a biscuit and slipped it down under the table.

"I wasn't trying to be a smart aleck," I said. "I never met anybody that had an imagi ... uh, a dog nobody could see. It's pretty interesting. How'd you get him?"

"Like I said before, I was taking a shower. The bathtub got all slippery because I had knocked over a bottle of shampoo. I turned around for the soap and Bam! I slipped and cracked my head open on the tub. My brains were oozing out my ears. I was unconscious for about a week and I had to have two brain operations."

"You don't you have a scar on your forehead like Frankenstein?"

"All my scars are back here," Alvin said, patting the back of his round head. "So, anyway, when I woke up in my hospital bed, Fermac was laying right there beside me."

"And you couldn't smell nothing?"

"And I couldn't smell a thing," he said, slipping another piece of biscuit under the table.

"What's Fermac look like?"

"He looks kinda like a big German shepherd, but he's got a lot of brown on him," Alvin said. "I don't think he's full-blooded."

"Can Fermac talk?"

"Who ever heard of a dog that could talk?"

"Yeah, I guess that was a silly question," I said. "And Fermac's always right there with you?"

"Yep!"

"Even when you go to the bathroom?"

"He waits outside the door," Alvin said, as he sneaked another chunk of biscuit under the table.

"Does he eat?"

"Sometimes I give him stuff," Alvin said. "Sometimes, late at night, when he's sure everything is okay, he might get out of bed and go catch himself a rabbit. But I'm not sure he even needs to eat. I think he might be some kind of a spirit or a ghost dog."

"What makes you think that?"

"Well, at night, when he jumps in bed with me, he shrinks down to a smaller size so he doesn't crowd me out of the bed," Alvin said. "But then he gets bigger again when we get up in the morning."

"Yeah, I never heard of a regular dog that could do that."

Alvin broke off another piece of biscuit and handed it under the table. He wasn't even trying to be sneaky about it now.

"Now, Alvin, I'm ain't trying to hurt your feelings," I started out slowly, "But have you ever considered that maybe Fermac ain't real?"

"But he is real." Alvin looked under the table. "I can see him sitting there right now. It doesn't bother me if no one else can see him."

"You know what? I'm right there with you on that deal," I said. "I was born part possum. I used to have a tail and everything 'til they cut it off. Except for my buddies, the Blount Brothers, and *maybe* our Development Tech, Mr. Anderson, nobody else believes me."

"Then you can see what I mean," Alvin said. "With Fermac around, I'm never lonely. My best friend is always right here beside me. I used to get scared at night. But now, I never get scared of anything or anybody because Fermac is always here protecting me. My life has gotten a lot better ever since Fermac started living with me. Maybe he's not real. But I can still see him." He cast a glance under the table. "And I choose to believe in him because he makes me happy."

"The way you describe it, makes me wanna go crack my head on a tub," I said.

"I could not recommend it," said Alvin. Then he glanced at the white plastic clock hanging on the wall above the serving line. "I better go," he said, "I have to go dig turnips."

"Gross! I hate turnips!" I said.

"Yeah, me too," said Alvin. "See you around, Delphus."

"Good talking with you, Alvin," I said.

"Fermac, come!" Alvin said to the empty space underneath the table.

"Bye, Fermac," I said quietly as Alvin walked toward the door.

Just out of curiosity, I decided to look under the table. I figured that Alvin must have broken up and dropped at least a whole biscuit under there, pretending to feed Fermac. I was feeling sorry for the cafeteria worker that was going to have to clean all that mess up. So I looked under the table.

And there was nothing there!

Okay, now there might have been a few tiny crumbs, but not even close to a whole biscuit-worth. Where had Alvin put that dern biscuit? If he had been stuffing the pieces into his blue jeans pocket, I would of seen him doing it.

And then it come to me! Alvin must have been dropping the pieces of biscuit into the rolled-up cuffs of his blue jeans. That little stinker! But did Alvin have the cuffs rolled up on his blue jeans? I wasn't really paying attention to that. But everybody, and I mean everybody, at Clover Bottom had to roll up their britches legs because they always bought our britches with "room to grow." So I'm sure that's how he did it.

Why did Alvin put on that little show for me? He made sure that I seen him slipping pieces of biscuit under the table. He didn't even try to be sneaky about it that last time. Was Alvin trying to bamboozle me into believing in his imaginary dog? Maybe he was trying to bamboozle hisself into believing in Fermac. Can you bamboozle your own self?

On the other hand, maybe Fermac *was* real and he liked homemade biscuits. I reckon anything's possible.

I sat there, swooshing my eggs between my teeth, and turning these notions around and around inside my head. Then for no reason that I can think of, I looked over at the dining hall door. And who should walk through the door that very second but Mr. Anderson! I jumped out of my chair and ran over to see him. "Mr. Anderson!" I said, sticking my hand out for him to shake, "It sure is good to see you!"

"Well, it sure is good to see you too, Delphus," he said, giving my hand a shake. "How've you been doing?"

"Fine as a frog hair," I said. "You coming into work today?"

"No, we just had to drop off some paperwork at Johnson Hall and I thought I'd stop in and see if you were here."

"Is Miss Zelda with you?"

"Yeah, she drove me here," he said. "She's dropping off the paperwork for me. I didn't really feel like talking to them in the office"

"You're not retiring, are you?"

"No, not quite yet. When you're out on extended medical leave, you have to give them periodic updates. I still have tons of sick leave."

"You gonna have some breakfast?" I asked.

"I've already had mine, but I'll sit with you while you eat yours."

We headed back to where I left my tray, which was the table where we usually had our breakfast. I walked alongside Mr. Anderson because he looked like a soft breeze might blow him over. His tan jacket sagged down off his shoulders and his britches were all bunched up in the back. It was hard to believe that this same man clobbered a 600-pound boar three or four months ago.

When we reached our table, Mr. Anderson practically collapsed down into his chair. I set down and took a swallow from my box of milk.

"You sure you don't want some milk or juice or something?" I asked. "I could run and get it for you."

"No, I'm good. I'm good," he said.

"The Blount Brothers will be here 'fore too long," I said.

"I can't wait to see 'em," he said, "Them, and all the other boys. But I especially wanted to talk to you today."

"Me?"

"Yeah, I've had a good life, Delphus, better than any one man deserves. I've got a wonderful wife that I'm crazy about. I've seen my kids grow up to be people that I am proud of. I got beautiful grandchildren. But, lately, with all this time on my hands, I been thinking about all the things I've left unfinished. I came up here today to share my testimony with you one more time and hope you'd think about getting baptized."

"Oh, Mr. Anderson, do we have to talk about this right now?" The Blount Brothers never had to listen to this stuff because they got Washed in the Blood of the Lamb before they was brought to Clover Bottom. The other boys were too little.

"I worry about you, Delphus," Mr. Anderson said. "You're a smart little man, the smartest little feller I ever saw. But I'm afraid all them smarts will lead you down the wrong road, if you don't have The Lord in your life."

"I try to be a good person, Mr. Anderson."

"I know you do. I know you do," he said. "And you do a good job of it. But I've told you about some of my hard times back during the War. There were days when I didn't think I could take one more step, and my faith in The Lord was the only thing that kept me going. My faith gave me a...a strength to contend with whatever burdens life threw at me." Mr. Anderson took off his glasses and looked me straight in the eye. "I'm afraid you're gonna have days like that too, Delphus. Hard times. And I just don't see how you're gonna make it through 'em if you don't have The Lord to lean on." His eyes were kinda watery and he put his glasses back on.

Mr. Anderson had climbed out of his sickbed and ridden all the way from Nolensville just to share his testimony with me. What in the world would possess a man to do such a thing?

"You know, to me," Mr. Anderson continued, "The worst part about passing on is how long I'm gonna be away from Miss Zelda. I sure am gonna miss her. But I know I'm gonna be seeing her again. Someday I'll see her again in the Kingdom of Heaven." He pulled a faded blue bandanna out of his back pocket and wiped his nose. "You're my friend, Delphus. You are. And I'd like to think I'm gonna see you up there too, someday. Someday --not too soon." He smiled.

"Mr. Anderson, you know I would do anything to make you happy," I said. "But I don't think you would want me to lie about it. I can't get baptized until I believe. Mark 16:16 says, 'Whoever believes and is baptized will be saved, but whoever does not believe will be condemned.' And all through the Acts of the Apostles, it says the people *believed* and *then* they got baptized."

"Delphus, I know you have the Scripture pretty much memorized," Mr. Anderson said. "I always coveted your ability to do that." He chuckled a bit.

"Never could get all them 'begats' though," I said, shaking my head.

"So, basically, the problem is you don't believe in The Lord?"

I did not want to reply to that question because I knew my answer was gonna hurt his feelings. I searched for a way to tell him what he wanted to hear without straight-up lying to his face. Finally, I just said, "No, sir," as I stared down at the partitions in my food tray.

"Delphus, I can't see how you can believe in Superman and Batman and not believe in The Lord."

"I dunno."

"Come on, son, talk to me. We're having an important conversation here," he said. Then he leaned forward a bit and lowered his voice. "Tell me what you're thinking. There ain't no wrong answer. I ain't gonna get mad at you or judge you."

"Mr. Anderson, I don't really believe in Superman. I just pretend to. If Superman was real, he'd be on the News every night. They'd be saying, 'Superman fought a giant robot,' or 'Superman rescued the President.' But you don't never see him on the news. So I know he's not really real."

"That's good," said Mr. Anderson. "Being able to tell what's real and what's not real is important." He took off his glasses again and rubbed the bridge of his nose. "But you're having trouble believing in The Lord. Talk to me about that."

"Well, sometimes I think there is a God but he just don't care about us little people down here on Earth. He don't care about what happens to us or about what we do. Other times, I just don't think there's a God at all."

"Tell me about that, Delphus."

"Well, like when terrible things happen," I said, "Like that flood they had over there in China. It was on the news a while back. They said that flood killed tens of thousands of Chinese people.[43] Tens of thousands! Surely all of them people didn't deserve to die. I know they

---

[43] According to the Chinese government, *Typhoon Nina* and the attendant collapse of Banqiao Dam killed approximately 26,000 people in August 1975. Another 145,000 people died during the subsequent epidemics and famines. Unofficial estimates place the disaster's death toll as high as 230,000.

was all Communists, but they couldn't, all of 'em, have been bad people. Why would God let that happen to them?"

"Delphus, I believe The Lord has a plan for each and every one of us," Mr. Anderson said. "And everything that happens in our lives, good or bad, happens according to that plan."

"And you think it was God's plan for all them people in China to die?"

"Everything that happens is according to The Lord's plan," Mr. Anderson said.

"I can't see no kind of good in a plan like that," I said.

"See, that's the thing," said Mr. Anderson. "I have to vaccinate my dog Spanky for rabies every year. I have to give him shots for parvo and distemper too. I don't give Spanky those shots to hurt him. I give him those shots so he'll stay healthy and don't get rabies and die on me. Now, Spanky's just a dog, he don't understand why I'm doing that. All he knows is that I'm sticking him with a needle and it hurts! And that I'm the one who's hurting him!"

"Now, compared to The Lord," Mr. Anderson continued, "People ain't even as smart as a dog. Most of the time, we can't see His plan. Sometimes He sends us blessings. Other times He sends us hardships. But even when He sends us hardships, it's like Spanky getting stuck with that ol' needle. It's for our own good, or for the greater good of all creation--the ultimate fulfillment of The Lord's plan. We may not be able to see what that ultimate good is, because, like Spanky, we just ain't smart enough. We can't see the big picture the way The Lord can."

Then Mr. Anderson pulled a Bible from a pocket inside his jacket. It was dog-eared and taped up with black electrical tape. Flipping to the page he wanted, Mr. Anderson read, "'For I know the plans I have for you,' declares the Lord, 'Plans to prosper you and not to harm you, plans to give you hope and a future.'" Then he snapped the Bible shut with a grin. "See there?" he said. "'Plans to give you hope and a future.'"

"But, Mr. Anderson, there ain't no hope or future for them Chinese people."

"I hear what you're saying, but those people are with The Lord now. I won't pretend to you that I understand it all. No man can understand the mind of The Lord. We just can't think on that level. We aren't smart enough," Mr. Anderson said. "Even you, Delphus. You may be a genius the way you can memorize Scripture and books and things, but even you can't be as smart as The Lord. And just because you can't see The Lord's plan or can't understand it, that don't mean that the plan don't exist. Any fella who thinks that he's smarter than The Lord is getting a little too big for his britches, don't you think?"

"I don't think I'm smarter than God, Mr. Anderson," I said.

"But don't you, though?" he said, patting my arm. "Now, I don't mean for this to sound too harsh, but when you criticize what The Lord does, aren't you really saying that you know better than Him what things ought to happen?"

"I ain't thought about it like that." I said. "But are you saying we ought to just sit back and not try to understand why things happen the way they do?"

"Oh, no," Mr. Anderson said, "The Lord gave us eyes to see, and ears to hear, and brains to figure things out. He wouldn't have give 'em to us if he didn't want us to use 'em. I just wish you could have faith in The Lord and know that he has a special plan for you, and that plan is full of hope. You don't have to shoulder your burdens all by yourself."

"I don't want you to die, Mr. Anderson." I burst into tears right there in the middle of dining hall.

"It's The Lord's will, Delphus," he said, patting my hand. "Everybody gets born and everybody dies. But I'll be going to a better place."

I wiped my eyes on my sleeve. I wanted to tell Mr. Anderson that I had found my faith in The Lord and I would get baptized straight away, but I couldn't chase Alvin Elliott and Fermac out of my head. Was Mr. Anderson bamboozling his own self too?

It seemed awful coincidental how right before Mr. Anderson comes in, all eager to share his testimony with me, that I meet Alvin, who tells me all about his belief in an invisible dog. All on the same morning! Almost like it was *planned* or something. Was it God's plan for me not to believe in God's plan?

Finally, I just said, "Mr. Anderson, you give me a lot to think about. Why don't we go drag them Blount Brothers out of bed?"

CHAPTER SIXTEEN

"Christmas is not a time for you to be out patrolling—
'Tis the season to be jolly!"

At Christmas, Clover Bottom was like a ghost town. The residents that had families got to go home. That is to say, if their families came and got 'em, they got to go. Of course, I didn't have no family and the only kin the Blount Brothers had was a mean old uncle who wanted to steal their family farm. Of the little boys, nobody had showed up to claim Skippy Dean. His people was all from Bristol and that was a long way away. He stood at the window at the end of C-Wing's hall, holding his pillow under his arm.

"Whatcha looking at, Skippy Dean?" I asked him.

"I'm jus-jus-just looking," he said.

"You reckon it'll snow?"

"I do-do-don't know," Skippy Dean said, "You reckon it sno-sno-snowed in Bristol? That's where I'm fr-fr-from."

"I don't know," I told him, "Bristol's way up in the mountains. They get a whole lot more snow than we do here."

"Maybe that's why my sis-sis-sister Doris didn't come to get me. Maybe it sno-sno-snowed too much and she couldn't get her tr-tr-truck out."

"I bet that's what it was," I told him. "But, listen, Skippy Dean, we're gonna have a real nice Christmas right here. We have a big party. Folks from the Methodist church come and sing Christmas carols. We have lots of good food to eat and there's a ton of presents."

"We used to always have a bi-bi-big par-par-party at home, we did," he snuffled.

"I bet y'all did," I said, "But we're sure gonna have a good one right here. It's gonna be fun!"

"I worry if Sa-Sa-Santy will know I'm he-he-here."

"Santa Claus? Why, he always comes to the party! He hands out the presents!"

"Sa-Sa-Santy will be here?"

"Oh, yeah! He's the star of the show!"

"Okay then," Skippy Dean said, but he still kept staring out the window, waiting for his sister's truck to pull into the driveway.

"Me and the Blount Brothers was fixing to walk down to the Walgreens to get Mr. Anderson's Christmas present," I said, "You wanna come? Sure is a nice day for a walk."

"N-n-no," he said, "I think I'll just sta-sta-stay here."

"Suit yourself then," I said. "Let me know if you change your mind. See you later, alligator."

"After while, cro-cro-crocodile," Skippy Dean said.

"Too soon, baboon!" I called back over my shoulder as I went to find the Blount Brothers.

Walgreens Drugstore was about two miles away. Me and the Blount Brothers cut through the grassy field that separated Progress House and the Blind School.[44] When we reached the fenced-in part of the Blind School, we crossed over to the sidewalk.

As soon as we walked through the door of Walgreens, the first thing I noticed was that there was a brand new issue of *Detective Comics* on the comics spinner rack. The cover was all black and had Batman standing over an unconscious Alfred and a Dracula was springing out of a coffin right at Batman! Obviously, he had already bitten Alfred! In the upper

[44] This field is now the campus of Middle Tennessee Mental Health Institute, a State psychiatric hospital. The facility opened in 1995.

left-hand corner, the price said "25¢." I dug in my britches pocket and counted. I had eight quarters.

Now, to be honest with you, I ain't very good at counting money. I am okay at math, but "making change" is not exactly the same thing. See, we don't have a need for money at Clover Bottom. So I don't get a lot of practice with it and I kinda forget which coins count for how much. I do know you can't just go by whichever one is the biggest. They have classes at Clover Bottom about making change and I've took 'em, but without practice, it just don't stick with you.

Anyway, I needed to save what money I had to help pay for Mr. Anderson's Christmas present. I was going in with the Blount Brothers on Mr. Anderson's present like we always did and we was gonna get him a bottle of aftershave like we always did. Now, maybe you think that's a dumb gift, but when you work around hogs all day, aftershave can come in pretty handy.

By the time I caught up with them, the Blount Brothers had already found the aisle where they kept the shaving cream and the razor blades and the aftershave.

"Yessir! Walgreens sure has got a right smart of aftershave," Ferlin Blount said. "What kind do y'all wanna get?"

"I think Mr. Anderson uses Old Spice," I said.

"Hai Karate!"[45] said Sammy Blount, executing two knifehand kung fu chops in the air.

"I dunno," I said, "In his condition, Mr. Anderson may not be able to fight off a bunch of sex-crazed women."

"'It is nature's law that rivers wind, trees grow wood, and, given the opportunity, women work iniquity,'" sighed Sammy, shaking his head. "Still," he continued, "We gave Mr. Anderson Hai Karate before and he didn't have no trouble."

[45] Hai Karate was an inexpensive aftershave best known for its television advertisements in the 1960's and 1970's. The commercials featured a nerdy character applying the aftershave and then having to employ martial arts to fend off amorous women. A self-defense instruction booklet was included with every bottle.

"Yessir," said Ferlin, "Since we know he's already got Old Spice, maybe he'd like something different so he could switch 'em up depending on how he's feeling."

"Hai Karate!" said Sammy again, punctuating it with two more kung fu chops.

"You just like the name," I said.

"Yes, I do," said Sammy, leaning his head back to peer at me beneath the rims of his spectacles, "What of it?"

Before I could respond back, Frank Blount reached up to the top shelf and loudly tapped his finger on the top of a small black-and-green box.

Ferlin lifted the box off the shelf and held it close to his face so he could read it. "'Hai Karate Gift Collection,'" he read, "'Contains aftershave and cologne, four fluid ounces each.'"

"What's the difference between aftershave and cologne?" I asked.

"Yessir, aftershave is what you put on after you're done shaving," said Ferlin. "You can put on cologne any time you just want to smell better."

"So it'd be like two gifts in one!" said Sammy.

"How much is it, Ferlin?" I asked.

"Yessir, it's $3.75. With tax, that'd be about four dollars. A dollar apiece from each one of us."

"I still ain't sure about that Hai Karate in Mr. Anderson's condition," I said, "But you can't beat that price, two bottles for four dollars. It works out perfect. Good eye, Frank!"

We all give Ferlin our money and I knew that I still had enough left over to go back and get that copy of *Detective Comics.* So I went back and picked out a copy that wasn't already creased and bent. It was issue number 455 and was drawn by an artist I didn't recognize.

The Cash Register Lady, Mrs. Sofer, had jet black hair stacked up layer-upon-layer. Mrs. Sofer was nice, but she always talked to me in a very loud voice, like I couldn't hear good or something. Ferlin was ahead of me in line and Mrs. Sofer talked like that to him too.

"Is this gonna be it, hon?" she said.

"Yessir-uh-yes Ma'am," said Ferlin.

Mrs. Sofer punched some keys on her cash register and said, "That's gonna be three-ninety-four, darlin'."

Ferlin had a double-handful of coins from all the change we had give him. After shifting it between his hands a few times, trying to count it, he finally just dumped it all out into a little pile on the counter. Ferlin bent over the counter and scrutinized each coin as he slid it across the counter, adding the value to the total cost.

"Somebody is sure gonna be tickled with this nice Christmas present," Mrs. Sofer said.

Ferlin stopped.

Had Mrs. Sofer made him lose count?

After what seemed like forever, Ferlin started right back sliding the coins across the counter. Ferlin was a whole lot better at making change than I was. Eventually, the pile of coins in front of Ferlin became a pile of coins in front of Mrs. Sofer. Mrs. Sofer quickly sorted them out into her drawer, put the Hai Karate in a paper bag and handed it to Ferlin.

"You have a Merry Christmas, darlin'!" she said.

"Yessir-uh-yes Ma'am!" said Ferlin, "Thank you! You have a Merry Christmas, too!" Ferlin hurried out the door with Frank and Sammy trailing right along behind him.

I carefully laid my *Detective Comics* No. 455 onto the counter. "Good morning, Mrs. Sofer," I said, "How are you doing today?"

"Well, hello, Delphus," she said, "I'm fine. How have you been doing? We haven't seen you in a while."

"I been kinda busy lately," I said, sliding my *Detective Comics* No. 455 towards her. "How are Dick and Liz?" Mrs. Sofer kept a photo of her two Welsh corgis, Dick and Liz, taped up by her register.

"Oh, they're fine. Mean as ever," she said, tapping at her register. "That'll be twenty-seven cents, hon," but then she glanced down at her register and said, "Hey, somebody left me two extra pennies so you can just give me a quarter and we'll call it even."

I handed her my quarter and said, "Thanks, Mrs. Sofer."

"Now, I know you'll want a bag," said Mrs. Sofer, slowly placing my *Detective Comics* inside a brown paper sack. "And, see? I'm being real careful with it, darlin', not bending it or nothing."

"Thank you so much, Mrs. Sofer," I said, "I hope you and Dick and Liz have a very Merry Christmas."

"Thank you, sweetie," she said, "You too."

When I caught up to the Blount Brothers, they was feeding coins into a Coke vending machine just outside the door. Sammy and Frank had already drunk half of their cokes.

"Yessir! Cokes is just a quarter!" said Ferlin, pulling his bottle out of the machine. "Yessir! Delphus, I got some extra change if you need it."

"Naw, thanks, I got it," I said, inserting my quarter into the machine and pulling me out a Dr Pepper.

Sammy said, "On the way back, why don't we go up Donelson Pike and then cut over and walk through the neighborhoods? 'Those who are mindful do not tarry in the same place.'"

So we headed up Donelson Pike. Ferlin and Frank walked in front, with me and Sammy bringing up the rear. After we had walked a while, our cokes began to kick in.

"Urrrrrrrp!" Sammy Blount loudly burped.

"Three jacks!" I yelled and punched Sammy on the shoulder. Sammy hadn't called "Otis!" And then, just to show off, I loudly burped, "Ohhhhhtiss!" The rules allowed you to say "Otis!" while you was burping, so Sammy couldn't hit me.

"Urrrrrrrp!" Frank let out a huge belch.

"Three jacks!" yelled Sammy and he gave Frank a light jab on the shoulder. Frank swung around and shoved Sammy so hard, he went tumbling down the embankment into somebody's front yard. Without saying a word, Sammy stood up, struck a Kung Fu Golden Rooster Stance, and then he come running hard at Frank. Just before Sammy reached him, he executed a spin-kick and drove the heel of his tenni'shoe right square into Frank's balls. It pained me just to see it.

Frank dropped down on all fours. Ferlin knelt over him and pushed Sammy back with one hand. "Frank," said Ferlin, "Just breathe now. Try to catch your breath. That's good. Just breathe in." Then Ferlin wheeled around to face Sammy. "Nossir! Nossir!" he shouted at Sammy, "You know Frank don't play The Game! Nossir! You could of hurt him bad, kung fuing him like that. Nossir! Here I thought you was all 'enlightened' and everything."

"'One should not yield to anger,'" Sammy said to himself, "'But control it as a driver controls a chariot.'" Then Sammy faced Frank and bowed. "I'm sorry, Frank," he said, "I didn't mean to hurt you. I strayed from the Path."

Helping Frank to his feet, Ferlin said, "Yessir! Now you fellers shake hands." Frank seemed a bit reluctant at first, but he and Sammy went ahead and shook hands. "Yessir! We got to stick together," Ferlin said.

And so it was over, just like that. But if I was Sammy Blount, I would clear everything off the bottom shelf of my locker. I figured Frank would be leaving him a smelly souvenir in the next day or so.

We cut across to McCampbell Avenue and walked through the neighborhood, looking at all the houses. We might as well of been walking on the surface of the moon. Each house looked pretty much like the next one, one-story and red brick. I wondered about all the families who lived in them houses. What kind of jobs did the daddies have? Did they operate a crane like Fred Flintstone? Or did they wear neckties to work like Ward Cleaver? I wondered if the mommas always had cookies baked every afternoon when the kids came home from school. Did every kid have a bedroom all to hisself? All the houses had nice green yards where you could have a dog named Rex, but I didn't see no dogs around.

A metal trash can sat at the end of each driveway, waiting for the garbage men to come along and empty them. Even their garbage cans gleamed like they was brand new! The tops had blown off a couple of the trash cans, and as we walked by, we glanced down inside them. Who knows? Maybe even their garbage was different than ours.

I spotted a black leather jacket laying inside one of the shiny cans. "Hey, y'all, look at this," I said to the Blount Brothers, pulling the jacket out of the can, "This is real, honest-to-goodness leather!" After I pulled it out, I saw that both sleeves had been ripped off. "This is perfect!" I said, "I have a brilliant idea."

About that time, a fat man stepped out onto his little concrete porch in his undershorts and yelled, "Hey! Hey! What are you boys doing out there?"

"Thank you!" I yelled back at him and I waved for good measure. And then I took off at a dead run, clutching the jacket in one hand and my bag with *Detective Comics* No. 455 in the other.

My hasty exit caught the Blount Brothers off guard. Standing around the can, they looked at each other, reached a silent consensus, and then took off chasing after me. They caught up with me in short order. Possums are not known for their speed. We didn't stop running until we reached Stewarts Ferry Pike.

"Way to take off and leave us, Delphus," said Sammy Blount, when we had stopped running. We was all out of breath.

"Sorry, boys, I couldn't think of anything else to do," I said, "I hoped y'all would just follow my lead."

"'He who walks with fools has a long journey of sorrow,'" said Sammy Blount.

"I said I was sorry."

"Yessir, if that fat feller calls the po-lice on us, we're gonna be in big trouble," said Ferlin.

"He don't know we're from Clover Bottom," I said, "I mean, how could he?"

"Well, he sure knew we didn't belong around there," said Sammy.

As we got a little closer to Progress House, tempers seemed to cool a little bit.

"Y'all wanna hear my brilliant idea for the leather jacket?" I said.

"Nossir," said Ferlin.

"Well, the last time I talked to Mr. Anderson, he had his Bible with him." I said, "And it was all worn out and in rough shape. So I figured we could take the leather from this jacket, cut out a square from this back part right here, and make him a book cover, so his Bible would look brand new."

"Lemme get this straight," said Sammy, "You want to make a book cover for Mr. Anderson's Bible out of a leather jacket that you just stole."

"I did not steal it," I said. "That fat man had thrown it into the garbage. He didn't want it no more."

"But he didn't give it to you," said Sammy. "The Second Precept says, 'I will refrain from taking what has not been given to me.'"

"And what did you have for breakfast this morning, smarty-pants? Bacon?" I asked. I had read one of Sammy's books one time, and saw that kung fu men were not supposed to eat meat.[46] But Sammy loved bacon.

"That coat smells like a rotting fish," said Sammy.

He had a point. The jacket was a bit stinky. I had been holding it at arm's-length since I pulled it out of the garbage can. But I wasn't about to let him have the last word. "Well, sometimes when you *find* things, out on the street, that people have throwed away, they can smell a little bit," I said. "I figured I can clean it up after I get it back to Progress House."

"No amount of saddle soap can wash the iniquity from that garment," said Sammy, folding his arms across his chest.

"You think you're so holy," I said.

"At least I believe in *something,*" said Sammy.

"Nossir!" shouted Ferlin. "That's enough outta both of you! Nossir! I'm tired of listening to you two idjits bicker!"

The holidays had made us all a little cranky.

I went to work on the book cover as soon as we got back to Clover Bottom. A pair of sharp utility scissors was hanging on the pegboard in the barn, so I used them to cut out two big squares out of the back of the jacket, where there wasn't no seams. Then I stuffed the rest of that coat down into a garbage can and closed the lid down tight. I hoped them two squares didn't include the stinky parts. To be honest, possums ain't known for their keen sense of smell.

I scrubbed them two squares of black leather down really good with some saddle soap and warm water. I didn't really need but one square,

---

[46] This is not strictly true. Although Buddhist theory does tend to equate killing animals with killing people, most Buddhists do not observe a strict vegetarian diet, the most notable exceptions being the monastics of China and Vietnam, who refrain from eating all meat.

but I wanted a spare in case I rernt the first one. Finally, I just soaped them up real good with saddle soap and left them hanging over the backs of the chairs in Mr. Anderson's office. I figured they could air out overnight.

Back at Progress House, I drug out my copy of *The Three Musketeers,* which I figured was the closest-sized book I had to Mr. Anderson's Bible. It might not have been the exact same size, but it was pretty dang close. Placing the opened-up *Musketeers* down on a piece of newspaper, I cut me out a pattern that I could transfer over to the leather later on.

The next day, after I got done with all my hog watering chores, I checked on the pieces of leather in Mr. Anderson's office. I carried them out to the workbench in the hallway, got me a damp washrag, and started buffing them off again. The leather seemed to smell okay, but everything inside a hog barn pretty much smells the same way, that is, like a hog. As I stood there buffing away, Ferlin Blount wandered in through the barn door carrying a faded cardboard box in one hand.

"Yessir," he said, "I took a leather crafting class a few years back and they let me keep some of the tools. Yessir, you're welcome to use any of 'em that you want to." Ferlin set the box down on the workbench. "Yessir, I can show you how to work 'em."

I looked inside the box and saw spools of thick black thread, some big needles for stitching, a thing that looked like a cowboy's spur on a wooden handle, a metal tweezer-looking thing, an awl, a bottle of something, and I don't know what-all.

Sliding one of the pieces of leather toward him, Ferlin selected a metal tool out of the cardboard box. It looked like a screwdriver with a little black L sticking out of the side. "Yessir, this right here is called a groover," he said, holding it up so I could see it. Then pointing to the little L, he said, "Yessir, this part here is the blade. It's sharp and it sure can cut you." Ferlin hunkered down over the workbench so he could see better, and said, "Yessir, You just run this groover alongside the edge of your leather and it will cut a little groove in the leather that's parallel to your edge. See that? Yessir, that will keep your stitching line straight." Sure enough, he had cut out a perfect parallel line.

Then Ferlin pulled out the tool that looked like a spur off of a cowboy boot, only it was fastened to a wooden handle. "Yessir, this feller here is called an overstitch wheel," he said. "You roll it down inside the groove you just made. Yessir, it'll make little dots that'll show you where to make the stitch holes, so they'll all be the same distance apart." Ferlin rolled it down the groove, pressing down hard.

Reaching into the box one last time, he produced an awl. "Yessir, this feller is called an awl."

"I know that one," I said, "I seen one of them before."

"Yessir," Ferlin said, nodding his head. "Yessir, you push the awl down through the little dots you just made with the overstitch wheel. Yessir, you push it all the way through," he said, his voice straining a bit as he pushed the awl down through the leather. "'Cause that's where the thread is gonna go through. Yessir, and after you push it through, you give it a little twist. See that? Nossir, you don't waggle it round-and-round, just a little twist. Yessir, did you get all that?"

"Watching you do it, you make it look easy," I said. "Mr. Anderson's book cover's gonna look like it was store-bought!"

"Yessir, you just have to take your time with it and be careful. Yessir, I'd practice on this 'un 'til I got the hang of it."

"I'll do that," I said.

"Yessir, when it comes time to stitch it up, I'll show you how to do that."

"I already know how to sew," I said.

"Yessir, leather stitching is a little bit different," Ferlin said, "You use two needles coming towards each other, both at the same time." He touched the tips of his index fingers together to demonstrate.

"Sounds hard."

"Nossir, it's not too bad once you get the hang of it."

That afternoon I laid out my pattern, trimmed the leather down to book-cover-size, and then wrapped it around my *Three Musketeers* book to make sure it would fit. I glued down the flaps where Mr. Anderson's Bible's covers would slide in. I didn't use too much glue, just enough to hold the leather seams together until they got stitched down tight.

Then I practiced cutting a groove and making holes on my spare piece of leather. It wasn't as easy as Ferlin made it look.

The next day, I had four humongous blisters on my thumbs and forefingers, but I put me on some Band-Aids and I got all the holes popped out for the stitches. With Phase I of my project completed, I gathered up all of Ferlin's tools and relocated operations back to Progress House.

CHAPTER SEVENTEEN

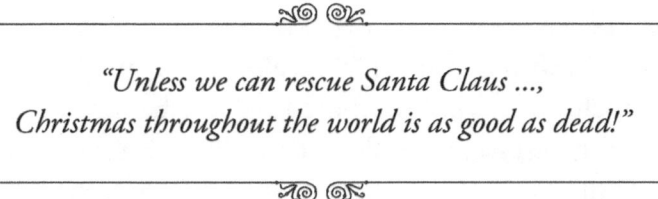

"Unless we can rescue Santa Claus ...,
Christmas throughout the world is as good as dead!"

Back at Progress House, the Bible cover still smelt pretty rank.

Sitting in our room, Ferlin Blount give me a lesson on leather stitching, which he called "saddle stitching." Just like Ferlin said, you used two needles on each end of the thread and they zigzagged across each other through the holes. Frank and Sammy drifted by to see what we was doing and they stayed to watch Ferlin. Holding the Bible cover between his knees, Ferlin stitched up one whole side just showing us how to do it. He showed us what you do when you got to a corner and how to make a splice when the thread ran out. When I tried it, I wasn't nowhere as near as fast as Ferlin, but I did get my stitches nice and tight. "One of you boys wanna try?" I asked.

Frank took the cover from me, sat down on the bed, and commenced to stitching away like a Singer sewing machine. He was even faster than Ferlin! I think it was because Frank was ambadect…ambidex… Frank could use his left hand as good as he could his right hand. We all just set there and watched Frank in amazement.

Finally, Sammy said, "Well, Frank, leave some for me to do."

"Ain't you worried about getting some 'iniquity' on you?" I asked. Yeah, I know I was a turd for bringing that back up again.

Sammy give me a serious look and said, "It is written that, 'Holding on to anger is like grasping a hot coal with the intent of throwing it at someone else; you are the one who gets burned.'"

"Well, I'm glad you ain't mad no more," I said.

Taking the Bible cover from Frank, Sammy sat down on Ferlin's bed, put the cover between his knees and said, "Seriously, Delphus, this thing really does stink."

"Yeah, I know," I said, "I'm working on it."

Sammy finished up the stitching, although Frank hadn't left much for him much to do. Ferlin put the final touches on the Bible cover, snipping off the last stray threads. After Ferlin completed his inspection, he propped the cover upright on his dresser. Mr. Anderson's Bible cover looked like it come from some fancy department store. But it still smelt like a dead dog that got squashed by a garbage truck.

Later that afternoon, I got a brilliant idea. Last April, Mr. Catfish got hisself a brand-new Wilson A2000 baseball glove and Mr. Anderson brought him some stuff to put on the glove to help break it in. Mr. Anderson called the stuff "linseed oil"[47] and said it would "condition" the leather. He brought Mr. Catfish a big Mason jar full of linseed oil from home. Inside the glass jar, the linseed oil was the color of pee, but when you touched it, it felt all slickery. And it smelled like a baseball glove ought to smell, which I think is one of the best smells there is.

So I went down to see if Mr. Catfish had any more linseed oil left over that he might let me borrow. Mr. Catfish lived on the A-Wing of Progress House, which is where the grown-up men lived. When I reached his room, Mr. Catfish was sitting on his bed, flipping through a copy of *Sports Illustrated* magazine. He was wearing his baseball cap.

"Hey, Mr. Catfish," I said.

"Well, hey nere, lil' possum mann," he said, smiling his broken smile.

---

[47] Linseed oil, also known as flaxseed oil, is a yellowish oil extracted from the dried seeds of the flax plant. Its superior drying properties make it useful as a varnish in wood finishing, a pigment binder in oil paints, and as a leather conditioner in leather finishing. Linseed oil use has declined over the past several decades with the increased availability of synthetic resins which function similarly.

"You doing alright today?"

"I'm nuing good, I reckon," he said, "What kanna do fer nu?"

"I was wondering if you might still have any of that linseed oil left over from when Mr. Anderson brought you some for your baseball glove," I said. "And if I might could borrow some of it?"

"I nighta nrowed nat stuff away," he said, "Lemme look." He bounced up off his bed and opened his closet door. Rummaging around on the top shelf, he held out his Wilson A2000 glove and said, "Ain't nat a beaut?"

"Boy, it sure is," I said, "I'm gonna get me one like that someday. Mine is an old, wore-out hand-me-down. The laces are all broken and tied together."

"Here's nat linseed oil!" Mr. Catfish said, pulling down the Mason jar. The pee-colored fluid sloshed around inside the jar, but it was still about half-full. "Nu kin have it," he said, handing the jar to me. "I non't need it no nore. I found some netter stuff to conn'ition ny glove with."

"Thanks, Mr. Catfish," I said, "I sure do appreciate it."

"Well, nu sure are welcome."

As I headed back to my room, Mr. Catfish called out after me, "Nu be careful, rags snoaked win'nat stuff nat nu use to wipe nown nour glove can catch far!"

I didn't hardly catch all that last part, so I just said, "Thank you! Merry Christmas, Mr. Catfish."

When I got back to me and Ferlin's room on C-Wing, I put some papers down on the floor, dipped a rag into the jar of linseed oil and globbed it all over Mr. Anderson's Bible cover. I worked the oil down into the leather real good and it made a pretty good dent in the smell.

"Yessir!" said Ferlin Blount as he walked through the door, "Smells like somebody got a new baseball glove."

"Naw," I said, "I'm just putting linseed oil on Mr. Anderson's Bible cover."

Inspecting my work, Ferlin said, "Yessir, I think next time you might want to go with a lighter coat. Yessir, linseed oil can dry a little tacky."

So I buffed off the excess oil and put on another light coat as soon as the first one had dried. I lost count of how many coats I eventually put on there over the next couple of days. But finally, the stink went away!

"It smells like a catcher's mitt," said Sammy Blount, as we was fixing to wrap Mr. Anderson's presents. We had drug the box of wrapping paper out of the closet and plopped ourselves down in the middle of the hall.

"Wh-Wh-What are y'all doing?" said Skippy Dean, coming out into the hall.

"Hey, Skippy Dean," said Sammy, "We're wrapping Mr. Anderson's Christmas presents. You want to help?"

"N-N-No, I'll j-j-just watch, I will." He set down beside us.

"That Bible cover smells like a catcher's mitt," Sammy said again.

"Well, I like that smell," I said. "It's one of the best smells there is."

"Maybe so," said Sammy, "But it's so strong that it makes your eyes water, Delphus."

"We could try putting some of that aftershave on it," I said. "You like the way that Hai Karate smells."

"Couldn't hurt," said Sammy, "'If a brightly-hued flower gives out an offensive smell, it is more than worthless in spite of its beauty.'"

So we opened up the aftershave bottle in Mr. Anderson's Hai Karate Gift Set.

"Let's just put the aftershave on the inside," I said. "'Cause I'd hate for it to stain the leather on the outside where it might show."

"Good idea," said Sammy and he sprinkled several drops inside the Bible cover. The scent of Hai Karate seemed to be winning the battle over the linseed oil.

Then I put the Bible cover into a little box left over from last year's Christmas and stuffed a bunch of white tissue paper into all the empty spaces around it.

"Mr. Anderson likes to shake his presents and guess what they are," I said, "I'm gonna stuff so much tissue paper in here, the cover won't slide around, and he won't never guess what it is."

"Why don't I sprinkle a little Hai Karate on the tissue paper too?" said Sammy. "Just in case that catcher's mitt smell tries to come back." He dribbled a few drops around onto the tissue paper. Then I mummified that box up tight with a roll of Scotch tape. It would take Mr. Anderson forever to tear it open.

"Why don't you pick me out some wrapping paper, Skippy Dean?" I said.

Skippy Dean crawled over to the big box that we had pulled out of the closet, carefully considered each tube of wrapping paper. Then he handed me a roll of red paper that had "Seasons Greetings!" printed on it.

"Good job!" I said, "Now pick out a big bow for me."

Skippy Dean rummaged around in the bottom of the box and tossed me a puffy red bow.

"Good choice, Skippy Dean!" I said and I had that package wrapped in nothing flat.

We only had one pair of scissors, so Sammy had had to wait 'til I finished wrapping Mr. Anderson's Bible cover before he could start. Sammy decided to use green wrapping paper on the Hai Karate Gift Set since it was already in a box that was mostly green. When we screwed the black plastic cap back down tight on the bottle of aftershave, you couldn't tell that we had hardly used any of it. We put name tags on both presents that said "To" and "From" and then wrote our names on there. We asked Skippy Dean to write his name on there too so he wouldn't feel left out.

Christmas Eve came at last and it was the night of the big party!

I dug out a bright red sweater that I got last year for Christmas, which I hated, but it looked "Christmassy."

Coming out of the bathroom with a towel wrapped around hisself, Ferlin said, "Yessir, you want to look sharp tonight. Yessir, they're gonna be taking pictures."

"Pictures of us?" I said.

"Yessir, pictures of everybody," he said "Yessir, they take 'em every year."

"Yeah, I had forgotten about that," I said. "You mind if I borrow some of your Brylcreem?

"Yessir, help yourself."

I went into the bathroom and got Ferlin's Brylcreem out of the medicine cabinet. If they was gonna be taking pictures at the party, I wanted my hair to look good.

My hair is like a stubborn ol' mule. It does whatever it wants to, whenever it wants to do it. My hair is stiff and white and always stands straight up in the air. I can comb it and comb it and Boing! It just pops right back up. I'd tried using Ferlin's Brylcreem before, but it didn't make a dent in it. I reckon I just hadn't used enough.

I squirted a big glob into the palm of my hand and then plopped it down on top of my head. I smeared it all around through my hair and then attacked it with a comb. I made a part, and combed my hair over to one side. The hairs laid down at first, but then, one by one, they started springing back up again like they was little tiny soldiers on the top of my head. The soldiers had ducked for cover when the shelling started, but now it was over and they was back reporting for duty! Clearly, they needed another barrage of Brylcreem to send them scrambling back to their foxholes. I squirted another glob on top of my head and massaged it around 'til I had Brylcreem streaming down my forehead. I wiped it off with a towel because I didn't want to get any on my Christmas sweater. I think the sheer weight of all that Brylcreem was what won the day. My hair was laying down!

We gathered up Mr. Anderson's presents and Skippy Dean and headed over to Roberts Hall, where they was having the party. It was already dark outside and the night air was cool as we walked along.

"Yessir," said Ferlin, "There's Nellybelle! Mr. Anderson and Miss Zelda made it in."

Whispering to me so Skippy Dean couldn't hear, Sammy said, *"Do you reckon Mr. Anderson will play Santa Claus this year?"*

"I dunno," I said, whispering back, *"He's played Santa for as long as I can remember. I sure would hate for him to miss it this year, but I don't know if he's got the strength."*

*"I reckon we'll find out soon enoug*h,*"* Sammy whispered.

When we got inside Roberts Hall, they had sure decked the halls! A humongous cedar Christmas tree sat in the center of the auditorium amongst all the dining tables. Colored lights and sparkly tinsel covered the tree and the smell of cedar filled the large room. Myself, I preferred the looks of a pine Christmas tree, but I had to admit that cedar-tree aroma sure was sweet.

A mountain of red and green and gold packages covered the floor underneath the tree. They was piled all the way up to the bottom limbs! Churches from around the city donated presents to us, mainly new clothes for the grown-up residents. Most of our toys come from the Marines[48] and a couple of Marines came to our party every year. Although they were always wore their sharp uniforms, they never brought their swords like me and Sammy asked them to.

After Sammy deposited Mr. Anderson's gifts under the tree, we looked around for Mr. Anderson and Miss Zelda. I spotted Miss Zelda already sitting at a table so we hurried over to her.

"Merry Christmas, boys!" Miss Zelda called out, waiving us over. "Little Sammy, come give me a hug!" Sammy gave her a big bear hug.

"Hi, Ferlin! Hi, Frank!"

"Yessi-yes, ma'am," Ferlin said. "It sure is good to see you. Merry Christmas."

Frank shot Miss Zelda with his index finger, crooking his thumb.

And Miss Zelda gave him a big wink and then shot him right back!

"Delphus, honey, what have you done to your hair?" Miss Zelda asked.

"I Brylcreemed it," I said.

"You sure did," she said. "But you know they say, 'A little dab'll do ya!'"

"Not my hair. My hair is like a stubborn ol' mule."

"Well, your hair is ...certainly in place," she said. Miss Zelda made like she was going to touch it, but then she thought better of it and decided to pat me sweetly on the shoulder instead. "And who is this little man you have here with you?" she asked.

---

48 Toys for Tots is a program run by the United States Marine Corps Reserve which distributes toys to children whose parents cannot afford to buy them gifts for Christmas. Founded in 1947, the program distributes many millions of toys to needy children every year.

"M-m-my name is Skippy Dean," he said, stepping closer to Miss Zelda.

"Well, you sure do have the red hair, don't you, Skippy Dean?" she said, leaning forward in her chair to be eye-level with him.

"Y-y-yes, ma'am," he grinned and his face turned as red as his hair.

"Is Santy going to come see you this year?" Miss Zelda asked.

"I-I-I hope so. I-I-I been good th-th-this year!"

"Then I bet he will."

"Where's Mr. Anderson, Miss Zelda?" I asked.

"Oh, he's in one of the side offices, talking with Mr. Jenkins."

I wanted to ask her if Mr. Anderson was going to play Santa Claus this year, but I couldn't do that in front of Skippy Dean. I wanted to go find Mr. Anderson. Plus, after the way Miss Zelda had acted about my hair, I wanted to go look in the bathroom mirror to see if it was doing something crazy. "If y'all will excuse me, I think I'm gonna visit the restroom," I said, "Save me a seat at the table." I casually strolled down the halls and Mr. Anderson was nowhere to be seen. I reached the restroom and checked out my hair in the big mirror.

Sure enough, my hair had betrayed me. Apparently, I didn't put enough Brylcreem on the sides of my head and the hair there was sticking straight up! It looked like I had two wings sticking out of each side of my head! I looked like Grandpa Munster! Or maybe like that new character in the *X-Men* called the Wolverine. Ferlin loved the *X-Men*.

Well, I still had plenty of Brylcreem on top of my head. I just needed to swoosh some around to the sides. So I started at the top and raked some of the Brylcreem down to the sides with my fingers. I didn't have a comb so I just pushed all my hair towards the back of my head. I looked like Dracula. Blah! I figured that was the best that I could do. I decided to just not worry about it. I needed to find Mr. Anderson. I washed the goop off of my hands real good and headed back outside.

As I passed one door, I heard Mr. Anderson's voice and it was raised! Like I told you before, Mr. Anderson was not a yeller or a screamer. It took a lot to get him riled. I decided to linger outside the door for a minute to see if I could hear what was going on inside. Possums are known for their stealth.

"Dad blast it, Jerry!" Mr. Anderson said, "I'm the only Santa Claus most of these kids have ever known!"

"Ed, we're just not sure that you're up to it this year," said Mr. Jenkins, who was some kind of bigshot in the Clover Bottom Administration.

"I'm having a good day today," Mr. Anderson said, "Plenty of energy. At least I was having a good day 'til you started all this . . . hogwash!"

"There are issues of liability," said Mr. Jenkins, "You could injure yourself."

"I have insurance," Mr. Anderson said, "And I have workmen's compensation. I am still an employee here!"

"Well, we just don't want anything unpleasant to happen."

"Jerry, I know every single one of them kids' names out there," said Mr. Anderson. "Can you say that?"

"No," Jenkins admitted, but then his voice got louder, "But what kind of trauma will it inflict on the residents if they see Santa Claus keel over and die right in front of them? On Christmas Eve?"

"I'm not going to die tonight, Jerry," Mr. Anderson said.

"You might overtax yourself and collapse."

"For months I been looking forward to being Santa Claus for them kids," Mr. Anderson said. His voice sounded tired and I heard the chair scoot as he set down into it. "These days, I need to have things to look forward to, to keep moving ahead. I've worked at Clover Bottom for 25 years and I haven't asked for much in all that time. The way I see it, y'all owe me this."

"Hold on now, Ed," Jenkins fumbled.

"Now this probably ain't the Christian way of handling this situation. I'm gonna need to pray about it tonight and ask The Lord's forgiveness, but, like I said, I reckon Clover Bottom owes me one." I heard the chair scoot again as Mr. Anderson rose to his feet and his voice had regained its strength. "That Santa Claus suit is in the cab of my truck! Both doors are locked! I realize that outfit belongs to the school and I'm gonna return it to the school. But not until *after* I'm finished playing Santa Claus and handing out the gifts!"

"But ..."

"You can call security!" continued Mr. Anderson, "You can call the police! And then we'll see what kind of trauma is inflicted on the residents when they see a bunch of jackbooted thugs strong-arming Santa Claus!"

"Okay, okay, have it your way," Jenkins gave in. "Hopefully, nothing will happen."

"You can play Santa Claus next Christmas, Jerry," Mr. Anderson said. "It'll be here before you know it."

I skedaddled away from the door because I didn't want Mr. Anderson to catch me eavesdropping. By the time I got back to the auditorium, the lines had already started forming at the buffet tables. So I went ahead and got in line.

Behind me I heard a deep voice say, "Ho! Ho! Ho! Merry Christmas!"

I turned around and there stood Mr. Anderson! His eyebrows and ear tufts was all white now and he must of lost about a hundred pounds altogether. His skin was dark now, not really yellow, but more like he had a dark suntan. I didn't even shake his hand, I went ahead and hugged him around the waist.

"Merry Christmas, Mr. Anderson!" I said.

"What have you been up to, young man?"

"Oh, just the usual, trying to keep the Blount Brothers out of mischief," I said.

"That's a full-time job," he laughed. "You ready to eat some turkey?"

"I sure am," I said, "I'm just glad I got in line ahead of you. You'd eat it all and there wouldn't be none left for me."

"Well, I might leave you a little."

We loaded down our paper plates and went to join Miss Zelda and the others at the dinner table. After a while, some carolers came in from the Methodist Church, which was just down the road from us. They sang some bouncy songs like "Santa Claus is Coming to Town" and some holy ones like "Little Town of Bethlehem." We all listened as we ate our turkey and dressing. Some people at the table sang along quietly with the carolers. A chubby man with a black handlebar mustache sang "O Holy Night," which is my favorite Christmas song. "O Holy Night" always gives me chills on the back of my neck, even if the singer is not the best in the world.

Most of the little kids, like Skippy Dean, could hardly eat, they was so excited about Santa Claus. They twisted around in their chairs and wheelchairs, looking left and then right, searching the room for a sign of him. There wasn't a whole bunch of little kids there because, like I said before, most kids at Clover Bottom got to go home. But their excitement was kinda contagious and it spread throughout the crowd.

When the carolers started singing, "Twelve Days of Christmas," Mr. Anderson leaned over to Miss Zelda and quietly said, "Well, that's my cue, Dear Heart. I gotta see a man about a reindeer." He squeezed her hand that was resting on the table.

"Do you need any help?" she asked him, placing her hand on his arm.

"No, ma'am," he grinned as he stood up from the table, "The situation is well in hand." And then he disappeared through the side door.

The carolers sang a couple more songs and I sipped on my sweet tea, which I loved, but didn't get to drink too often. Then I started worrying about Mr. Anderson. What if he did keel over and die tonight? He did look like he was feeling okay. Finally, the carolers started singing "Joy to The World," which was always their last number. Everybody sitting at the tables joined in! The older men boomed out the echo part, "And heaven and nature sing! And heaven and nature sing!" We was all singing so loud and so happy, I wanted to stand up in my chair and yell like I was at a football game! When the last song note sounded, the jingling of bells could be heard coming from outside.

Skippy Dean gasped in excitement.

The auditorium doors burst open and the man himself, Santa Claus, bounced into the room! His "Ho! Ho! Ho!" filled the auditorium and echoed off the walls! The kids squealed and some of the grown-ups clapped! Flashbulbs popped off around the room!

Now there's something I need to try to explain here. I'm not sure if I can. Every year, when Mr. Anderson played Santa Claus, he didn't just *play* Santa Claus, he *became* Santa Claus. He knew the names of every kid and every grown-up, no matter whether they was a resident or a staff member. He knew if you'd been good or bad, but he treated you like you'd been good anyway. When you looked at him, you didn't see Mr. Anderson in a Santa Claus suit, you saw Santa Claus. The eyes that was looking out at you from behind that white beard was not Mr. Anderson's, they was Santa's.

This year, Mr. Anderson had had to use a pillow to fill out his Santa Claus outfit. Before he never needed one. I don't know if it was the magic of the Christmas season, or some kind of power in that Santa Claus suit, or maybe Mr. Anderson's doctors had give him some "pep pills," but Mr. Anderson's Santa Claus was like he always was. And Santa Claus never got older, he never got sick with cancer, and he would never die.

It was a sight to see Santa Claus greet each guest, shaking their hands, or patting their heads or slapping their backs, as he made his way to the Christmas tree. Santa waved his arms and called out "Merry Christmas!" to everyone and every single eye was fixed on him. It was like he was a movie star! As he handed out the presents, he visited with each kid, asking them if they'd been good this year and stuff like that. Sometimes, he'd pose for a photo with them. With the kids who were severely disabled, who didn't even know who Santa Claus was, he would call their name softly and pat them on the cheek or the arm and then place their gift on their lap. But for every kid, whether they was sitting in a chair or a wheelchair, he would kneel down so he could talk with them face-to-face. All of that getting up-and-down had to have been killing Mr. Anderson, but Santa Claus had boundless energy.

Santa joked with the grown-up residents, sometimes pretending like he wasn't going to give them their gift because he had heard that they had been naughty this year.

Santa fetched a gift from under the tree and brought it over to Skippy Dean. Kneeling down, he said, "Merry Christmas, Skippy Dean! I hear you have been a very good boy this year."

"I sure have!" said Skippy Dean.

"Then this is for you!" said Santa Claus. He tousled Skippy Dean's hair and he was off for another delivery. Skippy Dean tore into the wrapping paper and found a fat teddy bear whose red fur was exactly the same color as Skippy Dean's own hair. He squealed with delight!

Santa approached me with a package and squatted down. "Delphus," he said, "Have you been good this year?"

"Mostly good."

"Well, that's an honest answer," said Santa, nodding his head, "I suppose I can let you have this gift if you promise to try harder."

"I promise."

"Then, here you go," he said, handing me the gift. "Merry Christmas!"

"Merry Christmas to you too, Santa," I said and he was off to hand out another one. I ripped the wrapping paper off my present and it was a Hot Wheels "Mongoose & Snake" Drag Race Set! It had a starting gate, a loop-the-loop, and 32 feet of track! It came with a red car that belonged to the "Mongoose" and a yellow car that belonged to the "Snake." They was famous racecar drivers, but I didn't know hardly anything about racing.

Santa Claus kept on going like that for an hour or more, until, at last, he had visited with every single guest at the party. After a while, some of the staff pitched in and started helping him pass out gifts. Otherwise, I think he would of gone on handing out presents 'til the morning.

"Well, I have quite a lot of stops to make tonight," Santa announced, "I'd best be on my way!" He looked around the room at all the smiling faces. "Merry Christmas, everyone! Be good to each other! Ho-Ho-Ho!" And with that, he charged back through the auditorium doors. We heard the tinkling of the bells as he flew away on his sleigh.

Sammy Blount got a "Mongoose and Snake" Drag Race Set too! That meant if we put our tracks together, we could have 64 feet of race track! That's practically a mile! We also got a pair of blue jeans apiece and a couple of sweatshirts. Ferlin and Frank just got clothes, which they seemed happy with.

A red-headed woman in a quilted overcoat wandered in through the auditorium doors. She looked kinda lost. The room went quiet when everybody seemed to notice her at once. "Excuse me," she said, "I'm looking for my little brother, Skibbereen McCarthy II."

We all looked at each other like, "Who in the world is *that*?"

"Doris!" yelled Skippy Dean, as he went running across the room to her, his teddy bear in tow. Doris scooped him off his feet and hugged him close.

"Sa-Sa-Sanny Claus came and he brought me this b-b-bear!" Skippy Dean told Doris. "I na-na-named him Red 'ca-ca-cause he's got r-r-red hair!"

"Pleased to meet you, Red," said Doris.

"Let's go m-m-meet my friends," Skippy Dean said, pointing toward us.

Doris didn't seem to want to put Skippy Dean down, so she carried him over to where we was sitting with Miss Zelda. After Skippy Dean introduced all of us, Miss Zelda said, "Honey, would you care for something to eat? There's still plenty over there on the banquet table."

"Oh, no, I couldn't," said Doris.

"Well, I insist," said Miss Zelda, "If you don't go get you a plate, I'm gonna go over there and fix you one myself."

"Well, if you insist, I could do with just a bite," Doris said and she reluctantly set Skippy Dean on his feet and went to fix herself a plate. Skippy Dean tagged along right behind her.

While she was gone, Mr. Anderson came in and sat down at the table. He had the sleeves rolled up on his white shirt and sweat was beaded up on top of his bald head. The white hair around the back of his head was wet. But he looked as energetic as he had been when he was being Santa Claus.

"Do you need something to drink?" Miss Zelda asked him.

"Oh, I'll go get me a glass of sweet tea, here in a minute," Mr. Anderson said.

"Sit still, I'll go get it," Miss Zelda said and off she went.

"Thank you, ma'am," he called after her.

"Yessir, you missed all the excitement," said Ferlin. "Santa Claus was right here in this room!"

"And he did an awesome job," I added.

"When Santa came through those doors, I thought Skippy Dean was gonna have a conniption fit," said Sammy.

"Men, if you ever get offered the chance to play Santa," said Mr. Anderson, "Snatch it up! There ain't nothing like it."

Miss Zelda, Skippy Dean, and Doris returned to the table. Miss Zelda handed Mr. Anderson his sweet tea and said, "Doris, this debonair, older gentleman is my husband, Ed Anderson." Then she wiped the sweat off the top of his head with a paper napkin. Mr. Anderson arched one eyebrow like Mr. Spock does.

"Doris, it's a pleasure to see you again," said Mr. Anderson, rising out of his chair and then sitting back down. "We met last year at Parents' Day, I believe."

"That's right, we sure did," said Doris, "Like I was telling Miss Zelda, I planned to be here the day before yesterday. But I got stuck in the snow in Knoxville! We had eight inches of snow, can you believe it? Then when I got to the plateau, the snow just stopped, not even a flake."

"Well, we have guest rooms available here for family members," said Mr. Anderson, "You'd be welcome to spend the night here and then head back to Bristol in the morning."

"Oh, that's too kind," said Doris, "But I'd be in hot water for sure if I didn't get this 'un back in time for Christmas dinner." She laughed and hugged Skippy Dean close to her.

"Aren't you worried about getting stuck in the snow again?" asked Miss Zelda.

"They seem to have all the roads pretty well plowed now," said Doris, "And they've towed all the cars out of the way. It wasn't the snow that was giving me so much trouble, it was all the abandoned vehicles that were blocking the roads."

"Doris' truck has f-f-four-wheel drive," said Skippy Dean. "It's a Jeep!"

Finishing her meal, Doris said, "Are you ready to go, Skibbereen?"

"Can Red go w-w-with us?" said Skippy Dean.

"Absolutely," said Doris.

"I have to t-t-take my other presents b-b-back to my room," Skippy Dean said. "And also I have to g-g-get some clean socks and un-un-underwear."

"Well, we better go then," said Doris

"Do y'all want to wrap up some turkey to take with you to eat on the way?" asked Miss Zelda.

"Oh, we'll be fine, thanks," said Doris. "It was lovely meeting you all. Merry Christmas!"

We all said "Merry Christmas" and "Drive careful" and Doris and Skippy Dean walked out hand-in-hand, with Red the Bear tucked under Skippy Dean's arm.

Most of the guests had left the auditorium by now, but a few groups still sat here and there at the different tables talking. A man I recognized as Mr. Jenkins stopped by the table and eagerly shook Mr. Anderson's hand. "Ed, you did a remarkable job tonight," Jenkins said, "Like you always do. No two ways about it, the way you are with the kids, you were born to play Santa Claus."

"I really appreciate you saying that, Jerry," Mr. Anderson said. "I left the Santa Claus suit in its box on your desk. And, Jerry, I hope you enjoy playing Santa Claus as much as I did."

"I'll never be able to do it as well as you," Mr. Jenkins said, as he walked away.

Several other people stopped by the table on their way out to congratulate Mr. Anderson on his performance.

"Time for more presents!" said Miss Zelda, as she reached under the table and brought out a green-and-red package. "Sammy can go first."

Sammy Blount shook the package as he held his ear to it. "It looks so pretty, I hate to tear up the paper," he said. But his curiosity got the better of him and he ripped the wrapping paper to shreds. He tore open the box. "Is it a bathrobe?" he said to himself, lifting the white garment out of the box. Then he realized what it was. "It's a *gi*!" Sammy said excitedly, "A karate uniform!" He put his arms through the sleeves and shrugged it on over his shoulders. It was kind of a tight fit over his bulky sweater.

"That is a *karategi*," said Miss Zelda, being careful with her pronunciation. "I was flipping through a Butterick's pattern book at Mill End Fabric Store, and I saw this pattern for a *karategi*, and I turned to Ed and I said, 'Ed, this would be perfect for little Sammy.'"

“I love it, Miss Zelda,” Sammy said and he leaned over and hugged her.

“Now, the pattern called for a 14-ounce cotton, which is almost canvas cloth,” said Ms. Zelda. “That seems like it would get awful hot when you start jumping around, but that’s what the pattern called for.”

“The heavier cloth is actually cooler,” said Sammy. “The jacket is stiffer and you get more ventilation.”

“Well, I’m glad you like it,” Miss Zelda said. Noticing that Frank had got kinda shortchanged so far, having only got clothes, Miss Zelda retrieved another package from under the table and said, “Merry Christmas, Frank! This one’s for you!” and she slid the present across the table to him.

Frank Blount took forever to open a present. He refused to tear the wrapping paper! Frank unwrapped a present like he was defusing a ticking time-bomb. He would carefully remove the bow and then slide the ribbon off. Next, he would slowly remove the tape from the wrapping paper, being careful not to pull off any of the colored part off the paper. It drove me crazy to watch him do all this. When he finally got the wrapping paper off, he would lay it out flat and smooth out the creases. You could re-use the wrapping paper next year, which is why he did it like that, I reckon.

Frank’s gift was a squat, red-metal box about two feet wide. On the top was a decal that showed two boys building a shiny robot. The decal read, “Be an Erector Engineer!” Frank opened the box and inside the lid was another picture of “The Mysterious Walking Robot: He’s Made of Metal! He has Electric Eyes! He walks by Remote Control!” Frank lifted out the top tray and it was filled with wheels and gears and little metal girders. Another tray held an electric motor, wires, and little squares of metal with round holes drilled into them.

“That’s an Erector Set,” said Mr. Anderson. “You can take them parts and build anything you want to. Sounds like it’d be right up your alley.”

“Are you gonna build a robot, Frank?” I asked.

“Yeah, build a robot,” said Sammy, “We can make him do our chores for us.”

Frank looked at Mr. Anderson and Miss Zelda and gave them a big thumbs-up with both hands. Then he went right back to studying his gears and girders.

"You're next, Delphus," said Mr. Anderson, sliding two presents down the table toward me. "Merry Christmas!" The bigger one was kind of heavy and I tore into it. I opened the box and it was two black hardcover books. I opened them up and there was page after page of heavy, unlined, gleaming white drawing paper!

"Since you're always drawing and reading comic books, I figured you could use these to draw up your own stories," said Mr. Anderson.

"I already have a story in mind!" I said. Then I started unwrapping my other gift and it was a Corgi Batmobile with a Batboat on a trailer behind it. I was in such a hurry to get them out of the box that I accidentally tore one of the flaps a little bit when I opened it up. The Batmobile could actually shoot little red rockets out of its rocket tubes and even had a chain-cutter blade that popped out of its nose!

"This is so neat," I said.

"Delphus, we like-to-have-never found that thing," laughed Mr. Anderson.

"Ed had us driving all over Creation looking for that Batmobile," laughed Miss Zelda, "He was bound and determined to find one."

"Well, I sure do like it!" I said, aiming up a rocket shot at Sammy Blount. "Thank you so much!"

"And now last, but certainly not least, is Mr. Ferlin," said Miss Zelda, sliding two gifts across the table toward Ferlin.

Ferlin gently tore open his first gift, making a single tear down the side. He pulled a black football jersey out of the box. On the jersey's front, back, and each shoulder was a big white number 32. Gold stripes circled each sleeve and across the back, it read "HARRIS."

"Yessir!" said Ferlin, "Franco Harris! Yessir! He is The Man!" Franco Harris was a football player for the Pittsburgh Steelers and he was Ferlin's favorite player. Ferlin slid the jersey on over his sweater and it fit perfect.

"Don't forget this other one now," said Mr. Anderson, pointing to the other gift. Ferlin picked it up and shook it a little bit. It rattled like metal. He tore away the wrapping paper and it was a long, shiny red toolbox! Inside was a nice ratchet wrench set.

"Yessir!" said Ferlin, "I sure do appreciate it. Yessir, I been carrying around all my tools in cardboard boxes."

"Well, now, there's more," said Mr. Anderson. "I got a bunch of tools down in my office in the barn. They're not the school's, they belong to me. I brought them from home. I want you to have 'em. Now, you can loan 'em out to the other boys, but they belong to you."

"Nossir, I don't know what to say..."

"A year or two ago, I got me one of them 'label makers' and some of that, what do you call it? ... 'embossing tape.' And I stuck a label with my name on it onto every single tool that I had brought from home. That way, they wouldn't get mixed up and confused with the school's tools.

"Yessir, I seen them labels on there."

"Well, if you see a tool that's got a blue label on it that says 'ANDERSON,' that means it's yours."

"Yessir, I sure do appreciate this, Mr. Anderson."

"You sure are welcome, Ferlin," said Mr. Anderson. "I'll try to come by in the next week or two, so we can sort through 'em. Some of the labels might of fallen off. And if I can find that label maker, we'll re-brand 'em."

"Sweetheart, I think the kids got to playing with that label maker and used up all the tape," said Miss Zelda.

"Them little rascals, stealing my toys," laughed Mr. Anderson. "Well, I'll pick up some more tape before I come back."

"It's your turn, Mr. Anderson," said Sammy Blount, fetching Mr. Anderson's gifts from under the tree. Sammy handed Mr. Anderson the Hai Karate Gift Set first.

"From Delphus, Sammy, Skippy Dean, Frank and Ferlin," Mr. Anderson read off the name tag. He turned it around in his hands, then held it to his ear and shook it. "Oh, oh, what can it be?" he said. "I bet it's bandanna handkerchiefs."

"Nope," said Sammy.

"Y'all got me some Matchbox cars to play with," said Mr. Anderson.

"Not even close," I said.

"It's a golden comb and hairbrush to brush my beautiful hair," said Mr. Anderson.

"Oh, Sweetheart, just open it," said Miss Zelda. "Nobody thinks you're funny." But we were all laughing, including her.

I guess Mr. Anderson got tired of teasing us because he went ahead and opened his present. When he saw what it was, he said, "Uh-oh, Miss Zelda, you are in trouble now!" Mr. Anderson held up the gift set so she could see what it was. "Hai Karate! I'm gonna be irresistible now."

"Oh, you're already irresistible," laughed Miss Zelda.

"Boy, I better read these instructions," said Mr. Anderson, pulling them out of the back of the box. He read: "'Hai Karate Self-Defense Manual: Don't dare use without memorizing this!'"

"You can read that later on," said Miss Zelda, "I promise to behave myself."

"Well, I reckon there's a first time for everything," said Mr. Anderson.

"Here's the next one," I said, sliding the box with Bible cover across the table. "We all worked on it."

Mr. Anderson picked it up, read off each of our names, and then held it up to his ear and shook it. "Hmmm," he said, "It feels kinda warm. You boys got me an electric blanket!"

"An electric blanket wouldn't fit in that box, Mr. Anderson," said Sammy.

"Then, an electric handkerchief," he said.

"No way!" said Sammy.

"Well, let's just see what it is," Mr. Anderson said as he tore the wrapping paper off the box. But then he saw the taping job I had done on it. I had wrapped the tape around and around the box. "I can sure tell who wrapped this one," he said, pointing his finger at me and grinning. "I gonna have to cheat a little bit," he said, thrusting his hand into his britches pocket for his pocketknife. He opened up a blade and carefully inserted it between the lid and the box and cut the tape all around the edges. Then he closed the blade on the knife and returned it to his pocket. "And now, let's see what this rascal is," he said and he yanked the top off the box.

A ball of fire the size of a basketball exploded out of the box! With a flash, the box erupted into flames! Mr. Anderson immediately dropped the box onto the table. His face and glasses was covered in soot! Miss Zelda shrieked! Then the white tablecloth underneath the box began to blaze up. Smoke surrounded the table and a smell like burnt bacon grease filled the air. Mr. Anderson calmly removed his glasses, grabbed the edge of the tablecloth, and flipped it over onto the burning box, smothering out the flames. He picked up his glass of sweet tea and methodically poured the contents over the smoldering mound in the tablecloth. When it stopped smoking, Mr. Anderson leaned back into his chair. He put his hand on Miss Zelda's shoulder and smiled at her.

Mr. Catfish suddenly appeared with a silver fire extinguisher under one arm. He squirted some soapy water onto the scorched spot in the tablecloth. "I always wannted to be na firemann," he said. "Neverbody onkay?"

"Oh, yeah, we're all okay," said Mr. Anderson, waving the smoke away from the table, and then he broke into a smile, "Looks like the boys got me a box of exploding cigars and they went off prematurely. But we're all fine now." He looked around the table at each of us as we sat there dumbfounded. Frank didn't seem to be bothered though, he had already gone back to studying his wheels and gears.

After seeing what happened and then seeing Mr. Catfish, I realized what he had said to me when he give me that linseed oil: "*You be careful, rags soaked with that stuff you use to wipe down your glove can catch fire!*"[49]

"I'll go get some napkins," said Miss Zelda and she got up from the table.

"What in the world was that?" said Mr. Anderson, shaking his head. His face looked like he had just come out of a coal mine. It was

[49] "Drying oils," such as linseed oil, tung oil, poppy seed oil, and walnut oil, dry through the process of oxidation, as opposed to evaporation. The oxidation process generates heat. If the heat is not allowed to dissipate, it may eventually become hot enough to ignite a fuel source (in this case, tissue paper), causing spontaneous combustion.

all covered in black soot, but he had big white circles around his eyes where his glasses had been.

"It was a Bible cover for your Bible," I said. "It was made out of real leather."

"Yessir, we all stitched on it," murmured Ferlin, hanging his head.

"I must of put too much linseed oil on the cover," I said, "And then, it wasn't dried good when I wrapped it up in the box."

"Yeah, rags snoaked in linseed oil can snorntaineously conbust on nu, like I snaid," Mr. Catfish said.

"Rags or tissue paper too, I reckon," I said.

Miss Zelda came back with a stack of napkins and started wiping the black soot off of Mr. Anderson's face. "It's a good thing you were sweating so much," she said, "It doesn't look like you have any burns."

"Oh, skin can grow back, I was more worried about my glasses," Mr. Anderson said, taking a napkin from the stack and wiping off his frames and lenses. "There," he said, positioning his glasses back on face, "Good as new!"

"I guess I shouldn't'a give lil' possum mann here nat linseed noil," said Mr. Catfish, "But who woulda nought sumpin like nis coulda happen?"

"Oh, don't you worry about that, Catfish," said Mr. Anderson, "Or you neither, boys." He pointed to each of us sitting around the table. "This is just one of them freak accidents that happen sometimes. I've heard about rags soaked with linseed oil spontaneously combusting. Never have seen it 'fore now, though. I 'magine that heat was smoldering inside that box and then, when I yanked the top off, it got a big gust of oxygen and exploded. Spontaneous combustion."

"Mr. Annerson, I've heard of hay snorntaineously conbustin,'" said Mr. Catfish, "Burn ye barn right down!"

"Now, you know, I have seen that," said Mr. Anderson. "I've seen people bale hay when it's too wet, and a few months later, you bust open a hay bale, and the inside of that bale will be so hot you couldn't lay your hand on it."

"I've seen nat sure nuff," said Mr. Catfish. "Nell, it's nast my nedtime!" He raised his baseball cap off his head. "Nissus Annerson, alnays a neasure to see nu!" He put his cap back on his head and shook Mr. Anderson's hand. "Mr. Annerson, nu nid a wonnerful job as Sanny Claus." Then he waved to us. "Noys, nu have a Nerry Christnas!" Then he walked out the door with the silver fire extinguisher still under his arm.

"Mr. Anderson, I didn't mean to blow you up," I said. I felt terrible.

"I know you didn't, Delphus," said Mr. Anderson, "Don't you give it a second thought! Like I said, it's just one of those freak accidents that happen sometimes." He slowly pulled the sodden tablecloth back away from the charred box and said, "Why don't we take a look at this incendiary Bible cover?" He took the Bible cover out of the box. "Oh, look at this, Miss Zelda. Ain't that fancy?"

"Oh, that's lovely," said Miss Zelda, "Look at all that fine stitching."

The thread we used must of not all burned away 'cause the Bible cover was still holding together. Mr. Anderson took some napkins and wiped at the scorched leather. Since the leather was black in the first place, you couldn't really tell how much of it was burned.

"And y'all all worked together to stitch this up?" said Mr. Anderson. He turned the cover around in his hands.

"Yessir, we took turns stitching it together," said Ferlin.

"Ferlin showed us all how to do it," I said, "You should of seen Frank stitching. He could sew like The Flash!"

"And it smells nice, too," said Mr. Anderson. He held it up for Miss Zelda to smell. "Don't that smell nice, Miss Zelda?"

"Oh my, yes, it sure does," said Miss Zelda, sniffing. "It hardly smells burned at all. I believe I could take a little water and white vinegar and it'll clean up real nice. Your Bible will look brand new."

"Well, I sure do like this, men," said Mr. Anderson, holding up the Bible cover. "All of y'all working on it together is what makes it special. Thank y'all for all my presents. Merry Christmas."

So we gathered up all our loot from the evening. We was loaded down with all our clothes and gifts. Me and Sammy had our Hot Wheels racetracks tucked under our arms. Sammy was still wearing his *karategi* jacket and Ferlin still had on his Franco Harris jersey. Frank clamped down the lid on his Erector set and carried it like it was stolen pirate treasure.

As we walked toward Nellybelle, Miss Zelda and the Blount Brothers got way ahead of me and Mr. Anderson.

"Mr. Anderson," I said, "I just wanna say I'm sorry again for ruining your whole evening."

"Delphus, you didn't ruin my evening!" Mr. Anderson said, as he stopped walking. "I had a great night, the best one I've had in a long time. I got to make all them people laugh and smile for a little while." He squatted down to look me in the eye. "Sure, we had a little setback there at the end, but you can't let that ruin the whole night. Delphus, that's just a part of life. Sometimes, you have good days. Sometimes, you have bad days. But you can't let the bad days overwhelm you. The trick is all in how you look at it."

"I think I understand," I said and we moved toward the truck.

"Good man!" Mr. Anderson said.

"Mr. Anderson, when I grow up, I hope I turn out as good as you did," I said.

"Well, that's awfully nice of you to say," said Mr. Anderson, "I think you'll do fine."

When we reached Nellybelle, Miss Zelda was already sitting in the driver's seat, letting the engine warm up. She was talking to the Blount Brothers through the rolled-down window. Mr. Anderson opened up the passenger door and said, "Merry Christmas, Delphus, and have a Happy New Year."

"You too, Mr. Anderson," I said. I didn't shake his hand, I went ahead and hugged him for the second time that night. My books and Hot Wheels racetrack slid out from under my arms and clattered to the pavement, but I didn't care.

Mr. Anderson climbed inside Nellybelle, closed the door, and rolled down the window. I scooped my presents up off the ground and stood back up.

"Remember, Delphus," he said, smiling, "It's all in how you look at it."

I took a few steps back and I felt like I wanted to say something more to Mr. Anderson, but I couldn't think of nothing to say. So I just nodded my head to let him know I understood. Miss Zelda put Nellybelle in reverse, backed out of the parking space, and they drove off into the night.

CHAPTER EIGHTEEN

"For two thousand years, mystics have experienced the many mysteries surrounding Christmas. Today there is one more..."

As we watched Nellybelle turn onto the highway, Ferlin Blount said, "Yessir! That sure was a fine Christmas party. Yessir! You fellers ready to head back to Progress House?"

"Yeah, my books are getting kinda heavy," I said. "Hey, Sammy, you wanna put our racetracks together? We put 'em together, and they'll stretch about a mile!"

"Sounds good to me," said Sammy. "It's still early yet, I reckon." He turned around and said, "Frank, what time is it?"

Frank Blount held his presents to his chest with his forearms and held up nine fingers.

"It's just nine o'clock," said Sammy, "I think we can get some racing in."

Frank Blount always knew what time it was, even though he never owned a watch. If you just out of the blue, asked Frank what time it was, he would hold up that many fingers.

Just inside the front doors of Progress House was the rec room. The overhead lights was dimmed this time of night. I could make out a single dark figure crouched over the pool table. lining up a shot. It was Earz Grissom!

Since it was Christmas, and Earz was all by hisself, and I figured he wouldn't kill me on Christmas, I thought I'd go wish him a Merry Christmas. The Blount Brothers hurried on to their rooms, trying to avoid Earz' gaze. I headed on over to the pool table, still carrying all my presents.

"Merry Christmas, Earz," I said.

"Well, look-a-here, it's little Delly," said Earz, "Merry Christmas to you too, you crazy bastard." Earz picked up his roll-your-own cigarette off the pool table rail and took a deep drag. Smoking wasn't allowed inside any of the buildings at Clover Bottom. He blew the smoke right at me and then leaned over the pool table to make another shot. The loud clack of the balls made me jump. I was starting to think this was a bad idea.

"Nobody's here," he said, "It's quiet as a church! So I thought I would fire it up!" He held the cigarette straight up over his head and yelled, "Fire it up!" Then I remembered Earz had burned down a church. He extended the cigarette toward me and said, "You want a drag?"

"No, I'm good."

"Suit yourself," he said, circling the pool table, eyeing his next shot. "You get all that shit at the fuckin' Christmas party?"

"I sure did," I said. "You should of come. They had presents for everybody there. I'm sure there was some presents for you there."

"Well, Christmas is for little fucking kids, ain't it? It ain't really my kinda scene--Santa Claus, "Joy to the World," and all that shit."

"Well, I just wanted to wish you a Merry Christmas," I said.

Earz looked up from the pool table. His eyes met mine and his sneer shifted into kind of a crazy smile. Looking into his eyes, I was certain that at least one time, Earz had killed somebody. Them eyes was the eyes of a killer. "You too," was all he said.

When I got back to C-Wing, Sammy Blount was out in the hallway. He already had the pieces of his Mongoose and Snake Racetrack out on the floor and was putting them together. "What took you so long?" he said.

"I was just talking to Earz Grissom," I said.

I went into me and Ferlin's room and dumped all my presents onto my bed. I could hear Ferlin in the bathroom brushing his teeth. Setting in the chair by the door was a small red package that hadn't been there when we left for the party. The package didn't have a bow. I picked it up and I could tell by all the creases in the wrapping paper that it had been used to wrap something else before. A square had been cut out of notebook paper to make a nametag. In an awkward scrawl, it read, "TO DELFUS, FROM EARZ." The bundle was flimsy; I didn't think it could have any kind of explosive device inside it. I ripped open the paper and it was a pair of brown polyester socks.

Well, this didn't make any kind of sense at all! Was this some kinda threat? I'd heard that the Mafia would send dead fish to people in the mail to warn them they was gonna be "sleeping with the fishes." Was brown socks some kinda code? Would he have put his name on the package if the socks was some kind of threat? I reckon I was more confused than scared, because I decided to go ask Earz about it.

As I walked back through the hallway, Sammy said, "Are you racing or what?"

"I'm gonna be a minute, Sammy," I said, "I gotta see about something." With the socks in my hand, I hurried back toward the rec room. I felt the tingle of my *Possum Mode* humming at the back of my brain, but I didn't think it was gonna overtake me. Earz was slouched over the pool table, cigarette dangling out of the corner of his mouth.

"Earz?" I said.

"Hmmm?" He didn't look up.

"I-I just wanted to thank you for the socks."

Earz jerked the pool cue forward and the impact of the balls sounded like a gunshot. I didn't hear any of the balls drop into a pocket. I had made him miss his shot! Earz stood up and leaned back against the table. He looked at me with his cold-blooded-killer eyes.

"Well, you sure are welcome, Delly." Earz took his cigarette out of his mouth and broke into that crazy smile of his.

"I was just wonderin' why you got 'em."

"Well, I figured stompin' around in all that goddamn pigshit the way you do, you could always use an extra pair of socks. I was gonna get you one of your little funny books. I know you like Batman, but Shit! I couldn't tell which ones you had and which ones you didn't. Plus, I only earn six-fuckin'-cents-an-hour milking them motherfuckin' cows and I didn't have a whole shitload of money to spend."

"No, I like 'em. I'm sure they'll come in handy. I was just wonderin' why you got me anything at all."

"Shit, man! It's Christmas!" Earz said, "And you're the only fucking pal I got around this place!"

"Pal?"

"Hell, yes! You're all-the-time saying some kinda funny shit, making me laugh, 'painting class,' or some-such-shit!"

"Here, I been thinking you wanted to kill me all this time."

"Well now, I do play kinda rough sometimes," said Earz, nodding his head, "But you know, Delly, you are kinda... soft. You need to toughen up, buddy."

"Why'd you stuff me into the back of The Penguin's car?"

"Now, that was for your own fuckin' good," Earz said, taking the last drag from his cigarette and stubbing it out on the pool table rail. "I did that to get your ass out of Clover Bottom. You're real smart, Delly. You don't belong in here with all these fuckin' retards."

"There ain't no fences 'round here, I could run off anytime I want."

"Yeah, but I knew you didn't have the fuckin' gumption to leave on your own. So I thought I'd give you a little push in the right direction."

"Were you mad when I come back?"

"Nah, I just figured you was like me--nowhere to run to," Earz said. "Sometimes, the best deal you got is three-hots-and-a-cot."

"You made a rhyme."

"Hah! I'm a motherfuckin' poet and you didn't even know it."

"Me and Sammy Blount was fixing to race cars on our new racetrack," I said. "We got extra cars. You wanna race?"

"Whaddya mean, like Matchbox or Hot Wheels, some shit like that?"

"Yeah."

Earz looked around at the balls on pool table, thought for a minute, and said, "Well, I'm losing to myself pretty fuckin' bad here. Why the hell not?"

Me and Earz headed back to the C-Wing hallway, where Sammy had finished putting together his racetrack. "Hey, Sammy," I said, "You care if Earz races cars with us?"

"Of course not," said Sammy without looking up, "Be one more person for me to beat."

"Well, you're a banty[50] fuckin' rooster, ain't you?" said Earz.

"Sammy is a kung fu man," I said. Sammy still had on his *karategi* jacket.

"Kung fu, huh?" said Earz. "Reckon you could show me a little bit of that kung fu?"

Without a word, Sammy Blount stood up, straightened his jacket, took about four running steps down the hall, jumped up in the air, started into a backflip, kicked the top of a door casing with his heel in mid-flip, and then landed back down on both feet.

"Well, kiss my cracker ass!" laughed Earz. "That was the hands-down, no bullshit, god-damnedest thing I have ever seen. Could you teach me some of that shit?

"It takes a great deal of practice," said Sammy evenly. He was not even breathing hard.

"Well, let's get the rest of this fuckin' racetrack built then," Earz said.

I went and got my Mongoose and Snake racetrack and my Batmobile out of me and Ferlin's room. Ferlin was already snoring away. We had my track put together in no time.

"We're gonna need a sturdy, high place for the starting line," said Sammy. The orange racetrack ran almost the entire length of the C-Wing hallway.

"There's a bunch of empty filing cabinets in the old Social Worker's office," I said.

"Let's use one of them motherfuckers," said Earz. He wrestled and scooted a green metal filing cabinet out into the hallway, with a little help from me and Sammy. He opened the top drawer and clamped the

---

50 A bantam (often referred to as a "banty" in the Southern United States) is a small variety of chicken. Named for the city of Bantam, Indonesia (now known as the Banten Province), bantam roosters were commonly used in cockfighting. Although sometimes viewed humorously because of their "puffed-up" demeanor, bantams were smaller, faster, and more aggressive than their full-sized counterparts. In reference to a person, bantam means someone of small size but aggressive and spirited.

starting gate to the top of the cabinet. The starting gate had a big orange clamp made into the bottom of it. We had two tracks set up so only two of us could race at one time. Earz put a chair on each side of the cabinet, so me and Sammy could stand in them when we was racing. Earz didn't need a chair. We kept score on the blackboard behind us.

Sammy was racing the Mongoose's red Plymouth Duster. Earz took the Snake's yellow Barracuda. I was gonna race my new Batmobile.

"You little turds go first," said Earz, "It's y'all's track."

Me and Sammy climbed into the chairs and put our cars behind the starting gate. There was a single button that you pushed down which would open both starting gates simultaneously.

"You can push the button first," said Sammy.

"Atomic batteries to power! Turbines to speed! Ready to move out!" I said.

"You're not going to say that for every race, are you?" asked Sammy.

"No, but I did want to say it at least once."

"Push the dang button!" said Sammy.

I did and Sammy left me sitting in the dust. The Batmobile did not even make it as far as the finish line. One win in Sammy's column.

Earz and Sammy raced next and I kept the score. When Earz won, he yelled "Barracuda!" and did a kind of little dance.

When it was my turn to race Earz, he let me push the start button. But I didn't say, "Turbines to speed!" this time. This race was even worse than my first one. The Batmobile hadn't even gotten up enough speed for the loop-the-loop and fell off the track.

I rushed down to where the Batmobile was laying on the carpet beside the loop-the-loop. I was sure that the clear canopy had broke. When I got there, thankfully, there was no damage!

Earz stopped his Barracuda dance long enough to say to me, "You better switch cars, Delly, that Batmobile is slower than goddamn paint drying."

"All the specialized equipment, like the missile launcher and chain cutter, must be slowing it down," I said, inspecting the paint for scratches. "I think the Batmobile was built more for crime detection than for speed."

"Why don't you use that blue one over there?" Earz said. "It's gotta be faster than that fuckin' thing."

"I think I will."

"All right, Kung Fu," said Earz to Sammy, "You ready to face 'The Barracuda?'"

"Okay, Hotdog," said Sammy, "Let's see what you got!"

Sammy beat Earz in the next race and that quieted him down a little bit. I started winning a few races after I switched over to the blue Duster car. We must of raced cars for a couple of hours. We got tired of keeping score pretty quick and so we stopped doing it. In the end, though, Sammy had won the most races, Earz came in a close second, and I brought up the rear.

Through with racing, we laid exhausted in the middle of the hallway floor. "I better scoot," moaned Earz, "I gotta get up at three o'clock in the goddamn morning to milk them motherfuckin' cows. If I don't milk 'em, they'll fill up with milk and explode."

"Will they really?" Sammy said.

"No, not really," said Earz, "But if I don't milk 'em, they can get pretty fuckin' uncomfortable.

Earz got to his feet, leaned against the filing cabinet and began unclamping the starting gate. "You know, I used to race Matchbox cars with my little brother, Scotty," he said, looking down the length of the racetrack. "That little fucker used to beat me every goddamn time. But, I don't know, I still kept right on racing him."

We wrestled the filing cabinet back into the old Social Worker's office and put away the chairs. Then we started breaking down the racetrack.

"We can finish the rest of this, Hotdog, you get on to bed," Sammy told Earz.

"Alright then, you're not gonna have to twist my arm," Earz said. He looked exhausted. Then pointing at each of us, he said, "Delly, you have a Merry fuckin' Christmas. Mr. Kung Fu, you do the same!" We told him "Merry Christmas and Happy New Year" back as he walked out the door.

CHAPTER NINETEEN

"Vast unseen forces are at work in the universe"

One crisp January morning, after we had finished feeding and watering the hogs, I heard one of Bessie's little pigs screaming bloody murder! I run out of the barn and spotted the Mulefoot boar trying to pull one of Bessie's piglets through the fence. The Mulefoot had clamped his teeth down onto the tiny pig's head and his massive black haunches quivered as he strained to pull him through the wire mesh.

"Ferlin!" I yelled, running back toward the barn, "The Mulefoot's got one of Bessie's little 'uns!"

Ferlin come running out of Mr. Anderson's office with a wooden baseball bat. By the time Ferlin and me got to the fence, the piglet had stopped screaming. The Mulefoot had ripped him in two. The rear half of the little pig's body and one of his forelegs was wedged into the mesh of the fence. His tiny heart was still rhythmically spurting blood all over the ground. The Mulefoot backed up a few steps from the fence and bellowed! As he reared up his monstrous head, we could see the piglet's crushed skull inside his gory mouth. The other foreleg dangled from his bloody jowls. With a shake of his head, The Mulefoot spit the crumpled head and leg across the pen. Then he leisurely strolled back to his bodock tree.

"What's all the commotion?" said Sammy, as he and Frank come running up.

"Yessir, the Mulefoot just killed hisself another little pig," said Ferlin, "Dadgummit!"

"That's the third one he's killed since Sammy Davis Jr," said Sammy.

Frank kneeled down and gently freed the little pig's headless body from out of the wire mesh fence. It had stopped squirting blood. Frank headed to the barn, to get a bucket to put the body in, I 'magine. He had his head bowed as we walked along.

"He does it every time," said Sammy, "Some curious little pig will stick his head through the fence to say 'hello' and that ... monster chomps down on his head like a crocodile and tries to pull him through the fence."

"He don't even bother to eat 'em," I said, pointing to the little head across the fence. "He just rips 'em apart and then walks off. Surely, there's gotta be something we can do."

"Yessir, the only thing I can think of is to build a solid wooden fence between the Mulefoot's pasture and this 'un."

"Well, why don't we do that then?" said Sammy.

"Nossir, I ain't got no authority to purchase no lumber nor nails," Ferlin said, shaking his head. "Nossir, only Mr. Anderson can do that. "Nossir. I can't requisition nothing from the warehouse."

"I know Mr. Anderson would come by if he was able," I said.

"Maybe we can scrounge up plywood somewhere," said Sammy.

"Yessir, you fellers can go and see what you can find," said Ferlin, "Me and Frank will clean up this mess."

Me and Sammy walked up to the warehouse and found three sheets of four-by-eight plywood leaning right up against the outside metal wall. Near their bottoms, the plywood sheets was soaked through with water and they looked like they had been setting there quite a while. Since nobody seemed to be using them, we scooped 'em up.

As we carried the plywood back to the hog barn, I said "Sammy, are we stealing?"

"'Buddhas employ the power of expedient means,'" said Sammy. "This is a matter of life and death. We're doing a bad thing to stop a worse thing."

After we carried the plywood back to the barn without anybody stopping us, me and Sammy decided we'd go back to the warehouse and see if they'd just let us have some. When Sammy launched his "Charm Offensive," he could smooth-talk people pretty good.

The huge sliding metal doors of the warehouse were rolled wide open. As me and Sammy walked in, a short, plump woman came scurrying out of a tiny office. A white hardhat was perched on top of her head and frizzy orange hair stuck out underneath. "What you boys want?" she screeched at us. She needed a bigger-sized uniform. A white oval above her shirt pocket said, "Bronislava." She carried a clipboard in her hand like it was a battleax.

"Good morning, Miss Bronislava," said Sammy, "And what a lovely name that is too. I'm Sammy Blount and this is my associate, Delphus White. We work down the hill at the hog operation..."

"What you boys want?" Miss Bronislava interrupted.

"Well, we have an emergency need down at the hog operation for a few sheets of plywood, preferably four-by-eight feet, and we were wondering if we might be able to just go ahead and borrow a few sheets."

"Where is paper?" she said, pointing to her clipboard.

"I'm sorry?" said Sammy.

"Requisition paper," said Miss Bronislava, stabbing her finger into the sheaf of papers clamped in her clipboard. "Pink requisition paper. No thing goes out door without pink requisition paper."

"You see, there's the catch," said Sammy, "Our operations manager has been out of the office with a serious illness, so we can't really provide a requisition form right now. That's why we hoped you might be able to let us just go ahead and borrow a few sheets of plywood now, and then we'll clear up the paperwork later."

"Borrow?" said Miss Bronislava, "How long you 'borrow?'"

"I'm afraid we would need to hang on to the plywood for quite a while," said Sammy, smiling sweetly, "But this is a matter of life and death, and we hoped you might be able to make an exception."

"Whose 'life or death?'" said Miss Bronislava.

"Well, you see, we have a boar that has killed four of our little pigs..."

"Peegs?" said Miss Bronislava, "I hate peegs! No paper, no plywood!"

"But, you see ..."

"No papers, no plywood!" shrieked Miss Bronislava, as she herded us out the door.

"And by that you mean..."

"No papers, no plywood!" Miss Bronislava squawked. When she had backed us all the way out of the warehouse, she spun around and stomped back into her little office.

"Where are *your* papers, you fat Commie?" said Sammy under his breath.

As we wandered back to the hog barn, I said, "Look, Sammy, I noticed that all them sliding doors had to lock 'em up was an old Yale padlock. Frank could have that lock picked in less than a minute. We come back here tonight, we can get all the plywood we need and no one's the wiser."

"We can't steal the plywood outright," said Sammy, "That's wouldn't be right."

"Sammy," I said, "I'm a little fuzzy on your kung fu rules, that is, when you can and can't do a bad thing to stop a worse thing."

"I'll try to explain it to you," Sammy said. "There was this rich guy and he had a humongous house. It's monstrous, but it's all dilapidated; the pillars are rotten and the ceiling is falling in."

"Why would a rich guy have such a run-down house?"

"I don't know," Sammy said, "I guess he was a cheapskate."

"So the house catches on fire," Sammy continued, "And the rich guy runs out of the house. He's standing out in the front yard and there's only one way in or out, the front door, but it's very narrow. So this rich man has a bunch of sons still inside the house--five, ten, or let's say twenty, little boys, still inside the burning house. And the flames are getting higher and higher. Smoke is everywhere! So the rich man yells to the boys, 'The house is on fire! Get out!' But the kids are too busy playing. They're just dumb little kids, they don't even know what 'fire' means. They don't pay no attention to the man."

"Why didn't the man just run in and grab the boys and carry them out?" I said.

"I don't know. There's twenty of them. That's too many to carry. They're all running around inside the house playing and he can't catch 'em. Plus, he can't carry them all through the narrow front door."

"He could make two trips."

"No, he couldn't," Sammy said, "For whatever reason, he could not go back inside the burning house to get the boys. Work with me here!"

"Okay, whatever you say. He couldn't go back inside the house to save 'em."

"Right. So the man gets an idea. He yells to the boys inside, 'Hey, boys! I got all kinds of wonderful toys out here for you! I got a bull-cart! I got a goat-cart! I got a deer-cart! Anything you want! They're awesome! You come out here in the front yard, you can have whichever toy you want! Who's gonna be first?'"

"But he didn't really have the toys?"

"No, he was just making that up," said Sammy. "So the boys, hearing about all these wonderful toys, come flying out of the house, scrambling all over each other to get to the toys. And so all the boys were saved!

"Good deal!"

"Later on, the man did give each of the boys a golden cart with fancy jewels, with real-live white bulls that could run fast as the wind!"[51]

"Bull-carts?"

"Well, they didn't have cars back then," said Sammy, "But the question is: Is the man guilty of telling a lie?"

"When he said he had all those wonderful toys, but he really didn't?"

"Yeah."

"I don't think so," I said. "He was just trying to save the little boys' lives."

"Exactly," said Sammy, "He employed *upaya*, or 'expedient means.' The man's intent was not to deceive the little boys, but to save their lives. He was 'prompted by no other motive but the love of his children.'"

---

[51] The parable related here is from Chapter 3 of the *Lotus Sutra*, one of the most important and influential texts in Mahayana Buddhism. The discussion here is largely out of context.

"Okay, Sammy, I guess I understand what you're saying."

"You shouldn't lie to somebody with the intent of deceiving them," he said.

"I gotcha," I said. But I didn't really.

Later that day, I found some blank requisition forms in a tray on Mr. Anderson's desk. The requisition form had a white page, a yellow page, a pink page, and then a golden page. Between each sheet of paper was a piece of carbon paper. All the pages was glued together at the top, but they was perforated to make them easy to tear apart. In a desk drawer, I found some white pages from some old requisition forms that Mr. Anderson had filled out before he got sick. I reckoned he got to keep the white pages. With my best penmanship, I filled in the blanks on a new form requesting ten sheets of four-by-eight plywood and three boxes of ten-penny nails. I filled in the blanks the same way Mr. Anderson had done it before. Then I tore the white sheet off of the form that I had filled out and put one of Mr. Anderson's pages right on top of mine. I lined up the edges precisely. Finally, I traced over the top of Mr. Anderson's signature, pressing down hard. His signature come through perfect on the pink page of my form. It was exactly inside the signature block! I could of forged Mr. Anderson's signature, but I thought, since I only needed the carbon copy, why bother?

I chased down Frank Blount to go with me to the warehouse so he could help me carry the plywood.

When we got to the warehouse, Miss Bronislava said, "So this time you have pink requisition paper, eh?" She looked down at me and smirked like she had really taught me a lesson. "Everyone have to follow rules. Let me see paper."

I handed her the pink sheet and held my breath while she studied it.

"I get nails," she said. "Plywood on Aisle 3. You get ten sheets. Ten!"

"I think we're gonna have to make more than one trip," I said to Frank as we walked to Aisle 3.

Sure enough, I couldn't carry more than four sheets at one time. Frank didn't have no problems with it though. I took the front end of our small stack and Frank carried the back end. As we was heading out the door, Miss Bronislava stopped us and counted the number of plywood sheets we were carrying.

"Four sheets of plywood," she said, "Three box of nails." She dropped the boxes of nails onto our load. As we walked away, Miss Bronislava said, "Smooth-talky boy not so talky now, eh?"

I realized that Miss Bronislava had confused Frank Blount with Sammy Blount, who had visited her earlier that day. Frank was two heads taller than Sammy, but other than the height difference, they did look exactly alike. Me and Frank just ignored the old cow.

We made our second trip without incident, although Miss Bronislava made sure to count the number of plywood sheets we was carrying out. On our third and final trip, we pulled three sheets of plywood down off the shelf, set them on the floor, and then leaned them back up against the racks of shelving. Then Frank held up one finger as if to say, "Wait a minute," marched down to the end of Aisle 3, and disappeared around the corner. I waited for what seemed like forever. I imagined Miss Bronislava prowling around the warehouse like an evil bear. Finally, my curiosity got the better of me and I had to go see what Frank was up to. As I rounded the corner of the aisle, I saw Frank squatted down with his britches around his knees. He was taking a poop right there in the middle of the floor! As soon as I spotted him, I spun around on my heel and went back to wait beside the lumber.

I reckon Miss Bronislava had hurt Frank's feelings with that "not so talky now" remark she made earlier. So he decided to leave a calling card for her to remember him by. You had to admire anybody who could just drop a "Number 2" on command like that.

When Frank was done, he rejoined me by the plywood. He nodded his head at me with a satisfied grin. We quickly picked up our load and hurried towards the front entrance. Miss Bronislava stopped us at the door, counted the number of boards, and sent us on our way. "Next time, you get pink paper first!" she hollered after us. All the way back to the barn, we listened for the scream when she found the surprise Frank had left her. But we never heard anything. I hoped that she would step in it.

The next day, when he saw the boxes of nails and stack of plywood, Ferlin said, "Yessir! You fellers sure did a good job of scavenging. Yessir, this plywood ain't gonna burn my hands, is it?" By that, he meant, "Was it 'hot' or stolen?" Ferlin had been watching too many police shows on TV.

"Naw, it ain't gonna burn your hands," I said, "Nobody's gonna come looking for it."

"Yessir! Then let's get these hogs fed and watered and we'll get started on building that fence."

Me and Sammy Blount drug the hosepipes around to all the watering troughs and filled them up. Then we snaked a hosepipe through the hole in the barn wall to fill up the Mulefoot's water trough. As the Mulefoot's trough was filling up, I stepped outside the barn door to make sure he wasn't trying to grab one last little pig before we fenced him in. But the Mulefoot wasn't anywhere near the common fence. He was back under his old bodock tree, stomping the ground, whirling around in circles, and snarling like he was crazy. Standing outside the fence, a few feet away, was Alvin Elliott, the kid with the imaginary dog. Alvin stood there serenely watching The Mulefoot pitch his fit. I decided I better go see what was going on.

"Hey, Sammy, can you finish up?" I said, "I need to go check on something."

"Sure, go ahead," said Sammy. "The trough's almost full."

Rushing through the gate, I hurried along the outside of the fence until I came up to Alvin Elliott. Although it wasn't especially cold that day, he had on a red-checked hunter's cap with the ear flaps flipped down.

"Don't get too close to that hog!" I yelled to Alvin, "He'll bite you!"

"Oh, hello, Delphus," Alvin said calmly, "You can rest assured that I'm staying on this side of the fence. I'm terrified of that scoundrel beast."

"What's going on?" I asked. The Mulefoot boar was still spinning around, snapping his teeth, snarling, and then whirling back around again. White foam splattered from his jowls each time he jerked his head and he had kicked up an awful lot of dust.

"Well, Fermac and I were out on our morning constitutional and we decided to take a different route. Fermac caught the scent of this awful hog-monster, chased off after it, jumped the fence, and now I believe he's trying to kill it."

"You mean Fermac is fighting the Mulefoot boar?" I said.

"Yes, I know you can't see Fermac," Alvin said, "But surely you can see how that hog-monster is putting up a fight."

"You know, Alvin, now that you say it," I said, "It does look like The Mulefoot is fighting *something*." At that moment, The Mulefoot leaped forward and snapped his teeth, then immediately whirled back around in the opposite direction.

"Fermac sure hates that thing," said Alvin, "It must be evil. Fermac's got a nose for evil. He never fights for sport. Fermac never harasses the cows and we walk by them every morning."

"Who's winning?"

"See, that's the thing. Fermac seems kind of hesitant to actually bite down onto the hog-monster's flesh. He's had plenty of opportunities to do so," said Alvin. "On the other hand, the hog-monster hasn't bitten Fermac either. Fermac is much too fast for him. I believe Fermac is trying to wear the hog-monster down, until he finally just collapses from exhaustion."

"Listen, Alvin, I hate this boar with all my might. I wish that he was dead more than anything. He bit Mr. Anderson and he tried to eat me alive," I said, "But, reckon you ought to call off Fermac? I mean, this seems kinda cruel watching two dumb animals fight each other to the death."

"Well, I've been thinking about that," said Alvin. "I'm concerned that if I call Fermac off, he's going to have a difficult time getting back across the fence. I fear he won't be able to get up his speed as he did the first time he jumped it. Fermac's back will be facing the hog-monster as he scrambles back over the fence and that's when the hog-monster will take him."

"How about if you go down that way about forty yards?" I said, pointing down towards a long stretch of the outside fence, "And you call Fermac to come? I 'magine Fermac can outrun The Mulefoot, and then Fermac can get up some speed, and jump over the fence."

"You think that'll work?" said Alvin.

“Yeah, I’ll create a diversion to get The Mulefoot’s attention.”

“How will you do that?”

I looked around to see what might be useful. I noticed a big mess of hedge apples laying on the ground right outside the fence. They had dropped off The Mulefoot’s bodock tree whose limbs stretched out overhead.

I dunno if you know what a hedge apple is or not. They are about the size of a softball and they look like a lime-green monkey brain, or maybe an alien monkey brain. They’re pretty hard when they start dropping off the trees around September, but then they get mushy as they lay on the ground. Hedge apples are poison and they will break out your skin if the juice gets on your hand. Luckily, I still had on my work gloves.

“Okay, when you get in place down thataway,” I said, “I’ll throw some of these hedge apples at The Mulefoot to get his attention.”

“I can do that,” said Alvin and he trotted off down the fence line in a clumsy run. After he had gone a-ways, he stopped and waved to show he was ready.

I had gathered up about a half-dozen of the least-mushy hedge apples and put them in a little pile at my feet. I yelled at The Mulefoot, “Hey, Mulefoot! Hey!” and let go at him with the hedge apples. The first one exploded when it hit his side. The second one missed him completely, but the third hedge apple got him right in the face. The Mulefoot charged at the fence toward me, but the fence kept him back.

At this same time, Alvin started yelling, “Come, Fermac! Come! Now, Fermac!” The Mulefoot suddenly sprung back from the fence and thundered off toward where Alvin stood. Was he fast enough to catch Fermac? As I ran towards Alvin, I could see him grasping at the top of the wire mesh fence, like he was helping Fermac get back over it. The Mulefoot crashed up against the fence and I heard a little yelp! Alvin fell backwards onto the ground. Had The Mulefoot bit Alvin? Maybe he got ahold of Fermac?

When I reached Alvin, I said, “Are you okay? Did The Mulefoot bite you?”

"No, no, I'm fine," Alvin said, getting to his feet, "I think he nipped Fermac though." Then he kneeled down to inspect the imaginary dog. "Fermac, are you okay, boy? That's a good boy. Let me see." After examining the invisible wound, Alvin said, "He's got a tiny nip here on his back leg. Not bad at all, is it, boy? Just a little scratch."

The Mulefoot stood on his side of the fence glaring at us, huffing and puffing like an angry bull. His black ears pointed at us like they was horns.

"Thank you for your help, Delphus," said Alvin, "This could have turned out much worse. We were probably lucky to get away with just a tiny bite."

"You're welcome," I said, "You probably want to keep Fermac away from 'round here."

"Yes, I think we'll stick to our usual path. See you around," he said. "Fermac, heel, heel. You ignore that hog-monster."

I watched them make their way back towards the dairy barn and then I looked over at The Mulefoot. His malevolent red eyes bore into mine. As he pawed the ground, I could see the massive muscles in his front shoulder moving underneath his glistening black skin. I started walking back towards the barn and he matched my pace, staying right beside me. He was so close to the fence, he brushed up against it sometimes. He started making a low rumbling sound. Suddenly, pale-green puke exploded from his jaws and splattered all over the ground. Slimy chunks of chewed-up hedge apple floated around in the vomit. The Mulefoot had been eating them hedge apples!

Then it hit me! That Alvin Elliot had bamboozled me again! The Mulefoot wasn't fighting no invisible dog. He got poisoned from eating them hedge apples. Like I said before, hedge apples are poison.[52] Most

[52] Although the fruit of the Osage orange tree (commonly referred to as hedge apples, horse apples, or monkey balls) were traditionally believed to be poisonous, various studies have shown that the fruit is not harmful to livestock. (e.g. Johnson, H.W., R. Graham, and J.P. Torrey. 1935. "A note on the non-poisonous properties of Osage Oranges [*Maclura pomifera*]" Journal of the American Veterinary Medical Association 86:667-668) However many authorities continue to list the fruit as poisonous (e.g. Joseph M. DiTomaso, "List of Plants Reported to be Poisonous

animals won't even eat them. The Mulefoot got more than enough hog feed every day, but I guess he just wanted some variety. So he ate some of them hedge apples laying around on the ground and poisoned hisself. Then Alvin Elliot walks up on the Mulefoot having some kind of conniption fit and decides to watch him. So I come up, and Alvin decides to tell me another invisible dog story.

On the other hand, maybe the hedge apples didn't have nothing to do with it. Maybe all that spinning around and chasing after Fermac got the Mulefoot dizzy. Maybe the Mulefoot got so dizzy, it made him puke. Or maybe getting a taste of Fermac's "magical" blood made the evil Mulefoot sick to his stomach.

Whew! I decided to go help the Blount Brothers work on the fence.

---

to Animals in the United States, Department of Soil, Crop and Atmospheric Sciences, Cornell University, Ithaca, NY). Some scholars speculate that when the fruit begins to rot, it develops a mold that is harmful to livestock.

CHAPTER TWENTY

"And a darkness fell over the cosmos..."

I was sitting at my desk in me and Ferlin's room drawing a story in one of the hardback books I got for Christmas. Ferlin was laying on his bed reading a *Spider-Man* comic. The story I was writing was *The Hellbeavers*, a superhero group I came up with. The Hellbeavers was a group of innocent beavers who unwittingly foiled Satan's plan to conquer the Earth.

Freed after a thousand years, Satan exploded out from under the rocky ground onto the Plain of Megiddo, or Armageddon, and he needed a lake that he could transform into the Lake of Fire. See, Satan couldn't create a lake because he wasn't The Creator. But it would be easy work for him to transmute one element (water) into another element (fire).

But the lake was gone!

"But, Master, the lake was right here last week," whined his demonic ambassadors.

A quick investigation revealed that the Beavers, doing what beavers do, had completely dammed up the river that flowed into the lake. The Lake of Megiddo had completely dried up. One of his diabolical ministers, Duke Chronoabdominu, pointed out to Satan that his window of opportunity had closed and he would have to wait another thousand years before he could try to conquer the world again.

In a fit of rage, Satan aimed his trident at the Beavers and blasted them all straight to Hell. But in his haste, he forgot to kill them first!

This is all in Revelations Chapter 20, except the part about the Beavers.

The Beavers were gifted to various demonic overlords to do with as they pleased. Some were kept as pets, some were experimented on, and others were made to fight in the Gladiator Pits. Whether by magic or maybe by just the passage of time, the Beavers learned to talk and developed distinctive personalities. But they escaped from Hell into the present day and now they fight Evil wherever it rears its monstrous head. They are known as The Hellbeavers!

The leader of the Hellbeavers is Dr. Stygio, "Master of the Thaumaturgical Arts." Dr. Stygio can fly and perform magic. He can shoot lightning bolts out of his fingertips and he wears a long red cape with a stand-up collar. I draw the hem of his cape all raggedy because it drags on the ground.

The next Beaver is Col. Bogey. He is the oldest member of the group. Col. Bogey is a master golfer and wears a golfing outfit. His golf bag is filled with trick golf balls that he uses to fight crime. He has a golf ball that shoots out a net to ensnare his opponents. One golf ball explodes when it reaches its target, another sprays tear-gas, and another golf ball sprays out glue and sticks you down right where you're standing.

Cybeave is 50% beaver, 50% machine and 100% hero! Cybeave got ripped to shreds in the Gladiator Pits, so his owner gave what was left of him to the Infernal Scientists. They built him a robot body. The scientists thought it would be pretty cool if he could also turn into an automobile so they designed his robot body to do just that. The car they decided on was a 1947 Buick Roadmaster Estate Wagon. The scientists never got the car transformation part to work, but Cybeave still has real wooden panels on his short robot legs and chrome trim on his sides. He can shoot laser beams out of his headlights.

The Grenadier is the micro-member of the Hellbeavers, like The Atom or Ant-Man. He is about one-sixth the size of the other Hellbeavers. Because of a botched experiment, The Grenadier's body is highly explosive, with the same destructive power as 500 pounds of TNT. After The Grenadier explodes, his body re-assembles itself. He has to live in a special containment suit that keeps him from exploding all the time. The containment suit has a firing pin ring that ejects him from the suit. In a battle, one of the other Hellbeavers just pulls the firing pin and then hurls The Grenadier at the enemy.

Nausicaa is the girl of the group. As you might can guess from her name, she makes people nauseous. With a single look, she can make the bad guys sick as a dog! She either makes them vomit or poop in their pants. But don't misunderstand, Nausicaa is not ugly. She is a very beautiful lady beaver. I think it is her beauty that makes men so anxious around her.

Last, but not least, is Jake. He is the "bad boy" of the group. He wears a motorcycle vest and an eyepatch, having lost an eye in the Gladiator Pits. I usually draw him with a cigar sticking out of his mouth because he is a "tough guy." Jake's wounds heal superfast. You know them two big teeth that beavers have sticking out in front? Well, when Jake is fixing to fight the bad guys, he can make them two front teeth grow out to about three-foot long. Then he rips them out and fights with 'em like they was katanas, or kung fu swords. When he gets done fighting, he just drops them. His new teeth grow right back in, like Dixie Cups.

In their first adventure, the Hellbeavers are inadvertently summoned to the Vatican by the Pope. The Vatican is in an uproar because the true Holy Prepuce[53] has been stolen from the *Sancta Sanctorum*. The theft is believed to be the work of the terrorist group known as The Skid-Marxists...

---

[53] The Holy Prepuce, or Holy Foreskin is a holy relic attributed to Jesus Christ, allegedly the product of his circumcision. Charlemagne presented the Holy Prepuce to Pope Leo III on December 25, 800 CE. Pope Leo III placed it into the *Sancta Sanctorum* of St. John's Basilica. The foreskin was allegedly stolen during the Sack of Rome in 1527, but reappeared in the Italian village of Calcata later that same year. Although as many as 18 villages have claimed to be in possession of the Holy Prepuce, only the Calcata foreskin was officially venerated by the Church. In 1900, the Church ruled that that anyone writing or speaking of the Holy Prepuce would be excommunicated. The Calcata foreskin was reported stolen in 1983.

"Good afternoon, boys," said Mr. Birdwell as he stepped inside the doorway. "How are you today?" Mr. Birdwell was the Development Technician who had been keeping an eye on us while Mr. Anderson was out. Although Mr. Birdwell never took off the khaki baseball cap that he wore with his uniform, today it was off and he was rolling the bill around and around in his hands. His hair was pretty thin on top. "Delphus, would you mind getting Frank and Sammy from their room? I need to talk with you boys about something."

After I went and got Frank and Sammy and we was all set down, Mr. Birdwell said, "Well, boys, I'm sorry to give you this bad news, but Mr. Anderson passed away on Sunday night. He passed away at home, in his own bed, surrounded by his family. They say he went peacefully in his sleep." Mr. Birdwell lowered his head.

Frank Blount slammed his fist into Ferlin's bed, which he was setting on. None of us knew what to say.

Raising his head, Mr. Birdwell said, "I've already sent some flowers to the funeral home and had all our names put on the card. That'll let Ed's family know that they are in our prayers."

"Yessir," said Ferlin, "When is the funeral going to be?"

"The funeral will be tomorrow at two o'clock, down in Nolensville," said Mr. Birdwell. "Now, I know you boys will want to go and I'll be glad to give you all a ride over there. Of course, I'll need to get approval from Johnson Hall, but hopefully they shouldn't have any objection. I believe the other boys are probably too small to be going to the funeral."

"Yessir, we sure would appreciate a ride over there, Mr. Birdwell," said Ferlin.

"I know you boys will want to look sharp when you pay your respects to Mr. Anderson," said Mr. Birdwell, "I don't know if any of you own neckties or not, but I can bring a few from home if you need them. They were my son's from when he was in school and his mother never throws anything out. I believe we may also have some sport coats that might fit you boys. So I'll bring those along tomorrow, in case any of you need to borrow one."

"I'd like to borrow a necktie, Mr. Birdwell," I said.

"Me, too," said Sammy.

Frank raised up his index finger, meaning he'd like one as well.

"Yessir, I got a coat and necktie that'll look okay, I think," said Ferlin, "But I appreciate it just the same."

"Okay, then," said Mr. Birdwell, standing up and putting on his cap, "I'll see you all tomorrow right after lunch. If you need anything before then, just come find me." Then he walked out.

I felt the tears well up in my eyes and start rolling down my face. Snot started pouring out my nose. I couldn't make 'em stop. I thought, there for a minute, I was gonna go into *Possum Mode*, but I didn't. None of the Blount Brothers was crying. Sammy was doing some kind of kung fu exercise. He had his eyes closed and he was breathing in-and-out real slow and loud. Ferlin and Frank just looked down at the floor.

I think we had all been counting on a miracle to save Mr. Anderson at the last minute, especially after he felt so good at the Christmas party. Even though we had plenty of time to get used to the idea of him being gone, it was still a shock. I thought of poor Miss Zelda being alone. She wouldn't have nobody to cut up with. At least I had the Blount Brothers.

"I ain't never been to a funeral," I said, "Have any of you boys?"

"Yessir, I been to one or two," said Ferlin.

"Do we need any money to get in?" I asked.

"Nossir, it don't cost nothing to get in," said Ferlin.

"Do we need money for the concession stand or anything like that?"

"Nossir, we shouldn't need no money for nothing."

"Well, that's good," I said. "What do they do at a funeral?"

"Yessir, they sing some songs and the preacher talks about what a good life the person lived, then they sing some more songs, and the preacher preaches a sermon."

"I hope they sing 'Knoxville Girl,'" I said, "That was Mr. Anderson's favorite."

"Nossir, they don't really sing that kind of song," said Ferlin, "It's more like church songs."

"Well, then they oughta sing "Precious Memories," I said, "Mr. Anderson used to sing that one a lot. He never could remember all the words. He just sung 'Precious Memories, how they linger ...' over and over."

We were all setting in exactly the same place when Mr. Birdwell came back more than an hour later. He kept on his baseball cap this time and his face was beet red. "Well, boys, I'm sorry to tell you this, but the Administration folks at Johnson Hall won't allow me to drive you to Mr. Anderson's funeral. They claimed that since I don't have a chauffer's license, it creates too much liability for the school if I drive you over there."

"Nossir, that don't make much sense," said Ferlin.

"I agree," said Mr. Birdwell, shaking his head, "I explained to them that I have full liability coverage on my vehicle and I believe Ed would have wanted you all to be there. I know Miss Zelda and the rest of the family would want you to be there as well."

"The Administration don't want us freaks parading around out in public," I said, staring at the floor. "They want to keep us retards locked away in here, out of sight and out of mind."

"Oh, I don't think it's anything like that, Delphus," said Mr. Birdwell.

"Sounds about right to me," Sammy Blount said.

"Well, in any event, I have to follow the School's orders," said Mr. Birdwell. He bit his lower lip. "They're my employer, and more importantly, they're your legal guardian. They could have me arrested for kidnapping if I disregard their orders."

"Sounds like you thought about doing it anyway," I said.

"I did consider it, there for a moment," said Mr. Birdwell.

"Well, thanks for considering it," I said.

"Yessir, we appreciate it, Mr. Birdwell," Ferlin said, "But we sure don't want you getting fired or arrested."

"I'll give Miss Zelda your condolences," said Mr. Birdwell, "And I'll let her know that you all wanted to attend the funeral, but that circumstances just didn't allow it."

"The Administration didn't allow it," I said.

"Yessir, Mr. Birdwell, we sure do appreciate everything you have done," said Ferlin, standing up and shaking Mr. Birdwell's hand. Then we all shook Mr. Birdwell's hand, even Frank, and Mr. Birdwell left.

"Reckon we could sneak out and take a bus to the funeral home?" said Sammy.

"Nossir, Nolensville's out in Williamson County and the buses don't go out that far," said Ferlin.

"Reckon what a taxi cab would cost?" I said.

"More than we got," said Sammy.

"We could try to hitchhike to Nolensville," I said.

"I doubt we could get there by two o'clock if we tried hitchhiking," said Sammy.

"Reckon we oughta call Miss Zelda on the phone?" I said, "And tell her we'd like to come to the funeral, but can't."

"Nossir, I don't believe we oughta bother Miss Zelda right now while she's grieving," said Ferlin. "Mr. Birdwell said he'd tell her we was thinking of her."

And so we didn't go to Mr. Anderson's funeral. I'd like to think they buried him with his exploding Bible cover.

CHAPTER TWENTY-ONE

They had a nice write-up in the paper for Mr. Anderson.
Nolensville, Tenn.

ANDERSON, Edmund Alexander, Sr.—Age 62 years. Sunday, February 8, 1976, at his home. A graduate of Scotts Hill High School and the University of Tennessee at Martin, he was a Development Technician at the Clover Bottom Hospital and School for more than 25 years. He was a member of the Nolensville First United Methodist Church and the Elks. Mr. Anderson was a veteran of World War II, holding the rank of Platoon Sergeant in the United States Marine Corps. He was attached to the 1st Marine Division and participated in the Guadalcanal Campaign. Mr. Anderson was awarded the Navy Cross for extraordinary heroism in combat. Surviving is his wife, Mrs. Zelda Pillo Anderson; 2 sons, Edmund Alexander Anderson, Jr. of Franklin and Harvey Randall Anderson of Lavergne; 2 daughters, Mrs. Daniel Brady of Nashville, and Miss Faith Anderson of Nolensville; 10 grandchildren; and sister, Mrs. Robert Ashley. Remains rest at Woodbine Funeral Home, 3620 Nolensville Rd. where visitation with the family will be (this) Monday evening 8 to 10 o'clock. Funeral services Tuesday afternoon at 2 o'clock at the above funeral home conducted by Pastor B. D. Weathers. Pallbearers selected from the Nolensville First United Methodist Men's Group. Internment at the Anderson Family Cemetery, Nolensville. WOODBINE FUNERAL HOME, Directors 832-1948.

CHAPTER TWENTY-TWO

*"Trudging through the murky swamp,
unseen tendrils clutch at his ankles."*

Everything changed after Mr. Anderson died. Or maybe it was me that changed. Nothing seemed real no more. Life felt like it was a 24-hour television show that played on and on and on. I wasn't the star of the show, I was just a background character. And there was this feeling like, just any second, somebody was gonna turn off the television set.

I was laying in bed one day after we had finished feeding and watering the hogs.

Ferlin peeped around the edge of the door and said, "Nossir, you ain't asleep."

"Hey, Ferlin. Yeah, I been sleeping funny lately," I said. "Seems like at night, I can't go all-the-way to sleep, and then when I get up in the morning, I can't wake all-the-way up."

"Yessir, it's suppertime!" said Ferlin.

"Funny, I ain't been able to keep track of time lately," I said. "Seems like one day blurs right into the next, and it all feels like it's just one long day. You know what I mean?"

"Yessir, I guess so," said Ferlin. "Yessir, it's been two months since Mr. Anderson passed. He wouldn't want you to be grieving this-a-way."

"I know. I just can't stop thinking about Mr. Anderson dying and being gone forever," I said. "It makes me think about *me* being gone forever. There don't seem to be no reason to do nothing if you're just gonna haul off and die."

"Yessir, it seems like to me that if you know the end is a-coming, you oughta hurry up and try to have as much fun as you can before it gets here."

"Yeah, Mr. Anderson would say, 'You're not looking at it the right way. It's all in how you look at it.'"

"Yessir, that sure is what he'd say," said Ferlin, grinning. "Delphus, you know, if you don't start getting out of this bed more, the nurse's aides are gonna send a doctor around to talk to you. Yessir, I'm surprised they ain't done it already."

"Yeah, I know."

"Yessir, and Delphus, nothing personal, but you're starting to smell kinda bad."

Now, when a person who works around hogs all day tells you that you're starting to smell bad, you probably should listen to him.

"Sorry," I said.

"Yessir, I tell you what--you're gonna go to supper with me and Frank and Sammy tonight if we have to wrestle you up out of that bed and carry you all the way to the dining hall."

I did go to supper with the Blount Brothers that night and they didn't have to carry me. I even took a shower. In the food line, I got me a Salisbury steak and some mashed potatoes, which is one of my favorites.

After we all got set down at a table, Ferlin said, "Yessir, we're getting a new Development Tech tomorrow. His name is Richard Eubel Phillips."

"He sounds like a presidential assassin," I said, "Or maybe a serial murderer."

"Yessir, now I know we all miss Mr. Anderson, but we oughta at least give this Phillips feller a chance."

"Where's he come from, Ferlin?" said Sammy.

"Nossir, I don't know anything else about him," said Ferlin, "'Cept his name."

"Well, I don't like his name," I said.

"Yessir, let's just give him a chance."

Earz Grissom sauntered by our table carrying an empty tray. "Howdy, boys," he said. "Well, look who's back from the fucking dead! Delly, I ain't seen you in a fucking coon's age, boy. The Kung Fu Man said you been feeling poorly."

"Yeah, I was a little under the weather."

"You okay now?"

"Well, I'm above ground and taking nourishment, I reckon."

"Alright, alright, alright!" said Earz, "Sounds like you just needed an ice-water enema with a shot of Tobasco sauce," He smacked Sammy on the shoulder. "How you been getting along, Kung Fu?"

"'Silently I endure abuse as the elephant in battle endures the arrow sent from the bow,'" said Sammy.

"Sheee-it!" laughed Earz. Then looking at Ferlin, he said, "Big Man, what are you gonna do with these crazy motherfuckers?"

"Nossir, I can't do nothing with 'em," said Ferlin, grinning and shaking his head.

Earz shot his index finger at Frank, who shot him right back. "Well, I'll see you boys on down the road," said Earz, "I got me a hot date." On his way out the door, Earz casually dumped tray-and-all into the garbage can.

Sitting there, eating my Salisbury steak, I realized I was feeling better. The smells in the dining hall, the homemade rolls and the macaroni and cheese, the hum of conversation from all the other tables around us, they seemed to calm me down some kinda way. Maybe it was just the change of scenery. I hadn't been anywhere other than the hog barn and me and Ferlin's room in the last month or two. I hadn't gone on a night patrol since Christmas. But right now, I was feeling okay.

When we had finished supper, me and the Blount Brothers scraped out our trays and put them on the conveyor belt. As we was heading out, I spotted Alvin Elliott sitting at a table all by hisself. He looked like he hadn't slept in days.

"You boys go on ahead," I said to the Blount Brothers, "I'm gonna holler at Alvin Elliott a minute."

"Yessir, we'll see you back at Progress House," said Ferlin.

"Hey, Alvin," I said, sitting down across from him. "How you doing?"

"Hey, Delphus," he said, looking down at the untouched food on his tray. "Not so well, to tell you the truth."

"What's the matter?"

"Fermac is gone."

"He's gone?" I said, looking under the table, "What happened?"

"Fermac's dead. He got sick and then he just sort of drifted away."

"What made him sick?"

"It was that Hog Monster he fought with," said Alvin. "Remember that day we watched them fighting?"

"Yeah."

"That Hog Monster bit Fermac."

"But you said Fermac just had a little nip on his hind leg?"

"It didn't look that bad to me, there was hardly any blood at all. I didn't even bother to put a bandage on his leg," Alvin said. "But Fermac was never himself after that day. He just got weaker and weaker. He didn't want to go on our morning constitutionals. Then one night, he shrunk down to bed-size, climbed into bed, and never got back up."

"I sure am sorry to hear that, Alvin," I said.

"He just faded from my sight," said Alvin. "It was like he evaporated. I'd like to think he went back to the Old Country." Tears rolled down Alvin's cheeks.

"Well, you never can tell with magical dogs, Alvin," I said. "Maybe Fermac realized you was tough enough now to make it on your own."

"No, it was that satanic Hog-Monster that killed him," Alvin said, sniffling. "That thing is pure evil. I'm sure that's why Fermac didn't want to touch it. He would snap at its heels, but he didn't want to sink his teeth into its skin."

"I'm sorry, Alvin," I said. "It was my plan that got Fermac bit."

"Oh, it's not your fault, Delphus," Alvin said. "There was no good outcome coming out of that fight. Fermac was doomed the minute he jumped that fence to battle that Hog-Monster. The wickedness of that monster is just too great."

"Do you think maybe there's a chance that Fermac might come back?" I said. "Maybe he's off somewhere healing up, and then when he's back in fighting shape, he's gonna come back?"

"No, Fermac's gone for good," said Alvin. "I don't know how I know--I just do."

I didn't know what to make of any of this. If Alvin had conjured Fermac up out of his imagination, why couldn't he just imagine Fermac getting better again? Or why couldn't he just conjure hisself up a new guard dog? Maybe when Alvin banged his noggin in the shower, it re-wired his brain somehow. Maybe he really could see and hear things other people couldn't.

"I sure am sorry, Alvin," I said.

"He was my best friend, Delphus," Alvin said, and tears started rolling down his face again.

"I know how you feel. I lost my best friend a little while back," I said. "Mr. Anderson, our Development Technician." I felt like crying too, but my tears had all dried up.

"Mr. Anderson?" said Alvin. "That's the man who was bitten by the Hog-Monster?"

"Yeah. But Mr. Anderson died of cancer."

"Hmmm," said Alvin. Then, after thinking a minute, he said, "I wish I could kill that Hog-Monster. But I'm just not tough enough for a job like that."

"Yeah, I hate that Mulefoot monster too," I said and stood up to leave. "I hope you get to feeling better, Alvin. Hang in there, buddy."

"Thanks, Delphus."

As I walked back to Progress House, I reckoned that this was the first time I had talked to Alvin Elliott and he hadn't bamboozled me.

CHAPTER TWENTY-THREE

"Another menacing figure looms large on the dark horizon."

Richard Eubel Phillips looked exactly like the Evil Twin of Popeye the Sailor Man.[54] Although our new Development Technician had regular-sized forearms, Phillips had the same squinchy eye as Popeye the Sailor Man and he snarled his words out of the side of his mouth. Phillips kept the center of his mouth occupied with a big glob of Bruton Snuff. And I never saw him spit one time! He must of been swallowing every drop of that nasty tobacco juice! I reckon that would explain his sour disposition.

We was all just milling around the pen in front of the barn when Phillips come stomping out of Mr. Anderson's office. "My name's Dick Phillips," he barked at us, "And I'm the new head of the hog operation." Instead of a white sailor hat like Popeye had, Phillips wore a black baseball cap with a patch that read "CAT Diesel Power." He pulled the greasy cap down low on his forehead and glared at us out of his good eye. "I been working around hogs my whole life, so I reckon I know a

54 Popeye the Sailor was a comic character created by E. C. Segar (1894-1938). First appearing in the syndicated newspaper comic strip *Thimble Theater* on January 17, 1929, the character quickly became the focus of the strip. A tough, one-eyed sailor, Popeye was featured in animated theatrical short films, comic books, a feature film, and cartoon television programs.

little bit about 'em," he growled the words out the side of his mouth. "And I raised up four boys and ain't none of 'em ever wound up in jail, so I reckon I know a little bit about that too." Phillips paced back and forth in front of us as he ranted. "The big boss man made it damn clear to me that my number-one job was watching out after that Mulefoot boar out yonder," he said, jerking his thumb over his shoulder toward The Mulefoot, who stood scowling at us from underneath his bodock tree. "They say he's an 'endangered species' and the school's getting' a whole lotta money to look after him. So you little turds better keep that in mind."

Phillips fished a white metal can out of his front shirt pocket and tapped some more snuff down into his bottom lip. A tiny black line of tobacco had already formed at the corners of his mouth.

"Now, everybody 'round here thinks that Anderson hung the damn moon," Phillips said. "But look at what a sweet set-up he had here. Anderson got everything for free or on-the-cheap 'cause y'uns are some kinda charity. He got his hog feed at a discounted price, he got his hauling at a discounted price, he got his processing at a discounted price, he didn't have to pay no boar fees, and he didn't have no labor costs at all." Phillips made a big show of ticking off each item on his fingers as he went along.

Phillips stopped his pacing and turned around to face us. "But if y'uns ask me," he growled, "Thangs around here look pretty damn slipshod. Look at that fence over yonder!" He pointed toward the plywood barricade that me and the Blount Brothers had built to keep The Mulefoot from reaching the little pigs. "That fence looks like a bunch of niggers built it!"

Me and the Blount Brothers stared at each other in shock! *Did he really just say that?* When Mr. Anderson was here, that was *the one word* that would get you spanked sure 'nuff.

Phillips marched over to Ferlin Blount and peered up at him with his good eye. Phillips had to look up at Ferlin 'cause he wasn't as tall as Ferlin was. He snarled, "What's your name, boy?"

"Yessir! Ferlin Blount's my name and this here's my brother, Frank Blount."

"That your name, boy?" Phillips snapped at Frank.

But Frank just stared down at the muddy ground in front of Phillips' shoes.

"Deaf and dumb, huh?" said Phillips.

"Nossir!" said Ferlin. "Frank's just not a big talker."

"'Freeing oneself from words is liberation,'" observed Sammy, who was standing next to Frank.

"Say what now?" growled Phillips.

"That's from the teachings of Master Bodhidharma," said Sammy, as he balled up his right hand into a fist, covered it with the palm of his left hand, and then held them in front of his chest. That was a kind of kung-fu salute.

"What? You some kinda Commie, boy?" shrieked Phillips, his good eye boring down on Sammy.

"Nossir!" said Ferlin, "That's my other brother, Sammy. We was born over in Smith County. Yessir! We's all raised up right around here!"

Phillips backed up a step and bellered to all of us, "Now, y'uns better know right now, that I hate a damn smart-aleck and I won't stand for no backtalk." Then he walked up to me and leaned down so we was face-to-face. His good eye blasted into me like a laser beam and I smelt the snuff tobacco on his breath. "So what are you?" Phillips growled, "Some kind of albino?"

Now, if you're like me, when somebody insults you, you never think of a snappy comeback until about thirty minutes later. And after thirty minutes, it's way too late to go back and say your snappy comeback. But even though I hadn't slept for more than two hours straight in several months, my brain did not let me down on that particular occasion.

"So, you an albino, boy?" Phillips repeated.

I looked Phillips straight in his good eye and said, "I yam what I yam and that's all what I yam!"[55]

I reckon this wasn't the first time somebody had compared Phillips to Popeye the Sailor Man. And clearly, he didn't think it was anywhere near as funny as I did.

---

[55] This phrase was popularized by the comic strip character, Popeye the Sailor Man.

I never even saw Phillips' hand coming at me. I just felt a sudden explosion inside my left ear as he made contact, and then the fire spreading across the side of my face.

And Possum Mode in 3, 2, 1 . . . .

While I was in *Possum Mode*, Phillips could slap me, punch me, and kick me all he wanted, I wouldn't feel a thing. I was invulnerable, just like Superman.

I woke up back in my bed at Progress House. Somebody had taken my shoes off. The Blount Brothers was all sitting around the edge of the bed.

"How long was I in *Possum Mode*?" I asked.

"Yessir, I'd say about thirty minutes," said Ferlin.

"You sure scared the daylights out of that skunk Phillips," laughed Sammy.

"Yessir, when you dropped into *Possum Mode*, he thought he'd done killed you for sure," said Ferlin.

"That oughta teach him," I said, "Hitting a little kid like that."

"Yessir, Mr. Phillips didn't know what to do," said Ferlin. "He knew if he carried you to the clinic, he'd get in trouble for what he did."

"Yessir! Sammy told Mr. Phillips that he ought give you mouth-to-mouth resuscitation!"

"No way! You didn't!" I cried.

"I thought it would be funny," said Sammy. "I was curious to see if he would spit out his tobacco cud before he tried to do it!"

"Yessir! Phillips finally got the idea to spray you down with the hosepipe, thinking maybe that would wake you up," said Ferlin. "Yessir! He yelled at Frank to go run and get the hosepipe and Frank took off after it."

"Traitor!" I said to Frank.

Frank nodded his head and smirked.

"If he'd of sprayed me with that hosepipe, I'd of caught pneumonia."

"Yessir! Before Frank got back with the water hose, we told Mr. Phillips that if we just left you alone, you come out of your *Possum Mode* all by yourself."

"Then we carried you back here to Progress House," said Sammy.

"Well, thanks for not leaving me there, laying in the pig poop."

"We was worried the hogs might come along and pee on you," said Sammy.

"That Phillips ain't nothing but a polecat,"[56] I said, "And a bully."

"Nossir. He shouldn't of never hit you like that," said Ferlin.

"Y'all realize, of course, this means war."

[56] A Southern U.S. term for the North American skunk, *Mephitis mephitis.*

CHAPTER TWENTY-FOUR

So the demons begged Him, saying, "If you cast us out, permit us to go away into the herd of swine." And He said to them, "Go." So when they had come out, they went into the herd of swine.

I tossed and turned in bed all night and the bedcovers got tangled up around my neck. One time, I read a story about this guy who was sleeping and he was having a nightmare that he was getting hanged. Then the guy accidentally twisted his bedsheet around his neck and strangled hisself. Now, I didn't reckon that could happen in real life, but I smoothed out all the covers just in case.

Finally, I just give up on trying to go to sleep. I pulled on my britches and slipped on my tenni'shoes. I was too tired to go out on patrol, so I went out into the lobby and turned on the television. All four stations had signed off for the night and snowy static filled the screen. Using the TV screen as a nightlight, I pulled a volume of the *World Book Encyclopedia* off the bookshelf and flipped through it. As I was reading about presidential assassin Lee Harvey Oswald, I dropped off to sleep sitting straight up in my chair. As I was dozing, the *World Book Encyclopedia* slipped out of my hands. The book smacking the floor sounded like a rifle shot! It jarred me wide awake!

I scooped *World Book Encyclopedia Volume N-O* up off the floor and slid it back onto the bookshelf. I decided to get me some fresh air. So, using the spoon skeleton key that Frank Blount had made me, I unlocked the door and let myself out. I didn't have a jacket on, but the temperature was warm enough. A blanket of fog had drifted up from the Stones River and filled the basin where Progress House stood. Bedford Circle looked like a Sherlock Holmes movie. As I climbed down the steps of Progress House, it was like wading out into the Stones River itself.

Under the streetlight, right across the parking lot, sat an old aluminum park bench. Setting myself down on the bench, I decided to watch the fog swirl around on the ground. I couldn't even see my feet.

"Good evening, Delphus," said a voice behind me.

A man I didn't recognize was standing behind me smoking a pipe. He was wearing a Dick Tracy hat and a buttoned-up Dick Tracy coat. I hadn't never seen anybody wearing anything like that except on television.

He walked around to the front of the bench where I could see him. He was slender man who I guess was probably in his fifties. His hair was cut short and he was wearing a necktie and suitcoat underneath his Dick Tracy coat.

He gestured with his pipe towards the bench and said, "Do you mind if I join you?"

He looked like a college professor, I decided. He talked funny, but he didn't have a Yankee accent exactly. It was more like the men on the TV news, who don't really have no accent at all. How did he know my name? Maybe he was a new administrator at the school? I reckoned I could outrun him if he tried any monkey business.

"It's a free country, I reckon."

"Ah, there are those who would dispute that statement," he said, sitting down at the other end of the bench, "But I would not be among their number. Indeed, it is a free country."

"Who are you? And how'd you know my name?"

"My name is David St. John," he said, puffing on his pipe, "And we've been closely following your progress since the first day Deputy Hicks brought you to Clover Bottom Hospital."

"Who's 'we?'"

"I work for the Central Intelligence Agency."

"A spy, huh?"

"In the strictest sense, I'm a 'contract agent,'" said St. John. "I retired from the Domestic Operations Division five years ago." He blew out a puff of smoke and watched it disappear. The sweet smell of pipe tobacco drifted toward me.

"Why would the CIA be interested in me?"

"The Agency is monitoring you as part of its Pre-Adult Training for Singular Youth initiative," he said. "You, Delphus, are a remarkable young man. We believe you have the potential to be a very valuable asset to us someday. You're an autodidactic polymath and before your ... supernumerary appendage, that is to say your tail, was amputated, you displayed an unprecedented level of motor skills for an individual your age."

"Did y'all cut my tail off?"

"Certainly not. That was a *fait accompli* before we had an opportunity to intercede."

"Do you know why I'm ... different?"

"Possibly," said St. John. "Let me point out at this juncture that I will relate only the objective facts, nothing else. First, do you know what Oak Ridge is?"

"Sure, it's a town right outside of Knoxville," I said. "They made part of the Atomic Bomb there."

"That's correct," said St. John. "Originally designated the Clinton Engineer Works, the site was an installation of the Manhattan Project and enriched the uranium ore that was employed in the development of the Atom Bomb. The Army Corps of Engineers constructed the entire city of Oak Ridge around the processing plants. After World War II, Clinton Engineer Works was renamed the Oak Ridge National Laboratory and continued its research under the Atomic Energy Commission."

St. John took another long puff on his pipe and leaned toward me. "The following information is classified," he said. "That means you are not permitted to share this information with anyone."

"I understand."

"In late 1962, early '63, Oak Ridge National Laboratory conducted an experiment on fifty-four individuals without their knowledge. The test subjects were patients from the clinical program at the Oak Ridge Institute and ranged in age from seven to seventy-six years. They were selected because they had normal intestinal tracts, which had not been affected by their illness.

"The purpose of this study was to measure the movement of radioactive material through the human body and to determine how much radioactive material would be absorbed by the large intestine. The patients were fed ten to twenty microcuries of Lanthanum-140, a potent source of gamma radiation.[57] The subjects received no medical benefit from this experiment. Although the study was reported in *The Journal of Nuclear Medicine*, it was never published in any mainstream publication."[58]

"I read that article!" I said. "That one about Lanthanum. I found a copy of that magazine in a Dempster Dumpster."

"Yes, I directed that the journal be placed in the Dumpster," said St. John, blowing out a plume of smoke.

"Whaddya mean? The blind school turns them books and magazines into Braille books and then they throw them away in the Dempster Dumpster!"

"That's not the way it works, Delphus. A non-profit corporation in Louisville, Kentucky, publishes hundreds of Braille textbooks, popular fiction and audio recordings every year.[59] The School for the Blind wouldn't need to do that."

---

57 *American nuclear guinea pigs: three decades of radiation experiments on U.S. citizens.* Report prepared by the Subcommittee on Energy Conservation and Power. Committee on Energy and Commerce, U.S. House of Representatives: Washington, D.C.: U.S. Government Printing Office. November 1986. p. 32

58 Hayes, R.L., Carlton, J.E., and Nelson, B. (1964) Lanthanum-140 as a measure of the completeness of stool collections demonstration of delayed excretion of Iron-59. *Journal of Nuc. Med* 5; pp. 200-208.

59 American Printing House for the Blind

"The blind school don't put them books in the Dempster Dumpster?"

"No, for the last six years now, the Agency has been depositing books and periodicals into that waste bin for you to ... discover. Although, Delphus, you're going to have to learn some geography if you're to be of any use to us at all. I chair the committee that selects the books that are to be placed in the dumpster.

"But to get back to the beginning here," St. John continued. "The Company's top analysts postulate that you are the progeny of a Lanthanum-140 test subject. Lanthanum isotopes produce gamma rays. Unlike some forms of radiation which are non-penetrating and cause only radiation burns to the skin, gamma rays permeate throughout the body, causing radiation sickness, DNA damage, cell death, and cancer.

"When gamma radiation breaks down DNA molecules, the cells may be able to repair the damaged genetic material. Sometimes the repair is imperfect, and in extremely rare cases, the cells can overcompensate in their regeneration.

"You do understand what I mean when I refer to DNA and genes?" St. John asked.

"Of course, it's the code in your cells that you inherit from your momma and daddy. It's the blueprint that decides whether you have blue eyes or brown eyes or red hair."

"Exactly," St. John said. "Our analysts believe that one or both of your parents were Lanthanum-140 test subjects and, as a result of their exposure, they sustained a change in a base-pair sequence of their DNA."

"And that's why I was born with a tail and special Possum Powers?"

"*In utero*, all human embryos have a tail. It measures about a sixth of the entire length of the embryo itself. As the embryo grows into a fetus, the tail is absorbed into the body, usually within eight weeks. In your case, we expect because of the genetic damage, your tail was not absorbed. True human tails are extremely rare. But what made your tail so unique was that it had nerves, muscle and vertebrae. It was prehensile. That means you could use it to hold and grasp objects, such as a tree limb, and even briefly support your weight!"

"I can still remember swinging through the trees with my possum brothers and sisters by our tails."

"Delphus, I'm not certain that an opossum can actually do that."

"Sure they can!"

St. John took a long draw on his pipe and he looked like he was thinking about what I'd said. Then just deciding to ignore it, he said, "Our analysts' hypothesis is supported by the fact that the first reported sighting of the 'Opossum Boy' was twenty miles east of Oak Ridge."

"So do you know who my momma and daddy are -- who my kinfolks are?"

"I'm afraid not, Delphus. Most of the Oak Ridge records were destroyed before CIA had any cause to investigate. The extant records identify the test subjects only by a numerical designation. We attempted investigative interviews with the townsfolk of Oak Ridge and the surrounding communities, but the denizens of that region are a tight-lipped folk. Finally, we examined the birth records of every hospital and clinic in the area for a four-year interval. No record of your birth exists. The evidence suggests you were born at home and delivered by a midwife. Then, circumstances unknown, you were separated from kith and kin, and maintained a feral existence."

"Alright, Mr. St. John, you ain't told me a whole lot that I didn't already know."

"You had only supposition, my boy! Conjecture!" St. John said. "I have related the facts -- the truth. As we say at CIA, 'And ye shall know the truth and the truth shall make you free.'"

"So now I'm free?"

St. John wheeled around to face me full-on, his eyes boring into mine. "You are a phenomenal young man, Delphus, capable of extraordinary accomplishments!" he said. "We cannot allow our thinking to be governed by the conditions that surround us!"

I thought about what he'd said for a minute. "I reckon you didn't come here just to tell me about my Secret Origin."

"That's rather astute, Delphus," St. John said. "You're quite correct. The matter that brings me here concerns the Mulefoot boar."

"The Mulefoot?"

"That creature represents an immediate threat to the health and safety of our Nation. His official designation is Calydon-A57. Before coming to Clover Bottom Hospital and School, he was quartered in Peking, China."[60]

"China?"

"China is a country of considerable social, political and economic complexity. I was stationed in the Yunnan Province of China during the last year of World War II, leading forays against the Japanese forces. This now seems ironic, as nine years later, I would relocate my family to Tokyo, Japan, as a civilian adviser to the North Asia Command.

"Three years ago," St. John continued, "President Nixon effectuated a détente with the People's Republic of China. In February 1972, both governments jointly issued the 'Shanghai Communique,' which encouraged 'people-to-people contacts and exchanges' between the US and the PRC, specifically in the areas of 'science, technology, culture, sports and journalism.'

"The population of the People's Republic of China has soared to more than 916 million people. The society, taken as a whole, has an obvious shortage of meat protein in its diet. Merely keeping its populace supplied with food is a major challenge for the Communist government.

"In mid-March, in connection with my work as a government consultant, I learned that NASA had initiated a program for the development of improved food sources for astronauts on deep-space missions. NASA scientists were attempting to grow meat in a laboratory. This meat, referred to in the classified prospectus as *in vitro* meat, or cultured meat, would be virtually indistinguishable from conventional animal meat. Again, you understand that this information is classified?"

"I know, I know, I can't tell anybody."

"The *in vitro* meat process involves extracting muscle cells from an animal and applying a protein that causes the cells to grow into large portions of meat..."

"So they're just cloning the cow, or the pig, or whatever it is?"

---

60 Peking is now more properly Romanized as Beijing.

"You're aware of cloning technology?"

"Sure! The Jackal cloned Spider-Man and his girlfriend, Gwen Stacy."[61]

"I'm not familiar with Spiderman," said St. John. "I take it that's a comic book."

"Oh, yeah!" I said, "It's a pretty good one, but I am more of a DC guy, myself."

"Well, my understanding of the *in vitro* meat process is that it does not involve actual cloning. Scientists have projected that, once the process is perfected, 50,000 tons of *in vitro* meat could be produced from ten pork muscle cells in just two months. Think of what that could mean to a starving country like China!

"Accordingly," St. John continued, "A few of my colleagues and myself concluded that decisive action could produce the most beneficial of results. We clandestinely acquired copies of NASA's research papers ..."

"You stole their research?"

"We merely made copies. NASA never even realized that they had been penetrated."

"But you stole their ideas."

"Bear in mind, these documents were created by scientists working for a Government agency, therefore the Government was ultimately the rightful owner. Bear in mind further, that the Shanghai Communique of 1972 specifically encouraged exchanges of information in the areas of science and technology. The Shanghai Communique was executed by President Richard M. Nixon and I was operating under the highest authority!"

"I still think you're a big stealer," I said.

"Perhaps when you're older and more mature, you'll understand what I'm attempting to explain to you." St. John refilled his pipe, lit it and took a deep draw. It seemed to calm him down a bit. "In any event, we subsequently made the NASA research available to Dr. Zhū Yīshēng of Peking, China. Dr. Zhū is China's leading researcher in the field of genetics. Channeling the initial operating funds through our contacts

---

61 *Amazing Spider-Man* No. 149 (October 1975)

in the city of Wenzhou, we had the Peking Genetics Research Institute fully operational in a matter of weeks. And Dr. Zhū was completely unaware of the true source of his funding.

"In April 1972, PGRI set about the task of creating *in vitro* pork. Early on, Dr. Zhū recognized that the procedure would require something akin to a circulatory system in order to deliver nutrients and oxygen to the growing cells, as well as to remove the waste products. Once the *in vitro* process was perfected, this function would be carried out in a 'bioreactor.' But in these preliminary stages, Dr. Zhū resolved that the best place to grow *in vitro* pork was inside a hog."

St. John pronounced the word *hog* funny. The way he pronounced it, it rhymed with *nog*, like in *eggnog*.

"PGRI had previously ascertained that the ideal swine breed for their purposes was the American Mulefoot Hog. Apparently, the Mulefoot breed has a high incidence of 'null alleles' in their genetic makeup."[62]

"What are 'null alleles'?"

"As I understand it from the requisition documents, a null allele is a mutant duplicate of a gene that completely lacks that gene's normal function."

"Do what now?"

"Delphus, I would be disingenuous if I told you I appreciated all the technicalities of these genetic issues," said St. John. "But according to the briefing I received, an example of a null allele in humans would be the 'O' blood-type. A person with type 'O' blood is a universal donor, he can donate blood to individuals of any blood-type. PGRI believed this genetic characteristic in the Mulefoot breed would help facilitate their work.

"Named for its syndactyl, or fused, toes, the American Mulefoot was quite popular at the beginning of the century because the breed had a great deal of intra-muscular fat, which resulted in a more tender meat. Additionally, breeders claimed that the Mulefoot was immune to

---

[62] *see, e.g.*, Kapke, Paul; Jorgensen, Hans Peter; and Rothschild, Max F., "A Study of Genetic Diversity in a Rare U. S. Pig Breed—The Mulefoot Pig" (1997). *Swine Research Report, 1996*. Paper 14. http://lib.dr.iastate.edu/swinereports_1996/14

cholera and many other hog diseases prevalent at the time. More than 235 herds of American Mulefoot Hogs were registered across the U.S.

"However, the breed is slow to reach maturity, which is problematic for large-scale commercial breeders. And the claims of extreme immunity had less appeal when vaccines became cheaper and more readily available. The popularity of the American Mulefoot declined and the population dwindled. The Mulefoot breed was all but extinct. Then, in 1961, a hog breeder named R.M. Holliday purchased a purebred Mulefoot boar and three purebred gilts, that is, young female pigs . . ."

"I know what a gilt is."

"From those four animals, Mr. Holliday built a purebred Mulefoot herd that now spans over a hundred pigs. Today, Holliday's herd is the only purebred Mulefoot herd in the world!

"Furthering our objective to procure the Mulefoot hogs required for Dr. Zhū's research, we contacted Mr. Holliday at his farm in Louisiana, Missouri. We presented credentials identifying ourselves as Agents of the Animal and Plant Health Inspection Service of the USDA and informed him that we were there to confiscate ten of his hogs for medical testing. However, Holliday appeared highly suspicious of us. He demanded to see a document called a 'Notice of Intent to Confiscate Animals,' which we could have easily fabricated, but we were operating on a strict timeline and did not have the opportunity to familiarize ourselves with USDA procedures. Ultimately, I threatened to have his entire herd quarantined and destroyed. Holliday relented and we confiscated ten pigs -- six boars and four sows."

"You stole them ..."

"No, we compensated Holliday for his hogs. We paid him twice the amount he usually charged for them," said St. John. We loaded the hogs onto a trailer, trucked them to Scott Air Force Base, and using covert military transport, the Mulefoot hogs landed in Peking, China the next day.

"Once the Mulefoot hogs were settled in, Dr. Zhū began his research in earnest. Extracting cells from a Taihu pig, a Chinese domestic breed, he transplanted the cell package inside the Mulefoot hogs. Dr. Zhū quickly noted that the female Mulefoot hogs absorbed the foreign Taihu pig cells into their own bodies, as if they were healing an infection. However, for reasons he could not immediately identify, the male Mulefoot hogs did not assimilate the Taihu pig cells in the same way."

"How did they get the Taihu pig cells inside the Mulefoots?" I asked.

"The doctors surgically implanted two plastic re-sealable ports into the sides of the Mulefoot hogs. This port is referred to as a fistula. The fistula provided researchers access to the inside of the Mulefoot's body without the necessity of repeated dissection and suturing. They could simply unseal the port. This explains the scar that runs from Calydon-A57's right shoulder to his ham. That is where the fistulas were implanted."

"It's awful to do that to an animal, even to a mean one like The Mulefoot."

"You must appreciate the larger picture, Delphus," St. John said. "Consider the Chinese people. Surely, the privation of 900 million human beings outweighs the discomfort of a few dumb animals. If the goal is sufficiently important, any method to achieve that goal is acceptable."

I don't know if he was trying to convince me or hisself.

"The work of the PGRI continued apace," said St. John, "But then in May 1972, disaster struck. Four hogs: Erymanthos-A23, Calydon-A57, Henwen-S06, and Porky-A35 became violently ill. They developed diarrhea and lost a remarkable amount of weight. Veterinary examination of the animals revealed anorexia, jaundice, and an accumulation of fluid underneath their lower jawbone. The pigs had become infected with a parasite."

"Sounds like some kinda worms," I said. "That swelling under the chin--that's called 'bottle jaw.' Never heard of a pig getting it. Goats and sheep get it mostly."

"Dr. Zhū maintained an absolutely sterile laboratory. When I visited PGRI, I was required to wear sterilized surgical attire. The hogs' pens were as clean as possible and were hosed out daily.

"However, adjacent to the laboratories, lay a small abandoned Chinese garden, complete with a moon gate and lily pond at its center, fed by two shallow streams. Forlorn goldfish darted up and down the streams. Although the wooden pavilions had been dismantled and vines had overtaken the granite shrines, the garden still retained plenty of lush grass and a stand of bamboo. Every afternoon, the PGRI researchers would herd the Mulefoot hogs into the Chinese garden for a daily sabbatical. The hogs delighted in rooting with their snouts in the streams, chasing after the goldfish, and wallowing in the lily pond. Sometimes, they would scrub their bodies by rubbing against the bamboo."

"Hogs can get too hot real easy," I said, "That's why they like to wallow in the mud. It keeps 'em cool."

"Had we known the danger lurking in the Chinese garden, we could have easily avoided the calamity altogether. The goldfish in the lily pond and its tributaries were infected with a parasite known as the 'liver fluke.'"

"What's a 'liver fluke'?"

"In China and indeed all of Southeast Asia, there exists a parasitic flatworm classified as the Chinese liver fluke. [63] When fully grown, the Chinese liver fluke is only about a half-inch long and a quarter-inch wide. They cause cancer."

St. John relit his pipe and let that sink in for a minute. "It is estimated that 15 to 20 million people are infected by the Chinese liver fluke. Eighty-five percent of the cases are found in China. Many other species of liver flukes exist, even in the United States, but they generally infect livestock and only rarely infect humans. The Chinese liver fluke has a complicated life cycle. The eggs are ingested by snails ..."

"Where do the eggs come from?"

"They are excreted into the water with the feces of an infected animal."

"Gross."

"Yes, as I was saying, the eggs are ingested by snails. After the eggs hatch, the fluke larvae bore their way out of the snail's body and into the water. The larvae then attach themselves to the scales of a freshwater fish

[63] Clonorchis sinensis

and bore into the fish's body within a matter of six to thirteen minutes. Inside the fish, the larvae develop a hard covering called a cyst. Finally, a human, or in this case, a hog, eats the fish."

"So you figure the goldfish in the Chinese garden had these liver fluke cysts inside them?"

"We have ruled out all other sources of contamination."

"And the four sick Mulefoots, they ate the goldfish?"

"Exactly so," said St. John, exhaling a long plume of smoke down into the fog billowing around our knees. "Once inside the hog, or inside a human for that matter, the digestive acids break down the hard cyst shell covering the larvae. The larvae penetrate the host's intestinal mucosa and enter the bile ducts."

"What are bile ducts?"

"Bile is a fluid that is produced in the liver and is necessary for the digestion of food," said St. John. "Bile ducts are long tube-like structures that carry bile from the liver to the small intestine."

"I gotcha. The fluke larvae move to the bile ducts."

"Indeed. Inside the bile ducts, the larvae feed on the bile secreted from the liver and begin to grow. In about a month, they reach full maturity and begin laying eggs. Remaining within the bile ducts, the flukes consume all the bile created by the liver, inhibiting the ability of the host to digest foods, particularly fats. Most importantly, the flukes induce hyperplasia, or an increase in abnormal cell growth. This hyperplasia frequently develops into cholangiocarcinoma, or cancer of the bile ducts."

"So these Chinese liver flukes cause cancer of the bile ducts?"

"Exactly so," said St. John. "Cancer researchers have long recognized the carcinogenicity of the Chinese liver fluke.[64,65] The cancer usually metastasizes to the liver itself and the surrounding tissues. The liver flukes infecting the Mulefoot hogs seemed especially virulent. Although

---

[64] *see, Yoshitaka, Komiya (1967). "Clonorchis and clonorchiasis". In Dawes, Ben. Advances in Parasitology Volume 4. Burlington: Elsevier. pp. 53–101.*

[65] Belamaric, J. (1973) "Intrahepatic bile duct carcinoma and C. sinensis infection in Hong Kong." *Cancer*, 31, 468-73.

three of the diseased hogs, Henwen, Erymanthos, and Porky, died almost immediately, Calydon-A57 did not.

"Calydon-A57 began to thrive. And to change. The cartilage in his ears thickened and his ears grew erect, which is not characteristic of the American Mulefoot breed. His weight grew to tremendous proportions. The blood vessels in Calydon-A57's eyes continually ruptured, giving his eyes a distinctive reddish hue. Always ill-tempered, Calydon-A57 grew overtly aggressive, and the PGRI researchers had a great deal of difficulty controlling him."

"Why didn't Calydon die like the others?"

"Dr. Zhū was at a loss to explain it," St. John said, "Whether it was the special nutrients given to Calydon-A57, the antibiotics, the hormones, the genetically modified proteins, or possibly just the natural immunities of the Mulefoot breed, Calydon-A57 did not succumb to cancer. In fact, it appears that Calydon-A57 and the liver flukes inside him reached a state of symbiosis."

"What's symbiosis?"

"Symbiosis is two dissimilar organisms living together where each individual benefits from the activity of the other. One noted example is the oxpecker bird and the rhinoceros. The oxpecker bird feeds on the ticks, horsefly larvae, and other parasites that it finds on the rhinoceros. This feeds the oxpecker and cleans the rhinoceros. Both the oxpecker and the rhinoceros benefit."

"Yeah, I seen pictures of rhinoceroses with them birds on their backs, but I didn't know they was eating bugs off of 'em," I said. "So The Mulefoot teamed up with the liver flukes that was inside him?"

"In a manner of speaking, yes," St. John said. "The flukes appeared content to survive on the bile that Calydon-A57 produced and slowed their exponential growth. But what was most startling, Calydon-A57 took on many of the genetic properties of the flukes. The DNA of the liver flukes contain many pathogenic molecules that cause hepatobiliary disease.

"Microscopic examination of tissue samples taken from Calydon-A57 indicated that every living cell in his body was aggressively carcinogenic.

This carcinogenicity extends to Calydon-A57's bodily fluids, such as his blood, urine and saliva."

"His saliva?"

"This discovery was made quite by accident. Calydon-A57 crashed through the aluminum gate of his enclosure. In the tumult of returning him to his quarters, he bit one of the researchers, one Èyùn Pàohuī, Ph.D. In just a matter of weeks, Dr. Èyùn contracted widespread cholangiocarcinoma and liver cancer."

"Liver cancer?"

"Dr. Zhū speculated that the genetically modified proteins administered to Calydon-A57 to encourage the growth of the *in vitro* pork cells allowed him to absorb the genetic properties of the liver flukes infecting him. Calydon-A57's immune system couldn't distinguish between the good cells and the bad cells."

"So The Mulefoot bit this Èyùn guy and it made him get liver cancer?"

"That's correct," said St. John, looking up at the stars.

"The Mulefoot bit Mr. Anderson on the leg," I said. "And then Mr. Anderson got liver cancer right after that. It's what killed him."

"Precisely! Edmund Anderson's untimely death is what brought this matter to a head."

It took a minute for that to sink in. God didn't kill Mr. Anderson. It wasn't just bad luck. It wasn't "God's Will" for Mr. Anderson to get cancer and die. It was because that Mulefoot hog bit him. While he was saving me. That wasn't right no kinda way. I could feel my face getting hot and my eyes watering, but I wasn't about to cry in front of this St. John guy.

"Why didn't y'all just leave that monster in China?" I was barely able to keep my voice from breaking.

"The Chinese in vitro meat enterprise was perceived as an unqualified disaster, an embarrassment to the Central Intelligence Agency. One young, envious wag at the Company christened the operation the 'Bay of Pigs II,' referring to another inefficacious operation with which I was associated. Eventually, the China Operation was referred to around the

Agency colloquially as the 'Bay of Pigs.'"[66] St. John blew out a plume of smoke that looked like the exhaust coming out of a car's tailpipe and he stared down into the fog swirling around our knees.

"Why didn't y'all just leave The Mulefoot in China, or go ahead and kill him?" I repeated.

"I convinced my principals that the failure of the Chinese Operation could be mitigated, that the Agency might still realize a dividend on its investment. Calydon-A57's vital fluids are a lethal, untraceable carcinogen..."

"You wanted to turn The Mulefoot into some kinda poison-making machine."

"Think of the value in espionage work, Delphus! A surreptitious introduction of Calydon-A57's bodily fluids, and a week later, the subject develops terminal liver cancer – to all appearances, a death by natural causes."

"That's just evil!"

"Delphus, an instrumentality in and of itself, cannot be evil. If the instrumentality is put to a nefarious purpose, then certainly, the intent of the user can be considered 'evil.' For example, guns can be used to kill people, but policemen use guns every day to save lives."

"It ain't the same thing."

"Poison from Calydon-A57 could be used to neutralize an Evil Dictator and liberate the millions of innocent people he oppresses. Not a single American serviceman would have to lose his life to accomplish this."

"You never did answer my question," I said. "Why did you bring The Mulefoot here to Clover Bottom? Why ain't he in some kinda super-secret Government laboratory?"

---

[66] The so-called Watergate "smoking gun tape" of June 23, 1972 documents President Richard Nixon telling his Chief of Staff H.R. Haldeman to approach CIA director Richard Helms to intervene in the FBI's investigation of the Watergate break-in. Nixon instructed Haldeman to tell Helms that "[T]his will open up the whole, the whole 'Bay of Pigs thing,' and the President just feels that...[this]... would be very unfortunate for CIA and the country . . . and for American foreign policy."

"My principals approved my recommendation that Calydon-A57 should be returned to the U.S. and evaluated for potential National Security value. However, the President dismissed the Director of Central Intelligence, Richard Helms, in February 1973. His successor, James Schlesinger, did not share Director Helms' vision. He ordered Calydon-A57 destroyed. But I believed that Calydon-A57's potential value was simply too great to be squandered. I was able to delay the implementation of Director Schlesinger's order through 'bureaucratic resistance.' Relying upon my various Agency operating accounts, I paid Dr. Zhū to keep and maintain Calydon-A57 at the PGRI facility for almost two years. Dr. Zhū is a geneticist. He had no interest in studying Calydon-A57's toxicological potential."

"Y'all should have left The Mulefoot over there."

"A year or so ago, I encountered a professional setback. An operation that I had initiated on behalf of the White House was blown. Five of my colleagues were arrested and my name was found in the address book of one of the operators. Instantly, I was subjected to an unprecedented level of press scrutiny. The government, perhaps the CIA itself, revealed to the press that I had been a career CIA officer. My cover employer dispensed with my services summarily and I lost all access to operational funds. My actions, my movements, even my communications, were all closely monitored. My plan was to temporarily quarter Calydon-A57 here at Clover Bottom Hospital and School, and then when my difficulties abated, have him transferred to our facility at Fort Detrick, Maryland. A generous block grant to Clover Bottom School, arranged before the onset of my predicament, subsidizes Calydon-A57's stay here."

"Can't you just get him out of here?"

"Unfortunately, that's not possible," St. John said. "All my Agency resources have dried up and attorney's fees have depleted my personal funds. Calydon-A57 is stranded here. I am unable to effect his transfer to a secure facility. Although Calydon-A57 could be the key to protecting freedom around the world, he is simply too dangerous to remain in an unsecure location."

"That's for sure."

"Delphus, do you love your country?" St. John whirled around to face me again.

"You bet I do."

"Good boy!" St. John leaned over and patted my knee. He smiled, but he only used his mouth. His eyes wasn't involved any kinda way. "The United States of America is the greatest institution ever devised in the history of man. Our wonderful country stands as a shining beacon of freedom throughout the world. Over the last 200 years, thousands of young men and boys have answered our Nation's call to defend against threats to our way of life."

"Yeah, Mr. Anderson answered our Nation's call," I said.

"He certainly did and he was decorated for bravery," St. John said and took a long draw on his pipe. "Delphus, we did not anticipate your recruitment for a number of years yet, but the Central Intelligence Agency needs an individual in your unique position and with your exceptional abilities. It's unconscionable to place this burden on one so young, but your country needs you. You are the only person who can do this."

"Do what?"

"The Agency needs Calydon-A57 terminated with extreme prejudice."

"Terminate? You mean like in 'kill?'"

"Exactly."

"Well, I hate that monster," I said. "Let's go! I'll take you down to the hog barn right now! I bet you got a gun under that Dick Tracy coat." I hopped up off the aluminum bench and the mist swirled around my knees.

"No, Delphus," St. John said, motioning for me to sit back down, "The Agency needs you to do this."

"Does the CIA need me to do this? Or is it just you, your own self? To keep you out of trouble?"

"No, my brief comes directly from the Director of Central Intelligence. If the circumstances of the China Operation ever came to light, it would be very embarrassing for CIA and could seriously impair our relations with China." St. John turned his pipe upside-down and tapped it against the armrest of the bench. "Officially, I am stationed at Auxiliary Field 6, Eglin Air Force Base in Florida for the next twenty-two months. The Agency brought me here clandestinely just to bring you this assignment. I must return to Eglin to establish an alibi before Calydon-A57 is terminated. This action cannot be traced back to CIA in any way, shape or form."

"I'm not sure I can do it," I said, "Kill him, I mean."

"Who will be The Mulefoot's next victim?" St. John asked. "Maybe your young pal, Sammy Blount? Perhaps his brother Ferlin? What if The Mulefoot transmits his liver fluke disease to other hogs? What if his liver fluke disease finds its way into our Nation's food supply? Millions of Americans will die, Delphus, just like your friend Mr. Anderson. How many people must The Mulefoot kill before you decide to do something about it?"

"Okay, I'll do it!" I said. "Give me your gun and I'll probably need a silencer too."

"I'm unarmed," St. John said, pulling back the lapels of his coat, "But that brings us to the innate complexity of your Assignment. The Mulefoot's death must appear to be an accident or at the least, simple misfortune. In the ideal scenario, he must appear to die by natural causes. Simply put, we must not arouse suspicion. The Agency cannot allow local law enforcement to go snooping around The Mulefoot's remains or allow them to transport said remains to the state Department of Agriculture for an autopsy."

"Are you kidding me?"

"Absolutely not. This Assignment will require a certain creative approach, Delphus. That is why the Agency needs someone with your exceptional skillset."

"So, I gotta kill The Mulefoot and make it look like an accident?"

"Precisely. Or by natural causes."

"How long do I have to get this done?"

"It should be done sooner rather than later." St. John said, pointing at me with the stem of his pipe. "Every day that The Mulefoot continues to live is one day closer to every man, woman, and child in America contracting liver cancer."

"I'll do the best I can."

"CIA will be monitoring your progress," St. John said. "Your Country is counting on you, Delphus." Then he stood up, shot me a crisp military salute, turned on his heel, and disappeared into the mist.

I was plumb wore out. This here was a lot to take in. I waded back through the fog and dragged myself up the steps of Progress House. Once inside, I dropped back down into my chair. The television screen lit up the lobby with a weird white light. Shaking my head, I picked up World Book Encyclopedia Volume N-O off the floor and slid it back onto the shelf. I turned off the television and went back to bed.

I slept like a dead man.

CHAPTER TWENTY-FIVE

"The Villain stays True to Form ..."

I woke up the next morning feeling okay. It was the first decent night's sleep I had had in months. While I was eating my breakfast in the cafeteria, I cogitated on how you might go about killing a hog. At the processing plant, I think they just shoot 'em in the forehead with a .22 rifle. But that definitely was outside my Mission parameters.

The day went okay, I reckon. Phillips wants to change everything about the hog operation. He wasn't making nothing no better, he's just changing things for the sake of changing 'em. I reckon he wants to put his "stamp" on things. For example, he told me and Sammy to spray more water on the ground so the hogs will have plenty of mud to waller in. But the way I see it, it's still cool this time of year and the hogs don't need no mud to cool off. So why make all that mess? Mr. Anderson sure didn't do things that-a-way.

"Yessir, I'm gonna show you how to change out them sparkplugs today," Ferlin told me, as I clambered up onto the bumper of the School truck.

Ferlin had brung along the red metal toolbox that Mr. Anderson had give him for Christmas. Ferlin carefully spread a faded shop rag out on the gravel and set his toolbox down in the middle of it. Ferlin was keeping that toolbox spick-and-span, just like the tools that was inside of it.

After Ferlin got the valve cover off, he said, "Yessir, this here is what they call a 'straight-six.' See? It's got one, two, three, four, five, six cylinders all in a row." He pointed out each cylinder with the screwdriver as he counted them off. "Yessir, at the top of each one of them cylinders is a spark plug and we're gonna change out each one of them fellers today."

"What are y'uns doing with that truck?" Phillips hollered from behind us. I dropped down off the bumper and we turned around to face him.

"Yessir, the truck has been missing real bad, here lately," said Ferlin, "And we had a brand new box of sparkplugs in the barn, so I figured I'd just go ahead replace the sparkplugs."

"Who told you to do that?" growled Phillips.

"Yessir, well, me and Mr. Anderson used to always keep this old truck a'runnin' so I just thought I'd help out."

"You didn't answer my question, boy," snarled Phillips. "Who told you to change them sparkplugs?"

"Nossir, nobody told me to do it," said Ferlin, "I just seen it needed doing' and took a notion to do it my ownself."

Phillips stomped over to Ferlin's toolbox and looked down inside. "Where'd y'uns get them tools?" he barked.

"Yessir, Mr. Anderson give me them tools before he passed away," said Ferlin.

"That's a goddamn lie!" snapped Phillips. "I see'd that wrench and them pliers hanging on the pegboard in the barn! I hate a goddamn liar, boy, and I hate a thief even more!"

"Nossir, them tools don't belong to the School. They, ... they was Mr. Anderson's," stammered Ferlin. "Yessir, Mr. Anderson give me them tools for Christmas. See right here?" Ferlin picked the pliers up out of the toolbox. "They got these little blue tags on 'em that says 'ANDERSON.' That means Mr. Anderson brought 'em from home and they belonged to him. Nossir, they don't belong to the School."

"Well, ain't that a fine-how-do-you-damn-do?" barked Phillips. "Y'uns are stealing tools from the School and then turning around and blaming it on Ol' Man Anderson."

"No, sir," I said. "I was there. I heard Mr. Anderson give them tools to Ferlin."

"I wasn't talking to you, Whitey," roared Phillips, and he swung at me with a grease-stained hand. But I saw it coming at me this time! I ducked and he just cuffed me a little bit on the side of the head.

"Nossir! Nossir!" mumbled Ferlin Blount. He grabbed Phillips up in a bear-hug, pinning his arms against his sides! Then Ferlin leaned back and slowly lifted Phillips' feet up off the ground. Phillips' feet kicked in the air as Ferlin held him like that for a minute or two. "Nossir!" grunted Ferlin, louder this time. "Nossir, you ain't a-hittin' these little fellers no more!"

After a while, Phillips stopped kicking, and Ferlin set him gently back down on the ground.

Phillips spun around to face us. "Spruce Building!" he bellowed, "Attackin' a staff member will get y'uns' ass sent to the Spruce Building! I ain't been here long, but I know that!"

"What about hittin' a resident?" I said. I reckon Ferlin's courage had rubbed off on me and I stepped in front of him, but I stayed close. "That will get your ass fired! And I got witnesses! You ain't permitted to hit a resident like that."

"That's just discipline, was what that was," snorted Phillips. "I gotta right to discipline."

"Well, why don't we go see the superintendent?" I said. "Let's go see him right now! Me and him's buddies." I took a few steps in the general direction of Johnson House. "And we can also tell him about that time you knocked me plum unconscious."

Phillips smiled and I realized he didn't have no teeth. He spit some tobacco juice on the ground. "Y'uns don't need to go running to no superintendent," he said. "Everything's fine. Y'uns can go back to changing them sparkplugs. But y'uns better watch ye damn self." Then he stomped off, but he didn't seem hardly as feisty as before.

After Phillips was out of earshot, I said, "Thanks for sticking up for me, Ferlin. Ain't no tellin' what he would of done if you hadn't been here."

"Yessir, you sure are welcome, Delphus," said Ferlin, ducking his head in embarrassment. "Yessir, I'm sorry I didn't stick up for you that first time Mr. Phillips hit you, but it happened so fast, it caught me by surprise. Yessir, that Mr. Phillips ain't nothing but a bully."

"Boy! That's for sure," I said.

"Yessir, are you and the superintendent really buddies?"

"Well, he knows my name and I know his name, and we've talked a little bit, " I said, "But I was probably stretching the truth a little bit when I said we was actually 'buddies.'"

"Yessir, we're gonna have a hard time dealing with that Mr. Phillips," said Ferlin.

"I got a plan."

CHAPTER TWENTY-SIX

"And therefore think him as a serpent's egg,
Which, hatch'd, would as his kind grow mischievous,
And kill him in the shell."

I needed a candle for this kinda deal. I dunno why, it just seemed like the right sort of thing. When Batman swore he was gonna spend the rest of his life warring on criminals, he did it by candlelight. Robin had a candle when he swore his oath too.

I knew the staff kept some big white candles in the storage closet, which they used for the older residents' birthdays. When you get too old, they just put one big candle on your cake, instead of a bunch of little ones. The skeleton key that Frank Blount had made me would open the storage closet easy enough, but even standing on a chair, I still couldn't reach the top shelf where they kept them big candles.

"Ferlin!" I said, shaking his mattress with my foot. When Ferlin gets to sleeping, won't nothing wake him up. Boy, I wish I could sleep as sound as he does! "Ferlin! I need you to do me a favor!"

"Yessir? Delphus?" said Ferlin, sitting up. He had drifted off to sleep with his glasses still on. "Yessir, what's going on?"

"Come on, Ferlin, I need you to help me with something," I said. "Come on, buddy, wake up!" Ferlin slowly rolled out of bed. He still had on his work clothes, but he had kicked his shoes off.

"Yessir. Whaddya want, Delphus?"

"I need you to get me a candle out of the storage closet, Ferlin," I said. "I can't reach 'em."

"Nossir, you ain't allowed to play with them candles in the storage closet, Delphus."

"I ain't gonna play with 'em," I said, "I just need a big candle for our council."

"Yessir, we're having a council?"

"Yeah, and we need a candle for it," I said, "And some matches to light it."

Ferlin shuffled out into the hall toward the storage closet. I had already opened up the door and set a chair inside. "See, up there on top? I need one of them big white candles and that box of matches."

Ferlin stepped up in the chair, grabbed up the candle and matches, and handed them to me. "Yessir, here you go," he said, stepping down off the chair. "Now, I'm going back to bed."

"Thank you, Ferlin," I said. "You're a pal! Now, could you go get Sammy and Frank?"

"Yessir? Huh? Wonder who wrote that up there?" said Ferlin, looking at the small black chalkboard that hung in the hallway outside our room. The Development Technicians wrote announcements for C-Wing on that chalkboard.

"WAKE UP!" somebody had wrote on the chalkboard. The next line read, "GET TO WORK!"

"Nossir, I don't recognize that handwriting," said Ferlin. "Reckon there's a new Development Tech on the wing?"

"I don't recognize that handwriting neither," I said, but I reckoned I knew where it came from. David St. John, Contract Agent for the CIA, was sending me a message and he was trying to light a fire under me!

"Ferlin," I said, "Could you go get Sammy and Frank and tell 'em to come to our room? It's real important!"

"Yessir, I'll go get 'em," said Ferlin as he shambled down the hall.

I carried the candle back into me and Ferlin's room and lit it. Turning off the overhead light, I sat down and dripped a tiny puddle of wax onto the cool tile floor. Sticking the bottom of the candle into the pool of wax, the candle stood straight up by itself. Looking around the illuminated room, I reckoned it would of been better to hold this council in a cave or something, but I didn't know where there was a cave close by.

Ferlin came through the door, with Sammy and Frank Blount in tow. Sammy and Frank joined me on the floor and Ferlin set back down on his bed.

"Looks like we're holding a séance," said Sammy.

I had memorized my opening speech:

"Gentlemen... Welcome to the Council of Clover Bottom. Y'all have come and we are met, here in the very nick of time, by chance it may seem. But it ain't by chance! Destiny has decreed that the four of us, sitting right here, and not nobody else, must figure out how to save the world."

"Delphus, what the H-E-double-hockey-sticks are you talking about?" said Sammy.

"I been assigned a secret mission by the Central Intelligence Agency, and I need y'all's help."

They snickered.

"Yessir," said Ferlin, "Delphus, is this one of your games? Yessir, we gotta get up early in the morning."

"I am absolutely serious," I told them. "The night before last, I was contacted by one David St. John, a Contract Agent for the Central Intelligence Agency."

"How did he contact you, Delphus?" Sammy asked. "Did he send you a coded message written in invisible ink?"

"No, smarty-pants, I couldn't sleep, so I went outside and set on that bench across from the front door of the building. I was just sitting there and he walked up."

"So this CIA man was waiting in the shadows all night, hoping that you might take a notion to come out there and set on that bench?"

"I dunno," I said. "Maybe he was fixing to break into the building, but then I come outside instead."

"Delphus, are you sure you didn't just dream up this whole thing?" said Sammy. "'It is a man's own mind, not his enemy or foe, that lures him to evil ways.'"

"No, I didn't just dream it."

"How do know you didn't dream it?" Sammy said.

I thought for a minute and said, "I smelled his pipe! St. John was smoking a pipe and I could smell his pipe smoke. You can't smell stuff in a dream."

"You can so smell stuff in a dream," Sammy said. "I smell stuff in my dreams all the time."

"Well, I ain't never been able to smell nothing in my dreams," I said. "And that's how I know I wasn't dreaming."

"Yessir, Delphus, why don't you go ahead and tell us about this mission he give you?" Ferlin said.

"I gotta kill The Mulefoot," I told them, "And it's gotta look like an accident."

"Why in tarnation would the CIA, the most powerful spy organization in the world, want you to kill a dumb boar hog?" Sammy said. "That's crazy!"

"That Mulefoot hog is a threat to every man, woman, and child in the U.S. of A." I said. "He killed Mr. Anderson!"

Nobody said nothing for a minute or two, then finally Ferlin said, "Nossir, Delphus. Mr. Anderson died of the cancer."

"But The Mulefoot give him that cancer!" I said, "When he bit Mr. Anderson on the leg, he gave him liver cancer. Mr. Anderson was fine before that happened."

"Nossir, I don't think that's the way cancer works, Delphus."

"See, Ferlin, that's what this CIA man, St. John, explained to me. The Mulefoot got carried over to China and he caught these worms called 'Chinese liver flukes.' These Chinese liver flukes will absolutely give you liver cancer 'cause that's how they got their name. But they didn't kill The Mulefoot 'cause he was so mean and tough. He got 'symbiosis' and teamed up with them Chinese liver flukes. They didn't kill The Mulefoot, but now his spit, his pee, even his poop will give you cancer! That's how he bit Mr. Anderson and give him liver cancer."

"Why can't we just worm him?" said Sammy.

"Well, that's the thing," I said, "Because of all the serums and potions they give The Mulefoot, them cancer-causing germs are bound up in The Mulefoot's 'cells.' They're a part of him now. Worming him won't get rid of 'em."

"Why don't the CIA just kill The Mulefoot their own selves?" said Sammy.

"The Mulefoot wasn't supposed to be in China in the first place," I said. "If they kill The Mulefoot and it gets traced back to them, it'll cause an 'international incident.'"

"Yessir, so that's why they want it to look like an accident?"

"The CIA don't want no local authorities examining the body," I said.

"I hate that dang monster," said Sammy. "I ain't forgot what he did to Sammy Davis, Jr. But what's The Mulefoot gonna hurt just laying around inside his pen?"

"The CIA believes it's just a matter of time before The Mulefoot gives his liver fluke disease to other hogs, and then them hogs will transmit the disease into the national food supply. People all over America will get liver cancer just like Mr. Anderson did."

"Nossir, we can't let that happen," Ferlin said solemnly.

"So, are you wanting us to swear an oath or something that we'll help you kill The Mulefoot?" said Sammy.

"If you don't care nothing about the health and safety of every man, woman and child in the United States of America, I don't want your help. If the tears and suffering of all them millions of people ain't enough to get you to help me, you ought to get up right now and just go on back to bed. I'll do it by myself."

"Delphus, you gotta admit that this story sounds a little far-fetched," Sammy said. "And you ain't exactly been yourself since Mr. Anderson died."

"Sammy, I know I act goofy sometimes, but have I ever lied to you?"

Sammy thought for a minute, then said, "I reckon not."

"Yessir, reckon we oughta bring y'all's buddy, Earz Grissom, in on this deal?" said Ferlin, leaning forward on his bunk. "Yessir, I 'magine he's got a lot more experience with killing than all the rest of us put together."

"Earz is too much of a wild card," I said, "I'm afraid we're liable to get him started killing and then he won't want to stop. Also, I don't think Earz is much of a 'joiner.'"

"Well, while we're on a killing spree," said Sammy, "Why don't we go ahead and kill Phillips too? Since we're bumping off people we don't like."

"That's the thing," I said, "If we get rid of The Mulefoot, we'll be rid of Phillips too. What'd he say? 'My number one job is taking care of that Mulefoot.' If something happens to The Mulefoot, then Phillips will get in trouble, the Administration will fire him, and we won't have to worry about that dirty snake no more."

Frank Blount thrust his fist toward the center of our group. I slapped my hand on top of his. Ferlin reached over and placed his hand on top of mine. Then we all looked at Sammy.

"I'm sorry," said Sammy. "I can't go along with you boys. 'As all Buddhas refrained from killing until the end of their lives, so I too will refrain from killing until the end of my life.' That right there is Number One of the Five Precepts."

We unhitched our hands 'cause it felt dumb when Sammy didn't join in. I said, "Sammy, what do you think happens to all them hogs we raise?"

"I know, Delphus," Sammy said. "I'm sorry. I just need more than your say-so to kill something in cold blood."

"Just look at the facts, Sammy: A) Mr. Anderson was the picture of health, B) Mr. Anderson got bit on the leg by The Mulefoot. Then, right after that, C) Mr. Anderson got liver cancer. How much more proof do you need?"

"I just can't do it, boys," said Sammy. "Y'all will have to count me out."

"Yessir, Delphus, how was you figuring on doing away with The Mulefoot?"

"Well, Ferlin, we're still in the early planning phase of this mission," I said, "And I ain't quite made it that far yet."

"You said it just a minute ago, when you was talking about Phillips," said Sammy. "A snake. You catch a rattlesnake and you throw it on The Mulefoot. The snake'll bite him and it'll look like an accident."

"That right there is a brilliant idea," I said.

"'He who foresees calamities suffers them twice over,'" said Sammy. "It's three o'clock in the morning! I gotta go to bed. It's too late for me."

Sammy headed out the door and Frank tagged along behind him. "Okay, everybody act normal tomorrow," I said, following them out the door and calling down the hall. "Put on a happy face. Don't do nothing to tip Phillips off that we got something planned."

By the time I stepped back into our room, Ferlin had already gone back to sleep. This time, he had took off his glasses and got under the covers. I reckon he didn't have no guilty conscience about planning The Mulefoot's murder.

I blew out the candle and then realized I wasn't gonna be able to put it back on the top shelf of the closet by myself. But I didn't have the heart to wake Ferlin up again. So I hid the candle in my chest o' drawers and went to move the chair out of the closet. After I scooted the chair out and locked the door, I saw Skippy Dean padding down the hallway. He had wrapped his blanket all around him and pulled it up over his head like a hood. He looked like a tiny ghost. "Hey, Skippy Dean," I said, "What are you doing up, walking the halls so late?"

"Red c-c-couldn't sleep," said Skippy Dean. "His sto-sto-stomach hurts." Skippy Dean pulled Red the Bear out from under his sheet.

"Did he eat something that upset his stomach?"

"N-n-no, he's sc-sc-scared and it makes his sto-sto-stomach hurt."

"What is Red scared of?"

"Mr. Ph-Ph-Phillips," said Skippy Dean. "He ma-ma-makes Red ner-ner-nervous. He do-do-don't like to be-be-be around him."

"I tell you what, Skippy Dean," I said, squatting down, "You tell Red not to worry. Me and the Blount Brothers are working on a plan to get Mr. Phillips replaced. So maybe he won't be around here too much longer."

Skippy Dean slid the hood back off his head. "F-f-for real?" Skippy Dean said. "Mr. Ph-Ph-Phillips ain't gonna be here f-f-forever?"

"Now, it may take a while, Skippy Dean," I said, "But you need to tell Red that things around here are gonna change. He just needs to hang in there."

"Oh-Oh-Okay," said Skippy Dean, nodding his head. "I'll te-te-tell him that."

"Skippy Dean, 'til then, if Phillips ever hits you or *anything*, you come tell me right away, okay?"

"I wi-wi-will."

"Does Red feel better?"

"Yeah, a li-li-little bi-bi-bit."

"Okay, Skippy Dean, go back to bed," I said, "And try to get some sleep."

CHAPTER TWENTY-SEVEN

Slowly a huge, hideous, wedge-shaped head took form before his dilated eyes, and from the darkness oozed, in flowing scaly coils, the ultimate horror of reptilian development

Frank Blount knew where there was some bad snakes. So that next Saturday, me, Ferlin, and Frank went snake hunting. We went tromping down past the dairy barn and the hog barn toward the Stones River.

As you get closer to the Stones River, the ground starts sloping downhill pretty quick. Over the ages, water streaming down them slopes had cut V-shaped gorges into the landscape. Rocky limestone bluffs formed the sides of these gorges and small creeks ran at their bottoms. Ancient cedar and maple trees, peeking over the edge of the bluffs, kept the creeks in perpetual shadow. Them creeks flowed over limestone shelves. Some of them shelves was only a foot tall, but some of 'em was waist-high. Sometimes, the water couldn't make it over the lip of the shelf and it just puddled up, forming a murky, brackish pool. A few silver minnows darted beneath the surface.

"Yessir, this place sure does look snakey," said Ferlin.

"What is that smell?" I said.

"Yessir, that's the river," said Ferlin.

"It don't always smell like that, does it?"

"Nossir, just sometimes."

"Frank, I think you're right," I said, "It sure looks like there ought to be some snakes around here."

"Nossir, I don't like snakes."

"Well, I don't like 'em either, but I ain't afraid of 'em," I said. "Possums are invulnerable to rattlesnake bites. So I reckon it's the same with any other kind of poisonous snake."

"Yessir, you ain't never tested that out, have you?"

"No, but I have faith in my Possum Powers."

If Frank Blount was paying any attention to us, he didn't let on. He was peering intently into the water at the bottom of a limestone ledge. Suddenly, Frank flopped down on his belly and started thrusting his arms up under the shelf! In an instant, he shot to his feet with a snake in his hand! The snake was about a foot-and-a-half long and Frank had it by the tail. The snake tried to coil hisself up as if to strike at Frank's arm, but with a simple spin of his wrist, Frank expertly twirled that snake around-and-around so that the centrifugal force would keep the snake from striking at him.

"Twirl 'im, Frank!" Ferlin cried out, "Twirl 'im. Don't you let that snake bite you!"

After the initial excitement was over, we evaluated the snake's suitability for our Mission. Frank continued to hold the snake up and twirl him in little circles, but slower now. If the snake was dizzy or just exhausted, I don't know, but he dangled there limply in Frank's hand.

"I dunno. He's pretty small," I said, "He looks like he's just a baby."

"Yessir, now, I heard that babies have got more venom stored up in 'em than regular grown-up snakes," said Ferlin.

"He just looks kinda small to take on a mean, six-hundred-pound boar."

Frank Blount shrugged his shoulders and released the snake back into the water. We watched it zigzag away.

Frank motioned for us to follow him to another gorge further down the hill and closer to the river. This gorge looked a lot like the first one, but the creek was a little deeper. The murky water come up to my waist.

"Look over there!" I said, pointing to the bank, "That's a snapping turtle!" A snapping turtle has a little beak that looks like a hawk's beak.

"Yessir, stay away from him," said Ferlin. "Yessir, if a snapping turtle bites you, he won't let go 'til it thunders."

"What if it don't never thunder?"

"Nossir, then he won't never let go."

Like before, Frank was ignoring us. Intently, he scanned the water beneath a rock ledge. Suddenly, Frank dove beneath the water! After a second or two, he splashed up above the surface, snake in hand. And this snake wasn't no baby! The water on the snake's dark gray scales glistened in the sunlight. Frank tried to do his whirling trick, but the snake was so long, its head was still in the water, but Frank run his hand down the length of the snake and kept it from biting him. All three of us splashed our way over to the dry creek bed.

When the snake was fully out of the water, Frank could do his whirling trick on him. Even with all the diving and thrashing around, Frank had kept his spectacles on, but there was so much water on the lenses, I don't know how he could see. Frank spun the snake around whenever it made like it was going to strike at him. After a while, the snake calmed down and just kinda hung there.

This snake was huge! Frank held it at arm's length and it came down below his knees. This snake was as big around as my arm. Its scales was dark, almost black, but out of the water, I could see faint bands of yellow running along its sides. Brown and yellow scales formed a checkerboard pattern on its belly. The snake's beady eyes watched us carefully, but it didn't seem too angry.

"Yessir, that right there's a water moccasin!" said Ferlin, squatting down to inspect it. "Yessir, that's one of the most poisonous snakes there is! You be careful now, Frank."

Frank gently rubbed his hand along the snake's body. I think Frank would have kept a snake for a pet if Clover Bottom allowed us to have pets.

"Gosh! What's that smell?" I said.

Frank switched hands holding the snake and held up his right hand, showing some runny white poop on it. He quickly jerked his right hand to his side and slung the poop off of it.

"Yessir, sometimes water moccasins will poop as a defense mechanism," observed Ferlin. "Yessir, I think this one's a female. Female water moccasins get bigger than the males."

"Let's call her 'Charlotte,'" I said, "After Charlotte in *Charlotte's Web.*"

"Yessir, I think Charlotte was a spider."

"Yeah, but I don't know any girl snake names," I said. "Whaddya think, Frank?"

Frank nodded his head yes.

"Yessir, then Charlotte it is."

"Charlotte looks like the kinda snake that can take down a 600-pound hog!" I said. "Let's go right now and sic her on The Mulefoot!"

"Yessir, I reckon there ain't no time like the present," said Ferlin.

By this time, Charlotte had calmed down and Frank was cradling her in the palms of both hands. We headed toward the grassy bank to make the long trek back to the hog pens.

The muddy slope going up the creek bank was as slippery as wet ice. I grabbed a muddy root for a handhold and it just pulled right out of the ground! I flipped backwards and went tumbling head-over-heels down the bank! Frank had been coming up behind me and I slammed right into him, knocking him over like a bowling pin!

We was all laid out flat on our backs on the dry creek bed: me, Frank, and Charlotte. Ferlin stood a few feet away frozen in place. Our crash had upset Charlotte pretty bad and she had coiled herself up, getting ready to strike at Frank! I thought maybe I could grab her and toss her out of striking distance if I was fast enough.

I lunged for her, but her head arched up in the air like lightning, avoiding my grasp. In an instant, her head crashed back down, burying her fangs into my forearm. Pain like fire flashed up my arm! With my left hand, I wrenched Charlotte's fangs out of my arm and threw her into the bushes. She weaved her way through the weeds and disappeared. Me, Frank, and Ferlin all just stared at each other with our mouths hanging open.

"Boy, that sure was something," I said.

And Possum Mode in 3...2...1

CHAPTER TWENTY-EIGHT

Fire can't burn him, knives can't cut him, bullets can't hurt him ... In fact, there's nothing known to man that can even harm a hair of his head!

When I come out of *Possum Mode,* Ferlin and Frank Blount was carrying me. Ferlin had me up under the armpits and Frank was holding me around my ankles.

"Put me down!" I cried.

"Nossir, no can do," said Ferlin over his shoulder.

Frank Blount violently shook his head no.

"Put me down!" I repeated. "I can walk by myself!"

"Nossir, you got that Water Moccasin venom coursing through your veins, and you don't need to help it along by joggling around."

"Well, just set me down for a minute so we can talk."

"Yessir, I reckon I could use a breather."

They gently lowered me to the ground. The grass felt itchy on my back, so I sat up.

"Yessir, you oughta stay flat on your back, Delphus," said Ferlin, as he and Frank dropped to the ground. "That venom is working its way through your system and you need to stay still."

"Listen, I've told y'all possums are invulnerable to rattlesnake bites and I'm sure it works the same way with Water Moccasins."

"Nossir, we gotta get you to a hospital."

"Ferlin, you know I'm a possum mutant, just like they got in the *X-Men*. Oh, Man! What is that on my britches leg?" My britches leg had a huge reddish-orange stain just below the knee. It smelled terrible.

"Yessir, you missed the show while you was getting your beauty rest," said Ferlin. "Yessir, right after Charlotte bit you, Frank heroically leaped over and commenced to sucking that venom right out of your arm! Yessir, I told Frank to quit that right now and for him to spit out that poison! Yessir, then I told him to go over to the creek and wash his mouth out. Yessir, then I did the best I could, trying to suck out the venom, but I reckon either Frank had sucked it all out or else it had already moved on through your system. Nossir, I couldn't get nothing but blood."

"So this is blood on my britches?"

"Nossir, after Frank washed his mouth out with the creek water, I reckon it didn't agree with him. Yessir, he started puking everywhere! So when I seen Frank puking, I started puking my ownself! Yessir, some of my puke got on your britches leg. I'm sorry about that. Nossir, I wasn't aiming to puke on you. It just kinda came on me sudden."

"Don't worry about it," I said, "You boys was trying to save my life. I sure do appreciate it."

"Yessir, we probably need to be heading on back," said Ferlin.

"Y'all don't need to carry me no more though, I feel fine." I held out my hand to show that it wasn't shaking, like they do on TV. "See? Look at that! Steady as a rock!"

"Yessir, you seem to be okay," said Ferlin, "But if you get to feeling weak, you just let us know."

I was lying. I felt weak as water and my stomach was doing flip-flops. But I reckoned it would probably take a while for my Possum Powers to start kicking in. Once my Regeneration Factor started percolating, I would be just fine. There was no way I was gonna go to a hospital.

As we were hiking back to Progress House, I said, "You know, after drinking my blood, you boys will probably turn into were-possums. 'Even a man who goes to church, And honest as honest can be, Can become a were-possum when the moon is full, And swing by his tail from a tree!'"

"Yessir, heh, heh, that's a good 'un," said Ferlin. "Yessir, I think one were-possum is all the world can stand."

When we got back to Progress House, I took a shower, hoping that maybe it would perk me up and also because I had been puked on. I was still feeling pretty pukey myself. My Possum Powers still hadn't kicked in, and to tell the truth, I was starting to get a little bit worried.

I went out in the hall, lifted the phone up off the hook, and dialed one of the few numbers I knew by heart.

"Hello?" said Miss Zelda.

"Hey, Miss Zelda!" I said, "This is Delphus V. White at Clover Bottom Hospital and School."

"Oh, Delphus, how are you doing, darlin'? It's so nice to hear from you!"

"Well, I hadn't talked to you in a little while and I just thought I'd see how you was doing."

"Oh, I'm doing fine, Delphus," said Miss Zelda, "I'm keeping the grandkids during the day now and I spend most of my time chasing after them. Plus, I'm still managing the boys' furniture-moving business and doing their books. So, I'm stayin' busy. Are you keeping the Blount Brothers out of trouble?"

"Yes, ma'am, but it's a full-time job."

"Have they found y'all a new Development Tech yet?"

"Oh yeah, and he's great!" I lied. "He knows all kindsa stuff about hogs."

"You know, Ed was so worried about what would happen with you boys once he was gone."

"Well, we're doing fine," I said. "I sure do miss Mr. Anderson though."

"I do too, Delphus," Miss Zelda said. "But I know I'm going to be seeing him up in Heaven."

"Yes, ma'am!"

"Delphus, honey, have you joined the Church yet?"

"No, ma'am, not yet."

"Ed worried about you not joining the Church."

"Yes, ma'am, I know he did. That's the kind of man he was."

"Well, you'll think about it, won't you?"

"Yes, ma'am, I sure will. Do you need anything?"

"No, honey, my boys are taking real good care of me."

"Well, I'll let you go then," I said. "I just thought I'd check on you."

"Thank you, sweetie, I'll try to get by there and see y'all real soon."

"Bye, Miss Zelda."

"Bye-Bye, darling."

I went back into my room and laid down on my bed. I felt like poop. I was starting to worry that maybe my Regeneration Factor only worked on rattlesnake bites, but not on Water Moccasins. I closed my eyes for just a minute.

"Hey, Delly, whatcha doing?" Earz Grissom was leaning in the doorway.

"Hey, Earz, I was just laying here."

"I hear you got yourself bit by a motherfucking Water Moccasin."

"Yeah, she was about to bite Frank."

"Lemme see it," said Earz.

I extended my forearm where Charlotte had bit me.

"Well, it don't look too goddamn swollen," Earz said, inspecting my arm.

"Nah, I think my Possum Powers are gonna take care of it."

"Why won't you go to goddamn clinic?" Earz said. "Them Blount boys are awful worried 'bout you, you little dumbass."

"You know, I'm part possum, Earz," I said, "And possums are invulnerable to snake bites - well, rattlesnake bites anyhow."

"Well, I don't know about all that shit, but I do know a Water Moccasin bite ain't nothing to fuck around with."[67]

---

[67] By this point in the narrative, it should be fairly obvious that the snake, "Charlotte," was not, in fact, a venomous Water Moccasin (*Agkistrodon piscivorus*). Charlotte was almost certainly a *Nerodia rhombifer,* commonly known as the Diamondback Water Snake, which is a nonvenomous species. The two species are frequently confused with one another, as they share the same habitat and general appearance. Additionally, the scales of the *Nerodia rhombifer* darken with age, so that the older adult snake will end with a body that is almost entirely black, a trait of *Agkistrodon*

"I'm gonna be okay, I promise. My Possum Powers are going to kick in here 'fore too long."

"How 'bout if I wrassle your ass up out of that bed and carry you down to the goddamn clinic? How about that?"

"Please don't do that, Earz," I said. "You know I ain't brave a'tall. If I thought I was in any kinda danger, I'd be running to the clinic."

"You sure, you little bastard?" said Earz. "'Cause if you fucking die on me, I'm gonna stomp the living shit out of you."

"I'll be fine."

"Alright then, goddammit!" Earz said, reaching into his back pocket. "In that case, I brought you some snakebite medicine. Here, drink some of this shit." He handed me a rectangular glass bottle. It didn't have no label on it and was about three-quarters-full with a golden liquid.

I took a sip from the bottle and it started burning in my mouth, burned all the way down my throat, and then when it got to my belly, the heat just kinda spread out all over my body. I had a coughing fit.

"Alright, pass that sumbitch back over here," said Earz, taking the bottle from me. "I might get bit by a motherfucking rattlesnake on the way home and I wanna inoculate myself just in case!" He took a huge draw from the bottle and his body shook as the medicine coursed through his system.

"Alright, knucklehead, now you need to take another swig, a big swaller this time," Earz said, handing the bottle back to me.

I took a big gulp like Earz had said, but this time, I didn't let the medicine linger in my mouth. I swallered it down into my belly as fast as I could. Then the heat, or the numbness, or whatever it was, spread through my body like lightning!

Friends, I am here to tell you, that right then and right there, my Regeneration Factor finally decided to kick in! I reckon my Possum Powers needed a jump-start and Earz' medicine was just the thing! I felt like Popeye the Sailor Man and somebody had just give me a big

---

piscivorus. The Narrator's symptoms are merely the product of an overactive imagination.

can of spinach! "Earz," I said, bolting upright up in bed, "I think your medicine worked!"

"Yeah, it always works for me," Earz grinned from ear-to-ear and took another swig out of the bottle.

"I knew my Possum Powers wouldn't let me down!" I said, jumping out of bed. "I gotta go tell the Blount Brothers!"

"Alright then, since you're feeling so goddamn spry, I'm gonna go and inoculate myself some more," said Earz, raising his bottle in a toast. "You can't be too careful with them fucking rattlesnakes." Earz swaggered out toward the front door.

I bounded down the hall to Sammy and Frank Blount's room, where Ferlin was setting across from Frank and Sammy. "Boys, my Possum Power finally decided to show up!" I announced.

"Yessir! Smells like Jack Daniels finally decided to show up," said Ferlin Blount.

I flexed my arms up over my head like Superman. "Earz Grissom give me some snakebite medicine and I feel like a new man!"

"You shouldn't drink anything that'll run a car," said Sammy.

"Well, it worked," I said. "That's all I care about."

"Yessir, you sure you're feeling better?" said Ferlin.

"I am absolutely, one-hundred percent positive."

"Yessir, that there's great news," said Ferlin. "Yessir, we was getting a little worried about you." He shook my hand and clapped me on the back. And since we had started shaking hands, we all just shook one another's hands all around.

"Yeah, I reckon this is all my fault," said Sammy, "Since I'm the one who gave y'all the idea about using snakes in the first place."

"No, everything was going smooth 'til I crashed into Frank while he was carrying Charlotte."

"Well, now maybe we can forget about all this foolishness," said Sammy.

"Oh, no," I said, "We gotta get back to The Mission as soon as we can. It's just a matter of time before The Mulefoot spreads his disease out into the national food supply. We are setting on a ticking time-bomb."

"Delphus..." said Sammy.

"No, I mean it," I said. "Just because we had one little setback don't mean we can ignore our duty to the men, women and children of the United States of America. Mr. Anderson didn't ignore his duty when he got called to fight in World War II."

"'People of this world are deluded,'" Sammy sighed.

"Now, Sammy, I know you don't want no part of The Mission, but we gotta do what we gotta do," I said. "Now, I'm going out on patrol."

Later, back in my bed, I slept peacefully, despite Ferlin's snoring.

Frank Blount woke me up three times that night to make sure I was still alive. Frank would tiptoe into the room, poke me on the arm a couple of times, and wait for my response.

"I'm fine, Frank," I replied all three times, and then satisfied, Frank Blount would turn around and tiptoe out the door.

CHAPTER TWENTY-NINE

"Of all the horrors of the universe,
man's inhumanity to man is the most vile!"

Like most days, Phillips was hollering. He bellered at Ferlin, "I done told you once to put more feed in that hog feeder, Big Blount!" Ferlin hustled away to get the wheelbarrow. Next, Phillips turned on Frank, "Fer the last damn time, get yer thumb outta yer ass and pick up them goddamn pallets!" Phillips kicked at Frank as he scrambled away to collect the plywood handling panels. Then Phillips aimed his sights at me and Sammy, yelling, "Don't you little turds drag the hosepipe through that pig shit!" Finally, Phillips glared over at Skippy Dean, who was just standing there, and snarled, "What're you looking at, Red? Why don't you go do something and make yourself useful?"

Skippy Dean's eyes started welling up and he turned around and started running back toward Progress House. Me and Sammy looked at each other. We wanted to go after Skippy Dean and check on him, but we couldn't drop what we was doing, or else Phillips would yell at us or hit us.

I got to thinking. This here is what it must of been like for Johnny McCline, the slave boy who escaped from Clover Bottom Plantation -- people yelling at you all time, "Do this!" and "Do that!" and then if you didn't do it just exactly right, they'd hit you with a leather strap. I believe technically we got paid for our work on the hog farm, but we never did see very much money out of it. We got a ten-dollar allowance each month. I was starting to get a feeling what it must have been like for Johnny McCline.

When me and Sammy got done watering the hogs and put the hosepipes away, we starting heading back to Progress House to clean ourselves up. We was planning on getting back to work on a log cabin that we was building out of popsicle sticks.

"Hey, Little Blount," Phillips called after us. "Come here, boy, I wanna talk to you." Me and Sammy looked at each other nervously and turned back around and stared walking back toward Phillips. "Naw, I wasn't talking to you, Whitey," Phillips grumbled, pointing his finger at me, "You get on. Mind yer own business." I froze in my tracks.

"Me and you need to have us a talk, Little Blount," Phillips sneered at Sammy as he motioned him toward Mr. Anderson's old office at the front of the barn. As Phillips followed Sammy through the door, he laid his hand on Sammy's shoulder and I didn't like the looks of that a'tall, not one bit.

Mr. Anderson's office didn't have no windows, so I couldn't see what was going on inside there. I painstakingly twisted the doorknob, but it was locked from the inside. I smooshed my ear up against the wooden door, and while I could hear the murmur of voices, I couldn't make out a single word that was being said.

I wasn't about to desert my pal, Sammy Blount, to the clutches of that monster Phillips. I thought maybe I should set the barn on fire, but I couldn't find no matches or gasoline. When I couldn't think of nothing else to do, I just started banging my fist on the door real hard.

"Go away! Get outta here!" yelled Phillips through the door.

I banged my fist against the door even harder this next time and kinda rammed my shoulder up against it too, just for good measure.

"Get yer ass away from that goddamn door!" shrieked Phillips.

And then it hit me! I didn't really have to set the barn on fire, I could just pretend that I had!

"Fire! Fire! Fire!" I screamed. "Oh, Lord have mercy! We gotta fire! Oh, merciful barbeque in Heaven! The barn's on fire! We're all gonna die! Oh, Sweet Baby Jesus! We gotta fire!" I keeled over and started squirming around on the dirt floor like the flames was consuming me.

"Oh, Dear Merciful Lord! The barn's on fire! All the hogs are gonna burn up!"

Phillips jerked open the office door. "Where's the goddamn fire?" he roared. He had taken off his navy work-shirt and was wearing a dirty white T-shirt underneath.

"I think the smoke is coming from that-a-way!" I said, pointing toward the back of the barn. I was still laying flat on my back on the dirt floor.

Phillips squinted toward the rear of the barn with his good eye. "I don't see no goddamn fire!" he grunted. "Stop fucking around!" Phillips roared, as he gave me a backhand slap across the face.

Laying on the ground, I didn't have much room to maneuver. I took the full brunt of his slap.

And Possum Mode in 3..., 2..., 1

Who knows how long I was out?

The next thing I knew, Sammy Blount was shaking me out of *Possum Mode*. "Come on, Delphus! Get up, buddy!" he said, helping me to my feet. "We gotta go now! Hurry!" Sammy pulled me along a few steps as my head started to clear. By the time I knew what was going on, we had run half-way back to Progress House.

When we got back to Progress House, we didn't work on the popsicle-stick log cabin. We just went to our rooms and got washed up. Sammy didn't say two words the rest of the day.

Around five o'clock, Ferlin stood up and said, "Yessir, I reckon it's time to round up the fellers for supper." I tagged along behind him.

When we walked through Sammy and Frank's door, Sammy was setting cross-legged in the middle of his bed with his eyes closed. He wasn't wearing nothing but his jockey-shorts.

"Yessir, you fellers ready to get some supper?"

Frank stood up and nodded his head a single time.

"I don't reckon I'm gonna eat supper tonight," said Sammy, opening his eyes. "I suffered an injury to my karma today."

"Yessir, I got some Absorbine Jr.[68] in the medicine cabinet," said Ferlin. "If you wanna borrow some...?"

"No, I just need to meditate, said Sammy. "'Once you appreciate that the nature of anger and joy is empty and you let them go, you free yourself from karma.'"

"Alright, then, I'll bring you back an apple or banana or something from the dining hall," I said.

The next morning, we was all milling around in front of the barn, fixing to start our day. A couple of the little boys was laughing and throwing clumps of mud at each other.

The door to Mr. Anderson's office flung open and Phillips come stomping out. A huge white plaster cast encased Phillips' right arm. Running from above Phillips' elbow to the tips of his fingers, the cast practically gleamed against his dusky skin and dingy clothes.

"You do that?" I whispered to Sammy.

"Yes, I did," said Sammy. "I can't abide no monkey business."

When Phillips reached us, he barked, "Yeah, y'uns can see I got a cast on my arm," and brandished his cast around. "I got my arm caught in a piece of goddamn machinery yesterday."

I wanted to ask Phillips what kind of machinery it was, but I kept my mouth shut.

"They had to put a metal rod in my goddamn arm," yelled Phillips. "So y'uns had better be careful. Y'uns had better do exactly like I say!" Phillips paced back and forth in front of us. "When I say, 'Jump!' Y'uns had better say, 'How High?' When I say, 'Go!' Y'uns better take off! I don't wanna hear no backtalk! I want y'uns to do what I say, when I say it!"

I noticed that Phillips wouldn't look at Sammy at all, but he had stopped his pacing and was standing right in front of Skippy Dean. Phillips' good eye was fixed on little Skippy Dean. "Y'uns better do what I say!" Phillips growled. Then Phillips cast his evil eye at the rest of us and snarled, "Now, you little turds get to work!"

---

68 Absorbine Jr. is a liniment introduced in 1892 that relieves minor joint and muscle pain.

Sammy immediately run over to Skippy Dean with me right behind him. "Skippy Dean!" said Sammy, squatting down. "You go back to Progress House right now. You go there right now and you can play for the rest of the day."

"I get lo-lo-lonely by myself all d-d-day, Sammy," Skippy Dean said. "I wa-wa-wanna help y'all with the pi-pi-pigs."

Sammy thought for a minute. "Alright then, Skippy Dean, you can help me and Delphus water the hogs, but you gotta stay right beside us the whole time," Sammy said. "You can't never get out of our sight. You understand?"

"I uh-uh-understand."

"Say it back to me so I know you understand."

"I have to st-st-stay in y'all's sight the wh-wh-whole time."

Sammy knew that Phillips was avoiding him like the plague. Sammy reckoned that as long as Skippy Dean was right by his side, Phillips wouldn't even think about going near him.

With Skippy Dean a few steps ahead of us, we tramped over to the wooden bin where the hoses was stored. As we unloaded the hoses, Sammy said quietly, "I'm in, Delphus."

"In?"

"Your Secret Mission... We gotta get rid of that skunk Phillips, and if killing The Mulefoot hog is the only way to do it, then I'm all in."

CHAPTER THIRTY

The criminal is then seated in a square room amid four mirrored walls that reflect his features and make them glow with an eerie red fire...Now the faces turn an unhealthy green pallor, betraying the sickness of mind that has gripped the criminal!

Me and the Blount Brothers was all setting in Ferlin and me's room.

"We gotta tell somebody about that polecat Phillips right this second!" I said.

"Yessir, but who can we tell?" Ferlin said.

"Delphus, you used to call Commissioner Jordan on the telephone all the time," Sammy said. "Reckon we could try that?"

"Naw, I ain't been able to get through to the Commissioner in a long time," I said. "He's got a new secretary and she don't understand that me and him are pals. Plus, he may still be sore about the Halloween party."

Frank Blount snapped his fingers. Then he interlocked his thumbs and flapped his fingers like the wings of a bird.

"Yessir! Mr. Birdwell!" said Ferlin. "That's a great idea, Frank! Yessir, Mr. Birdwell's always been good to us."

"I ain't seen Mr. Birdwell in a long time," I said. "Where's he been?"

"I heard he got transferred over to the Spruce Building," said Sammy.

"Where they keep the bad boys?" I said. "Them mean boys will eat Mr. Birdwell alive."

"I dunno, Mr. Birdwell was in the Army," said Sammy. "He ain't gonna take no guff."

"Yeah, but he ain't the kinda guy that would punch a resident back neither. Nor beat one up, for that matter," I said.

"Whaddya think?" said Sammy.

"Mr. Birdwell was gonna drive us to Mr. Anderson's funeral. He was even gonna bring us jackets and neckties to wear," I said. "I think we can trust him."

"Yessir, then let's go over to the Spruce Building and see if we can find Mr. Birdwell," Ferlin said. "Frank, can you stay here and keep an eye on Skippy Dean and the little fellers?"

Frank shot Ferlin a "thumbs-up."

The Spruce Building was only two buildings down from Progress House, but I always avoided it on my night patrols. I was always afraid that they would catch me in there and keep me. The Spruce Building had red brick walls and steel grates over all the windows. I fished in my pocket for my spoon skeleton key, but the front door was open and we just walked right in. There wasn't nobody at the reception desk and the halls was empty.

"How 'bout you boys go down the hall that way and I'll go back up this way?" I said.

"Yessir, sounds like a plan to me," said Ferlin.

All the doors had glass panels in them so you could see inside. The first door was locked and the lights was turned off inside. The second door was unlocked and I stuck my head inside.

"Whatcha doing, Delly?" said Earz Grissom. He was setting at the end of a wooden table with his hands folded in front of him. Other than the table and chair, the room was completely empty.

"What are you doing in here, Earz?"

"Aww, them motherfucking screws caught me partying with one of my girlfriends and dragged my ass in here," Earz said. "And I mighta punched one of 'em's ticket when they caught me. But, you know, Delly, when a man gets caught with his pants down, he ain't thinking too goddamn clear."

"How long you been in here?"

"A couple of weeks, I guess," Earz said. "It's hard to keep track of time when you're just staring at four fucking walls all day."

"You sit in here all day?"

"Fuck, yeah, from the time I get up in the morning 'til the time I go to bed."

"What do you do all day?"

"I'm supposed to sit here quietly and think about what a terrible fucking person I am."

"All day?"

"Sometimes when I get bored, I tell 'em I need to go to the can and I rub one out."

"I could sneak you in some books."

"Yeah, you know, Delly, I ain't much of a reader."

"I could bring you some comic books," I said. "You can tell what's going on in them just by looking at the pictures."

"Nah, they catch you smuggling books in here to me and they'll have your ass setting in the room next door," Earz grinned. "I fucking appreciate it though."

"Can't I get you anything?"

"Nah, I'm good," Earz said. "Now, you better get your ass out of here before they catch you."

"How long you gotta have to stay in here, Earz?"

"'Til I'm fucking reformed, I reckon."

"I sure hope they let you out before then."

"Ha-ha, me too!" laughed Earz. "Listen, Delly, before you go, there's something I want you to know. You know how I'm here 'cause of how I burned down that church?"

"Yeah."

"Well, I didn't really burn that fucker down. My old man did it."

"Your daddy?"

"Yeah. He burned down that church because it was a colored people's church and he hates colored people. I dunno why. He just hates colored people. I don't think he even knows any colored people, but he hates 'em just the same. Me, I ain't got no problem with colored people. When I played Little League, there was this colored guy on our team named

Donald Bailey. I played shortstop and Donnie played first base. I would scoop up that goddamn ball and I'd shoot it over to Donnie and he would catch that motherfucker every goddamn time--like clockwork. As long as I got it anywhere near close to Donnie, he would catch that fucker. He could stretch like a motherfucker – and never take his foot off the goddamn bag. Our team, Dan Hall's Grocery, won the whole goddamn championship two years in a row. Two fuckin' years! Me and Donnie was buddies. Naw, I ain't got nothing against colored people."

"What happened with the church?"

"Well, my old man started reading these little yellow pamphlets from the KKK, them bedsheet-wearing faggots. The old man gets it in his head that he's gonna burn down a colored people's church. So, one night, he gets hisself liquored up, buys hisself a couple cans of kerosene, walks over to a colored church which is just a few miles down the road from our house, and he burns that sonovabitch to the goddamn ground."

"There wasn't nobody inside the church, was there?"

"No, but that's beside the goddamn point," said Earz. "It's still a shitty thing to do."

"Yeah."

"So the Sheriff, the Highway Patrol, the FBI, and every other kind of motherfucking cop you can think of, hire a fucking bloodhound and that sonovabitch leads 'em straight back to our front door. The cops haul the old man in and they start sweating his ass hard. The old man completely pussys out! He tells 'em that I burned down the colored people's church. Then, the sonovabitch tells 'em that I'm always starting fires around the house and that they ought to take it easy on me 'cause I'm not 'right in the head'... That asshole!"

"Wasn't there nobody you could tell?"

"Hell, no, and I had had my share of run-ins with Johnny Law before, so they was ready to believe any fucking thing he told 'em about me."

"Why didn't you tell the cops that it was your daddy that done it?"

"Well, the old man was the only one bringing in a goddamn paycheck. My momma is disabled and she sure-as-shit couldn't support the family. I wasn't old enough to get a goddamn driver's license, so I couldn't get no fucking job. I got a little brother named Scotty and a little sister named Tena. I reckoned they could all get along a whole helluva lot better without me than they could without the old man. So I kept my mouth shut, took one for the fucking team, and here the hell I am!"

"Man! That sucks, Earz."

"Yeah, it sure does," said Earz. "But, anyways, I didn't want you thinking I was the kinda asshole that would burn down a colored-people's church."

"Okay."

"I'm a completely different kind of asshole!" laughed Earz. "Now, you get your ass out of here before you get caught!"

Ferlin and Sammy met me at the door. "Mr. Birdwell ain't here!" said Sammy. "He left to go work for the Department of Employment Security." Then, noticing Earz, Sammy said, "Hey, Earz!"

"Hey, Kung Fu, Big Man!" called Earz, and hearing our conversation, added, "Birdwell? Yeah, Birdwell split. I always liked Birdwell. He left a pack of smokes laying out on the table one time and I helped myself to couple of 'em. Birdwell never snitched me out, though I'm pretty sure he knew it was me."

"Yeah, we was looking for him," said Sammy.

"You boys better scoot before the screws catch you in here," said Earz. "Y'all will get in a shitload of trouble!"

"Yessir, we'll see you around, Earz," said Ferlin.

"We're gonna race again, Hotdog!" said Sammy, pointing at Earz.

"You take care of yourself," I said.

"Alright! Alright! Alright! You motherfuckers take it slow!" said Earz, grinning ear-to-ear.

We never saw Billy "Earz" Grissom again.

CHAPTER THIRTY-ONE

The warder of men, The worm's destroyer,
Fixed on his hook The head of the ox;
There gaped at the bait The foe of the gods,
The girdler of all The earth beneath.

The Blount Brothers was already waiting for me out in front of Progress House.

"Yessir, are we ready to go?" said Ferlin. "Do we have everything we need? Yessir, after last time, we ain't taking no chances."

Frank Blount held up a wooden stick about four feet long. He had twisted a thick piece of wire around one end to form a U-shaped crook. Slung over his shoulder and tucked under his arm, Frank had a coil of baling twine with a big shiny fishhook tied to the end. Finally, Frank reached into his back pocket, pulled out a stick of Bull's Head Beef Jerky, held it up, and then stuffed it back into his pocket.

"I got an old tow sack out of the barn," said Sammy, holding up a burlap bag. "It ain't got no holes in it."

"Yessir, I got me this machete from the barn," said Ferlin, sliding the blade out of his belt loop and brandishing it for us to see. "Me and Mr. Anderson made it out of a leaf spring from an old Ford truck."

"Is it sharp?" I asked.

Ferlin extended his fist and shaved some hairs off the back of his forearm. "Yessir, it'll do," he said, sliding the machete back into his belt loop. "Now, let's go catch us a bad snake."

We was silent as we hiked down towards the river, each man lost in his own thoughts.

"Scobey!" called Sammy, giggling.

"Dadgummit! Sammy, you crop-dusted me!" I said when the stench hit me. "Something crawled up in you and died!"

"Oh, don't be such a baby!" said Sammy.

Frank Blount led us to a gorge that bottomed out right into the Stones River. I reckon the snakes got bigger and meaner the closer to the river you got. Gray limestone shelves surrounded the pitch-dark pool at the bottom of gorge. In one corner, the water overlapped the craggy ledge and churned down into the river.

As we gathered on the pebbly bank ledge, Frank immediately pointed to the head of snake swimming through the clear black water. Only his head poked above the surface, cutting a V-shaped ripple in the black water as he swam along.

Suddenly, The Serpent arched his back and broke the surface of the pool! Drops of water sparkled across his black scales like little diamonds! The Serpent began coiling hisself up into one big, round circle and his body seemed to stretch longer and longer as he did it! He looked like he could of stretched all the way around the world if he took a notion! Then, face-to-face with his own upturned tail, he began studying it, like he was fixing to strike at it.

Springing into action, Frank tossed me his wooden crook. Then he reached into his back pocket, broke off a piece of Bull's Head Beef Jerky, doubled it up, and speared it onto the fishhook. Then Frank shrugged that coil of baling twine off his shoulder and let it fall to the ground. Using the baited fishhook as a weight, Frank began twirling that twine around-and-around. Frank looked just like Thor in *The Avengers*, twirling around his hammer, Mjolnir.

Then Frank let go of the rope and it shot out like a comet blazing through the sky! The rope formed a perfect arc across the length of the pool, splashing into the water right next to The Serpent's triangular-shaped head! The Serpent instantly struck at the beef jerky before it sank beneath the surface! Frank expertly jerked back on the twine to sink the fishhook deep into The Serpent's jaw!

The Serpent snapped his head around to glare at us on the bank. Then in a flash, he bolted beneath the water and soared toward the bottom of a limestone ledge, trailing the twine rope behind him!

As we watched the coils of twine disappear into the water, Frank deftly grabbed the rope and wrapped a length of it around his clenched fist. Almost instantly, Frank was wrenched off the bank and into the water! We watched helplessly as The Serpent towed Frank behind him, splashing and coughing!

Ferlin Blount leapt off the bank, crashing into the water. Me and Sammy looked at each other and then bailed off right behind him. As we stomped along behind Ferlin, the water splashed up to me and Sammy's chests. Our shoes sank deep into the sandy gravel at the pool's bottom, slowing us down.

By the time we reached Frank, he had found his footing. He was working his way hand-over-hand up the length of the twine. Frank heaved at the rope in a tug-of-war with The Serpent as The Serpent wedged hisself deeper and deeper into a fissure at the bottom of the limestone shelf. Now, no more than three feet away from the rocky ledge, Frank's feet sank through the gravel and reached the solid shale bottom.

Ferlin Blount slid the machete out of his belt, holding it high above his head! Me and Sammy stood ready, holding the burlap sack and the crook over our heads so as to keep them above the water level.

The Serpent began to weaken, and inch by inch, Frank began hauling The Serpent out of the crevice. Then, all of a sudden, the thin shale rock beneath Frank's feet splintered and gave way! Frank's head disappeared beneath the black water! Although a lot of silt and sediment got kicked up, we could still see that Frank had a good hold on the rope and he was still pulling for all he was worth! Air bubbles seeped from between Frank's gritted teeth and exploded on the surface of the water! Frank seemed to be under the water for hours!

Ferlin, Sammy and me stood there frozen, not knowing what to do next. Then without saying a word, Ferlin plunged the machete down into the water, slicing the rope in two!

Frank shot up out of the water! Gasping for air, he looked over at Ferlin like he was ready to kill him. But before The Serpent could disappear into his hidey-hole, Frank grabbed him bare-handed and commenced to pulling for all he was worth. Then, without even taking the time to think about what we was doing, Me, Ferlin, Sammy dropped our equipment and grabbed ahold of The Serpent too.

Now, I never had held a snake before. The Serpent's scales were smooth and slick, but even under the water, they wasn't so slippery that I couldn't keep a good tight grip on him. I could feel The Serpent's muscles tensing underneath his skin and straining against the grip I had on him.

My face was squashed up against Ferlin's back, and his T-shirt was wet and fishy-smelling. Sammy was right behind me, tugging on The Serpent, and screaming some kind of kung-fu yell right in my ear. We all strained against The Serpent, but it was like trying to pull a tree root up out of the ground.

Frank hiked his foot up flat against the limestone ledge to gain more traction. Luckily, he had selected a worn-out pair of Chuck Taylor All-Stars for this expedition. His tenni'shoe was caked with sand and muck and it made a muddy footprint against the pale gray limestone. Even crowded in behind Ferlin, I could see Frank's face turning purple from the strain. Above his spectacles, the veins had popped out on Frank's forehead. Frank gave a mighty heave and The Serpent broke loose!

All four of us splashed backward into the cold water! I bet we was a sight to see, thrashing around, struggling to get back on our feet, each man trying to get his head back above water.

When I reached the surface, I rubbed the stinging water out of my eyes and then I stood stock-still.

The Serpent's slitted eyes was locked onto me and they looked as big as dinner plates. The twine was still dangling out the side of his mouth, with the severed end floating around on the surface of the water. The Serpent's forked tongue licked his lips like he was fixing to eat me. Even if you are invulnerable to snake bites, it was a scary thing!

The Serpent slowly reared his head back, getting ready to pounce. The water around my waist turned warm as I peed on myself. Then, I felt my *Possum Mode* coming up on me ...

The Serpent sprung!

But before The Serpent could reach me, Frank Blount snatched up the end of that twine and jerked The Serpent's head back! I swear I felt The Serpent's tongue flick the end of my nose before Frank snapped him back! And when I looked up, Frank had caught that Serpent's head with his free hand! I am here to tell you that Frank Blount had caught The Serpent right behind his jawbones!

Now, if you are going to handle a poisonous snake, that right there is exactly the right place to do it. If you put just a little bit of pressure right behind the hinges where the snake's upper jaw meets his lower jaw, then he can't bite down. And he can't bite you.

The Serpent thrashed and splashed around in the water, but there wasn't nothing he could do. Frank had a good hold on his head and he couldn't bite nobody. The Serpent finally just give up and started coiling hisself around Frank's body like he was gonna squeeze him like a python. But Frank didn't pay that no mind, he was already working to extricate the fishhook out of The Serpent's mouth. Keeping a dadgum-good hold behind The Serpent's jawbones, Frank took his other hand and reached into the front pocket of his britches. Taking out a small pair of pliers, Frank snipped the fishhook in two. Then, he gently removed each part of the fishhook without doing any more damage to the insides of The Serpent's mouth. It was close work. The twine dropped out the side of The Serpent's mouth and floated down to the corner of the pool. If The Serpent was thankful at all, he didn't let on. He just kept on trying to squeeze Frank.

My *Possum Mode* had come and gone so fast, I didn't even lose consciousness. I just stood there kinda dazed. Frank waggled his finger at me for the wooden crook I had been carrying for him. I had dropped it in all of the commotion. Drawing in a deep breath, I squatted back down underneath the water and felt around for the crook. It was right beside my foot. I stood back up again, squeezed the yucky water out of my nose, and handed the crook over to Frank.

Frank placed The Serpent's neck into the U-shaped bend of wire at the end of the crook. The fit wasn't too tight, but The Serpent couldn't slide his head backwards out of it. Then Frank carefully extended the crook, with The Serpent's head, away from all of us. Frank lifted The Serpent's midsection and draped it over his shoulder. A right smart of The Serpent's body was still dangling in the water. There ain't no telling how long he was! The light bounced off his shiny black scales like little mirrors and he practically glowed! The Serpent had just a small yellowy patch running along his belly. He didn't have that nice checkerboard pattern on his belly like Charlotte had had.

"Yessir, why don't we wade down to the shallow end of the creek?" said Ferlin.

I got to feeling a lot more comfortable when we waded down to where the water only come up to our knees. I couldn't swim and I don't think Sammy could neither. Even in the knee-deep water, The Serpent's tail still hung below the surface. How long was he?

"Yessir, Sammy, you still got that tow sack?" said Ferlin.

"Got it right here," Sammy said, holding up the burlap sack. Water was dripping out of the bottom of it.

"Yessir, now, are you absolutely sure there ain't no holes in it?"

"'One should not seek perfection in a changing world,'" said Sammy, "But there ain't no holes in it. Not even a ripped thread."

"Frank, is the snake ready to get put in the sack?" Ferlin asked.

Frank, who was watching The Serpent twist hisself around the wooden stick, nodded his head.

"Yessir, Sammy, open 'er up good and wide," said Ferlin.

Frank carefully lowered The Serpent's head, which was still draped in the wire bend of the crook, down into the burlap bag.

Like lightning, The Serpent bolted into the sack and coiled hisself up at the bottom. I reckon he was eager to get shet of us! The Serpent was so heavy inside the bag, Sammy almost dropped the whole thing! Sammy instantly snapped the top of the sack closed. Ferlin helped him twist the top of the sack good and tight so The Serpent couldn't get out.

The piece of twine that Frank had cut out of The Serpent's mouth was floating around my knees. "Here's a piece of twine to tie it up good and tight," I said, picking it up and handing it to Ferlin.

Once we had The Serpent locked up good and tight, we stopped to catch our breath. We was all huffing and puffing, and out of breath, Everybody except Frank. Frank was just calmly standing there, examining his workmanship on where he had fixed the wire crook onto that wooden stick. I 'magine he was considering ways to improve his design.

When we had caught our breath and our hands wasn't shaking no more, Ferlin Blount stood up. "Yessir!" he said, "We got us an appointment with a killer hog."

CHAPTER THIRTY-TWO

Then the dreadful dragon advanced him, and came in the wind like a falcon, giving great strokes to the boar; and the boar hit him again with his grisly tusks, that his breast was all bloody, and that the hot blood made all the sea red of his blood.

"This ol' snake is getting kinda heavy," Sammy said, as we tromped back toward the hog barn. Sammy was holding the sack at arm's length so that The Serpent couldn't push one of his fangs through the weave of the burlap and stick him.

"Yessir! Give 'im here, Sammy," Ferlin said, as Sammy handed over the bag. "I reckon I can carry him for a little while."

"We ought to give him a name," I said.

Nobody responded.

"We could call him 'Fin Fang Foom.'"

"What's a 'Fin Fang Foom?'" said Sammy.

"He's kind of a dragon monster in Marvel Comics," I said. "This kid in China awakened Fin Fang Foom in his secret chamber, and then he sicced him on the Communists."

"'Fin Fang Foom' is dumb and hard to say," said Sammy.

"Well, then, what about Kaa, like the snake in the *Jungle Book?*" I said. "Remember when Mr. Anderson took us all to go see that?"

"Nah, that was a mean snake, he tried to eat that little boy," said Sammy. "This here's a good snake."

I tried to think of some more names for The Serpent as we walked along.

Sammy asked Ferlin, "Ferlin, you reckon after this snake gets done biting The Mulefoot, we can take him back to the creek?"

"Yessir," Ferlin said, "If we can ever catch him back up again, we oughta be able to put him right back where we found him."

"Good!" said Sammy. "That's what I wanna do."

We all took turns lugging the burlap sack back to the hog pens, with Ferlin and Frank taking the longest turns. The Serpent really was pretty heavy.

"I ain't too excited about all this killing business," Sammy said. "'All tremble at violence; all fear death. Putting oneself in the place of another, one should not kill nor cause another to kill.'"

"We all know how you feel about killing, Sammy," I said. "You already done more than your share. Why don't you head on back to Progress House? Nobody'll think a thing!"

"No, I reckon I better see this through," Sammy said.

Nobody said nothing as we hiked back up the hill. A cool breeze was blowing, and it dried out our damp clothes pretty quick. My shoes and socks was still soaked though and it felt like I might be getting a blister on my heel.

By the time we reached The Mulefoot's pen, the sky was an inky gray. Them cool breezes had blowed in black, rolling clouds and they completely blocked out the noonday sun. It smelt like a rainstorm was coming in. By then, I was carrying the burlap sack that was holding The Serpent. As we stood around a fencepost outside The Mulefoot's pen, nobody knew exactly what to say or do.

Finally, Ferlin said, "Yessir, it's blowing up a storm. We better get to work before it gets here." Looking down at the sack, he said, "Yessir, Delphus, you want me to do it?"

"No, that's okay, Ferlin," I said. "The CIA assigned me this mission and I roped you boys into helping me, but I reckon I oughta be the one that does it." I climbed up a few rails of the hog panel fence like it was a ladder. I was right beside a wooden fencepost so my weight didn't bend down the wire too much. "You could help steady me up here though."

"Yessir," Ferlin said, as he hooked his thumbs through the belt loops on either side of my britches.

A crack of thunder exploded in the skies behind us. "Come on out here, you Godforsaken Abomination Unto The Lord!" I yelled at The Mulefoot's house. "You are a plague on this Earth and we are here to put an end to you!"

The Mulefoot lunged out the door of his oak-board shack and spotted us by the fence. He reared back his head and a furious roar blasted from his slobbery jaws! The Mulefoot charged at us! With each leap, his shiny black hooves pounded the ground like sledgehammers and every blow echoed through our chests! A cloud of kicked-up grass and clumps of dirt swarmed in his wake!

The Mulefoot bowed his neck and kept on a-charging! He looked like he was fixing to crash through the fence at us, fencepost and all! My heart was pounding in my ears and I felt the *Possum Mode* coming on! I started grabbing at Ferlin's wrist to let me down 'cause I decided right then and there to dump that Serpent on the ground and run for my life!

But The Mulefoot halted his charge and pulled up just short of the fence, showering us with dirt and grass. Somehow, The Mulefoot seemed to know that it was me who had issued the challenge. Lazily, he leaned back his massive head and his red bloodshot eyes bored right into mine. The Mulefoot gave a contemptuous snort that sprayed stinking, white slobber over all of us!

"Alright, big boy," I said, from my perch on the fence. "I got something for you." With my free hand, I grabbed a fistful of loose burlap in the bottom corner of the bag that held The Serpent. "This is for Edmund Alexander Anderson!" I hollered and I heaved that bag at The Mulefoot with all my might and then I immediately yanked back hard on the corner of the bag! The Serpent slingshotted out of the burlap sack!

The Serpent was a bolt of black lightning as he sliced through the air! His pale fangs sank deep into the sleek black hide of The Mulefoot's neck! The Mulefoot bellered with rage! Keeping his fangs still buried in

The Mulefoot's neck, The Serpent coiled hisself up into a huge pile on top of The Mulefoot's back, resting just between his shoulders.

Over and over again, The Mulefoot reared back onto his hind legs and then smashed his front hooves onto the ground, trying to dislodge The Serpent. The Mulefoot's terrible stomps made the ground tremble! His monstrous head jerked left-and-right, as he struggled to snatch The Serpent in his mighty jaws! But The Serpent stayed on top of The Mulefoot's back, keeping his fangs sunk firmly into The Mulefoot's powerful neck. The Serpent was riding The Mulefoot like a bronco buster!

Frustrated, The Mulefoot lurched his mammoth frame into a kind of barrel roll. It was like watching a car wreck in slow motion, only it was just three feet away from you! The Mulefoot slammed down onto his side and it jarred the earth! Sammy Blount was knocked off his feet! I would of fell off the fence if Ferlin hadn't been holding me steady.

The Mulefoot violently wallowed around on his back to-and-fro, trying to crush The Serpent into a pancake! But The Serpent darted out from under The Mulefoot's massive bulk just in time! He zigzagged through the grass until he was good and clear of The Mulefoot's hysterical thrashing around.

"Well, I don't reckon Fin Fang Foom's got any more fight left in him," I said.

"Yessir, after that long a bite, I can't imagine he's got any venom left!" said Ferlin.

Almost like he understood what we said, and felt insulted by it, The Serpent stopped dead in his tracks! He raised his head about a foot above the ground, and then out of the corner of his slitted eye, he shot an angry glance at me and Ferlin. Then, The Serpent methodically coiled hisself up into a circle and faced back toward The Mulefoot.

The Mulefoot was back on his feet, his shiny black hide now flecked with pale gray dust. Thunder crackled again in the sky and a gust of cold wind blew past us. As the wind swept the dust off The Mulefoot, he appeared to be on fire and smoke was rising up off him.

For a moment, their eyes locked on each other.

The Serpent sprang toward The Mulefoot, keeping his head high as he raced along the ground! When he reached The Mulefoot, The Serpent leapt like an arrow shot out of a bow! He just barely missed The Mulefoot's fiery red eye! The Mulefoot's ivory teeth snapped after The Serpent, but didn't connect! Then, twice in rapid succession, The Serpent struck at The Mulefoot's snout, but didn't sink in his fangs! The Mulefoot leaned back on his hind legs and roared at The Serpent! You could hear the air furiously rushing in-and-out of The Mulefoot's flared nostrils.

Why didn't The Serpent quit? He had to know that he had injected all the venom he had into The Mulefoot and it wasn't showing no signs of taking effect yet.

But The Serpent struck again, this time aiming for The Mulefoot's snout! It was a bad move! The Mulefoot was ready for him. His powerful jaws snapped down on The Serpent's head like a bear trap! With a quick jerk of his savage head, The Mulefoot snapped The Serpent up into the air like he was cracking a whip! The Serpent's body dropped to the ground with a dull thud. He did not move.

A thunderclap exploded behind us and the wind picked up. The Serpent began to gingerly slither away from The Mulefoot. Clearly, the battle was over for him.

And then for some reason, The Serpent made one last strike at The Mulefoot's fierce red eye! But The Serpent was sluggish now and The Mulefoot caught him easily. With his head clamped in The Mulefoot's viselike jaws, The Serpent writhed in the grass. The Mulefoot's front hoof crashed down onto The Serpent's body like an axe! The blow mangled The Serpent's skin and bright red blood pooled up around The Mulefoot's gleaming black hoof.

With a mighty wrench of his neck, the Mulefoot ripped The Serpent's head off! An explosion of blood erupted from The Serpent's body, showering us all in specks of red! They kinda stung as they hit your skin! My pale arms looked like I had the measles.

The Serpent's now-lifeless body contorted rhythmically in the dust. And then, as calm as you please, The Mulefoot laid down on his fat belly and started devouring The Serpent, one bite at a time.

A cold, fierce breeze wind blew over us, and with a crack of thunder, the sky opened up and poured down the rain! Although the rain was chilling to the bone, none of us hurried back to Progress House. We let the cold rain wash The Serpent's blood off our faces and our hands and our clothes.

"That was a horrible thing to watch," murmured Sammy Blount.

CHAPTER THIRTY-THREE

I know you thought him dead. He was. But he is no longer. How could any of us know that Mistress Death would resurrect this Monster?

I woke up the next day and I felt like a ton of weight had been lifted up off of my shoulders. There wasn't a cloud in the sky and the warm sun beamed down on my face as I rushed to the hog pens. The Mulefoot monster was dead and every man, woman, and child in America was safe! I was a hero! 'Course, nobody knew that I was a hero, but I reckon that's all part of working for the CIA!

First, I visited the battleground where The Serpent and The Mulefoot had waged their momentous battle. The overnight rainstorms had washed the battlefield clean. No bloodstains marked the spot where The Serpent got ripped to shreds. I squatted down and looked around in the dirt to see if there was anything left of him. I couldn't find a single scale. It was like the battle had never happened. Where The Mulefoot's sharp hooves had ripped into the ground, now it seemed there wasn't a single blade of grass out of place.

I stood up and thought about The Serpent for a minute. I felt sorry for him. The Serpent was a brave Water Moccasin who had sacrificed his life to save everybody in America from liver cancer. And now, there wasn't a lick of evidence that he had ever existed. I looked around for a rock, or maybe even just a dandelion, that I could use to mark the spot where The Serpent had died, but I couldn't find a thing.

Finally, I just broke a piece of wood off the fencepost and jabbed it into the ground. Maybe later, I could find me a big rock and set it right here. I bet Frank Blount could make me some kinda tool that I could use to chisel a cross, or maybe his name, onto the rock.

But I needed to focus on the Mission. I had to make sure The Mulefoot was dead. "Confirming the kill" is what we call it in the CIA. The Serpent's fangs had been buried in The Mulefoot's neck for at least five full minutes, pumping deadly venom into his bloodstream that whole time. There's no way The Mulefoot could have survived that, even at his massive size.

****

The Operation commenced at twelve-hundred hours, Zulu time. I moved stealthily around the corner of the fence and proceeded to the large bodock tree situated behind The Asset's oak-wood domicile. As I approached the rear of The Asset's dwelling, I observed approximately two-dozen hedge apples that had fallen onto the ground from an overhanging limb of the aforementioned bodock tree. I carefully inspected each hedge apple, evaluating them for operational suitability. I designated three hedge apples, and one alternate. The selected hedge apples were the approximate diameter of a regulation-size softball and all were in varying degrees of mushiness.

Next, I manually detached a thorn, approximately six inches in length, from a limb of the bodock tree, a species known for its needle-sharp thorns. Employing surgical precision, I pricked the tip of my left index finger with the thorn and immediately drew blood. This procedure indicated that the thorn would be the ideal instrument for confirmatory prodding.

Having requisitioned the necessary materiel, at twelve-fifteen hours, Zulu time, I initiated the Auditory Engagement Phase of the Operation. Pitching my voice at 90 to 120 decibels, I verbally accosted The Asset, stating, "Come on out here, you big fart head! I got another snake for you to fight!" This patent falsehood was merely an attempt to arouse The Asset to determine if he had, in fact, been conclusively abrogated.

The Asset did not exit the domicile as instructed and no audible sound could be detected emanating from within the structure. Having achieved the intermediary objective, I resolved to intensify the Auditory Engagement Phase with the introduction of a Percussive Component.

Arming myself with one of the pre-selected hedge apples, I forcefully launched the projectile in the direction of The Asset's dwelling. Sortie Number One met with only limited success: the hedge apple missed the shack completely.

Taking the operational setback in stride, I prepared for Sortie Number Two. I rotated my arm and shoulder repeatedly, loosening them up to ensure a more accurate throw. Arming myself with the second of the pre-selected hedge apples, at twelve-seventeen hours, Zulu time, I launched Sortie Number Two. I observed said hedge apple explode as it made contact with the oaken surface of The Asset's domicile. The explosion of Hedge Apple No. 2 was accompanied by a report that should have reverberated within the interior walls of The Asset's dwelling house.

Again, The Asset did not emerge from the structure and no detectible sound emanated from inside.

Having achieved the second intermediary objective, I escalated the Operation to the Tactile Engagement Phase at twelve-twenty hours, Zulu time.

I readily observed that the fence was too high for me to negotiate by either of the regulation "high vault" or "low vault" techniques. Accordingly, I employed the non-regulation "ladder maneuver" to effect my ingress, opting to climb the fence as one would climb the rungs of a ladder. My point of entry was at the interstices of the prefabricated fence panels, i.e. a fencepost.

Achieving the apex of the fence, I dropped to the ground on the other side, employing the regulation "tuck-and-roll" maneuver. Having now crossed into the free-fire zone, I stealthily approached The Asset's domicile.

At twelve-twenty-one hours, Zulu time, I made visual contact with The Asset. Maintaining a discreet observational distance of fifteen feet, I observed The Asset's rear legs and hindquarters through the entrance of his dwelling place. The Asset appeared to be in a lying posture, facing the interior wall. Listening intently, I was unable to detect any audible sounds issuing from The Asset that are normally indicative of respiration.

At twelve-twenty-two hours, Zulu time, I initiated what would be the final leg of the Operation, the Tactile Confirmation Phase. I had held the third of the pre-selected hedge apples in reserve for the final sortie. The third hedge apple exhibited the most advanced stage of mushiness, but still maintained structural integrity. Taking careful aim, I forcibly propelled the hedge apple at The Asset. The projectile made contact with the surface of The Asset's left rear hindquarter with a violent splat. The hedge apple's pale green innards oozed down The Asset's buttocks.

No discernible motion or audible sound could be detected coming from The Asset.

At twelve-twenty-three hours, Zulu time, I prepared myself for the realization of the Operation's Ultimate Objective: to conclusively determine whether The Asset had been fully neutralized. Reaching into my back pocket, I retrieved the pre-selected bodock thorn. Moving noiselessly and deliberately, I crossed the distance to the entrance of The Asset's dwelling. Kneeling down, I quickly plunged the needle-sharp bodock thorn into the left buttock of The Asset.

The Asset roared! His roars echoed within the walls of his oak-board shack!

At twelve-twenty-four hours, Zulu time, the Operation was aborted and the Operator lost complete urinary continence.

****

I could feel the *Possum Mode* coming up on me and I knew I had to get back over that fence! All that pee was making my britches feel as heavy as concrete. So I grabbed me a big handful of jeans right ‘round my straddle and made a bee-line straight for the fence!

The Mulefoot's hog house was just wide enough inside to let him turn completely around in a circle, but there wasn't much room to spare. He couldn't just spin hisself around on a dime, he had to maneuver a little bit. So I took full advantage of them precious seconds that The Mulefoot was using to get hisself turned around. By the time The

Mulefoot came clambering out the door, I was half-way to the fence. I was keeping a tight grip on my wet jeans 'cause I didn't want them to drop to my ankles and trip me up.

I could hear The Mulefoot's hooves pounding the ground as he closed the distance between us. I could hear his grunts of exertion as he pushed hisself to catch me. I didn't look behind me 'cause I knew that would just slow me down.

As I reached the fence, I could feel the pressure of his heavy breaths on my back. I let go of my wet britches so I could use both hands to scramble up the fence. They immediately dropped right down to my ankles.

As I scrambled over the top of the fence wire, The Mulefoot's savage white teeth clamped down onto my jeans right between my ankles! He had hisself a good hold and he started pulling me back over to his side of the fence. He was stretching me out like a rubber band, but I was holding on to the top fence wire for dear life! I started kicking and wiggling my feet trying to slip out my britches. When I finally kicked them off, it catapulted me back over the top of the fence!

Sprawled out on the ground outside the fence, I looked down to assess the damage. I still had my drawers on, but I had lost my blue jeans and a shoe in the process. I lifted up my head and saw The Mulefoot prancing across his pen, waving my britches around like they was some kind of flag. "How are you still alive?" I thought to myself.[69] I could feel the *Possum Mode* coming on hard now. I looked over at the wooden stob I had stuck into the ground to mark The Serpent's gravesite. I reckon he had died for nothing.

Possum Mode in 3...2...1

---

[69] All evidence suggests that "The Serpent" snake (Fin Fang Foom) was, in fact, a venomous Water Moccasin (*Agkistrodon piscivorus)*, unlike the earlier "Charlotte" snake, which was clearly a non-venomous Diamondback Water Snake (*Nerodia rhombifer)*

However, pigs are largely immune to snakebites because their bodies are covered with a thick layer of adipose (fat) tissue. This adipose layer has minimal vascularization (blood vessels). Accordingly, any venom that is injected underneath the pig's skin does not seep into the bloodstream.

CHAPTER THIRTY-FOUR

When his investigation hits a brick wall, The Batman returns to the shadowy night in search of clues...

"Delphus, you lose your britches?" Sammy Blount said, nudging me awake with the toe of his shoe.

"Huh? Yeah," I said, sitting up. "The Mulefoot ripped 'em right off of me."

"He didn't try no 'monkey business' on you, did he?"

"No, he did not!"

"Yessir, also looks like you also threw a shoe," said Ferlin Blount.

"Yeah, I kicked it off when I was wiggling out of my britches."

"Yessir," said Ferlin, "The Mulefoot didn't bite you, did he?"

"Naw, I got over the fence just in time," I said. "Ain't y'all even surprised that monster's still alive?"

"Nossir, not really," said Ferlin. "Anything that big and mean, takes a whole lot to kill it."

"'There must be Evil in the World,'" said Sammy, "'So that Good can prove its purity above it.'"

Frank Blount had been walking around the outside of The Mulefoot's fence. He walked back up to us, looked at Ferlin, and shook his head.

"Nossir, Frank couldn't find your britches, nor your missing shoe, neither," said Ferlin. "Yessir, looks like The Mulefoot ate 'em up, zipper, buttons and all."

"Well, I'm just lucky The Mulefoot didn't sink his cancer teeth into me," I said, climbing up off the ground. "I reckon I'll walk back to Progress House, as is."

"Yessir, you know, Delphus, in your current state, you ain't exactly modest," said Ferlin. "You're liable to scare the womenfolk and the hogs too, for that matter. Yessir, I could give you my T-shirt and you could stretch out the neck hole and make yourself a little skirt."

"I ain't wearing no skirt."

"You could call it a kilt, if that would make you feel better," said Sammy.

"I ain't wearing no 'kilt' neither!" I said. "I'll just run on back to Progress House, stay off the main path, and hide if I see any girls coming."

I felt a little lopsided as I run back to Progress House, since I didn't have but one shoe, but it took my mind off of the fact that I wasn't wearing no britches. I made it back without running into no girls or hogs.

That night, I couldn't sleep at all because I kept thinking about The Mulefoot and what I was gonna do about him. The clock was ticking! How long would it be before The Mulefoot spread his liver fluke disease out into the world? I needed to get my mind off him for a while. I thought about reading something, but I was fresh out of books to read.

I wanted another Conan the Barbarian book. I know they made a bunch of 'em. In this last story I read, Conan had just finished up a battle with a bunch of guys who had claws for hands. He was all cut up and covered in blood and one of his ears was half tore off. So he says to the heroine, "Come on over here, baby, and give me a big kiss!" And then he swoops her up off her feet in one massive arm and lays a big smackeroo on her! Dang, ol' Conan was cool!

I decided to go out on patrol. I scooped up my book bag. I figured I might pay a visit to the Dempster Dumpster behind the Blind School. Maybe there was another Conan book in there.

I hiked over to the Blind School and slipped right under the metal fence. The big security light was so bright, I didn't need no flashlight. I sneaked over to the green Dempster Dumpster and somersaulted right in. The books in there was knee-deep! The first book that caught my eye was a red-and-white hardback that had a dejected-looking cougar on the front of it. He had a knot tied in his tail! But what really caught my eye was the author – Robert E. Howard! That's the guy who writes Conan! But this book wasn't about no musclemen sword fighting, it was funny cowboy stories[70]. After reading the first couple of pages, I knew it was bound to be good, so I immediately stuffed it down into my book bag!

And then, about six-inches deep into the pile, a white paperback book locked down on me like a tractor beam! The top of the book read *Conan the Adventurer* and it had a cover on it like I hadn't never seen before! It was a painting of ol' Conan standing on a pile of dead guys that he had just wiped out. He had just freed a beautiful slave girl from them boys and now she was setting on the ground clutching onto Conan's leg for dear life. Conan looked exactly like I pictured him in my head! He wasn't no pretty boy. He looked tough as nails and he had big scars on his arms and his face from all the fighting he had done. Even his muscles had muscles! I carefully placed *Conan the Adventurer* down into my book bag to make sure that front cover didn't get bent[71].

And then I locked in on another book. It was a tan hardback with a caveman drawing of a wild prehistoric boar on it. The boar was reared up on his hind legs and his snout was too long to be a regular modern-day hog. This book was called *Swine Production in Temperate and Tropical Environments.*[72] If there ever was a book that could help me out with my Mulefoot problem, this was it! I flipped through it. It

---

70 Howard, Robert E. *A Gent from Bear Creek.* West Kingston, RI: Donald M. Grant, Publisher, Inc., 1966.

71 Howard, Robert E. and L. Sprague de Camp. *Conan the Adventurer.* New York: Lancer Books, 1966. (The cover illustration was painted by noted fantasy artist Frank Frazetta [1928-2010]. The Narrator's reaction to the cover was typical of many adolescent boys in the late 1960's and early 1970's)

72 Pond, Wilson G., and J.H. Maner. *Swine Production in Temperate and Tropical Environments.* San Francisco: W.H. Freeman and Company, 1974.

had everything you could ever want to know about raising pigs! Mr. Anderson would of loved this book! There was stuff in there about breeding and nutrition and vitamins. Surely, there had to be something in there about what it would take to kill a 600-pound boar! I stuffed *Swine Production in Temperate and Tropical Environments* right down in my book bag, but I was careful not to mess up the cover of *Conan the Adventurer*.

I had to get back to Progress House and read this book right now! Surely, this swine production book had the answer to all my problems! All I had to do was find it. I dove out of the Dempster Dumpster and did three tuck-and-rolls as I hit the ground. I was under that metal fence like sauce through a goose!

As I jogged back to Progress House, I thought to myself, "Well, Agent St. John sure came through for me! He left me a book that'll show me all about how to take out The Mulefoot, plus two Robert E. Howard books."

But then I thought, "How did he know them snakes wasn't gonna do the trick?" I just found out myself earlier this morning that Fin Fang Foom didn't kill The Mulefoot. How could the CIA get that *Swine Production* book into the Dempster Dumpster so fast? St. John said the CIA had been monitoring my activities. Just how closely was they "monitoring" me? Reckon they had "bugs" in me and Ferlin's room?

Then I realized I hadn't visited that Dempster Dumpster in several weeks. Them books must of been dropped in there three or four weeks ago! Agent St. John had probably meant for me to use that *Swine Production* book in my Mission all along. Wonder why he didn't just give it to me? I bet it was some kind of test of my resourcefulness as a CIA Agent!

When I got back to Progress House, I slid off my tenni'shoes and climbed into bed. I wanted to dive right into the *Swine Production in Temperate and Tropical Environments* as soon as I could, so I used a flashlight to read it. I didn't want to wake up Ferlin.

The first thing I thought about was salt. Mr. Anderson always said you could kill a pig if you give him too much salt. But according to the *Swine Production* book on page 394, we would have to load The

Mulefoot up on salt, then we would have to haul off and deprive him of any water to drink. That sounded like a long, drawn-out process that would take a lot longer than a weekend, which was all the time we'd have without Phillips watching our every move. Plus, Mr. Anderson also said that a hog was too smart, he generally wouldn't eat enough salt to kill him, unless he had to.

As I flipped through the pages of the book, I found an envelope pasted inside the back cover like they have in library books. Folded up inside was a four–page pamphlet. Its pages had turned yellow the way a comic book page will turn if you don't keep it out of the sunlight. Across the top it read, "UNITED STATES, DEPARTMENT OF AGRICULTURE, DEPARTMENT CIRCULAR 283," and then, "LIVESTOCK POSIONING BY COCKLEBUR.[73]"

The circular began, "For many years there have been persistent reports of the poisoning of livestock, more especially swine, by cockleburs. These reports have come to the Department of Agriculture in general correspondence and in special reports from field inspectors." Then the circular went on, "Experimental feedings made on swine, cattle, and sheep showed conclusively that the plant is poisonous to all those animals.[74]"

Bingo!

---

[73] Marsh, C. Dwight, G.C. Roe and A.B. Clawson. "Livestock Poisoning by Cocklebur." *Department Circular 283, U. S. Dept. of Agriculture.* Washington, D.C.: Government Printing Office, 1923

[74] Marsh, C. Dwight, G.C. Roe and A.B. Clawson. "Livestock Poisoning by Cocklebur." *Id* at p. 1.

CHAPTER THIRTY-FIVE

... All idealisation makes life poorer. To beautify it is to take away its character of complexity—it is to destroy it. Leave that to the moralists, my boy. History is made by men, but they do not make it in their heads.

"Delphus, I still think you just dreamed up that CIA agent," said Sammy Blount.

It was another meeting of The Mulefoot Assassination League. Everybody was asleep on C-Wing except for me and the Blount Brothers. I had dug out the big white candle again and the orange glow shined on our faces. The rest of the room danced in shadows.

"But I also think that killing that evil Mulefoot is the fastest way to get rid of that skunk Phillips," Sammy continued. "I don't want that bastard trying no 'monkey business' on Skippy Dean or none of them other little boys. We can't be around to watch them all the time, so Phillips has got to go!"

"You're absolutely right," I said. "And killing The Mulefoot is fastest way to get rid of him."

Frank Blount slid his index finger across his throat mimicking a knife cut.

"If there was only some way I could get up under The Mulefoot and face his chest," said Sammy, "Then I could stop his heart with the *dim mak*[75]."

"You mastered the Quivering Palm Technique?"

"Yeah, I'm pretty sure I have," said Sammy, "Something like that is kinda hard to practice."

"Yessir, I think Count Dante is a big phony," said Ferlin.

"And yet," said Sammy, "I have mastered the *dim mak*," And then Sammy did that thing where he balled his right hand up into a fist and then placed the fist into the palm of his left hand and closed the fingers down over the fist. He made a slight bow with his head.

"Yessir, well then, we could dig us a hole in the ground, deep enough to hold Sammy," said Ferlin. "Then we could lower Sammy down in the hole and lure The Mulefoot to come stand over it. Yessir, then Sammy could pop up out of the hole and put the *dim mak* on him and explode his heart!

"Be hard to dig a deep-enough hole without Phillips catching us," I said. "Also, it'd be hard to trick The Mulefoot into standing right exactly over the hole."

"Yessir," said Ferlin, nodding his head. "That's true."

"It's a good plan, Ferlin, but I think I have a better one."

"What's that?" said Sammy.

"We poison The Mulefoot."

"Poison is a dishonorable weapon," said Sammy. "Only ninjas use it."

"Well, we would be doing a dishonorable thing for an honorable purpose," I said. "Like that man in your burning house story."

"Okay," said Sammy, nodding his head, "But what are you gonna poison him with?"

"Cocklebur plants."

---

75 *Dim mak,* (or touch of death, quivering palm, vibrating palm) refers to a legendary Chinese martial arts technique. *Dim mak* is reputed to cause a lethal disruption of heart rhythm by applying minimal force to specific pressure points on the opponent's body. *Dim mak* was first popularized in Western culture by Count Raphael Dante in 1960's American comic books advertisements. (*see*, Chapter Nine, FN. 2)

"Yessir, they's a ton of cockleburries around Red Creek."

"You bet there is," I said.

"How do you think we can get The Mulefoot to eat cockleburs?" said Sammy. "Them things are all scratchy, they'll hurt his throat. He won't never eat enough to poison him."

"Well, it ain't the actual cockleburs that The Mulefoot has to eat," I said. "It's the cocklebur plants. See? I found this Department of Agriculture Circular and it talks about cockleburs being poisonous to hogs." I pulled the circular out of my back pocket and handed it over to Ferlin.

"Yessir, looks like cockleburries will do the trick," said Ferlin, craning his head back to study the circular through the lower section of his eyeglass lenses.

"This is the kind we need right here," I said, pointing to the picture on page three, "Them little two-leaf seedlings. They look like little T's."

"Yessir, it says the plants get bitter-tasting when they grow bigger." Ferlin handed the circular over to Sammy. Frank looked over Sammy's shoulder. They both leaned their heads back to peer through their spectacles like Ferlin had done.

"It says here," said Sammy, "'A pig weighing 50 pounds would be poisoned by about 12 ounces of the green plant.' Then how much would it take to poison a 600-pound hog, Ferlin?"

"Yessir, that would be 144 ounces."

"How many pounds is that?"

"Yessir, that would be ..." Ferlin looked up at the ceiling and then said, "Nine pounds."

"That's a whole lot of cocklebur plants," said Sammy.

"But think about it, Sammy, a five-pound sack of flour ain't that big."

"But flour is heavier than these plants'll be."

"Not if we smush 'em down real good," I said.

"Yessir, they's a ton of cockleburries around Red Creek," repeated Ferlin.

"Well, then, count me in," said Sammy and he extended his fist out between us. Then we all placed our hands on top of his, sealing the deal.

Frank pinched the wick of the candle, extinguishing its flame, and Ferlin flipped on the overhead light. When he did, we saw Skippy Dean standing in the doorway, clutching his teddy bear, Red. Skippy Dean's eyes were as big as saucers and his bottom lip was quivering.

"What's the matter, Skippy Dean?" Sammy said, kneeling down.

"I-I-I heard y'all talking about k-k-k-killing, and poi-poi-poisons and explo-plod-plod-ploding hearts, and it sc-sc-scared me."

"Oh, we was just playing a game, Skippy Dean," I said. "It's just pretend. There ain't nothing to be scared of."

"I'll take him back to his room," Sammy said, and he walked Skippy Dean back down the hall.

Ferlin put the big birthday candle back in the closet and turned out the light. I took off my shirt and britches and then walked over to the window. The security light had gone out in the back yard and it was pitch black outside. I pressed my forehead up against the windowpane and it felt cool. So I rolled my whole face up against it, side-to-side, like I was rolling a fingerprint. When I leaned back, the imprint on the glass looked like a skull screaming in terror. "You know, Skippy Dean was right," I said, "What we're doing is pretty cold-blooded."

Ferlin's only response was a deep, relaxed snore. He had drifted off to sleep.

CHAPTER THIRTY-SIX

But as for you, turn you, and take your journey into the wilderness by the way of the Red Sea.

Red Creek was just down from the hog barn. Red Creek wasn't actually a creek. Although it was long and narrow, the water didn't flow at all. Depending on whether or not the Dam[76] was generating, sometimes the water level would be up high and sometimes it would be low. We called it Red Creek because the only thing that could live in that putrid water was some kind of algae that was the color of a rusty nail. Now, a little bit of lime-green algae did live around the edges, but the whole creek was pretty much that rusty red color. Here and there, jagged gray tree stumps poked up through the red muck.

The area around Red Creek did have one thing though, and that was plenty of cockleburs. That was the main reason we shied away from Red Creek. If you just walked by to pitch a rock into it, you'd have to spend a dadgum hour pulling them cockleburs off of your clothes.

We started early that day 'cause it was gonna be a hot one. I thought about wearing short britches, but I knew them cockleburs would eat my legs up! Frank Blount was wearing his rubber work boots 'cause he didn't want to mess up his Chuck Taylor tenni'shoes.

---

[76] J. Percy Priest Dam is a hydroelectric dam located at river mile 6.8 of the Stones River. Completed in 1968, it is named in honor of J. Percy Priest (1900-1956), a Congressman from Tennessee.

Ferlin Blount reached down and pulled a cocklebur seedling out of the ground and held it up for all of us to look at. “Yessir, this right here is what we need, fellers,” said Ferlin. “It looks kinda like a whirlybird[77] off of a maple tree. Yessir, it’s got a little bud here in the middle and then it’s got these two skinny leaves sticking out on each side.”

I pulled U.S.D.A. Circular Number 283 out of my back pocket and held up the picture for emphasis.

“Yessir, this ‘un here is about the size of a quarter and that’s exactly the size we need,” said Ferlin. “Yessir, any bigger than that and they ain’t poisonous a’tall. Plus, they get bitter-tasting and The Mulefoot won’t eat ’em. We gotta collect nine pounds of these things today. Yessir, let’s get to work.”

It was long, hot, boring work. I started out by squatting down and pulling up them cocklebur plants, but then my back started aching pretty bad. So finally, I just plopped myself down on the ground and started pulling up the plants that was within arm’s reach. Then when I had picked everything clean within my reach, I’d scoot on over to a different spot. It made me think about all them slaves who picked cotton on plantations. I bet they didn’t get to set down like I was doing. I tried to remember if Clover Bottom Plantation raised cotton or not. I don’t remember Johnny McCline ever mentioning cotton in his story.

After about an hour, I was soaked with sweat, I was muddy as a little pig and my arms was all scratched up from the cockleburs. I only had gathered about a double-handful of seedling plants in my burlap sack. This was going to take forever!

“Hey, knock it off!” yelled Sammy.

I looked over at Sammy and he had a big clod of mud stuck right in the center of his eyeglasses. Frank was bobbing his head and grinning evilly.

“Frannnk!” hollered Ferlin, “You cut that out right now! Sammy’s liable to come over there and put the kung-fu on you! And if you don’t behave, I might not even try to stop him.”

---

[77] Samara -- a dry, usually one-seeded, winged fruit, as of the maple or elm tree. The wings cause the samara to autorotate as it falls to the ground. The samara is also known as a key, helicopter, wingnut, polynose, whirlybird, or whirligig.

After another hour or so, Ferlin called us all in so we could pool the contents of our tow-sacks and see how many cocklebur plants we had collected. Everybody else's bag had way more than mine did. Ferlin poured them all into one big burlap sack and squashed them down. They hardly filled up one bottom corner of the bag. Ferlin handed the bag over to Frank. "What do you reckon, Frank?" Ferlin asked.

Frank held the bag at arm's length, made a long face, and then shook his head "no."

"How much?" said Ferlin.

Frank held up four fingers.

"Four pounds?" said Ferlin. "Yessir, fellers, we still got a long day ahead of us then. Luckily, there's still a lot of ground that we ain't covered yet. Yessir."

"I need a break," said Sammy. "Ain't it about dinnertime?"[78]

"Yessir, it is," said Ferlin. "Why don't we head on up to the cafeteria and get us some dinner? Delphus, they might not let you inside with them mud-caked britches. Yessir, when we get into the shallow grass, why don't you waller around on the ground a little bit and rub some of that mud off of you?"

"That's a good idea," I said. "Ain't no point of taking a shower if I'm just gonna haul off and get muddy again." My clothes was soaked through-and-through with sweat. "Whew! I just can't take this heat like you boys."

"Yessir," said Ferlin, lifting his fist, "That's 'cause we got Cherokee blood."

When we got to the cafeteria building, we all spent more time drinking water at the water fountain than we should have. We had meatloaf for dinner, which I hate. It was a gray square of meat covered with a about a half-inch of ketchup. Ugh! But I was so hungry I ate it all up. Since we was allowed to drink all the milk we wanted, I drank about six of them little square cartons of milk. Sammy had five. Frank also had six chocolate milks. I couldn't even count how many Ferlin had. Needless to say, we was parched!

---

[78] The speaker is referring to the mid-day meal here. In southern U.S. culture, the mid-day meal is often referred to as *dinner,* rather than *lunch.* The evening meal is called *supper.*

As we was hiking back to Red Creek, the heat started getting to me. All of a sudden, my belly heaved and a spew of milk and meatloaf erupted out of my mouth like it was blowing out of a volcano! The puke splattered onto Sammy Blount, who was walking up in front of me. It hit him right square between the shoulder blades, and then slithered down his back and into the top of his britches.

Sammy Blount spun around to face me and there was a murderous look behind his spectacles! But then he calmly leaned backward like he was just surveying the landscape around us. Then suddenly, his body pitched forward and a white jet of milk blasted out of Sammy's mouth. Sammy's puke hit me full force, square in the chest, knocking me back a few steps! And Sammy swiveled just a little bit and sprayed some more onto Frank's left shoulder.

Frank Blount was not a man to be trifled with, nor puked on intentionally, for that matter. Frank kicked wildly at Sammy, missing him completely, but his rubber work boot flew off and hit Sammy in the shinbone! Then Sammy took out running, cackling like a maniac! Frank took off after him and caught Sammy pretty quick, despite having only one boot! Hooking a finger into the back belt loop of Sammy's blue jeans before Sammy could put the kung fu on him, Frank crooked a finger into the corner of his mouth and completely showered Sammy with pale brown puke! I reckon it was all that chocolate milk that turned it that color.

"Nossir! Nossir! Nossir!" hollered Ferlin, as he pulled Frank and Sammy apart. "I ain't about to stand here and watch you two idjits puke all over each other!"

"Delphus started it," said Sammy, pointing at me.

"Nossir, I don't care who started it, I'm a-stopping it."

A brownish-pink glob of chewed-up meatloaf was stuck onto the back of Sammy's hand, which was left over from Frank's puking assault. With a quick jerk of his hand, Sammy swatted that lump of meatloaf onto Ferlin's bare forearm. Where it stuck.

Ferlin's eyes locked down on that chunk of meatloaf. "Huuagh! Huuagh!" he started gagging. He doubled over, but to his credit, he spun around and did not vomit on either Sammy or Frank.

I'll have to say, that puking spell seemed to hit Ferlin Blount a lot harder than it did any of the rest of us. Gallons and gallons just seemed to pour out of him. We couldn't do nothing but stand there and watch. Frank Blount patted Ferlin on the back a little.

"Yessir," said Ferlin, regaining his footing, but still unsteady. "Yessir, I reckon we need to get ourselves cleaned up. Nossir, there ain't no point in walking all the way back to Progress House." He coughed a little and then spit. "Yessir! Let's head on over to the hog barn and use the water hoses there."

When we reached the hog barn, me and Sammy dragged out the hosepipes. When me and Sammy got the water turned on, Ferlin took a long drank out of the hosepipe. I was worried that he might drank too much and make hisself sick again, but Ferlin was careful and started spraying the water on Frank.

I turned the second hosepipe on Sammy Blount, and Sammy started skipping around, trying to avoid the spray.

"That water is colder than Nirarbuda[79]!" yelled Sammy.

"Turn around!" I said. "I need to get that puke off your back."

After I got Sammy cleaned off, I held the hosepipe over my own head and sprayed myself. I didn't have much puke left on me, but I was nasty from all the sweat and mud.

After me and Sammy put the hosepipes back on their hooks, Ferlin said, "Yessir, this time, why don't we take a jug of water back with us in case we get thirsty?"

Mr. Anderson had brought one of them plastic gallon milk jugs from home and we kept them in the barn just for that very thing. What you would do is fill the jug up half-way with water, then put it in the freezer. Then, when you was ready to use it, you would fill it up the rest of the way with water. The frozen bottom half would keep the whole jug cold for a great long while. Some people used Clorox bottles, but I was always leery of them. I don't think you could ever get that Clorox taste out of 'em.

We was still dripping wet when we headed back to Red Creek. But by the time we reached the cocklebur patch, we had pretty much dried out. It was that hot!

---

[79] Nirarbuda is a frozen hell realm in Buddhist cosmology.

I looked around to see if I could find me a shady spot, out of the sun, where I could pick cocklebur plants. But I didn't see none. So I just set down on the ground and started back to pulling plants.

A little while later, I glanced up from my plant-pulling and seen Alvin Elliott coming up towards us. I could tell it was Alvin because he always walked kinda funny. Alvin walked with his hands clasped behind his back. As he got closer, he looked like he had lost even more of his hair since the last time I'd seen him.

"Good afternoon, Delphus," said Alvin Elliott. "How are you today?"

"Hey, Alvin," I said. "Doing pretty good. I ain't seen you in a while. You been doing okay?"

"As well as can be expected," Alvin said, nodding his nearly-bald head. "I must confess I am still grieving the loss of my companion Fermac, but I am coping."

"Yeah, it sure is hard losing somebody like that. I miss Mr. Anderson every day."

"What are you all doing in this dreadful heat?"

"We're picking these little cocklebur plants here," I held one up to show him what I was talking about.

Alvin took the plant and inspected it closely. "Hmm, *Xanthium echinatum*," he said. "You are going to poison all the hogs."

"What makes you think that?"

"My grandfather owned a hog farm. I used to get to visit him in the summertime. Poppa allowed the hogs to graze in the pastures and invariably, a few pigs would be poisoned by eating *Xanthium echinatum*. Sometimes, if we caught the symptoms early enough, we could give them lard to eat and they would pull through."

"Well, we ain't poisoning all the hogs," I told him. "Just one of 'em—The Mulefoot!"

"The Hog Monster?" said Alvin. "The one that killed Fermac?"

"Yeah, he killed Mr. Anderson too," I said. "And if we don't put a stop to him, he's gonna kill a whole lot more people."

"I want to assist you in any way I can!" Alvin said.

"Well, Alvin, all we're doing right now is pulling up these cocklebur plants and it's pretty hot work. Plus, you got on them nice, tan-colored britches and you're liable to get 'em awful dirty."

"Oh, I don't mind," insisted Alvin. "I want to help."

"Hey, Ferlin!" I hollered at Ferlin, who was twenty or thirty yards away. "You care if Alvin Elliot helps us pull cocklebur plants?"

"Nossir, not if he feels like it!" Ferlin hollered back.

"He says he feels like it!"

"Yessir, then tell him there's an extra tow sack laying on the ground over by the water jug."

I took Alvin over to where the water jug was and got him a tow sack. "Now, Alvin, I don't want you to make yourself sick," I said. "If you get too hot or too tired, you just take yourself a break. You hear?"

"Thank you, Delphus. I will be fine." And with that, Alvin waded out into the cocklebur patch, carefully avoiding the cockleburs as best he could. Then, all of a sudden, he jammed the edge of that tow sack into his teeth and dropped down on all fours. He started creeping amongst them cocklebur bushes like he was a spider, or maybe a crocodile. Alvin commenced to pulling up cocklebur seedlings! He would pull up a cocklebur plant with his left hand and put it in the sack, then he would pull another one up with his right hand and put it in the sack. Whichever hand wasn't supporting his weight, it was pulling up a cocklebur plant. It was something to see!

But I had to get back to work myself. I took a sip out of the water jug and headed back to my picking spot.

After what seemed like an eternity, the blazing sun slid in behind the tall cedar trees. Ferlin hollered out, "Yessir, let's bring it in, fellers, and see what we got!"

We all dragged ourselves over to where Ferlin was and collapsed onto the ground, dropping our tow sacks down in front of us. Except for Alvin Elliott, who just stood there with a silly grin on his face, holding his burlap sack in front of him.

"Alvin, why don't you take a load off?" I said.

“Oh, no, I’m fine, Delphus,” grinned Alvin. “This endeavor has been most invigorating! Moreover, I don’t really wish to further soil my khaki trousers.”

I looked over at Alvin Elliott and I couldn’t see a speck of dirt on him nowhere. He hadn’t even broke a sweat. There wasn’t even a single cocklebur stuck to him!

I picked up the water jug and held it towards him. “Alvin, you want a drink of water? It’s still good and cold.”

“Oh my, no. Thank you, Delphus,” Alvin said. “I wouldn’t care for any, but thank you just the same!”

I think Alvin may of been afraid of me and the Blount Brothers’ germs.

As me and the Blount Brothers passed around the water jug, we suspiciously eyed the size of the others’ burlap sack. We was all curious about who had gathered the most cocklebur plants.

But then we stole a glance over at Alvin Elliott’s sack, and there wasn’t no doubt that his bag was twice as full as any of ours.

After catching his second wind, Ferlin started pouring the contents of our tow sacks into the big main sack. After he poured the cocklebur plants into the main sack, he would mash them down and squash them together. And I tell you what, it sure is disheartening to watch a half-day of your hard work get squashed down into the size of a softball.

When he got to Alvin’s sack, Ferlin sifted through the contents with his hands. He wanted to make sure that Alvin had picked the little seedlings that we needed and not full-grown cocklebur plants. It was kinda suspicious that Alvin’s tow sack was twice as full as any of ours. But, sure enough, Ferlin didn’t cull a single plant! They was all seedlings just the right size! Ferlin dumped them into the bag.

“What do you figure?” Ferlin said, handing the bag over to Frank.

Frank Blount held the bag at arm’s length, concentrated for a minute, and then held up both thumbs.

“How much?” said Ferlin.

Frank held up nine fingers.

“Yessir, fellers, looks like we can call it a day,” said Ferlin. “Looks like we got everything we need.”

CHAPTER THIRTY-SEVEN

Then, venom, to thy work!

The pale sun was just barely peeking out over the tops of the cedar trees when I woke up the next morning. Even the Blount Brothers got up early. We took a notion to head over to the hog barn before we eat our breakfast. As we left out for the day, I snatched up the burlap sack that held all the cocklebur plants we had pulled the day before.

As it dangled from my hand, that tow sack felt a lot heavier than any nine pounds. It felt like I was carrying a cannonball inside there, or maybe some kinda bomb. There was death in that burlap sack! As we tramped down to the hog barn that day, not a one of us mumbled a single word. When we got there, we spoke in hushed tones, not much louder than a whisper.

"I say we complete the Mission, first thing."

"Yessir, we might as well get it over with," said Ferlin, nodding his head. "The Mulefoot generally eats about 18 to 20 pounds of feed per day. Yessir, I usually give him about six or seven pounds in the morning, six or seven pounds for dinner, and then the same amount for supper."

"You reckon we ought to give him the whole nine pounds of cocklebur plants all at once?" I said.

"Yessir, it depends on whether or not he likes the way they taste," said Ferlin. "If you give him too much feed at once, he'll eat what he wants and then he'll start playing with the rest. Yessir, he'll just strow the rest of that feed out on the ground and stomp on it."

"'To cherish our blessings means to not waste food,'" said Sammy.

"Yessir, I'm gonna go get him some corn to mix in with it," said Ferlin. "Yessir, he loves that corn."

While Ferlin hustled off to the barn to get him some corn, Sammy, Frank and me headed on over to The Mulefoot's feeder. The feeder backed up to the fence between his and the other hogs' pens. Phillips had criticized the workmanship of the plywood barricade that me and the Blount Brothers had built to separate The Mulefoot from the other hogs, but in the whole time that he had been here, he hadn't so much as raised a finger to fix it. The feeder was so close to the fence, you could just reach over the wooden barricade and pour the feed right into the back side of the feeder. That way, you didn't have to get inside the pen with The Mulefoot.

Ferlin come back carrying a five-gallon bucket that was half-full of dry kernel corn. In his other hand, he had a cracked wooden scoop. He lifted up the hinged metal flap and let it rest against the back side of the feeder. Motioning toward the burlap sack, he said, "Yessir, you want me to do it?"

"Naw," I told him, "It's my responsibility. I oughta be the one that does it. Just give me a boost up, will you?"

Ferlin hoisted me up by my belt loops until I could reach over into the hog feeder. I dug my hand down into the tow sack, grabbed me a big handful of cocklebur seedlings, and scattered 'em across the shiny bottom of the feed trough. After a couple more handfuls, I had emptied out about half the bag. "Reckon that's enough?" I asked Ferlin.

"Yessir, that oughta be enough for right now," Ferlin said, as he lowered me down. "Let's see if he likes 'em first. Yessir, I'll flavor it up with some corn." He scooped his wooden scoop into the bucket and carefully sprinkled the dry corn over the bed of cocklebur plants. "Yessir, and here's another scoop for good measure."

Then Ferlin flipped down the hinged metal door, letting it slam shut. The door fell into place with a loud CLANG! and the clamor pierced the morning's quiet like a gunshot!

The sound must of woke up The Mulefoot and he come stomping out of his wooden shack. As he sauntered toward the feeder, he stared us down like a gunfighter in an old cowboy movie.

When he reached the feeder, The Mulefoot raised up his head and gave us a contemptuous snort. Jamming his bristly black snout underneath the metal cover of the trough, he viciously flipped the cover open! When the cover smacked against the top of the feeder, it sounded like somebody had smacked it with an iron skillet!

As The Mulefoot ate his breakfast of cocklebur seedlings, he snorted a kind of a rhythmic snort. It sounded like a slow drumbeat.

"That's for Mr. Anderson," I whispered, "And for every man, woman, and child in the United States of America."

"Is he eating it, Ferlin?" Sammy said.

Ferlin quietly lifted the back door of the feeder an inch or two and peered inside. "Yessir," he said. "He's already eat almost all of it."

"Reckon we oughta give him the rest right now?" I said.

"Yessir, I think that'd be alright," Ferlin said. "Looks like he loves them cockleburry plants. Yessir, I 'magine he'd eat 'em up right now and not strow 'em around on the ground."

"Well, give me another boost up then" I said, and Ferlin quietly raised the back door of the feeder. Then he hoisted me up so I could reach over the plywood barricade.

As soon as I came into The Mulefoot's view, he stopped chasing the stray kernels of corn around the shiny bottom of the feed trough. He lifted up his head and shot me a deadly glare beneath his coal black brows. His dark reddish eyes burned into mine. Did he know I was poisoning him? How could he?

As I began dumping the remainder of the cocklebur seedlings out into the feed trough, they wasn't coming out of the burlap sack fast enough to suit The Mulefoot. He thrust his head up inside the bag and wrenched the plants out between his teeth. I held up the tow sack by its bottom corners and shook the last few stragglers out of the bag. The Mulefoot licked the bottom of the feed trough clean, chasing the last few remaining plants around the bottom with his sleek black tongue.

Setting me down, Ferlin said, "Yessir, I think I'll give him a little bit more corn to chase that down." The hard corn made a rattling noise as it bounced off the bottom of the feed trough. The Mulefoot gobbled it up in no time and then stalked off toward his water trough to get hisself a drink.

"Well, that was easy enough, I reckon."

"Yessir, fellers, it's time to get back to work," said Ferlin.

After the hogs was watered and fed, the Blount Brothers hiked up to the cafeteria to eat their breakfast. I decided to hang back and keep an eye on The Mulefoot. I pulled out U.S.D.A. Circular 283 from my back pocket and read it for the umpteenth time: "The symptoms ordinarily appear within 24 hours after the plant is eaten and commonly continue for only a few hours."

The circular said that "The symptoms of poisoning are depression, nausea accompanied with vomiting, rapid and weak pulse, and a low temperature. Before death there are, frequently, spasmodic movements, but animals sometimes die very quietly."

I set down on the ground outside The Mulefoot's lot and watched him through the fence. The grass was still wet with the morning dew and soaked the seat of my britches. I had to move a couple of times to stay in the shade of the bodock tree.

The Mulefoot plunked down on his belly outside his wooden shack and glared at me with his reddish black eyes. Did he realize I had just poisoned him?

A few hours later, Sammy Blount come along and set down beside me. "Whatcha doing, Delphus?" he said.

"I'm standing a vigil on The Mulefoot."

"What's that mean?"

"You know, like knights in the old days used to do, to purify themselves before a big fight."

"You expecting a big fight?"

"Naw, just getting ready for what happens."

"What do you think's gonna happen?"

"I reckon The Mulefoot's gonna die," I said, "And I wanna see it when he does."

"Could take a while," Sammy said.

"I'll wait for as long as it takes."

"Delphus, I'm your buddy, you know that, but I still think you dreamed up that CIA man. I don't believe The Mulefoot had anything to do with Mr. Anderson getting cancer."

"Maybe," I said, staring directly at The Mulefoot, "But he's mean. He deserves to die. He killed Sammy Davis, Jr. and them other little pigs. He tried to eat me, but Mr. Anderson stopped him. The world will be a better place without The Mulefoot in it."

"I reckon," said Sammy. "And I still figure it's the fastest way to get rid of Phillips. But if they don't fire Phillips, you gonna poison him too?

"Only as a last resort."

"Dang, Delphus! I was just joking!"

"I wasn't."

"We can't just haul off and kill him!"

"We gotta protect the little boys," I said. "Mr. Anderson's gone. Mr. Birdwell's gone. I can't get Commissioner Jordan on the phone no more. There ain't nobody left but us. Somebody's gotta do something."

"Well, maybe this plan'll work."

"I hope so," I said. "I'm ready for things to get better around here."

"I'm fixing to go play cars with Skippy Dean," said Sammy, nodding his head. "You wanna come?"

"Naw, I reckon I'll stay here and keep an eye on The Mulefoot."

"Good luck with that," Sammy said, as he got up and left.

By now, the sun was high overhead and the only shade was directly underneath the bodock tree. The Mulefoot's fiery black eyes was fixed on me from his spot in the shade, and he had not moved a muscle. Then suddenly, The Mulefoot lurched to his feet and staggered forward a few steps. His mighty black shoulders heaved and trembled! He lowered his massive head and deep retching sounds echoed from his throat! His blazing eyes was squinched down tight! His dark lips snarled back and I could see that his gleaming white teeth was clamped together like a vise! Except for a little bit of vomit that squirted out between two of his teeth, The Mulefoot did not puke at all! After a long minute, he reared up his head and I reckon he swallowed that puke back down. Gross! Then he stumbled back to his original spot and toppled down onto the ground.

Why would he do that? It ain't natural. Why wouldn't he just puke that poison right out of his system? Reckon that's something they trained him to do in China? I bet all them hormones and chemicals they give him at the Peking Genetics Institute made him sick to his stomach. I wonder if they punished him for puking inside his stall. But then, The Mulefoot didn't have no trouble puking up them hedge apples after he fought Fermac.

The Mulefoot didn't go eat when Ferlin put feed in his feeder at dinnertime or at supper. Ferlin even banged the feeder door up-and-down like he was ringing a dinner bell, but The Mulefoot never moved from his spot underneath the big bodock tree. The Mulefoot's gaze never left me that whole day. I'm pretty sure he knew it was me that had done this thing to him.

A couple of hours later, The Mulefoot almost puked again. He jerked hisself up onto his feet, took a few faltering steps, and then he roared that awful choking, gagging noise. His heavy jaws clamped shut, The Mulefoot's monstrous head swayed to-and-fro, but he did not puke. Then he collapsed with a thud that jarred the ground.

The Mulefoot laid on his side now instead of resting on his belly like before. His black eyes remained locked on mine, but their fiery glow had burned out.

The sun drifted back behind the treetops, but there was still plenty of daylight left.

Another puking fit come up on The Mulefoot. This time, he didn't even climb to his feet. He just rolled over from his side onto his belly. His massive black shoulders heaved and a hoarse retching sound croaked out of his throat. The Mulefoot dug his black snout down into the dry dirt, his jaws clamped shut. Jets of dark red puke spurted out of The Mulefoot's noseholes! God A'mighty! Why did he not just go ahead and puke? The Mulefoot slowly lifted up his head like he was looking at the sky. But on the other hand, he might of just been swallowing all that puke back down.

After a while, The Mulefoot staggered to his feet. He stumbled toward his shack. About half-way, he got tripped up and crashed onto the ground. The Mulefoot lay there for a minute, then hauled hisself back onto his feet. When he reached the door of his shack, he turned his head and stared at me for a minute. With a quick snort, he disappeared through the door.

It was starting to get dark now. As I walked over to the barn to get a flashlight, I kept wondering, "Why in the world would The Mulefoot not let hisself puke out them poison plants?"

And then, an idea hit me. Maybe The Mulefoot *wanted* to die! Maybe he had been in pain this whole time! Could be that them liver flukes crawling around inside him made his whole body ache, all the time, every day. I know them exploding blood vessels in his eyeballs must of hurt. Maybe The Mulefoot just got tired of all the pain.

I found a shiny metal flashlight in Mr. Anderson's old office. The batteries was fresh and the light beam was bright and strong. As I headed back to The Mulefoot's pen, I passed the big bodock tree. I broke a long sharp thorn off of a limb and stuck it in my back pocket, just in case I might need it.

I switched off the flashlight and sat down in the quiet dark. Crickets was chirping and a hoot-owl hooted out loud from somewhere. I never could tell where the hoot-owl was perched at. Not a single, solitary sound came from The Mulefoot's shack.

After about thirty minutes, I decided to go in. I climbed The Mulefoot's fence and quietly dropped down on the other side. I switched on the flashlight and headed for The Mulefoot's oak-board shack.

I peeked around the corner of the door and shined the flashlight inside. I knew right then I wasn't gonna need that bodock thorn. The Mulefoot was laying on his side and he was not breathing. Runny black poop had leaked out of him and spilled out onto the floor. The stench made my eyes water. I laid my hand down on The Mulefoot's back hip and he was already turning cold.

I shined the flashlight beam up towards The Mulefoot's head. He had something clutched between his two front legs and had it hugged up to his chest like a teddy bear. I took a step closer. It was a tenni'shoe – My tenni'shoe! Then, sticking out from underneath The Mulefoot's motionless head, I spotted the leg of my blue jeans – the blue jeans he had pulled off me when I stuck him with that bodock thorn. The Mulefoot had wadded up my blue jeans and was using them as a pillow. He hadn't eaten them after all!

What did any of this mean? I been so wrong about so many things, like Earz Grissom. I was terrified of Earz and I hated him, but Earz thought of me as his pal.

There was so many things I couldn't figure out. Was I wrong about The Mulefoot too?

I set down at the door of the shack and breathed in the cool fresh air. And for the first time in like, forever, I bowed my head and I prayed to God.

EPILOGUE

A couple of weeks later, me and the Blount Brothers was eating breakfast. Even Skippy Dean had gotten up early and tagged along! As I was peppering my eggs, a handsome colored man walked over to our table with a huge grin beaming across his face. His hair was shaped like a basketball.

"Good morning, fellas," he said, as he set down. "I'm Ronnie Halliburton. I'm going to be your new Development Technician!" He smiled again and I could see one of his front teeth was capped in gold. "You must be Delphus! Now, these three handsome fellas here have got to be the Blount Brothers, Ferlin, Frank, and Sammy," he said pointing at each one of us. "And that young man down there with the red hair, he must be Skippy Dean!"

"Yessir, you got us," said Ferlin, nodding his head.

Mr. Halliburton reached across the table and shook each of our hands. Except for Frank. Somehow he knew Frank didn't like to be touched. So Mr. Halliburton just shot Frank with his index finger, and Frank shot him right back! Sammy added his kung fu salute for good measure.

"Like I said, I'm going to be your new Development Tech," said Mr. Halliburton. "And I'm really looking forward to working with you fellas." Just being around this Mr. Halliburton put you in a good mood.

"What happened to Phillips?" said Sammy.

"Well, you know, the incident with the Mulefoot boar really upset the administration, so they decided to make a change," Mr. Halliburton said. "But he's down at the hog barn right now, collecting his things, if you'd like to say good-bye."

"He's probably stealing Ferlin's tools," I said.

"Oh, I'm sure it's nothing like that," Mr. Halliburton grinned.

“Let’s go see!” Sammy said, as we all jumped up from the table.

“You haven’t even finished your breakfast.”

“Yessir, we’ll finish it later!” said Ferlin, as we scrambled out the door.

“Nice to meet you Mr. Halliburton!” I yelled over my shoulder.

Sure enough, as soon as we reached the hog barn, we found some of Mr. Anderson’s tools, which was now Ferlin’s tools, laying in the bed of Phillips’ truck. It was a rusty maroon Dodge, but the passenger door and front quarter-panel was from a white truck. Phillips hadn’t even bothered to rip the “ANDERSON” nametags offa the tools.

We snatched them tools out of the back of the truck and pitched ’em all on the ground.

“Y’uns better get away from my truck!” Phillips shrieked, as he come stomping out of Mr. Anderson’s office with a claw hammer gripped in his left hand. He glanced down at it, saw the blue “ANDERSON” nametag on it, and tossed it onto the ground. “You little turds, just stay away from me. I’m getting in my truck and leaving.”

Phillips opened the door to his truck, got in and cranked the engine. He leaned out the window and snapped, “I’m glad to be rid of you retarded little shits!”

Frank Blount thrust out his fist toward Phillips. He lifted his middle finger into the air and yelled, “Screw you, you baby-raping bastard!”

www.ingramcontent.com/pod-product-compliance
Lightning Source LLC
LaVergne TN
LVHW041751060526
838201LV00046B/969
* 9 7 9 8 8 8 6 4 0 3 7 3 2 *